PAMELA MORSI

Suburban Renewal

MIRA®

$5.99 U.S.
$6.99 CAN.

**Also available from
bestselling author**

PAMELA
MORSI

and
MIRA® Books

EAN

LETTING GO

USA TODAY Bestselling Author

**PAMELA
MORSI**

"...Witty, wise
and wonderful!"
—Susan Elizabeth Phillips

USA Today Bestselling Author

**PAMELA
MORSI**

Doing Good

One more chance...please!

MPM0204IFC

Rave reviews for Pamela Morsi's

Suburban Renewal

"A stunning read. Looks deep into the heart to
find the truth about love—and marriage."
—Joan Johnston, *New York Times* bestselling author

"Reminiscent of LaVyrle Spencer at her finest,
Pamela Morsi pens a family saga jam-packed with
the emotional turbulence only life can bring. Be
prepared to laugh, to cry and to reexamine your
own choices. A must-read family saga that
kept me turning pages all night long."
—Carly Phillips, *New York Times* bestselling author

"Warm, witty, richly crafted, Pamela Morsi's books
are like unputdownable chocolate, and
Suburban Renewal will have readers licking
their fingers with every turn of the page."
—Kathleen Eagle, bestselling author

"Anyone who's ever been married
will relish the faith and love, the ups and downs
of Corrie and Sam's marriage. As always,
Pamela Morsi touches the hearts of her readers
with warmth, humor and grace."
—Debbie Macomber,
New York Times bestselling author

Also by PAMELA MORSI

LETTING GO
DOING GOOD

Watch for PAMELA MORSI's next novel

SONNY DAYS

Available from MIRA Books
February 2005

PAMELA
MORSI

Suburban Renewal

MIRA

ISBN 0-7783-2011-1

SUBURBAN RENEWAL

Visit us at www.mirabooks.com

Printed in U.S.A.

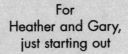

For
Heather and Gary,
just starting out

ACKNOWLEDGMENTS

The author would like to acknowledge
the gracious assistance of Jose and Valeria Lopez,
and the staff of Delicious Tamales,
San Antonio, Texas.

Corrie
2002

"The way I see it," I announced to my husband. "We either renew our vows and start this marriage all over again or we just call it quits and get a divorce."

Sam's jaw dropped open and he looked at me as if I'd lost my mind.

Maybe I had.

It might have been boredom or empty nesting or some weird premenopausal psychosis, but I got up that morning feeling like something had to change and that something *had* changed. It was as if my life, my marriage, was on some monumental precipice. All that was required was for me to give it a little push.

So I pushed.

"You want to renew our wedding vows?" The tone of Sam's question was conciliatory, almost condescending. "Then we'll renew our wedding vows. You don't have to get dramatic or threaten me about it. Number twenty-five is a big anniversary. A nice party with a little ceremony would be fine."

"I'm not looking for a reason to throw a party," I told him. "It's time to make it clear that we're together because we want to be."

He shrugged off that comment. "I'm here. I'm married to you," he said. *"Because I want to be goes without saying."*

My translation of those words from *Sam language* to plain English was "Hey, babe, I love you as much today as ever." But I was no longer certain that making up my own interpretations of his feelings was going to be enough.

We sat across from each other on the deck outside the family room. Sam had been here first, already showered and dressed before I'd even awakened. That was not unusual. Sam had always been a notorious early riser. Fit and tan, at age forty-five, he still had most of his abundant hair, though it was graying, especially at the temples. Dressed in khaki Dockers and a golf shirt, with the swimming pool in the background, Sam looked like a magazine ad for the successful middle-class businessman at his leisure.

He was that, of course, but he couldn't be summed up that easily.

Still in my nightgown, makeup free and bed-headed, I carried my coffee out to join him.

He leaned over to give me a good-morning kiss and handed over the Lifestyle section of the newspaper without me even asking for it. That was because he thought he knew me. He thought he knew what I wanted.

I thought I knew him, too. But I no longer knew what I wanted from him. Or if he still wanted anything from me.

"Still being here is not enough," I told him. "I refuse to have a marriage based on inertia. If we can't find a reason to stay together, then I'd just as soon start over by myself."

From the stunned look on his face, I could tell that

Sam was finally taking the discussion seriously. He weighed his response, carefully working out the appropriate words. He was like that. At home or on the job, he rarely allowed himself the luxury of being impulsive. When he spoke his tone carried just exactly the right amount of concern, question and curiosity.

"I didn't realize that you were unhappy," he said.

I frowned.

"I'm not unhappy," I told him defensively. "How could I be? I have a satisfying career, two healthy, well-adjusted kids and a wonderful home. I'm emotionally stable and financially secure. Any woman who has all that can't possibly get away with saying she's unhappy."

Sam let that sink in for a moment.

"So you're not unhappy."

"No, I'm not unhappy."

"Usually when the *D* word is mentioned, it's because something is terribly wrong," he said. "It's kind of the poster-child for unhappy."

"How would you know?" I asked him. "You've been married to me for almost twenty-five years, and as far as I can remember, this is the first time the *D* word has ever even dropped into a discussion."

I was right about that.

Sam nodded.

"So why has it dropped in today?" he asked.

That question momentarily stumped me. It wasn't that easy to explain. I took a sip of coffee and then looked thoughtfully into the eyes of the man who had been my partner for more than half of my life.

"Things are different now, Sam," I said. "With Lauren out of college, married, and Nate as settled as he probably will ever be, it's as if we've suddenly got our own lives back."

He shrugged. "We've worked hard, we've done our job as parents and, knock on wood, they've both turned out okay," he said. "We have every reason to be proud of that. And I'd say we've earned some time on our own."

"I agree, I totally agree," I told him. "But it's like a door is opening to a whole new life. I want to know why we should we spend that life together."

Sam tightened his jaw. I could tell he was getting annoyed.

"I don't understand what you're getting at," he said. "If it's something that I've done or not done, I think you're going to have to spell it out to me. You know how hard it is for me to figure out what you're thinking."

"If you met me today, now, this morning," I asked him, "would you choose to be married to me?"

"Of course," he answered too quickly.

"No, think about it," I insisted. "If we were total strangers, just starting out on our own in our midforties, forties, would you want to date me, sleep with me, spend the rest of your life with me?"

Sam folded up the newspaper and laid it on the mottled glass patio table with a snap of irritation. He leaned back in his chair and eyed me speculatively.

"Is this one of those 'no right answer' questions you women come up with?"

"*We women* didn't come up with this question, I came up with it. This is not some *Cosmo* survey, it's the rest of our life."

It sounded serious and I wanted it to be.

"So what's your answer?" I persisted. "If you

weren't already married to me, would you want to marry me?''

My husband, Sam, definitely requires some read-between-the-lines skills when expressing his feelings, but he isn't one of those inside-himself kind of guys who can only respond to relationship questions with *yes, no and I dunno* answers. He is actually fairly adept at verbalizing his inner concerns and conflicts. As a husband, Sam has always been able to share with me. I credit part of this ability to his having been raised by his widowed grandmother. He's also had some times when the surface of his life was so rocky that he's had to dig down deep to stay anchored.

And he's dependably honest.

"If you weren't already married to me, would you want to marry me?"

"How can I know?" he answered. "If I hadn't married you, I don't know what kind of guy I'd be. And I don't know what kind of woman you'd be if you'd spent the last twenty-five years somewhere else."

I nodded thoughtfully.

"Okay, that's a fair enough answer," I admitted.

He smiled and let out a little sigh of relief.

I shook my head. "But I have to let you know," I warned him, "I'm not sure that I'm willing to spend the next twenty-five years with you if our only reason for being together is that we always have been."

His brow furrowed with genuine concern.

"Was my pregnancy the only reason that you married me? Can you even remember how you used to feel about me? What was our getting together all about?"

Sam
1977

—▶ ◀—

What was our getting together all about? Well honestly, in the beginning, it was about sex. Or maybe it wasn't really about sex, it was just that time of my life when everything seemed to be about sex. But sex was a part of it, that's obvious. Sex is what changed everything.

It was already over. We were finished as a couple, both of us had moved on, that cool autumn day in October when the crew truck pulled up to the Burger Barn. Corrie was standing beside her mother's blue Lincoln. She glanced up at me, casual but smiling. I knew she was waiting for me.

She was dressed in what I think of as "college girl clothes." She had on a straight brown corduroy skirt that came to the top of her boots. Her sweater was sort of orange, but so dark that it matched the skirt. She'd tied some kind of long scarf thing around her neck and had a round hat, a beret or a tam-o'-shanter on the top of her head.

She looked good, real good.

I knew then, if I'd never known it before, that Corrie Maynard was way out of my league.

I'd known Corrie all my life, or at least since second

grade. She was two years behind me in school, so maybe the first time I really met her she was in kindergarten. Not that I paid much attention. Girls weren't really on my radar screen at the time, and kids younger than me were beneath my notice. But I knew all of them, of course.

Lumkee, Oklahoma, was a very small town. Everybody pretty much knew everybody. Maybe everybody didn't know me. I really sort of snuck into town and tried not to draw attention to myself. But there wasn't anyone who didn't know Corrie Maynard. Corrie's father was Doc Maynard, the druggist. Maynard Drug was a local Main Street business landmark. It had a long marble soda fountain, the old-fashioned kind where a kid could buy a real ice cream soda for seventy-five cents or vanilla-lime Coke for a quarter.

When we first started dating, Corrie's personal preference was cherry-chocolate Dr. Pepper.

It was football season my senior year when we began going out. I'd never had a real girlfriend. And Corrie wasn't the type that I would have normally even considered. But it was football season and I was riding high.

The great thing about A-conference high school football was that it was a far reach from elite athleticism. With only five hundred kids in the high school, every guy who could walk upright and didn't make the cut for marching band went out for the Varsity Eagles.

I was not exactly on my way to the NFL, but I was bigger than a lot of the guys in my class and I could pass and run pretty good and I was a very tenacious blocker. I made a few plays, got a few cheers. By the homecoming dance I thought I was major hot stuff. And I needed a date.

When that thought occurred to me I was at my locker looking for my Spanish book. I couldn't *habla* worth a flit. The only one in our class who really could was Corrie Maynard. A sophomore!

As it sometimes happens in my brain, those two un-related thoughts just happened to pop up at the same time, and got sort of weirdly fused together. And by the time I got to class I took the unprecedented step of walking up to her desk (she sat in the front row, of course) and saying, "Do you wanna go to the home-coming dance with me?"

I interpreted her stunned, slack-jawed silence as re-jection and had already turned to walk away when she grabbed my arm.

"Yes, yes, I'd love to," she said, very enthusiasti-cally.

That was the beginning of our high school romance. By the end of football season we were going steady. Over Christmas, we'd declared ourselves in love.

On New Year's Eve, it all came to an abrupt end.

Corrie and I had gone to a dance at the American Le-gion, and it was late when I took her home. All I re-member is driving up Main Street and then waking up to see a tree coming at me.

Although I was rushed to the hospital in Tulsa, I only suffered minor cuts and bruises. I thought Gram's car had taken the worst of it—that is until I was ar-rested. Because of the date on the calendar and the stu-pidity of hitting a tree in City Park, the officer assumed I'd been drinking.

Corrie's parents wouldn't let her speak up for me when my case went to Juvenile Court. Gram went with me. And a couple of guys from the team put in a good word. But when I was asked about my parents, I had no choice but to admit that my father was in prison.

I could see it in the judge's eyes—that settled it for him.

I think the prosecutor had his doubts. He talked to us and suggested that if I volunteered for the army, he'd drop the charges.

I'm sure Corrie's mom was praying I'd be shot dead in some lonely rice paddy. Fortunately, for me, Vietnam was ending. I did my military service in the Canal Zone.

I returned to Lumkee in the spring of 1977. Not to stay, just to see my grandmother, gather my things and head out to the big world. Of course, I couldn't not show up to hear Corrie make her valedictory speech at high school commencement.

She'd written me once a week from the day I'd left. She'd taken up the task of keeping me up to date with the news of Lumkee and its residents. I'd enjoyed her letters, but the gap between us had grown into a chasm. I thought I was a man. I thought she was just a little girl.

That night as she stood on the stage addressing a crowd of nearly a thousand people, she was completely confident, relaxed, persuasive, insightful, wise.

I was blown away.

I can't remember a lot of what she said. It was about how each of us have been touched by lives before us, our parents and grandparents, and we will share that experience through our own lives with the generations still to come. I don't recall much more than that, except at the end of the speech she held her hands out to the audience and said, "Touching me is touching history."

Suddenly touching Corrie was all I could think about.

I felt exactly the same way that chilly autumn afternoon at the *Burger Barn* when I saw her standing beside her mother's Lincoln.

The whole crew jumped off the back of the truck. Stopping to get a can of pop and a bag of chips for the ride back to town was a daily ritual. The rest of the guys hurried up to the window. I walked over to Corrie.

"Hey, babe, you're looking mighty fine, as always."

I lowered my mouth to kiss her. She turned her head and my lips landed upon her cheek.

That was troubling. We were, of course, officially broken up. But not because we were angry or finished. We were still in love. We were going to be together always. We just couldn't be together right then.

When she'd gone off to Oklahoma State, her parents had insisted that it didn't make sense for us to continue to see each other exclusively. It was the same argument they'd used when I was in the military. At that time we'd acquiesced without much argument. But it was a harder sell when she went off to college. It was harder because we'd been intimate. Over the summer, we'd started having sex.

Back then people talked about casual sex and free love. There was nothing casual or free about how I felt about Corrie. I was completely committed. I'd sworn undying love. I'd said that I would wait for her forever. And I'd meant it. But I wasn't that crazy about the follow-through.

Corrie professed to love me, but she also wanted to be a journalist. To write for a paper or work at a TV station. That was okay with me. Except that being a journalist required a four-year degree. She'd looked forward to college since childhood. I never told her not to go. I was at least smarter than that. But I wanted her to stay home. If she had to go away, I wanted her to do it as my girlfriend, already spoken for. I didn't want Corrie, *my Corrie,* taking her newfound sexuality and trying it out on college guys in Stillwater. And Corrie didn't want me hanging out at the beer joints among the honky-tonk honeys. We didn't want to break up.

But her mother insisted. College wouldn't be college if Corrie couldn't pledge a sorority, make new friends and date new boys. We'd talked it over for weeks. Corrie argued with her mother and I'd argued with Corrie. Finally we agreed to do what her mother wanted. Corrie always had to do what her mother wanted.

I still loved her, wanted her. When she turned away from my kiss at the Burger Barn, I was hurt.

"What's wrong, babe?" I asked her.

"We've got to talk," she replied.

"Okay."

"Get in," she said, indicating the car.

I glanced at the interior of the baby-blue Lincoln. "I'll get it dirty," I pointed out. My Sunray DX coveralls had smears of the thick black engine grease that was the daily experience of petroleum production. "And you know how your mother hates the smell of the oil patch in her car."

Corrie shrugged, unconcerned. "It doesn't matter."

I knew that it did matter, but I wasn't willing to argue the point.

I opened the driver's side door. Corrie got in and slid all the way across to the passenger's side. I was *never* allowed to drive her mother's Lincoln. And when we went in my grandmother's car (a blue '53 Bel Air), Corrie always sat in the middle. Something was wrong. Something was really wrong. And I wasn't all that eager to find out what.

I got behind the steering wheel and gazed over the vast expanse of hood between me and the front bumper. The ignition turned over easy and the powerful roar of the 460 V8 was muted in the plush interior. I loved that car. Normally I would have given my eyeteeth for a chance to drive it. But with Corrie so obviously distracted, I couldn't even enjoy it.

I put the automatic transmission in reverse, backed out of the parking spot and headed for the highway.

"Let's drive up to the river bluff," she suggested.

The little hill in the bend of the river was an infamous teen hangout and Lover's Lane. This time of day it would most likely be deserted and it would offer a great view of the sunset.

"I can't," I told her. "I've got to go home and get cleaned up. And Gram will have my dinner on the table. She'll worry if I don't show."

That last was undoubtedly true, though it was the kind of thing that I never spent a lot of time worrying about. The truth was, I didn't want to go up to the river bluff at sunset with Corrie. It seemed exactly the kind of site that she would choose to break bad news. She had met someone else. I was sure of it. Terrified of it. We were already broken up. I could bear that, because it was her parents standing between us. If she decided that she no longer loved me…well, I wasn't sure I could stand to hear it.

"I really need to talk to you," she insisted.

"We'll talk," I said. "But I need to get cleaned up first."

I drove us into town. I was so distracted that I actually went straight up Main Street, not even having the presence of mind to avoid being seen from the front of her father's drugstore. I went around the city park and turned left on West Hickory and drove the five black-topped blocks to my grandmother's little two-bedroom bungalow.

I had lived with Gram since I was four. That was the year that my mom died and my dad went away. That was the way that I always said it, "My mom died and my dad went away." That was the truth, but as they said at Daddy's trial it wasn't *the whole truth and nothing but the truth.* My father shot and killed my mother in the middle of an argument on a hot summer night as I lay sleeping in my bed. He said it was an accident. The police said it was murder. The one thing everyone agreed was that my father, Floyd Braydon, was very drunk at the time. From what I've gathered, that wasn't all that unusual.

My father got *twenty-five to life.* I got Gram. She was widowed, almost fifty and still in shock over the loss of her youngest daughter, but she took me in. She drove all by herself down to Odessa, Texas, to pick me up at the child welfare office. I didn't remember her. I'm not sure that we'd ever met. She walked into the building and she might as well have been a total stranger. But she loved me immediately, unconditionally. A kid couldn't have asked for a better deal.

I remember the caseworkers kept talking and talking. They talked about me, but nobody really talked to me. Finally Gram just took my hand.

"Let's go home," she said.

I didn't realize that she meant *her* home in Lumkee. But I already trusted her so much that I would have followed her anywhere.

Corrie and I didn't say a word to each other as I drove the Lincoln. She just stared out the window with a sad, almost lost look on her face. It was over between us. I was sure of it. And my heart was already breaking.

I pulled into the two rutted dirt tracks that served as the driveway beside Gram's little brown shingled house. I raced around the car to open the door for Corrie. I was almost too late, she had one foot on the ground already before I could offer a hand. She gave me a little smile. It was only tiny, but it gave me hope.

"Good manners will get you a long way in the world," Gram had taught me.

I hoped it would be enough to keep Corrie beside me.

I held open the white picket gate as she went through. And then clasped her palm as we walked across the yard and up the front porch steps. The screen wasn't latched so I opened it and stuck my head in.

"Gram!" I called out.

"Samuel Braydon," she answered from the depths of the kitchen. "Don't you be tracking through my house in those dirty work clothes!"

"I'm not," I assured her. "Corrie's here with me."

"Corrie?" Gram's tone changed immediately. A minute later she was walking through the living room wiping her wet hands on the hem of the apron tied around her waist. "Corrie! Get in this house, young'un. I have missed the sight of your pretty face."

Gram was delighted. Her eyes virtually disappeared among the wrinkles as she smiled. She was a little tiny woman, not quite five feet tall in sensible-heeled shoes. Her hair, as always, was pulled away from her face and twisted into a neat little bun at the nape of her neck. Pentecostal Hair, is what Corrie called it. Gram was a Baptist, of course. But her hair, left to grow as long as it would grow and bound up tightly by day, was definitely Pentecostal.

"What a wonderful surprise to see you," she told Corrie. "Now, I've only got some nice butter beans with a bit of ham shoulder. It's plain food, but it's filling and we'll dress it up with some chow-chow and some pickled beets. Would you like that? Come on in here and you can help me set an extra place. Samuel, if you don't get yourself cleaned up, we'll eat without you."

It was an empty threat, of course. But I was very willing to hand off Corrie to my grandmother. The two liked each other a lot. And I thought it might be good to remind Corrie that those guys she met at college might be smarter and richer and more her type, but they didn't have Gram. Gram came with me. If she dumped me, she'd lose Gram as well.

I walked back across the porch, down the steps, leaped over the picket pence and trotted around to the backyard. The old washhouse that my grandfather had built in the 1920s was still in use. Gram had her Maytag installed in the little room just off the kitchen, but she still had washtubs and a scrub board for my coveralls. I stepped inside the weathered tin-roofed shack and stripped off my clothes. I washed up with lava soap in a basin of hot water carried down from the house and rinsed in the cold water from the spigot on the wall. This was the same routine that my grandfather and my uncles had followed. Clean clothes, freshly starched and pressed, hung on the hook on the back of the door. I mixed my shaving cream in the same chipped cup my grandfather had used and brushed my teeth with his preferred Colgate tooth powder. The passage of time and changes in consumer choices had somehow passed Gram by. Either that or she saw no reason to change a system that had obviously worked. In a few minutes, I was clean and presentable. I stepped back outside and dropped the sweaty, greasy coveralls in the barrel of Gram's special oil-field cleaning solution that had to be kept out in the open, it's main component being highly flammable drip gasoline.

In the kitchen Gram and Corrie were getting dinner on the table. I knew that Corrie's family never ate before 7:00 p.m. But Gram always fed a working man as soon as he came home from the field.

I watched for a moment, unobserved. Corrie was helpful, soft-spoken, subdued. She'd only been at college for six weeks. In some ways it felt like yesterday, and in others, that she had been gone forever.

"There's our boy," Gram said as she caught sight of me. "Come on in and take your place at the table. Corrie, you sit down as well. I'll only be a minute until this corn bread comes out of the oven."

Corrie sat at my right. I smiled at her. She smiled back, but it was only a shadow of the happy expression I was accustomed to.

When Gram was seated we joined hands around the table as I said grace. Corrie's hand was so small in my own and it was cold. I couldn't resist giving it an encouraging squeeze. If this was the end for us, I knew I would be sick, miserable. There was no reason that she should be sick and miserable, too.

"Thy will be done," I told God. But I was fervently hoping that He would see things my way.

The meal seemed to last forever. Gram kept up a

steady stream of talk, including a long-winded, oft-told tale of Aunt Kate sewing flour-sack drawers with the advertising along the back so that the butts read SHAWNEE'S BEST. It was one of Gram's typical old-timey stories of her and her sisters growing up in Territory Days. I'd heard it a million times, I guess. But Corrie hadn't heard it and it made her laugh. It was a wonderful sound. So I told a story or two myself. By the time Gram served up the applesauce cake the tone had changed to being almost festive.

"Why don't you two sit out on the porch while I clean up this little tat of dishes," Gram said.

Corrie argued for a minute, but Gram shooed her away and reluctantly we found ourselves alone on the porch swing. Twilight was coming on and the overhead cloud cover made it seem even darker. I didn't switch on the porch light, but the house light seeped through the front window, giving just enough illumination for me to see Corrie's face.

She looked so sweet and pretty. Smart and sweet and pretty, Corrie had it all. It was no wonder that her parents wanted more for her than me. And no surprise that once she'd been out into the world, she'd discovered there were plenty of guys more suited to her.

I knew I would never do as well. I'd find some good-natured gal and we'd buy a mobile home on a fifteen-year lease and raise three or four kids. But I would always remember Corrie. I would always remember the girl who thought better of me than I did myself.

I pulled her close and kissed her. I wanted to taste for one last time the lips that by any reasonable accounting should never have been mine. As I moved back, I smoothed away a few strands of blondish-brown hair that strayed across her cheek.

"Don't be nervous or anxious or afraid," I told her. "Just tell me whatever it is you have to tell me."

A worried frown still creased her brow, but she raised her chin bravely.

"Sam, I'm pregnant."

I was momentarily speechless, but I'm pretty sure my jaw dropped open in shock. That disbelief was almost immediately followed by irrational anger.

Some son-of-a-bitch college boy had knocked up my Corrie!

Fortunately, before I could express that thought, I realized that if Corrie was telling me, then I must be the guy who'd knocked her up. Could that be true? I always used a rubber. The last time we'd done it was in August. It was October already. Is that how it worked? You did it in August and didn't find out things had gone wrong until October? Was she sure it was true? Was she sure it was me?

I wanted to ask her all those things, but I looked into those bright brown eyes, awash with tears, and I couldn't play twenty questions.

"I'm so sorry, Sam," she apologized. "I don't know what to do."

"I know what to do," I told her. "We get blood tests and a license, we say 'I do' and live happily ever after."

She didn't look as if she appreciated my humor.

I took her hand in my own and brought it to my lips for a kiss.

"Marry me, Corrie," I said.

When she hesitated, I added, "Please."

Corrie
1977

--- ◄◄

The worst day of my life. That's how I would have described it then. And since my life experience up to that time had been mostly pampered and sheltered, it probably was.

I hadn't wanted to believe that it was true. I couldn't imagine that it could happen to me. I was smart. I was careful. I had a great future ahead of me.

Okay, so I missed a period. Sometimes that happens. New surroundings, different foods, even a change in water might cause the body to get out of its normal rhythm.

Finally, my roommate, a foulmouthed, chain-smoking cowgirl from Altus made me face my denials.

"Hey," she said angrily when I'd unintentionally awakened her. "How many mornings are you going throw up before you trot yourself over to the infirmary and pee in a cup?"

I went that very afternoon.

"I'm sure it's not true," I told the nurse, smiling. "I mean. Lots of things can mess up your cycle."

She made no comment about that. She put a dropper into the cup of urine and drew out just a tiny bit. She put that on a card and swished it around for maybe ten seconds.

"Positive," she said, no inflection in her voice.

"It can't be," I said.

"It is."

"You can't know that fast."

She held up the card for me to see. There was a big circle and a small circle. Both of them had turned color.

"Sometimes we get false negatives," she said. "We never get false positives."

I left the building with a sense of unreality. My life had just made a terrible unexpected turn. I felt disassociated from it. I walked to the Student Union. Ate a burger on the Starlight Terrace. Talked to two of the other girls who'd pledged Tri-Delt with me. That afternoon the greatest concern of Lisa and Janice was Saturday's game with K State.

"You're going to be there, right?" Lisa asked.

"No, no, I think I have to go to Lumkee this weekend," I said.

"Eew, bummer," Janice said. "Well, hurry back as quick as you can."

"Yeah," Lisa said. "When I go home to Shidler, I always get this irrational fear that somehow I'm going to be trapped there."

We all laughed, but her fears were similar to my own.

But I had no choice. I had to go home, because I had to tell Sam. He was the person most concerned and also the one I felt closest to. I needed someone I could trust. I needed a calm, rational discussion to consider my options.

I could get an abortion. They were safe and legal

now in Kansas. And at less than eight weeks, the procedure would be simple and quick.

Or I could have the baby and give it up for adoption. In all honesty, I favored that idea. I imagined a happy little child, a part of me and Sam, growing up as the doted-upon only child of a loving, formerly childless family so blessed to get him. They would lavish upon our little baby everything that Sam and I had ever wanted. And they would tell him that his parents gave him up because they wanted the best for him.

The choice I gave the least consideration to was getting married. That would mean quitting school. That would mean telling my parents. That would mean public shame. That would mean the end of my life as I had known it, as I had planned it.

For me, wedding bells were the last and worst option.

It was the first thing out of Sam's mouth.

If I'd told him out on the river bluff, like I wanted to, I think I could have said no. But in the warmth and hominess that was Gram's house, somehow it seemed possible, it seemed almost desirable.

"Are you sure you want to marry me?" I asked him.

"Of course I am," Sam insisted. "I've always wanted to marry you. You know that. You know I love you."

"But to get married now, because of this, it just seems so wrong."

"Nothing has ever been so right," he assured me.

I don't remember ever actually agreeing. But I was swept along by Sam's enthusiasm.

"Let's go inside and tell Gram."

"What?" I was incredulous. "I can't. We can't."

"The longer we wait, the harder it will be," he said. "When your direction is clear, you've got to move forward. We don't want to waste time second-guessing ourselves and anticipating what might happen. Let's get it over with."

Like a zombie, I followed him back into the house.

Gram had finished washing dishes and was sitting out on her sunporch crocheting in lamplight. The banks of windows that surrounded the room on three sides were all open and the fresh night was alive with the scent of autumn. I had always associated that season with football games and pep rallies, youthful optimism and possibility. Now it just seemed decayed and melancholy.

"Gram," Sam said to her. "Corrie and I have some news."

She glanced up with a smile, but when she looked at me, her expression faltered.

Bracing herself with a chair, she rose to her feet and gestured for us to go back to the living room.

She sat in her overstuffed rocking chair with the lace doilies on the arms. I seated myself on the edge of the couch. Sam continued to stand, leaning his back against the wooden mantel that surrounded the gas heating stove.

He looked at me.

I was so scared, I was worried that I might faint. He smiled at me. He looked as if he was completely happy. He even gave me a little wink, as if to say, "Someday we're going to look back at this and laugh." For me it felt like no laughing matter.

"Gram," he said calmly, confidently, "Corrie and I are going to have a baby and we've decided to get married."

The old woman grew pale and her ever-smiling mouth drew into one straight unpleasant line. She moved to rise to her feet. Sam offered a hand to help her. She slapped his hand away.

"Samuel Braydon, I hope that you are writhing in shame," she said. "I did not raise you to take advantage of the affections of a sweet young woman!"

Her words were whispered, obviously not meant for me, but I heard them just the same.

"No, ma'am," Sam replied, his expression notably more solemn.

Gram came over and seated herself next to me on the couch.

"You poor thing," she said. "Are you feeling sick? I thought you looked pale."

She patted my hand comfortingly.

"Won't this be wonderful," she said. "A baby in the house is always such a blessing."

Gram cast all the blame for my out-of-wedlock pregnancy on Sam. At my parents' house, they did the same, eventually. My mother's first reaction was an irate scream.

"How could you do this to me!"

It wasn't posed as a question and I wasn't prepared to answer it.

"I can't believe it! I just can't believe it. Doc, do something!"

She looked at Dad as if she actually expected him to fix it. My father just looked sad.

"Sam and I have decided to get married," I told them.

My father nodded, Mom looked, if possible, even more distressed.

"You can't actually mean to marry him," she said. "It's bad enough that he got you into this mess. It would be stupid to compound the mistake by tying yourself to this...this low-class bad seed."

Mom made no attempt to hide her contempt for Sam. On the contrary, she said these awful things to his face. He should have gotten mad and told her to "go to hell," but Sam didn't behave like that. He stood, eyes downcast, taking all the venomous anger my mother could dish out. And I knew from long experience that when provoked, Edna Maynard could really dish it out. Like a mama lion protecting her cub, I furiously defended him.

"Sam is not low-class and he's not a bad seed," I declared. "He is a kind, generous, caring guy. Any woman would be proud to call him her husband and to give birth to his baby. And I...I love him."

"Of course you love him," Mom said with disgust. "Teenage girls always fall in love with the wrong guys. It's part and parcel of rebellion. But I will not allow you to ruin your life by getting married and having a baby."

"I don't know how you will stop us," I said. "I won't drive to Topeka to get an abortion."

"Of course you won't," Mom said. "You'll go to that home for unwed mothers in Tulsa. We'll tell people you're doing a semester overseas. You'll give the baby up to a nice childless couple and come home to get on with your life as if nothing happened."

Honestly, that didn't sound like such a bad idea to me. It was, in fact, what I really wanted. To go away secretly, have the baby quietly and give it away. It was the best solution.

If we'd been in a calm, rational discussion, if I hadn't talked to Sam first, if Mom hadn't used that determined "you'll do what I say or else" tone with me, my life might have been totally different.

As it was, I turned away from my mother and took my dad's hands in mine.

"Sam and I are getting married, Daddy," I told him. "I want you to give me away. Will you do that for me?"

"Of course I will, pumpkin," he said.

"George!"

"It's her life, Edna," he said. "If Sam suits her, then he suits the rest of us."

I rarely heard my father be firm with Mom. But he was that night. He was firm and resolute and supportive. And Sam and I got married.

Sam
1978

◄—►

The first year of my marriage was no easier than we deserved. Mrs. Maynard, once convinced that she couldn't stop us, took over the plans for the wedding. It was small, only close friends and family, held in the huge First Methodist Church. Corrie wore a pale blue suit with a matching hat. The outfit kind of reminded me of an Easter egg. But she looked real pretty, like always.

I asked her brother, Mike, to be my best man. Well, I admit, Mrs. Maynard suggested him as the best choice. I guess she didn't want to see any of the guys I hung out with standing up with us. That was okay with me. I couldn't have picked out any of my buddies as particularly special. Corrie was, and always had been, my best friend. And since she was standing on the other side of me, well, it really didn't matter.

Mike had come home from Kansas City where he was in pharmacy school. He was a tall, athletic, really nice-looking guy and a sharp dresser. So it seemed appropriate to ask him to help me come up with something to wear. My choices were a brown corduroy sports jacket or my high school suit, which was now way too tight across the shoulders.

"I've got some money," I told him. "I can buy a new suit. I just hate to spend my savings, knowing we've got hospital bills ahead of us."

He came down to see me, carrying an old suit of his. It was in perfect shape and the most expensive thing I'd ever had on my back. He claimed it didn't fit him anymore. It didn't fit me, either. But Gram got her pincushion out of the sewing box and by the morning that I slipped that plain, fifty-dollar gold band on Corrie's finger, I had the nicest, best-fitting suit I ever owned.

But the truth is, I have trouble thinking of that date, the wedding date, November 5, 1977, as the beginning of our marriage.

It wasn't just that I didn't get to have sex on my wedding night. I'm sure there are plenty of guys who share that bad luck. But I hardly saw Corrie before the ceremony or after. When the guests went home, Mrs. Maynard told me to go home, too. Corrie was sick. That was probably true. Corrie was sick a lot. That was why we hadn't bothered with a honeymoon. But she couldn't have been sick every minute!

The next day Corrie had to get back to school. Edna Maynard was adamant that her daughter finish the semester. So after one hasty, supervised kiss in the driveway of her parents' house, Corrie went back to Stillwater and I went back to Gram.

I was lonely, immediately lonely. It was really weird. I'd been single always and had never felt alone. Now I was barely married and she was sixty miles away and I felt this sad emptiness without her.

Since Gram believed that long distance was only used in emergencies, I stopped down to the phone booth on the park end of Main Street every day after work and called my wife. I knew she was scared and having doubts. I was scared, too, but I had no doubt about what I wanted. I wanted Corrie and our baby. I was determined to make it happen.

I had a lot of free time. A full-time job only takes forty hours a week. Now a married man with a child on the way, I quit wasting my nights in beer joints and honky-tonks. I was thinking about all that free time and about how hard I needed to work to keep Corrie and the baby with me. Those two thoughts sort of melded into the idea of making more of what I was doing. I started taking extra jobs after work; lots of independents couldn't really afford to pay time and a half for a well-service company on nights and weekends. So I picked up little jobs charging day rates. It wasn't that I loved oil wells so much, it's just that's what I knew how to do.

You might have thought that my boss, Cy Walker, wouldn't want the competition. But back then, there was more work than anyone wanted and he was glad to share some of it with me after I clocked out.

I gave my phone number to everybody I knew and told them that if they had an engine down, or they needed somebody after regular hours, I was available, even in the middle of the night. I jokingly began to call myself the Midnight Mechanic. I even had some cards printed up with that name. It was funny, but people remembered it. I got calls during the ten o'clock news or at three in the morning. I was young and strong and pretty much sleepless those days, anyway, so I never missed a call.

With the extra money, I surprised Corrie at Christmas with the keys to a two-bedroom furnished duplex only four blocks from her mother's house. I figured out pretty quick that Mrs. Maynard had decided that Corrie and I should be kept apart until the baby was born. Then once her grandchild was legitimate, a nice clean divorce would be the fix-up for Corrie's life. I was determined not to let that happen.

When Corrie came home for Thanksgiving, there was a question about whether or not I was even going to be invited for dinner. Fortunately, Corrie insisted. But every time I brought up any discussion about the future, Mrs. Maynard would change the subject. I finally just asked her straight out.

"Where is Corrie going to live after she comes home from college?"

Mrs. Maynard, always dressed up like she was going to church, and so smug in her superiority, managed to look down at me even across the table.

"In her condition, Corrie needs to be close to her mother," she stated.

I knew she meant that as an explanation of why Corrie would never live with me. Right then I took it as a challenge to find a place that we could afford, so near to the Maynard's house that nobody could complain.

I managed to do it.

The duplex was shabby and run-down. But I cleaned it up until it shone like a new penny. Gram took charge of the kitchen, getting all her friends from the Baptist Ladies' Auxiliary to each donate one pan. She embroidered dish towels with Sam and Corrie on them and hung them from the back of the chairs of the three-piece dinette. And she bought a secondhand high chair that she had me sand and stain to match the furniture.

When Corrie saw the place, she started crying. At first I thought it was bad crying, but then I realized it was happy crying.

"I love you, Corrie," I told her. "I will always take care of you. I will always provide for you."

I meant those words when I said them. She must have believed me. Because she moved in with me. I guess I'd say our marriage started that day. December 25. That's when we finally had a commitment.

Corrie encouraged me to continue doing the Midnight Mechanic work on the side, though now I really wanted to stay home with her. I wanted to spend my time talking to her. And I worried about leaving her alone at night. She wouldn't hear of it.

"Mom's four blocks away and I'm perfectly capable of using a phone," she assured me. "Besides, the only time a poor newlywed wife like me gets any rest is when her man isn't home!"

She was teasing, of course. But I let her get away with it.

As it happened, when she went into labor she didn't have to call her mom, I was neither at work nor on call.

It was a sunny spring Saturday. We were working together in our driveway. Corrie had given me the idea of putting Midnight Mechanic and our new phone number on the sides of my truck. We didn't want to spend the money for a sign painter, but we didn't want a really homemade job. So we cut a stencil on butcher paper, taped it to the door and we were dabbing the paint on. Suddenly Corrie doubled over in pain.

"What happened? Did you get a stitch in your side?"

"It's the baby," she answered.

"The baby!" I hollered. "It's not time for the baby. Is it the baby? Let's get to the hospital. Come on, get in the truck, get in the truck."

Corrie refused. "No, no, I don't want to go yet," she told me. "Let's finish painting this door."

"Finish painting the door?" I said. "While you're in labor?"

"Firstborns take forever," she assured me. "That's what everybody I've talked to says—labor averages ten to fourteen hours. I don't want to go to the hospital until it's closer."

"Are you sure?"

"I'm sure," she said. "Let's paint the door."

We painted the driver's-side door. Then she insisted that we paint the passenger-side door. I was so nervous I thought I might throw up, but Corrie took her time. She didn't get ahead of herself. When we were finished, I ran in and grabbed her suitcase and started up the truck.

When she didn't come out immediately, I went back inside to find her coming out of the shower.

"What are you doing?"

"I can't get examined if I'm dirty," she told me.

She called the doctor and assured him that she was fine. He agreed to meet us at the hospital.

"Aren't you going to call your mom?" I asked her.

Corrie shook her head. "I don't want them pacing the floor all day at the hospital," she said. "We'll call them when we know we're close."

I had to help her get dressed.

"These pains are coming really close together," I said.

Corrie waved away my concern. "It takes forever to have a baby, everybody says so."

She had me drive through the Sonic to get her a soda pop with extra ice.

"They won't let you have anything to drink in the labor room," she explained.

By the time we got to the hospital she was in a lot of

pain. We parked the car in the lot and walked in through the front door. Took the elevator to the maternity floor. Corrie was leaning on me pretty heavily. We made our way to the nurses' station.

"My wife's in labor," I told them.

The nurse looked up, gave us both a quick, unconcerned once-over.

"How close together are the pains?"

"They're pretty much constant, I think," I told her.

The woman's brow furrowed a bit.

"Let's get her into the labor room and examine her," she said.

We were directed into a small, windowless mauve room. All the clothes that I'd helped her get on at home, I had to help her get off now. She was suffering pretty tremendously.

After one long, tough pain, she looked up at me, frightened.

"I can't even imagine how bad it's going to be, if it hurts this much now," she said.

A nurse, different from the one at the desk, came in and we helped Corrie into the bed.

"The doctor is coming in to examine her," she told me. "This would probably be a good time for you to go down to the business office and fill out the admission forms."

"I'll be right back," I told Corrie.

She barely responded, concentrating hard upon the pain she was in.

I met Dr. Kotsopoulos at the door. We shook hands and I told him where I was headed. He told me not to worry.

I got directions from the nurses' station and was

standing at the elevator door when the nurse from the room came hurrying down the hall calling out to me.

"Mr. Braydon! Mr. Braydon."

"Yeah?"

"The doctor wants you to get scrubbed and suited up," she said.

"I haven't been to admissions yet," I explained.

"That can wait," she said.

Obviously not everything could.

The nurse took me to wash up. I was dressed in a paperlike yellow gown as well as a blue paper shower cap and shoe covers.

I heard Corrie before I saw her.

"You can do it," Dr. Kotsopoulos said. "Come on, Corrie."

"Where's Sam?" she screamed.

"I'm here, I'm here," I assured her, hurrying to her side. I grabbed her hand. Her palm was sweaty but cold.

"We're crowning," Dr. Kotsopoulos said. "Hold it, Corrie, don't push yet. Don't push."

"I gotta push!" she hollered back.

"Don't push!" he repeated.

She looked up to me, her eyes pleading. "I gotta push."

"Corrie, you can do anything you have to do," I told her. "If you have to not push, then I know that you won't."

She groaned like some animal and squeezed my hand so hard, I thought it might break my fingers.

"Okay," the doctor said. "Next contraction you can push."

The man had hardly gotten the words out of his mouth when she was bearing down.

"Here he comes," the doctor said. "Here he comes. You'd better look this way, Dad, or you're going to miss it."

The nurse tapped me on the shoulder. The doctor meant *me.* I glanced down just in time to see a big whoosh of something pop out of Corrie's body like soap in a shower.

Dr. Kotsopoulos caught her and the minute he turned her over, she began to cry.

"It's a girl," he said.

"It's a girl," I repeated, not sure I even believed my eyes.

"A girl," Corrie repeated with a sigh. "My mom will be so happy. She wanted a girl."

When I called Mrs. Maynard a half an hour later, she was anything but happy.

"You took Corrie to the hospital and let her have a baby without calling me!"

"It all happened so fast," I told her.

"Sam Braydon, I will never forgive you for this!"

I doubt seriously if she ever has.

Corrie
1979

It was bitter cold that morning. I'd dressed Lauren in the little pink snowsuit that my mother got her for Christmas. It was padded and thick, and wearing it, she looked like a stuffed sausage, with just her little round face sticking out.

Mom loved to see Lauren dressed in the clothes she bought. And it was cute, but the stores were about sixty degrees warmer than the sidewalk. So I had to get the snowsuit on and off of her every time we went in or out—which occurred about every twenty minutes. The routine was wearing thin. And worse, it was annoying Lauren. It could have been avoided if we were at one of the fancy shopping malls in Tulsa. With the new expressway opened they were less than an hour away. But for my mother, the February white sales were as much an annual tradition as any religious holiday. And tradition dictated that she celebrate in the meager downtown shops of Main Street, Lumkee.

"Honey, look at these sheets," she said. "They are thirty percent off and in plenty of colors. We can both buy a couple of sets."

Mom spent money with a carelessness that I was in no position to match.

"I don't need any sheets, Mom," I told her.

She looked at me skeptically. "Everybody needs sheets," she insisted.

"We're still using the ones we got for wedding presents," I said. "And if I bought more, I'd have to figure out where to store them."

Sam and Lauren and I were living in a garage apartment that was barely five hundred square feet.

Mom shook her head in disgust.

"Your husband makes you live in some rat hole and you act like a church mouse about it," she said. "It's time for you to demand your own house. If not for yourself, then for Lauren. A child needs a yard to run and play in."

"Mother, she can't even walk yet," I pointed out. "I don't think getting her a backyard is a high priority at this point."

"She'll be walking any day," Mom said. "She might have started already but realized there wasn't anywhere to go."

I rolled my eyes but spoke with deliberate reasonability.

"The apartment is a really good deal for us," I explained.

Mom sniffed with disapproval. She'd lost interest in the sheets, barely glanced at the towels and had moved on to the china and glassware section. A complete set of fake Christmas Spode was set on a table for ten percent off. Mom was giving it close inspection.

"I never liked that Mrs. Neider," she said, casually. "Her husband made his money in nightclubs and she didn't play bridge."

I wasn't sure which flaw my mother thought was the worst.

Mrs. Neider was pretty well off but, at ninety, she needed a lot of help. She allowed us to live in the apartment above her garage for only the cost of the utilities. We paid the rent by helping her out. I did her housework, laundry and cooking. Sam took care of the yard work and odd jobs. She could be cranky and crabby, but more often she was easygoing and kind. She loved Lauren and the two kept each other company while I cooked and cleaned.

"If you're thinking that women is going to die and leave you something, you know you're wrong," Mom stated emphatically. "She's got five children and a dozen grandkids. Once what she's got is divided among them, there won't be a pittance for any outsider, no matter how hard you've worked for her."

"We're not hoping to be left anything, Mom," I told her. "We've got a good deal now. With Sam just getting his business started, we need to keep our family expenses at a minimum."

Mom was dismissive. "I don't think you can call a truck and a couple of ne'er-do-well employees a business," she said. "He's a shade-tree mechanic without even a shade tree."

"It's an oil-well service company, Mom. There is no reason to have a big office somewhere if all their work is done out in the field."

"He doesn't have an office. He doesn't seem to even have a paycheck. What kind of *work* is this, anyway?"

"Mom, it takes time to get a new business off the ground," I tried to tell her. "Things are actually going great. He's building a reputation. He's got new customers every day."

"But he's not making any money."

"He has a hundred thousand dollars' worth of debt

tied up in equipment and he's got a weekly payroll he has to meet. Starting a business is always a struggle. That's why everybody doesn't do it."

"Yes," she said disdainfully. "I suppose most men's first concern is providing for their wife and child."

She was deliberately being disagreeable. Mom could always be this way, and when she was in the mood there was really no arguing with her. But I tried, anyway.

"Think about when Daddy started in business," I said. "Those first few years couldn't have been easy."

Mom turned to look at me. We were exactly the same height, so she raised her chin, making it possible to look down her nose at me.

"Your father waited until he could afford to support a wife before we married," she said. "He'd finished his degree, had his license and money in the bank before we even thought of starting a family."

We were back to that. Somehow we always got back to that. My mother's disappointment in my "lapse in judgment" never waned. It was as if every day that passed increased her regret of my failure to finish college. There was nothing I could do about that. No further apology that I could make. I hadn't lived up to her expectations then and I continued to be unable to do so.

Lauren began to get fussy and I suggested that we interrupt shopping for a little lunch. I wrestled the baby back into her snowsuit and we walked down the block and across the street to Cathy's Corner Café. The place was cute and girly but the food they served had to satisfy the appetites of working men, as well. The special of the day was obviously chili. As soon as I stepped inside the smell of it hit me like a brick wall.

The sweat popped up on the back of my neck and my legs felt as if they were made of jelly.

"Get Lauren out of her snowsuit, I've got to go to the bathroom," I told Mom.

I hurried toward the door marked *Ladies* at the back of the building. I barely got the door locked behind me before I was throwing up in the toilet. I felt better immediately, but that didn't stop the tears from running down my cheeks. I leaned against the cold white bathroom tile and just allowed myself the luxury of a good cry. It didn't last long, but it did feel good.

I washed up at the sink and then dug into my purse/diaper bag for enough makeup to repair the worst of the damage. I studied myself in the mirror. I looked tired. I looked old. I looked pudgy. I looked pale.

I rinsed out my mouth and brushed on more blush. It was the only help I could offer myself. I was twenty years old. I should be at college in the middle of my sophomore year. Instead, I was stuck in Lumkee living in a tiny garage apartment and working as a maid.

Mom wasn't the only one who was a little disappointed with my choices.

I gathered up my things and headed out into the café.

Mom and Lauren had a table in the corner. Lauren was strapped into a high chair and eating crackers. Mom was conversing with the waitress on the obvious beauty and brilliance of her granddaughter. I had to give Mom credit for that. She may have been upset about my pregnancy, but she adored the baby.

"Hi, Cindy, how you doing?" I asked, politely.

Cindy and I were in the same class in high school. But we'd never socialized. I was brainy, involved in everything and relatively popular. She was a lackluster student with no extracurricular activities who'd gotten pregnant in her junior year.

It was amazing how the distance between our lives had narrowed.

"Your little girl is a real cutey," she said.

"Thank you."

"I'm hoping my next is a girl," she told me, patting her belly. "Boys are absolutely the worst and there are no cute clothes for them or nothing."

I smiled.

"When are you due?"

"August," she replied. "Wouldn't you know it? I'm going to be big as a house through the hottest part of the summer."

"I'm sure it will be worth it," I told her.

Mom ordered the chili special. I chose a very bland grilled cheese sandwich.

"Can you believe that Cindy?" Mom asked when the waitress left. "Bringing another child into the world when she can't support the one she's got now. They say her husband went off on pipeline just to get away from her."

"That's what *they* say about every wife whose husband goes on pipeline," I pointed out. "Pipeline is a good living. Guys go on it to make money and their wives miss them when they're gone."

Mom's expression was skeptical, but she let the subject drop.

I got Lauren's juice out of the diaper bag and poured it into a sippy cup.

"She's drinking apple juice?" Mom asked.

"Yes, I'm trying to wean her," I admitted.

"Really?" Mom was genuinely surprised. "Well, that is good news. The way you bought into all that La

Leche nonsense, I was worried that the child would be carrying your breast in her lunchbox at school."

"It's not nonsense, Mother," I argued. "Breast milk is best."

"So says the most saggy-titted women in the world," she replied. "I raised both my children on formula and they've certainly turned out fine. And I did it without any damage to my figure."

I didn't even want to go into that. I changed the subject.

"What's going on with Mike?" I asked.

Mention of my brother, my all-so-perfect brother, was always guaranteed to distract my mother.

"Michael is doing wonderfully, of course," she related. "That big city must be a very exciting place for a good-looking single man. I just hope he's ready to settle down to small-town life when the time comes."

Mike was attending pharmacy school at the University of Missouri, Kansas City. My father's alma mater. He was making top grades and when he graduated next year he was coming back to Lumkee to become a partner in the business with Dad. That would free up Dad for travel. Mom went on lots of trips with widowed friends and tour groups. Dad always felt as if he had to stay home to take care of the drugstore.

"I'm sure Mike will settle right back into Lumkee," I assured her. "Mike always does the right thing."

"Yes, he does," she agreed. "He's smart, ambitious, hardworking, considerate and kind."

I couldn't argue that. The truth was, I would have loved to resent my brother or be jealous of him. But he was exactly as Mom described. And as a brother, he was unbeatable. He was three years older than me and could easily have made the life of a little sister miserable. But he was always caring and we were close. I could count on him for good advice or a sympathetic ear. I cried like a baby when he left for college.

"Mike's a great guy," I admitted.

"He is," Mom said. "And that's why all of this is so difficult to understand."

"What?"

"I raised the two of you in the same house with the same rules and the same expectations. And Mike has always done so well. While you seem so content to settle for such an ordinary, mediocre life."

"Mom!"

"You're so smart, so attractive, you have so much potential, yet you settle right into working-class motherhood like one of these no-neck sows with an IQ of ninety."

We'd been over this ground so many times, it was like a routine. I knew my lines perfectly. I would respond with assurance that a university degree could still be had after age twenty-five. That as soon as Lauren was safely in preschool and Sam was making a little money, I'd be starting back to college. My dreams and ambitions had not been given up, they were only temporarily dormant. They were altered, but they had not been destroyed.

I'd grown up thinking I would be a journalist. Like a young, intrepid heroine in one of those well-worn YA books in the public library, I'd be *Corrie Maynard, Girl Reporter*. That had seemed exciting and full of adventure. I would travel to distant places, meet unusual people. I would drink coffee in Paris cafés with artists and communists. Interview chieftains in the thin air of the high Andes. Report my observations of life on a junk in the Yangtze River.

With Sam and Lauren at my side, that life no longer held its appeal. I was not a girl anymore. I was a woman. As a woman, I had other interests. I'd learned so much from motherhood. My daughter was absolutely fascinating, much more so, I was certain, than any foreign potentate. Now I wanted to study Early Childhood Education.

But it seemed that I would not do that, either.

"Mom, I'm pregnant again," I said calmly.

It is hard to make my mother speechless, but that did it. Her jaw dropped open in shock and she just looked at me incredulously. After a moment, her expression of utter disbelief gave way to defeat. She sat back in her chair, a sigh of exhaustion escaping her.

"Oh, honey, that's impossible," she said.

"It certainly is possible," I assured her. "People get pregnant every day."

"I asked your father if you had a prescription for birth control," she said. "He assured me that you were up-to-date."

"Mom, I think it's illegal to spy into my pharmacy records."

"Yes, of course," she said, waving my words away. "So call a policeman. How did this happen?"

"In the usual way, Mom," I told her. "I don't think we need to alert the Vatican."

"But the pill…"

"I quit taking the pill," I admitted. "My girlfriends at La Leche explained that all those hormones were getting into Lauren's milk. That's not good. And breast-feeding is a natural contraceptive."

"Oh, for heaven's sake."

Mom's response was disdainful and dismissive.

"Anyway, it's happened and I'm happy about it," I lied. "I want you to be happy about it, too."

I glanced over at Lauren, who had finished smashing her crackers into crumbs and was now joyously sweeping them off the table in wide, enthusiastic strokes.

"How can I be happy when you're losing your life?" Mom asked.

I didn't know what she was talking about. "The doctor didn't indicate that there was any danger associated with this pregnancy," I assured her. "I didn't have any problems when I had Lauren."

"That's not what I meant," Mom told me. "It's not about dying, it's about not living. A woman with one child, that's a burden. A woman with two children…" She shook her head sadly. "That's the end of it. Any life that was your own is over."

On some level, I agreed with her. But I railed against it.

"Mom, that's ridiculous," I said. "I'll still have my own life."

"No, you won't," she said. "You'll be too busy. From here on out for the next twenty years you are somebody's mother and nothing more."

"That was your generation, Mom," I told her. "Women today, we can have it all. Husband, children, career and social life. We're not limited by yesterday's gender roles."

She was shaking her head. "Two children under age five is as limited as it gets in this world and that's the truth," she insisted. "I blame Sam Braydon for it. You're smart and pretty and you could have had a great life full of opportunity and possibility. He's stolen all that from you. He's low class, with a bad background. Good Lord, his own father is a murderer. He'll never make anything of his life and now he's dragging you down to his level."

I bristled immediately. "He's my husband, Mother," I told her sternly. "And the father of my children. If you are going to talk about him with disrespect, my daughter and I will leave."

It was no empty threat. Mom knew better than to bad-mouth Sam to me, though I was certain her bridge club was well versed in his shortcomings.

She didn't apologize, but she did acknowledge my words with a nod and a moment of silence. If we were to keep a relationship, she knew she had to keep her opinion to herself.

"What are you going to do?" she asked me finally.

"What am I going to do?" I repeated her question, puzzled. "Mom, I'm going to have a baby."

Sam
1980

➤ ◄

It's interesting that with all the up and downs, changes good and bad in the decade of the eighties, what stands out most for me are the two important men who walked into my life. Well, I suppose I couldn't say that Nate Braydon *walked* into my life. He sort of slithered in covered with blood and yuck.

"It's a boy!" Dr. Kotsopoulos announced.

"It's a boy," Corrie repeated with an exhausted sigh. She had wanted a boy.

"One of each," she'd said. And, "Every man wants a son."

Every man but me.

All the people that I cared about in the world, all the people that I'd loved and who had loved me…all of them had been women. I liked women. I understood women. Lauren's birth had been one of the sweetest moments of my life. And she continued to make even my worst day seem more bearable. With her little baby smile and the way she said, "Daddy," she made me feel as if I were some uniquely special being, a father. I couldn't have loved her more.

But a son. How did a man love a son? What was that all about?

"It's a boy!"

The doctor laid the little slimy guy on Corrie's tummy. I kissed her on the temple, careful not to block her view.

"He's perfect," I assured her.

"Perfect," she agreed.

I didn't share any of my worry, my concern, with Corrie. And I completely hid my anxiety from her parents out in the waiting room. But when I called Gram, it just came out.

"I don't know anything about raising a boy," I told her. "I don't remember anything about my own dad. I always considered that a blessing. But how will I raise a son? I don't have any idea."

Gram giggled, as if I'd said something funny. "You'll do fine," she assured me. "Just follow the example of your Heavenly Father, that's much better than anything you could have learned from Floyd Braydon."

It occurred to me to point out that *my Heavenly Father* had allowed his son to be crucified for the wrongs of other people. Of course I didn't. I would never have the faith that Gram had, the certainty of her convictions, but I couldn't help but respect her beliefs.

"God will guide you," she said. "Trust in him, do what you know is right. Things will always work out exactly as they are supposed to."

I tried to take comfort in Gram's confidence.

Two days later, we brought Nate home to our little garage apartment behind Mrs. Neider's house. Corrie's parents were waiting in the driveway. They snapped photos of us driving up, getting out, climbing the stairs. It was like having our own personal paparazzi.

By the time we got into the apartment I was wishing they were gone.

"I'm so sorry that Michael isn't here to see him come home," Corrie's mother said.

"He came to see us in the hospital," Corrie told her. "Babies aren't really on the top of the interest list for good-looking bachelors."

"Somebody's got to run the store, Edna," Corrie's dad pointed out.

"Here, have a seat, Doc," I said, offering him my worn easy chair with the hand towels pinned atop the threadbare arms.

Even after being married to their daughter for two and a half years, I still called Corrie's parents Doc and Mrs. Maynard. I was hoping to someday work my way to George and Edna, but I knew they would never be Mom and Dad.

The mother and grandmother were seated together on the couch, cooing over the little fellow's wide-eyed look at the world. I stood leaning against the doorjamb of my own house and feeling like the outsider.

Corrie's mom was chattering to Nate in the most nauseating baby talk possible. It was all oogy-boogy-ba-ba. It was all I could do not to roll my eyes. I caught Doc's glance. I was pretty sure he wanted to roll his eyes as well, but we both had the good sense to refrain.

Lauren, in pink shorts and a T-shirt decorated in butterflies, was going nuts, of course. Behaving as if she'd suddenly become hyper. She was talking too loud, banging her toys, demanding attention that she wasn't getting. My heart went out to her. I'd never had a little brother, but I could imagine that it might not seem like that much fun at first. She was so used to the care, the love, the admiration of everyone in the family. Nobody was looking at her today and that was infuriating. She was getting more noisy and boisterous.

Wordlessly, I held out my arms to her and she jumped at the opportunity to climb into them. I sat her upon my hip as she wrapped her arms tightly around me. Her stringy blond hair smelled like strawberries.

"Your baby brother is brand-new," I explained to her. "That's why everyone is looking at him. They've never seen him before."

She leaned close and whispered in my ear.

"He's ugly."

"I know," I admitted. "But don't tell Mom or Grandma. It might hurt their feelings."

She nodded solemnly, agreeing to keep our secret.

"Oh, dear," Edna complained as she glanced up and noticed us. "Look, Corrie, your husband and daughter don't even have a place to sit down. George, we'd better leave. There's just not room for everyone in this tiny place. I can't imagine how either of you can think that you'll be able to raise two children here."

The words stung, and even though they were typical, I couldn't help but resent them.

"People all over the world raise children in places smaller than this," Corrie defended. "I love keeping my children close."

Mrs. Maynard sighed in exasperation as she rose to her feet.

I said nothing.

In a way, it was a good thing that Corrie's mother was such a complainer. As long as she kept up her litany of my failings as a provider, Corrie would staunchly defend me. And if she was defending me, she couldn't reasonably be discontented as well.

The truth was, of course, that her mother was right.

The place was way too small for a family of four, but every penny I made was tied up in company expenses and equipment. Personal sacrifices were a necessity when trying to get a business off the ground. Corrie understood that. Unfortunately, her mother did not.

It was going to take a lot of long hours, hard work and thrifty living to turn Braydon Oil Field Service into a profitable company. But business was great.

With OPEC crunching the price of oil up to thirty-four dollars a barrel, producers were looking at secondary recovery as more cost effective than new development. I hadn't got my start on the ground floor, of course. But there was still a lot of money to be made, even by a small independent company like mine.

In truth, making money wasn't that tough. As the Midnight Mechanic I'd already established myself as reliable and dependable. I had a long list of clients who called me first when they had a well down. I actually had more jobs than I could reasonably take on. And I couldn't accept any more, because I didn't have the crews to do them.

The biggest challenge of my company was not making money, it was keeping up with the progress in technology and hiring good workers.

The boom was on in the oil fields, there was full employment. The statistics said there were three percent out of work. From my perspective, that three percent didn't particularly want to work. I was hiring guys straight out of high school, giving them top pay after a couple of weeks' training, and then watching them leave me for Big Four jobs with better benefits. It was frustrating. The ones that stayed on were usually too lazy to work or had trouble getting along. It wasn't the best of circumstances. And it kept me doing six twelve-hour days a week. I was paying down debt and growing my business, but I missed my family.

With a flurry of more picture-taking and lots of hugs and kisses all around, my in-laws finally left us alone. But I wasn't free to lounge around in domestic bliss. I'd already taken off the whole morning.

I kissed my wife and kids goodbye and went back to work.

When I said, "I missed my family," I guess I should explain that I didn't simply mean that I thought about them all day and wished that I was home. That was true, of course. But what I really meant was that in those early years of our marriage, my family was growing, changing, doing exciting, memorable things every day. And I was missing all that.

Most nights I'd come home very late. Lauren would already be sleeping. The baby would sometimes be awake, but he was growing so fast he looked like a different kid every time I saw him. Corrie would be exhausted, walking around like a zombie in a bathrobe. She kept her hair cut close to her head, like a boy's. And there was never so much as a smear of makeup. She bore little resemblance to the sexy college girl that I'd married. I suppose that was all right, though. We never got to have sex anymore, so if she'd looked good, I guess I would have *really* missed it.

When I did get a rare evening to be home, it wasn't like things went perfect. They had their routine and my presence was like a disruption.

"Let's go, Lauren, it's time for your bath."

"No! Daddy's home. I doan wanna baff."

"You have to have a bath."

"I doan wanna!"

Lauren would curl her little lip and stamp her foot.

She had the exact same expression on her face that Corrie got when she stood up to her mother.

"Why don't I give her a bath?" I suggested.

Lauren immediately complied.

Problem.

Routine bath with Mommy takes fifteen minutes, then ten minutes more to get into pajamas and into bed.

Bath with Daddy takes an hour of laughing and splashing. Ten minutes to get into pajamas and then two hours' worth of song, stories and threats to counter overstimulation before finally succumbing to sleep.

Corrie never complained of my intrusion or the fact that my help cost her more time. Not that she was a saint. She could be as cranky or whiney as anyone, but maybe she was too tired to complain. She'd just snuggle up against my chest and listen to me voice my dreams.

"What I really need is a frac truck," I told her one night.

"What's a frac truck?" she asked.

"It's a truck you use for fracing."

She giggled like a little girl. "Tell me what *fratching* is and maybe the truck will make more sense."

"Fracing, it rhymes with *cracking*. It's making fractures in the rock with high-pressure pumps. You inject those fractures with sand that holds the cracks open so that the trapped oil can work its way through to the main zone. It increases recovery to thirty, sometimes thirty-five percent."

She nodded thoughtfully.

"How much does a frac truck cost?"

I shook my head. "A half million bucks."

A sigh of exclamation escaped from her lips in one little puff.

"I know," I agreed. "That's a lot of mac and cheese. This is not a poor boy's business."

"Will the bank loan you that much?"

I nodded. "They are handing out checks down there like you wouldn't believe," I told her. "It's almost crazy."

"So would the oil companies pay you more for fracing their wells?"

"Fracing is very expensive," I said. "But if you're going to make these secondary recovery fields pay off, it's what you're going to have to do."

"Then go talk to the banker," she said. "If he thinks we can eventually pay all this off, then we should surely believe it."

"What about your house?" I asked.

"My house?"

"Our house," I corrected. "I know we've got to buy a house. We can't raise these kids cramped in this little place forever."

She shrugged. "We can last a little bit longer," she told me. Then glancing around at the toy-strewn main room, with Lauren's little screened-off bedroom/corner on one end, she added, "It will be less for the kids to mess up."

Corrie
1982

◆ ◀

If it hadn't been for my brother, Mike, I'm not sure that Sam and I would ever have gotten around to buying our own house. Dear old Mrs. Neider passed away on an exceptionally warm afternoon in February. She'd been sitting on the porch playing with Lauren and Nate. Nate was still shy and reserved with everyone except me, but she and Lauren were good friends. There were always having tea parties or playing mail delivery or grocery store.

I was washing up the lunch dishes. I had Mrs. Neider's harvest-gold kitchen wall phone pulled as far as its coiled cord would allow so that I could talk to Mom on the phone. It was an emergency meeting of the Maynard women. Mike had invited Cherry Dale Larson, the former Cherry Dale Pepper, ex-cheerleader and notorious local divorcée with two small children, to the Chamber of Commerce Citizens Banquet.

Mom was certain that they must be having a secret affair, which would explain why Mike did not seem to be particularly interested in dating any of the younger, more eligible women of Lumkee.

I was trying to both ease her fears and raise her level of tolerance.

"Mom, just because he's escorting her around town doesn't mean he's sleeping with her," I pointed out.

"I can't imagine any other reason he'd be willing to be seen with her, the little tramp," Mom responded.

"They have known each other since high school," I said. "And from what I've heard she's trying to get her new gym classes off the ground. Mike probably invited her as a prospective member of the Chamber."

"Oh, for heaven's sake, Corrie." Mom's voice was exasperated. "An empty dance floor with mirrors on the wall is not a gym. And she's not even providing classes for children. She says it's for women only."

I never really liked Cherry Dale, but at this point felt called upon to defend her. She'd rented the old Hay Biscuit Dance Hall and was opening a place right on the highway. The sign read Cherry Dale's Pepxercise.

"Mom, it is a business," I told her. "These fitness centers are springing up everywhere. They have them in Tulsa."

Mom made a haughty, derisive remark.

"I can't imagine that any woman in her right mind would want to waste her time going to some smelly gym, when she can get just as much exercise shopping on Main Street."

"Mommy."

Lauren walked into the kitchen and tugged on my shirt, distracting me from my conversation.

"Mommy, I have to show you something."

"Just a second," I told my mother. "Lauren, I've told you a dozen times, when I'm on the phone it is the same as if I were speaking to someone in the room. Interrupting is very bad manners. When you see that I'm on the phone, you should wait until I'm finished and then you can politely tell me anything you have to tell me."

"But Mommy…"

"You do understand what I'm saying?"

"Yes, Mommy, but…"

"I know that it's hard and that you're impatient, but you have to learn to wait your turn."

She stood then, waiting, though not so patiently, standing on one foot and then the other. I deliberately stalled her for about a minute. "Excuse me, Mom," I said into the receiver. "Lauren wants to tell me something."

I smiled at her proudly. She was very bright, and growing up to be so sweet and well behaved.

"What do you want to tell me, Lauren?" I asked.

"I think Mrs. Neider's dead, Mommy," she said. "She's still sitting in her chair, but she looks really dead."

I hung up on my mother without another word. I am certain that Lauren had never seen a dead body in her life, but she knew what she was talking about. Mrs. Neider was sitting in her rocking chair, eyes closed as if she were asleep. She was not asleep.

Nate, for once, had overcome his shyness and was struggling to climb into her lap.

I jerked him away and into my arms and led Lauren back into the kitchen. I picked up the phone and called Dr. Kotsopoulos. I didn't know that doctors don't even make house calls for the dead. The office told me to call her family and the funeral home.

We got through the next few days with only a fair amount of difficulty. Sam took off work the day of the funeral. Our intent was to go to the service to show respect for the dear old lady. The family asked us not to.

"Somebody has to stay here and guard this house," her daughter, Betty, told us. "Since everybody knows the family will be at the church and the cemetery, no telling who will show up here to try to take something out of the house."

So Sam and I honored Mrs. Neider by sitting in her house while she was eulogized and buried.

"You didn't miss much," Sam's grandmother assured us later. "It wasn't the best funeral. Her niece, Doris, did the music and it was very gloomy."

Since Gram had been to more funerals than most, we took her word for it.

Our immediate concern was for a place to live. The family made it eminently clear that we needed to vacate the premises as quickly as possible. In fact, the eldest son, Howard, suggested that we should begin paying rent retroactively. He said it in such a way that it sounded as if he thought we had been living off the kindness of an old woman, completely discounting all that we had done for her in the four years we'd lived in the garage apartment.

His attitude made Sam furious. He was ready to pack up and move into our car rather than spend another night in the little apartment that had been our home for so very long. I insisted that we had to have a place to go before we left.

I spent the next morning looking at rental properties. I didn't see anything that really felt like a home, but there were a couple of possibilities that I could probably bear to live in.

It was a gray day. The weather had turned and the wind blew through my coat. If I was cold, I figured the kids were shivering. We went to the drugstore to warm up. It was not really a good idea to interrupt the workday at Maynard Drug, so I made sure that we didn't do it often enough to wear out our welcome.

Dad was delighted to see us. He so rarely got to see Lauren and Nate when my mother was not around. He took them to the back, entertaining them while I stepped behind the soda counter to pour myself a cup of coffee. The saucer clanked loudly upon the marble, but it was a familiar sound. The drugstore was as much a part of my childhood as home or school. Every afternoon throughout the elementary grades, I came here to sweep up. By high school I was working two evenings and Saturdays.

The place was like an archeological site turned upside down. Near eye level it was a 1980s pharmacy with all the brightly labeled cold remedies and glossy magazines that represented. A little higher, however, were the sleekly modernistic plastic clocks of the sixties and the pants-down Coppertone advertisement and rock-and-roll motifs of the fifties. Up next to the fifteen-foot ceiling were sepia-toned panoramic photographs of Lumkee as a raw boomtown. There was even a brightly painted Gibson girl sipping a Coca-Cola.

I took my usual behind-the-counter seat on the Dr. Pepper cold box, leaving all eight chrome-and-vinyl bar stools available for paying customers.

A minute later my brother came up and joined me.

"I've always heard it's bad to drink alone," he said, gesturing toward the coffeepot.

I poured him a cup and set it and the little one-serving cream container in front of him.

"If you'd spent the morning driving around Lumkee with Raylene Wallace, you'd be looking to drown your sorrows as well."

He feigned abject horror and then laughed.

Mike had a great laugh. He and I looked a lot alike. Everybody said so. But somehow, it looked better on him. With honey-brown hair and green eyes, Mike was six foot two, long and lean, with ruggedly handsome features and a dentist-perfect smile. He'd played all the sports in high school but had settled on swimming by the time he got to college. It kept him fit and tanned. Even in the middle of winter, he drove all the way into Tulsa two or three nights a week to swim at an indoor pool where he had a membership. "So did you find the house of your dreams?" he asked.

I shrugged. "Most of the Lumkee rental market is more like a nightmare," I told him.

"Well, maybe you should take this opportunity to actually buy a house," he said.

I narrowed my eyes and gazed at him speculatively. "Are you a lobbyist for Mom these days?" I asked him.

He chuckled.

"No, she already has more influence than could ever be bought or sold," Mike assured me. "But it does seem like a convenient time to be going after something you want."

I shook my head. "Sam's business is just getting on its feet. I hate to put any more stress on him."

Mike was thoughtful for a moment and then he spoke in the soft, gently prodding way that he'd always used to encourage me to study hard and do my best.

"Buying a house isn't about Sam or his business," he said. "I know this might be a radical concept, sis, but you know you could go out and get a J-O-B."

He spelled out the last in a whisper, as if it were a subversive idea.

I chuckled and shook my head. "Oh, yeah, Mike,

that's why Mom thinks you're the smart one," I told him facetiously. "Maybe this has escaped the notice of a carefree bachelor like yourself, but I have two small children."

"And?"

"And it would cost more to put them in day care than the pay scale at Burger Barn currently allows."

"Then you should mark Burger Barn off your list of job prospects," he countered. "I hate to be the one to point this out, but you've been the one putting the roof over your family's head since you got married."

I waved off this observation.

"I just helped out Mrs. Neider," I told him. "I could do that on a flexible schedule and without leaving the kids."

"Then I'd suggest that you find a position that offers flexible work schedules and allows you to bring the kids along."

"What kind of job would that be?"

"You're asking me?" Mike replied. "Weren't you the girl who was valedictorian of Lumkee High."

"So were you," I pointed out.

"And look at me," he said. "What a success I am, still working at the drugstore for Dad."

I laughed and shook my head.

"Seriously, sis," Mike continued. "Get a house, get a job. Get some things that you want out of life. Sam will be behind you one hundred percent. The guy is crazy about you, you know."

I nodded.

"If Cherry Dale, who can't even string two coherent sentences together, can come up with a business plan that allows her to make money with her kids underfoot, I'm sure my brilliant sister can do even better."

"And speaking of Cherry Dale," I said. "What's the deal there? Are you two having secret rendezvous, planning summer nuptials or just trying to see if you can push the local gossips into busy-signal overdrive and shut down telephone service in the entire region."

Mike grinned. "Don't try to distract me," he said. "Cherry Dale and I are just two happily single people trapped in a community of Stepford wives who won't be happy until everyone is *till-death-do-us-part-ing*."

"Marriage is wonderful, Mike," I told him. "I can highly recommend it."

"And I can highly recommend working for a living and buying your own house," he countered.

I shrugged, feeling wistful. "Even if I could," I pointed out, "it would take me a year to save up the down payment. We have no choice but to rent again."

"Dad would loan you the money," he noted.

"And Sam would cut my tongue out before he'd let me ask for help," I said. "I'd cut my own tongue out before I'd mention it. If I even suggested it he'd sell one of the trucks or mortgage more of the equipment. He'd work himself to death to try to give me whatever I want, Mike, and I can't let him do that."

My brother nodded solemnly and I thought that was the end of it. But I should have known Mike better. He had that same bulldoggedness as my mother. Unexpectedly he stopped by the apartment that night when the ten o'clock news was on.

"What's wrong?" I asked immediately when I opened the door.

"Nothing," he assured me.

"Why are you here so late?"

He chuckled. "I've got to get here late if I want to talk to Sam."

"You want to talk to Sam?"

My question was skeptical.

"Hey, Mike, come on in," my husband said from behind me. "What's going on?"

"I wanted to talk to you about something," Mike said. "I want to talk to you both."

"Sure, come on in."

My brother's arrival awakened Lauren, who escaped from her bed and sleepily crawled up in Uncle Mike's lap, where she lay her tousled blond head upon his chest and returned to her dreams.

"That looks good on you, Mike," I told him. "You'd make some lucky little boy or girl a wonderful father."

He looked down at Lauren and gently smoothed a stray lock of hair from her cheek.

"I'm already making a couple of lucky kids a wonderful uncle," he told me. "I figure I should quit while I'm ahead."

I frowned at him and he grinned back.

"So what's up?" Sam asked.

"Well, I've got some money in the bank that's not making all that much interest and I was hoping you would give me some advice about investing it," Mike said.

I was immediately alert.

Sam was puzzled.

"I think you've come to talk to the wrong guy," he said. "I don't know anything about investment."

"You know about the oil business," Mike said.

Sam nodded. "Well, this might be a good time to buy some Big Four stock," he admitted. "The price of crude this week is down to thirty and a half a barrel. That's the lowest we've seen it in years. It's hard to imagine that OPEC is going to let it slide any further."

Mike was nodding thoughtfully.

"The value of fossil fuels can only go up," Sam continued. "It's a limited commodity and the industrial economy depends upon it. International production has become so risky and politically vulnerable that what's pumped here at home becomes increasingly more valuable. So you're looking at the Big Four?"

"Not really," Mike told him. "I'm not interested in putting my money in some faceless corporation that I hear from once a year in a slick report. What I'd like to do is invest in a small, well-run company that's expanding and growing. I want a place where I trust the management and know they're honest, hardworking and there's lots of potential for future earnings."

Sam's brow furrowed. "That's a good idea," he said. "I'm sure there are some very good opportunities just like that. I'm not sure I can really advise you, off the top of my head like this. If you'd give me a couple of weeks to look around, ask a few questions, I'll do what I can to come up with some choices for a good, safe situation for you."

"I appreciate that, Sam," Mike said. "But honestly, I've already figured out where I want to put my money. There's a local business that I've watched grow from nothing. It's well-managed, respected, and the guy running it is honest as the day is long and very careful about keeping things on a sound financial footing."

"Sounds good," Sam agreed.

"I'm absolutely certain that this is exactly where I want my money to be. I'm just hoping the guy will let me buy in."

"What company is it?" Sam asked.

Mike glanced over at me. I already knew the answer.

"Braydon Oil Field Service," Mike told him.

Sam
1982

We moved into our very own brand-new house in May. Fifteen hundred square feet in a new track of housing just east of town. We fenced in the backyard and put up a play set. In the front we planted two red oak trees with the symbolic assumption that they would grow tall and strong like our children. Just the idea of the mortgage made my palms sweat, but I was so happy to be able to move in. It was the nicest place I had ever even spent the night. And now it was ours, mine and Corrie's.

The first night we made love in our bedroom, I asked her afterward, "Can you believe we actually own our own house?"

She claimed that she always knew we would.

I have to admit, I was never so sure.

The kids both had their own rooms and Corrie and her mother worked day and night to get everything painted and papered and decorated the way that they wanted.

My part of this was to redouble my efforts on the job. The price of crude oil continued to inexplicably slump, though most people said that the Falklands War, down in Argentina, couldn't help but get things back on track.

I have to admit, I was feeling pretty dad-gummed good about myself. I was twenty-five years old. The owner of a successful business and a new home, married to the prettiest and brightest girl in town, father of two happy, healthy kids. When I walked down Main Street, I held my head pretty high.

I was in this frame of mind: proud, happy, blessed, the day my father showed up. He walked into the little eight-by-ten office shed I kept on my equipment lot. I was on the phone with Arnie Rayburn, trying to collect what was owed me. His struggling independent company was strapped and was getting slower and slower to pay. I just wanted to make sure that he didn't forget to pay at all.

The older man, thin and bent, nodded to me, biding his time looking at the photographs on my walls. They were all pictures of rigs we'd worked on and jobs we'd done. I kept family photographs on my desk. The ones I hung around the room were to display the breadth of my client list.

I didn't know the fellow, but I was certain that I'd seen him around, he just looked too familiar to be a complete stranger. He wasn't in the best physical shape. But old oil men can be tough and wiry. A lot of them could do a full day's labor well into their seventies. With good workers still at a premium, an employer would be a fool to overlook a proven, experienced laborer.

I finished my call with Arnie and rose to my feet, offering my hand.

"Sam Braydon," I said.

He nodded. "You're pretty young to be running a business like this yourself," he responded.

I shrugged. "There's money to be made in the oil patch these days," I told him. "And I've been lucky."

The man nodded. "I heard around town that you married Doc Maynard's girl," he said. "Did Maynard set you up in business?"

I was insulted, but I tried not to show it. I'm sure a lot of people probably thought the same thing. Most just had the good sense not to say it aloud.

"No," I answered, calmly. "I *set myself* up in business with a lot of hard work and some handy bank loans. Are you looking for a job?"

He shrugged. "Well, I don't have one."

"Did you quit or get fired?" I asked.

"Neither," he answered. "I been in prison."

"Prison?" I repeated.

He hesitated a moment, eyeing me speculatively before he nodded.

"Sam," he said. "I'm your daddy."

"What?"

The question came out before I could stop it. Not until that very moment did I actually recognize him. I don't think that I can express in words my feelings. I looked into his eyes and I could vaguely see the man I used to know. I couldn't call to mind even one specific incident of sitting on his lap or playing with him. I could remember looking at the back of his head the day that I'd seen him in court. That was it. But in his eyes there was something of my childhood, my past. Something that I wanted.

"Well…well hi," I finally managed to get out.

I didn't know if I should hug him. In my life, both with Gram and with Corrie, hugging of family mem-

bers was mandatory. But somehow it just seemed awkward and strange.

"Have a seat," I suggested. "Would you like some
coffee?"

"Sure," he said.

I turned my back as I got him a cup. It was a good
thing he couldn't see how my hands were shaking.

"Cream? Sugar?"

"Black's fine," he said.

When I turned back around he was holding the family portrait from my desk. We'd had it made the previous Christmas at the new Kmart just south of town.

"That's my wife and kids," I explained unnecessar-
ily.

He nodded. "The little girl looks like your mother,"
he told me.

I smiled. "That's what Gram says."

He glanced up quickly. "Is that old lady still alive?"

"Yeah, she's doing great. Still keeping her own
house and going to church every Sunday, whether she
feels like it or not."

He made a strange snorting sound.

"She never liked me," he said. "I suppose she's told
you all kinds of terrible things about me."

That statement was puzzling and made me vaguely
wary. "No," I replied honestly. "I don't think she's
ever said anything about you at all."

He raised an eyebrow as if he were momentarily
skeptical and then he nodded as if that made perfect
sense.

I sat down across the table from him. I was uneasy.
This was my father. He was to me what I was to Lauren
and Nate. I hadn't seen him in more than twenty years
and I ought to have plenty to tell him, questions to ask

him. There should have been a world of words to be spoken between us. I couldn't think of anything to say.

Silence seemed to be good for him as well. He drank his coffee. Glanced around the room. Occasionally he glanced at me.

"When did you get out?" I asked finally.

"Two weeks ago," he answered. "I been hanging around Tulsa for a few days."

"Oh."

"Got a few friends there," he said.

"That's good."

More silence.

"So, you got a nice-looking family," he said, pointing again to the photograph on my desk.

"Yes," I assured him, smiling. "Corrie is wonderful and the kids are great. Both of them smart and happy."

He nodded.

"And this business of yours, it's not too shabby, either."

"We're doing great," I agreed. "It's been tough getting myself established, but things are going along nicely now."

"I'd like to meet your children," he said.

This request actually surprised me. It was strange to imagine that he would be interested. I reminded myself that they were his grandchildren. His only grandchildren. He hadn't been involved in my life, but that really hadn't been possible. He'd been locked up. And I had never once gone to visit him.

Of course, he could have written me a letter or sent a Christmas card or acknowledged my birthday. For some reason, I didn't allow myself to dwell upon those facts, instead I heard myself inviting him to come to the house for dinner.

He suggested that I meet him downtown, but I didn't want to let him go. I'm not sure if I was afraid I'd never see him again or just eager to show off my life, but I begged him to hang around with me, visit the jobs, watch me work.

I don't ever recall consciously daydreaming about being with my father. I'd thought about my mother a lot and Gram had always talked about her. I remembered her, but only in the vaguest sense, and I'd imagined her to be a lot like Corrie. Of the circumstances surrounding her death, I tried not to think at all. I decided in childhood that it had been some terribly regrettable accident. I was sure that my father was as saddened by her death as I was myself.

However, as we went through the day together, I did not introduce him to my employees or clients. I had spent too many years keeping a low-profile past to suddenly present this stranger as my long-lost father.

It was after four in the afternoon before I finally called Corrie. I wasn't sure what to say and I didn't want to say it in front of my father. We were out at a well and he was taking a leak in the bushes when I radioed her on the CB.

"This is BOWS Patch Dog calling the home base. Come back at me, Daisy May?"

It took three or four calls before Corrie picked up.

"Daisy May, you're cool and clear Patch Dog. Talk to me."

I could hear the typical kid chaos in the background.

"I'm bringing somebody home for dinner," I said simply.

"Oh, gosh—" was her initial response. Followed by a more official "Roger, what's the time on that?"

"Two hours," I told her. "I can stall longer if you need it."

"No, it's fine," she assured me. "I was cooking chicken. Will that be okay?"

"Sounds good."

"Is it a client?"

I hesitated. The radio barked again.

"Repeat, is it a client?"

"It's my dad," I answered.

There was a long silence on the other end of the line.

"Okay," she said finally. "We'll see you when you get here."

As it turned out, Corrie had plenty of time. When I closed the office, my father suggested that rather than go straight home, we stop at the beer joint on the edge of town.

With the exception of my time in the army, I have never been much of a drinker. Gram never really approved of alcohol in any form unless it was rubbed on. But I do admit that after being outside in the hot summer sun, there is nothing better in the world than an ice-cold beer. Since it was on the cusp of summer, I figured a nice brew after a long day wouldn't be such a bad idea.

Inside the place it was dark and dank and smelled of cigarettes. I knew most everybody at the bar. If they were surprised to see me there, nobody commented on it.

Dad sat down at a table at the back, near the shuffleboard table. I went up to buy the beer. They had Coors on tap, but in the vague recesses of my memory I knew that Dad drank Lone Star and I asked for two bottles. I was so proud of this tiny sliver of knowledge that when I got to the table I revealed it.

"You drink Lone Star, right?"

He glanced up at me and shrugged. "I'll drink anything," he said. "With this damned Oklahoma three-two, it all tastes like horse piss, anyway."

Three-two referred to the mandated maximum alcohol content, 3.2 percent, which was about half what most beers contain. Oklahoma beer was pretty watered down, supposedly to keep guys from getting drunk. Of course, there always seemed to be plenty of drunk guys around, so I'm guessing it didn't work as well as the lawmakers in Oklahoma City had hoped.

I sat across the table from Dad. He was examining the old, faded photographs that hung on the walls.

"This place sure hasn't changed much in twenty years," he said. "I'd already spent a million hours in this place by the time I was your age."

This surprised me. I guess it shouldn't have, but I'd always thought of Lumkee as my town, as Gram's town, as my mother's town. That my father had lived here, knew the area and the people had completely escaped my notice.

"I guess you met Mom here in town," I said.

He glanced up. "Gloria? Oh, yeah, I met her here in town. You don't think her mother would have let her go anyplace else?"

"No, I guess not," I responded as he took a big gulp of beer.

"Half the reason that woman married me was to get away from her stifling mama and that damned holy-roller church."

"Half the reason?"

"You were the other half," he said, winking at me. "Did you know that? Did you know that she was knocked-up?"

I shook my head.

My father nodded. "I didn't think that old biddy would have fessed up to that," he said. "If I hadn't married her precious little daughter the damned church would have probably burned Gloria at the stake!"

The conversation was disturbing. I was unaccustomed to hearing anything bad about Gram or my mother. I didn't want to hear any more, but I didn't want to walk away, either.

"That kind of thing happens," I told him. "I mean, getting pregnant before you're married. It's happened to lots of people."

"Did it happen to you?" he asked.

"Yes."

He laughed uproariously. "Knocked up Doc's daughter," he said. "That's a stroke of brilliance, I'd say. You're pretty smart, son, even if I do say so myself."

The use of the term *son* was so strange and unfamiliar that the rest of the sentence was completely lost on me.

In all we drank five beers before we headed toward home. I had one, he had four. My father wanted to have another, as well, but we were already late for dinner and I didn't want Corrie to worry.

She looked very concerned when we walked into the door. The house was unbelievably quiet, but the smell of fried chicken was welcoming.

"Corrie, this is my dad," I said, introducing the two.

"Now, aren't you a pretty thing," he said. His voice was confident, charming, a bit too familiar, as if he were used to having women adore him.

"No handshake now, girlie. Give your father-in-law

a kiss. Why, you're as curvy as a mountain highway. Two kids, Sam tells me, but you sure haven't lost your figure."

Corrie's smile was tight, unwelcoming.

"Where are the kids?" I asked her.

"They're spending the night with my mother," she replied.

I'm sure my jaw must have dropped.

"Dad wanted to meet them," I told her.

She opened her mouth slightly, as if to make some sort of explanation, but none came out.

"Dinner's ready to set on the table," she said.

"No hurry," Dad told her. "I'll take another beer if you've got one," he said to me.

"Ah...I don't have any beer here at the house," I explained. "I can get you some..." I glanced over at Corrie for assistance.

"Iced tea," she said. "Or juice. I can make some coffee."

He shook his head. "No, that's fine," he said.

Corrie scurried off to the kitchen and my father was walking around the living room, looking everything over.

"This is a damn fine house, son," he told me.

I beamed with pride. "We just moved in May 6. It's brand new."

"Nice, real nice," he assured me.

"Have a seat," I told him, offering my new Naugahyde lounger. "I'll see if I can help Corrie."

"I always say, 'Leave the women's work to the women,' but go ahead if you need to. I am getting hungry."

I left him and went into the kitchen. Corrie was

spooning up mashed potatoes. A skillet of bubbling gravy was on the stove. She did not look happy.

"What's going on?" I asked her.

"You tell me," she replied.

"Are you mad because we stopped for a couple of beers?"

"I don't care if you want to drink a beer," she said. "Although I'm glad we don't keep the stuff in the refrigerator."

"Why are the kids over at your mother's?"

"Why do you think?"

"I have no idea."

Angrily, she handed me the bowl of potatoes and began pouring gravy into the boat.

"I didn't think the children should be here," she said.

"Why not?"

The cast-iron skillet banged loudly as she set it back down on the stove.

"Sam," she said, "sorry to be the one to point this out, but we have a murderer in the living room."

A low, humorless laugh came from the doorway. My father was standing there.

"Not only shapely, but feisty as well," he said. "You damn sure got yourself a wife, Sammy."

A look passed between the two of them. It was pure animosity and distrust on both sides.

"Did your husband tell you that he's offered me a job?" my father asked her. "Looks like I'm going to be working at Braydon Oil Well Service."

Corrie
1984

Our family, in the years that followed the arrival of Floyd Braydon in Lumkee, was plagued by an abrupt and seemingly insurmountable division of the sexes. It was Lauren and I versus what I called the "Men's Club."

My daughter, a pretty and precocious second-grader, had been one of the first children chosen for the elementary school's new gifted and talented program. She was tall for her age and a little bit awkward, but she was cute and sweet and bright-eyed. She looked very much like my mom. Therefore it was a certainty that she was going to grow up to be very attractive.

Our time together was golden. We were the perfect mother-daughter team. We cooked together. Read together. Discussed books and concocted science experiments. I was den mother for her Brownie troop. And the mom most likely to spend a Saturday at the amusement park. I loved it. My daughter was happy and biddable. Willing to sing to me as I scrubbed the bathrooms or to sit patiently while I styled her waist-length chestnut hair into a french braid, an elaborate crown or a punk-rock do.

She'd inherited my mom's love of shopping. And

fortunately, Sam's business was doing well enough for her to do a lot of it. We hardly wasted our time with the flimsy offerings of Lumkee's downtown Main Street. Lauren and I haunted the malls of south Tulsa where we could buy Calvin Klein jeans and Izod shirts. For Lauren that was the second-grade uniform. If, in the silence of my soul, I worried about the appropriateness of a seven-year-old wearing Charlie perfume and Lee Press-On Nails, I never voiced it aloud. Lauren was my gal pal, my best buddy.

I needed her.

Sam was no longer there for me, he was busy with his *dad*.

Floyd and I had nothing to say to each other. Sam and his father never stopped talking. They spent the weekdays together. Floyd was quickly promoted to superintendent. A position where he had the authority to watch everyone else do the work, not being particularly interested in actually working himself.

"He's an old man, Corrie," Sam responded when I pointed this out. "His joints are stiff and he doesn't see as well as younger men."

Floyd managed, however, to get drunk and dance at honky-tonks every Saturday night. And his vision was good enough for him to give the eye to every female between the ages of fifteen and fifty-five.

He ate dinner with us three or four times a week. I didn't like that, either.

"Dad appreciates a good meal, Corrie," Sam told me. "You should be flattered that he's so partial to your cooking."

Weekends for the guys were filled with hunting, fishing, watching sports or going to gun shows.

My disapproval made it all worse. I complained that

Sam was wasting his time. So he bought a freezer and filled it with dead birds, venison and bass. I didn't want the two of them sitting around my living room. So Sam bought his dad a big TV and spent his time there.

When I found out that Sam had bought his father a handgun (for protection), I threatened to contact Floyd's parole officer. Sam brought home the semiautomatic .45 to store in our bedroom closet!

The thing I hated most, however, was not Sam's idolization of the man he never really knew. I hated my father-in-law being with my son.

From the very beginning, I tried to keep the children away from Floyd. With Lauren that was no problem. He didn't even seem to notice her. But Nate and his paw-paw were immediately inseparable. Maybe it was some kind of genetic-link thing. Unlike Sam or Lauren, Nate actually favored his grandfather. He had Floyd's eyes and his big toothy grin. And they both had that sort of casual charismatic charm that attracted people to them.

The last thing that I wanted, however, was for my son to grow up to have a life that in any way resembled that of Floyd Braydon's. I did everything I could to separate the two of them. But it was a losing battle to try to protect my five-year-old from the influence of his grandfather. I fought it, anyway. I fought it daily. That actually made it worse.

Floyd took it as a challenge. Quietly, diabolically, everything Floyd did was designed to undermine my authority.

It wasn't like he said to Nate, "Don't listen to your mother." He was much too clever to do anything so direct. But in every interaction between the two of us, I felt diminished, disregarded. And my son picked up on that. All things female were disparaged. *Pitiful* was the word Floyd most often used for anything to do with the feminine gender. Nate began using the word to describe almost anything broken, intricate or pretty.

"Can't you see the way Floyd treats me?" I asked Sam. "Can't you see how he treats women?"

He just stared at me, clueless. "Dad goes out of his way to be polite. You're the one that's always making some nasty comment," he replied. "And women love Dad. Every single woman in the county has got him in her sights, and the ones in town are dogging him night and day."

That was an exaggeration, of course. But I could hardly argue that Floyd wasn't popular with the ladies. Even among those who knew of his prison record there was fawning and primping in his presence.

"He's driving a wedge between me and my son," I said.

"Little boys like to be with their grandpas. There is nothing wrong with that. It's natural."

"It's not natural to have a grandfather who's a murderer."

Sam rolled his eyes as if my statement were ludicrous.

"My mother's death was a terrible accident," he says. "Dad took responsibility for that. And he's paid his debt to society. You can't hold it against him forever."

I was pretty sure that I could.

I looked for natural allies in the family. My first choice was Gram. The two of us had grown close spending Sundays together. She was too frail to make her own way to church, so Lauren and I now gave up the relative chicness of First Methodist to accompany Sam's grandmother to the tiny clapboard chapel that housed the Ninety and Nine Baptist Fellowship. Despite the name, we rarely saw more than forty people at worship. After the service we would, as Gram put it, "scare up a little lunch" together. There was always potatoes and pickled beets, crowder peas and raisin pie. Lauren loved Gram's kitchen. And I have to admit, her home was somehow a haven of serenity and peace in my complicated world.

But her own life was not without flaw. She had good reason to hate Floyd Braydon. And she did.

"It's not Christian," Gram admitted to me one morning as she sat in her overstuffed upholstered rocking chair with the crochet arm covers. "But I still hate the man."

The last winter had been hard on her, that or Braydon's return to town. Though she always put on a smiling, cheery facade, I knew that these days she sat in her chair more than she puttered around her house. That long braid of silver hair twisted at the back of her head was pure white now and her hands trembled as they lay at rest upon her lap.

"Floyd Braydon turned my child away from me," she told me sadly. "He took that precious girl far from home and friends and family. He poisoned her life with whiskey and bad companions. And finally he killed her in a drunken rage." Gram shook her head and stared off into the empty depths of her stuffy, overheated living room. "'Vengeance is mine, sayeth the Lord,'" she quoted. "That's what my Bible tells me. Still, I lie in bed at night wishing I could see that man lying in a casket, cold as clay."

The pain in her words cut close to my heart, though my aspirations for his future were not as fatal.

"I just want him out of our lives," I told her.

She sighed heavily. "He will be, Corrie. I'm sure of that. His kind never really settle, they always move along."

Her submission to the status quo was not what I wanted. I needed her to actively work with me against Floyd Braydon.

"Aren't you worried about Sam?" I asked her. "It's not good for him to be around Floyd. The man is bad. Sam thinks he's rehabilitated, but we know that he's still the man he always was. What if he leads Sam into…into sin."

I felt weird saying that word, but I felt like I had to translate my fears, which were somehow wordless, into Gram's vocabulary.

"He will," she admitted nodding. "He's already brought a world of temptation into that boy's life. Sam is changing. He doesn't visit me like he used to. He doesn't believe as he once did."

"Doesn't that worry you?"

"The Bible says to 'train up a child in the way he should go. And when he is old he will not depart from it.' The part that a lot of folks fail to listen to is that teensy word *old*. I raised Sam to do right and I have faith that ultimately he will live up to his raising. I won't live to see it. I'm like an ancient Moses on Mount Nebo. I've got to trust that God keeps his promises in this world as I ready myself for the next."

The strength of her faith or her fatalism almost broke my heart.

Without Gram's assistance, I turned to my own family. That brought even less help.

"I'm not interfering between a father and his son," my dad told me.

"I don't like Braydon, either," my brother Mike admitted. "But he's your husband's father, Corrie. It's time you learned to get along with him."

The worst advice came from my mother.

"Honey," she said. "I think you'd feel better about everything if you'd lose some weight. When a women starts feeling pudgy, nothing in the world suits her."

I didn't actually feel pudgy, though I had put on about twenty pounds since high school. Since my body was one thing in my life that I could control, I began dieting.

I bought a gym membership to Cherry Dale's Pepxercise and began doing step aerobics and weight lifting. I quit marking my day around the hands of the clock and based my waking hours on calorie consumption. Monday through Friday, one thousand calories. Weekends twelve-hundred. Every third week, I did a liquid-protein fast.

I couldn't lose Floyd Braydon, but I dropped the twenty pounds, plus ten more in a little over two months. And it was really even more than that, because I had developed tremendous muscle strength and muscles weigh more than fat.

I loved being at the gym and I began spending more and more time there. Cherry Dale and I even began to become confidantes of a sort. Though she was three years older than me, she looked younger. She was as spirited and athletic as when she'd been a Lumkee High School cheerleader ten years earlier. And she wore the cutest workout clothes; rugged but revealing spandex, striped or printed in pink and lavender. It was like doing squats and crunches with Barbie herself.

At first we just shared exercise tips and diet warnings. But eventually that led to more personal discussions.

Her boys, Harlan and Rusty, were each one year older than Lauren and Nate. We were able to share frustrations and insights as well as personal gossip.

"Are you still seeing that guy from Perkins?" I asked her.

Cherry Dale shook her Princess Di hairdo.

"No, he's all tight with some giggly clerk in his office," she told me. "The woman's butt is as big as the grill on a Mack truck, but there is no accounting for what men want."

I nodded sympathetically.

"Well, you know my brother is still available," I pointed out. "You two are such good friends. It would be nice if that could blossom into something more."

She gave me a startled look. She was surprised, I assumed, that I looked favorably upon her relationship with my brother. I'm sure we both knew that my mother was no fan of hers.

Cherry Dale covered her surprise with a nervous laugh.

"Mike and I have already crossed the line," she said. "You know, that invisible line. We know each other too well as friends to ever get sappy in love with each other."

"A lot of good marriages are not based on being sappy in love," I pointed out, thinking about my own.

She nodded. "Yeah, that's true. But the ones that aren't eventually lose their luster and just fall apart."

That statement hung with me as the days passed.

Was that happening to my own marriage? Was my husband drifting away from me? Was our life together falling apart?

Certainly a case for that could be made. I was looking so good these days that teenage boys whistled at me when I stopped by the grocery store wearing my leotard. Yet my husband hardly seemed to notice. His attention seemed almost exclusively focused on his work, Floyd and the kids, in that order. I guess I was lucky to come in the top five.

If he was never home, then I decided that I should go to where he worked. I hit Sam up for a job in the office.

"You don't need to bother with that," he assured me. "You've got more than enough to do hauling the kids around and keeping the house going."

"I want to get a job," I assured him. "Mike's been telling me for ages that I should do that. If you won't let me work for you, I'll work for someone else."

Sam finally agreed and I found myself ensconced in the little office helping out part-time three days a week. The work was dull, boring monotonous filing. And my presence made Vicky, the office manager, nervous. I guess she thought I didn't trust her, or that I was after her job.

I saw my husband breeze in and out of the office twice a day. And I had Floyd Braydon hanging around constantly critiquing my work. It was hardly the solution I'd hoped for. Within a few weeks I gave my notice, telling anyone who would listen that I was completely content with my *real* job as wife and mother.

I don't think my brother believed me. But he didn't say so. Instead he offered other advice.

"Get a weekend away," Mike suggested. "You two never even had a honeymoon. Sam's making great

money these days. He can afford to take you somewhere first class."

The more I thought about it, the more I was sure that
Mike was right. We did need some time away. We did
need to have our honeymoon after all.

My first choice was New York.

Mike suggested San Francisco.

Sam and I finally agreed on San Antonio. Once that
was settled all that was left was making the time to go
there.

Sam
1985

—→ ←—

Corrie got it in her head that we needed some kind of vacation. It wasn't that easy for me to take time off. I didn't feel really comfortable leaving my business in someone else's care. But Corrie had been too quiet lately. And after the job fiasco it seemed to be worse. I know she missed the children, who were now in school all day. And in seven years of marriage, Corrie and I had never really gotten away together. We hadn't gone on a honeymoon or even so much as a weekend getaway without the kids. A little time away from our familiar life wasn't a bad idea.

I'd certainly earned some rest and relaxation. The price of Oklahoma crude was down to twenty-six dollars a barrel. Thirty dollars was what it had been a year earlier. But it was some kind of availability glitch. The North Sea reserves and Mexico had come into production at the same time. It was just a temporary unsteadiness in the market. Everyone I talked to was certain that by any estimation that made sense, oil ought to be selling at fifty dollars. There was war all over the Middle East. Two of the world's biggest suppliers, Iran and Iraq, were locked into battle while their assets went up in smoke. OPEC, led by Saudi Arabia, was actually curtailing production. The solution to the inevitable depletion of world oil reserves was no closer than it had been in the seventies crisis. Every economic formula in the world assures you that when supplies get pinched, the price goes up.

I was counting on that. I still had more work than I had men to handle it. And I was making money. However, I still owed money. Every piece of equipment, every improvement on the technology, had to be purchased with borrowed money. And the interest rates were higher at every renewal of the loans.

And my expenses were going up as well. The blame for that could be laid at nobody's feet but mine. Taking on Dad as supervisor had been bad judgment on my part. I guess I'd been blinded by the idea of having a family business, my dad and me working together. It was like I was grasping for some weird Kodak moment.

But it wasn't working. Dad wasn't working. As each day passed it was clearer to me that he wasn't very interested in actually working. He liked being the boss. He liked showing up at the jobs and pretending to be important. But he didn't know anything much about the machinery or the extraction processes and didn't try very hard to find out. He'd worked in the oil fields before he went to prison. But either he'd forgotten everything he ever knew, or he never learned that much. Either way, it didn't stop him from giving huge amounts of unrequested advice to the guys who did the work. His good-old-boy charm really wore thin among my employees and I lost a couple of really good workers who just got tired of putting up with it. Engine work was hazardous. The last thing a careful man needed was some blowhard running off at the mouth.

Dad must have known that they left because of him, but he never acknowledged it. By then, of course, I'd learned that he only revealed those things that it was in his best interest to reveal. I'm not saying my father was a liar, just selectively secretive.

Like the whole truth about his past. The first Thursday of every month he'd borrow my truck to drive to Tulsa to see his parole officer.

It was months before some niggling thought got through my thick skull to ask, *Why would a parole officer from the Texas Department of Criminal Justice be in Tulsa?* He wouldn't. In a couple of quick phone calls I found out that Dad saw his parole officer in Tulsa, because he was on parole from the Oklahoma State Penitentiary. He'd served only eight years in Texas at Huntsville penitentiary for killing my mother. He was released in 1969, when I was twelve years old.

There had been times back then when I'd daydream that he'd come by to see me. Not stopping or speaking or interfering with my life. But just sneaking into town to watch me ride my bike or hit a baseball.

If he did that, I'll never know, because he never spoke of it. But he could have done it. He could have done it anytime. It is still almost inconceivable to me that all through my teenage years I thought my dad was locked up in a faraway prison. He was, in fact, living most of those years in Yellow Jacket, a town only a hundred miles from Lumkee. He remarried and had two more children. Though he never once mentioned to me that I had two half sisters.

During that time he had two more run-ins with the law. One involved the sale of stolen property. The other was for a series of hot checks. Each netted him a few months in county jail. I might have driven past him picking trash up alongside the highway in an orange jumpsuit.

He was finally returned to prison for an incident in a Muskogee nightclub parking lot where he tried to run over his girlfriend with a pickup truck. Only the clumsiness caused by the level of Dad's intoxication kept the woman from being killed. It was that conviction for which he was now on parole.

That he hadn't told me any of this bothered me. That he was inept at the job I'd given him was annoying. The way he seemed to have taken over my life was downright scary.

I couldn't share any of my feelings about this with Corrie. She hated Dad and always expected the worst of him. My complaining would have been tantamount to saying that she was right. Maybe she was, but I wasn't ready to admit that.

Even if I did, what would that change? Floyd Braydon was my father. We'd been apart nearly all my life. For good or bad, a boy needs a father. After all this time, I wanted mine.

And there was Nate. I easily forgot all my father's shortcomings when I watched him with my son. Nate adored his paw-paw and Dad showered the little guy with love, attention, affection. I didn't see how that could be a bad thing.

Floyd Braydon was family. Lost family found at last. Corrie couldn't appreciate that because she'd always had hers close. I couldn't explain it to her, because I didn't really understand it myself.

So instead, I took her on a nice week-long getaway to south Texas. It was still cool and brisk in Lumkee. But in San Antonio it was already like summer. I anticipated a couple of quiet strolls along the Riverwalk, sipping champagne together from a balcony overlooking the moonlit water and retiring to the pleasures of a lust-filled bed at La Mansion Del Rio.

That wasn't exactly how it turned out.

Our first indication was the incredible traffic snarl we encountered as we exited the highway into downtown. Orange cones and barricades were all over the place. Every detour we took led to another detour. I'm sure I must have circled the entire city at least twice before I finally made my way to the hotel entrance.

The doorman hurried out to help me with the bags from the trunk of our shiny new Volvo. I tipped him generously and placed my hand against the small of Corrie's back, ushering her through the doorways of the street entrance.

I felt great. I felt important. I was a well-dressed businessman with a luxury car, walking into an expensive hotel with a very fine-looking blonde on my arm.

The blonde was, of course, my wife, but she didn't look much like the woman I had married. Corrie had trimmed up since the kids were born. She worked out every day. She'd had her pretty chestnut hair lightened and permed into a huge explosion of gold ringlets all over her head. She'd also started wearing a lot more makeup and it made her look really different. The change came from some woman-seminar thing she described as "having her colors done." I didn't quite understand it, but she told me that she'd turned out to be a summer which, apparently, was a surprise to her. Knowing that helped her decide what she should wear.

For myself, deciding what to wear was usually based on what happened to be hanging in the closet when I was getting dressed. Though that was changing, too. Corrie assured me that I was a True Autumn, whatever that means. What it meant to me was that all my favorite shirts disappeared and new stuff in yellows, greens and browns appeared in their place.

"You didn't even leave me one white shirt!" I complained at the time.

Corrie shook her head. "Autumns don't wear white, ivory is white for an autumn."

So she got me a couple of shirts in ivory. They looked white to me. I was wearing one that day.

Inside the lobby of the hotel, the noise and hubbub ceased immediately. The place was cool, dark and pretty much deserted.

"Where is everybody?" Corrie asked me, in a whisper.

I shrugged. "It's an exclusive hotel," I told her. "Maybe it's so exclusive, nobody comes here."

We walked over to the check-in counter. It looked empty, but as we got closer we could hear the click of plastic computer keys from behind the desk. I glanced over to see a clean-cut young guy, his eyes entranced on a brightly colored CRT as he put a little mustached cartoon character through his paces.

"Excuse me," I said, clearing my throat.

The guy jumped up, so startled he knocked his chair over.

"Sorry," he said, embarrassed as he tried to recover his composure. "Super Mario." He pointed at the computer screen. "I kind of get lost in it."

Corrie was smiling at him, sympathetic.

"We want to check in," I said.

He looked surprised. "Are you sure?"

"We have reservations."

"Really? Okay. You've come to watch the move? It's going to be totally awesome."

I didn't know what he was talking about. "We're just here for the six nights," I told him. "When I called I asked for a view of the river."

The kid laughed. "Hope you brought binoculars."

"What does that mean?" I was getting annoyed and apparently the guy could hear it in my voice. He immediately stood taller and his tone became serious.

"There's no water in this stretch of the river," he said. "They've drained it out."

We stood staring mutely at him for a moment and then beside me Corrie laughed.

"April fool! Right?" she said. "You're early, the first is Monday."

The young man shook his head. "No, the river's really empty. They drained out the loop portion of the river, the part that runs by here. Some kind of safety deal for the move."

"What move?"

"You don't know?"

"Would I be asking if I did?"

"They're moving the Fairmont Hotel, the whole building. It's this old three-story brick building. They've like wrapped these steel cables around it and put it up on wheels and they're moving it west from Bowie and Commerce Street around the corner and down on South Alamo to Nueva."

He was pointing as if giving directions.

"That's four city blocks, three ninety-degree turns and a bridge crossing," he told us. "It's the largest building ever to be moved. It is sure to make the *Guinness Book of World Records*."

"Really," I said. It wasn't really a question.

"My dad says it'll never make it. Anyway, that's why we haven't got so many tourists this weekend," he continued. "Lots of places have closed up. And the river is just this big muddy ditch."

He wasn't kidding. Within a few minutes we were standing together on the balcony of our very luxurious hotel room staring down at a big muddy ditch.

I was angry and disappointed. Guests were supposed to have been warned when making reservations. Somehow someone had slipped up and here we were, slated for our first romantic escape to what looked very much like a noisy, busy construction zone.

Corrie took the whole thing in stride. She was once more the sparkling teenage girl that I'd dated in high school.

"Come on," she urged, wrapping her arm around my waist. "Let's look at the whole thing as an adventure. And we've got a front-row seat."

We hung up our elegant nightlife clothes and changed into jeans and T-shirts—the uniform of mud observers everywhere. With the enthusiasm of children we left our room and headed in the direction of all the activity, just three blocks from the hotel. Onlookers flocked the area. It was a friendly, festive atmosphere.

The building had been jacked up and loaded on steel girders that formed a 280-ton-chassis. It was hooked up to three cranes and seven loaded dump-trucks. Having arrived late, we missed the start of the trek, but we were quickly filled in on what we'd missed by those who'd seen it all.

"The move of the hotel was blessed by the bishop," a woman told us.

"A rabbi and a preacher prayed over it, too," a nearby cowboy added.

"They've started late," another fellow told us. "They were worried about rain."

I finally found a place for Corrie and me to sit down near the edge of the sidewalk on Bowie Street. She was as happy and wide-eyed as a little girl at a parade. Immediately, she made friends with everybody within shouting distance of us. She held people's babies, listened to their stories. I fully expected all these strangers to show up on next year's Christmas card list. Two men sitting near her turned out to be employees of a Minnesota transport company who'd been sent down to observe the move.

They, at least, had some interesting observations on the engineering of the event.

"It didn't crack much when they jacked it up," one explained to me. "That's really harder on the building than the actual travel distance."

"The real question here is the bridge," his co-worker related. "Bridges are designed with a certain amount of give. Without flexibility they can't withstand temperature changes and the natural motion of the earth. But flexibility is a negative with this much weight. They are still shoring it up. If it won't hold, they lose the hotel, the bridge, the road and a whole section of the river. It will be tens of millions of dollars in cleanup."

He said the last with such enthusiasm, it was almost as if he relished the thought. I suppose it was like the lure of the auto race. You didn't really want anyone to crash, still the danger of it was part of what drew you there.

The comparison of a car race, however, was tenuous. As the hours passed, the rows of tires beneath the seventy-nine-year-old hotel barely rolled around and took long breaks between revolutions. We sat in the sunshine watching it move along the pavement at a snail's pace. It had all the thrill and excitement of watching paint dry.

The conservation society sold T-shirts and lemonade. I purchased both for myself and Corrie.

She was playing Frisbee with some teenage kids and their dog. She fit right in, looking to be as young as they were. Even with the rough start to our marriage and two kids. Things were now going great. And Corrie was the major part of that. She made the whole family thing work as well as it did. And she managed it without acquiring so much as a line on her face. I knew guys in the oil business who dumped their wives to get an expensive piece of eye candy that made them look more successful. I was lucky to have a great mom for my kids who was a looker as well.

My thoughts along this line were interrupted when a middle-aged Hispanic woman approached me carrying a big red-and-white cooler.

"Is that beer you've got there?" I asked her.

"No sir," she answered. "These are homemade tamales."

"Oh, yeah?"

"The ladies of our church are selling them," she said. "Three dollars a dozen."

I was hungry, and at three dollars, even if they were terrible, it wasn't much of a loss.

"Give me a dozen," I told her, reaching into my hip pocket for my wallet. She set the cooler on the grass and opened it to hand me a brown paper bag.

"We make the best tamales in San Antonio," she assured me as I paid her.

"What's your secret?" I asked her.

She laughed and pointed to her temple. *"Cabeza,"* she said.

I assumed she was referring to her own brilliance.

Smiling, I thanked her and opened my little brown bag. I'd eaten tamales before. They came in cans and they were wrapped in thin white paper. You removed the paper, smothered them in ketchup and they weren't half bad.

The contents of my brown paper sack did not in any way resemble what I'd previously eaten. For one thing, they were not nearly as wet. They were warm and wrapped in corn shucks, and though I looked through the sack, there was no ketchup to be found.

I unfolded one of the corn shucks and took a bite. I cannot describe that first taste. It was perfection. The texture was smooth, but not pasty. The filling was not too spicy, almost sweet but not exactly. It didn't compete with the breading, but complemented it. I savored the flavor with pleasure that had to be verbalized.

"Mmm."

I chewed slowly, holding back, trying to prolong the pleasure as if it were sex instead of food.

"What are you eating?"

"Tamales," I told her. "Try these. They are the best thing I've ever eaten in my life."

Corrie sat cross-legged beside me and I handed her one. She brought it up to her lips. When she bit into it her eyes closed in near ecstasy.

"This is fantastic," she agreed. "Where did you get these?"

"That woman with the cooler was selling them."

"I can't believe it," Corrie said. "This is too good just to be food."

Our romantic weekend had not turned out exactly as we'd expected, but clearly we had both fallen in love.

Corrie
1986

When things start to go downhill, sometimes they just career faster and faster until they are shattered to bits. That's what it was like that year. The bad news began on a cold, snowy morning in January. It was hardly dawn. I was lying in bed, snuggling down beneath the warmth of the comforter. I could hear Sam moving around the bathroom, getting dressed for work. Beside me the phone rang.

Sam opened the door.

"Whoever it is," he called out, "tell them I've already got a job ahead of them this morning, but get their name and say that I'll get there as soon as I can."

It seemed to me that he could have walked back into the bedroom, picked up the phone and told them that himself. But reluctantly, I snaked my arm out from under the covers into the cold of the bedroom and picked up the receiver.

"Hello."

"Corrie? This is Lurlene Bledsoe."

I was immediately puzzled. I hardly knew Lurlene. I probably hadn't spoken to her five times in my whole life. She lived next door to Gram. But I couldn't imagine why she was calling.

"The front room light has been on in Sam's grandmother's house all night," she said. "I called over there, but there was no answer."

It was as bad as she had feared. Gram had passed away the previous evening as she sat in her favorite chair reading her Bible.

The sense of loss I felt was like a huge emptiness inside of me. I don't think I had realized before that moment how much Gram meant to me, and how much I counted on her to be there.

The children were shaken as well. Lauren was sad, quiet, thoughtful. Nate's curiosity was almost morbid. And though he quickly went on playing, he was acting out and hard to control for weeks.

Only Sam appeared completely unfazed by her death. He took care of the funeral arrangements calmly and efficiently. He was stoic, yet sincere and dignified.

I did notice at the service that he seemed to talk about oil prices more than he talked about Gram.

But I didn't realize the level of his disconnect until two weeks after the funeral. Reverend Turpin, the pastor of Gram's church, called me.

"I hate to ask you this," the reverend said uneasily. "But I talked with Mr. Braydon about your mother-in-law's hymnal collection. She had indicated to me that she intended to donate them to the church. But Mr. Braydon is asking for three hundred dollars, and truly, we just don't have it."

The whole question surprised me completely.

"Sam told you he wanted three hundred dollars for Gram's hymnals?"

"No, not Mr. Sam Braydon," he said. "Mr. Floyd Braydon. He's the one handling the estate sale, right?"

"Estate sale?"

"Yes, they're having her estate sale this weekend."

Immediately I called Sam at work.

"Do you know anything about an estate sale?"

"No, well, yes, I guess I do," he answered. "Dad said he was going to get rid of the stuff he didn't want."

"What?"

"I gave Dad the house," he told me. "He said he was going to keep some of the furniture, but he didn't want all of it. I think it's more of a garage sale than an estate sale."

"What do you mean you gave your dad the house?"

"Well, we don't want it," he said. "We'd never live there. Dad's been paying rent. He was glad to get it."

"It's Gram's house," I insisted. "It's full of Gram's things."

"She didn't have anything valuable," Sam replied. "Old dishes, songbooks, knickknacks. If you want something, go over there and ask Dad. I'm sure he'd give it to you."

I went over there, all right. I couldn't bear the thought of Gram's house, Gram's things, being handled and bartered by the man she hated. The man who'd stolen her daughter's love and then taken her daughter's life.

It was as bad as I'd feared.

He'd gone through everything in the house, emptying closets and drawers, stacking everything in piles like so much flotsam. I was standing next to a box that was labeled WWII Mementos. Inside it were patches, insignias, medals and stacks of letters tied with ribbon.

"Well, if it isn't Ms. Corrie?" Floyd said, suddenly appearing at my side. "You come to supervise, honey?"

"Did you ask Sam's uncles about this military

stuff?" I asked him. "These are their medals, their letters."

Floyd shrugged. "Collectors pay top dollar for that crap," he said. "The old lady left it all to Sam. If the uncles wanted it, they should have carried it off years ago."

I thought about explaining to him that in real families, people don't come into their mother's house and "carry off" things. But I knew he wouldn't understand, he couldn't understand. He was incapable of any emotions beyond anger, selfishness and greed.

"There are some things that I want," I told him firmly.

He smiled. "I hope you brought your checkbook."

I began loading up the car. I was like a crazy person. Everything was an heirloom to me. It all said love, family, stability. The pillowcases embroidered with bright jonquils and the rolling pin woodburned with the prayer Give Us This Day Our Daily Bread, I needed to save it all.

Gram's worn Bible sat discarded on a footstool. A strip of masking tape had been slapped on the front with the price, seventy-five cents. It was too much. I grabbed the tattered leather volume up in my arms and began to cry. Once I started, I couldn't stop. People were staring at me. I didn't care. I didn't bargain. I didn't haggle. I didn't say anything to anyone. I was gathering up Gram's things and adding their price to my running total. I was, at times, almost zombielike, hardly cognizant of my actions. Then I'd be sobbing again, uncontrollably.

Having filled the Volvo's trunk and back seat, I was trying to wedge some metal TV trays into the passenger side when I felt a hand on my shoulder.

"Corrie? What are you doing?"

I looked up into the eyes of my brother, Mike.

"What are you doing here?"

"One of those damned gossips couldn't get Mom on the phone so she called the drugstore," he said. "Tell me what's happened."

I fell into his arms, pouring out the whole horrible story, all the anger and loss and aloneness I felt.

"Come on, sis," he urged. "Get a grip, it can't be as bad as all that."

"It is, Mike," I assured him. "It's a battle between good and evil. And evil is winning. He's winning without Sam even putting up a fight."

He held me tightly, just as he had when I was a little girl and had skinned my knee. Eventually, I managed a grasp on my composure. I was still shaking a little, but Mike held me at arm's length and looked me in the eye.

"You're going to be okay now," he said to me firmly, as if he could make it so.

I nodded.

"Wait here."

I watched him walk through the gate, across Gram's yard, up the steps to her porch and through her front door. From the corner of my eye I spied a covey of strangers watching me as if I were a sideshow. My tears were gone now. Letting them go made me feel freer, stronger, ready to take on anything that I had to.

Determinedly, with head high, I followed the path my brother had taken. I went around the picket fence to the gate and into the house. I couldn't find him there.

"I think they went out the back," Ernie Wingate told me. He was sorting through a box of Gram's hymnals.

"Those are not for sale," I told him. "They've already been donated to the church."

I didn't wait for him to respond. I walked on through the house and out the back door. I stopped on the back step. I didn't see anyone. I almost turned around and then I heard voices, raised voices, coming from the direction of the wash house.

I hurried in that direction.

I was still a few feet away when I heard Floyd Braydon's voice clearly.

"You sniveling faggot, you don't give orders to me."

"This time I do," I heard my brother answer. "Because believe it, Braydon, this is one sniveling faggot who would like nothing better than to kick your skinny balls so high they'll be choking you at the back of your throat."

I stood rooted to the spot.

I could hear movement as if one of them was walking around.

"Yeah, come at me, Braydon," Mike said. "Come at me. I'd love the excuse to beat you to a bloody pulp."

"Oh, yeah, you talk tough to an old guy," Floyd complained. "You've got twenty years on me."

"I do," Mike admitted. "And I'd like to use every day of it to smash your skull till there's nothing left but a greasy spot."

There was a moment. A long moment that was dangerous, pivotal, consequential. I held my breath.

Then Mike spoke.

"Come on, Braydon," he said. "Take the money. It's what this is about, anyway. Getting your greedy hands on everything you can. Take the money and get the hell out of my sight."

A second later, the door burst open. Floyd Braydon

hesitated at the sight of me. Inexplicably he raised his arm as if he were going to strike me. I was so surprised, I made no attempt to defend myself. Then he uttered a gender-defined expletive and swept past me.

Then Mike was there.

"What...what is going on?"

"I bought the household goods from him," Mike said. "I'll go take that estate sale sign out the front yard and you clear everybody out of the house. It's all yours, Corrie. To take care of it as you see fit."

I was still incredulous. "You were going to fight him?"

Mike shrugged. "He's a bully. I've known since first grade there's only one way to handle that. Don't look so shocked. There wasn't much chance of a fight. The man's a coward, as well. And if he wasn't..." Mike grinned with unconcern. "I can bench-press three hundred pounds, sis. I could snap that creep's neck like it's a chicken leg."

Mike called the moving company and made arrangements to have everything in the house packed up and delivered to my garage. I was grateful but still stunned by what had happened.

My husband had carelessly given away everything that Gram had valued to the one person in the world she had most reason to hate. My father-in-law was openly flexing his influence over Sam. And my sweet, unassuming brother had gotten what I wanted by threatening violence.

It was as if my world didn't make sense anymore. The loneliness I'd felt since the children had started school suddenly intensified.

I tried to get back to my exercise regime, to get those dopamines flowing again, to feel good about myself once more. But when I heard the rumor that Cherry Dale had struck up a relationship with Floyd, I couldn't believe it. I confronted her.

"He's a bad man, Cherry," I told her. "Even if he wasn't, he's way too old and far less than you deserve. He's a bad man."

"He's made mistakes in his life," Cherry responded. "Who hasn't? That doesn't make him bad, it just makes him human."

Her response left me almost speechless.

"Cherry, you've got to quit seeing him," I said. "Trust me on this."

She waved away my words and shook her head. "He warned me that you'd have nothing good to say about him," she said. "You see him as some kind of competition for the attention of your husband and son. That's totally crazy, Corrie."

Her spiral-permed blond curls bounced as she shook her head sadly and eyed me with pity.

"You've got to get a grip," she told me. "Floyd thinks it might be some hormonal imbalance or something, but whatever, you're losing touch with reality. The whole town heard about that fit you threw at the estate sale. You really need help. You should see somebody."

After that confrontation, I couldn't show my face at her place of business. I decided I'd just exercise at home, but I soon gave it up. I didn't want to exercise. It no longer offered any salve for the pain and disappointment I felt in my life.

More and more I found myself avoiding the chic, perfectly appointed rooms of my new home, to sit in Gram's rocker within the darkness of the garage. Surrounded by boxes and boxes of the relics of a woman's life, a life I hardly knew or shared. I would sit and cry for hours in the bleak shadows of inexplicable despair.

On January 31, I was eating cereal in front of the television and saw the explosion of the *Challenger* space shuttle.

Within twenty minutes, Lauren called me from school. She was sick and throwing up. I had to go get her. The entire school had been watching, the kids were inconsolable. Lauren cried more for Christa McAuliffe, a schoolteacher she'd never met, than she had for Gram.

As for myself, I identified completely with the victims. I felt as if I, too, were encapsulated in my own coffin, helplessly dropping to earth at accelerating speed.

Sam
1986

$\longrightarrow \longleftarrow$

It's amazing how one guy, getting up every day and going to work in Lumkee, Oklahoma, doing what he knows he should and playing by the rules, can suddenly have the whole world knocked out from beneath him from millions of miles away and by folks who don't even know that he exists.

It wasn't supposed to happen. Oil prices have always been controlled. In the nineteenth century, they were controlled by the robber barons. In the first half of the twentieth century, by the Texas Railroad Commission. Then OPEC was in charge. Things got scary for a while, but then they settled down. Or rather, they settled up. The price of domestic crude rose to $31.75 in November 1985, the highest price ever recorded. Then something happened. It was crazy and unexpected. Except maybe someone should have expected it. I wish I had.

In the mid 1980s OPEC slowed production to keep the supply of oil low and the price per barrel high. They did not, however, take into account two developing new production areas that were just taking off, Mexico and the North Sea. Neither of these new, abundant oil fields were members of OPEC.

Saudi Arabia, the Goliath of the OPEC nations, began to realize that their limited production policy was being eroded as they were losing market share. Their response was to turn on the spigot. Oil began to flow like water. And for about the same price.

All over the country consumers were jumping for joy. America was back where it should be, living large with gas-guzzling cars and a stock market headed for the stratosphere or what seemed more like the statusphere.

Every day the spot market price of crude was lower. Pumping domestic wells became less and less cost effective. At thirty dollars a barrel people had been getting rich, at fifteen dollars they were getting by. At ten dollars they were getting out. The multinationals were moving their production overseas where wages, regulations and ecodamage were less costly.

The small companies, the ones who were my clients, found their backs were up against a wall. First unable to expand, then unable to keep up their commitments, unable to pay their bills and finally declaring bankruptcy. Over and over my company's name showed up on creditors' list filings.

As quickly as the money had appeared, it was gone. Producing wells were suddenly not cost effective and were shut down. And oil equipment surpluses stood rusting in the countryside. There was so much of it for sale, it didn't pay to even crate it up and transport it to town.

People who owed me money avoided my phone calls. Those who were paid up had no new jobs to offer.

At first I refused to believe it was happening. I would go into work every day expecting things to be better. Then I'd walk the floor all night, fearing that they were only getting worse.

Even with businesses I knew going belly-up all around me, I convinced myself that it couldn't, it wouldn't happen to me. Many of the independents were run by wild guys, firecrackers, young men who'd stashed their profits in fast cars, expensive boats and fancy mansions. Compared to those guys, I was Joseph P. Suit. I'd kept the operating costs to a minimum, my salary modest, and had plowed all the profits back into the business. I had paid two small dividends to Corrie's brother, but nothing I'd done could have been characterized as lavish or risky.

Still, day by day, the situation worsened. I cut back on everything. I left my car in the garage and walked to work. I tried to schedule my paperwork for the afternoon, so that I didn't need to use the lights in the office. I cut down on toilet paper. I knew I was kidding myself when I yelled at Lauren for putting "more peanut butter than she needed" on her sandwich. It made her cry. And it forced me to admit that the crisis was too big to be solved with some thrifty belt-tightening. If I was going to operate on less money, I'd have to cut down on payroll. I hated to lay off my crews, but I reasoned that the sooner they got out there looking for new jobs, the better chance they might have of finding some. Overnight, every company within two hundred miles had more help than they needed. And the line at the unemployment office got longer and longer.

I couldn't let everybody go. If I got work orders, I had to have a crew to help me fill them. So I kept Dad and three of the older guys. I figured they'd have the least chance to find anything else. And I went out and beat the bushes from morning until night trying to find paying clients who needed something we could do. Nothing was too small or too far away for me to bid on.

I barely met payroll. I cut wages. It made very little difference.

During all of this, I was so alone. I think it was the first time in my life that I ever really felt that way. I hadn't been the most popular guy in town, but I'd always had a few buddies. All my friends were now in the oil business. Even those who weren't my clients or my competitors couldn't be expected to listen to my fears. And I think they must have felt the same way. All over town, it was like a conspiracy of silence. Guys might talk about the world market or the price of crude, but nobody talked about the stripper wells that were shutting down and the drilling contracts that were canceled.

I was as bad as the rest of them. When I got a question about how Well Service was holding out, I responded with what I knew about operations at Haliburton and Schlumber. I was far too proud, or too scared, to admit aloud that I'd taken a second mortgage on my house and was in negotiations with the IRS.

I was not, of course, accustomed to airing details of my business in public. Corrie had always been my confidant. It was Corrie who had offered her two cents in every plan, brainstormed with me on every new development and listened to every detail of our growth from the miraculous to the mundane.

These days, however, Corrie was not available to me.

Her life had somehow veered off in a different direction. I'm not really sure if she was even aware of how dire things had become. She'd taken Gram's death very hard. I know they had grown close over the last few years, when she and Lauren were seeing that she got to church. But Corrie's grief was pretty intense. And it had gotten mixed up with her dislike of my dad. Which somehow made the whole thing worse.

By spring, she was a basket case, crying all the time in the garage. The kids were weirded out and scared.

"Why is Mommy so sad?" Lauren asked me one evening when I arrived home late to find the two of them eating cereal for supper in front of the TV.

"I don't know," I answered.

"I do!" Nate offered, jumping to his feet with his hand raised as if he were in school. "I know, I know!" He was almost seven now, skinny as a rail, but a good-looking kid if you could get past the big excited grin that had several missing front teeth.

"How could *you* know?" Lauren's voice was disdainful.

"Paw-Paw told me," Nate replied, his voice dripping with superiority. "Mommy cries cause she's 'one bitch that's permanently on the rag.'"

Lauren's brow furrowed with question. My jaw dropped open in shock.

"What!"

Both kids immediately stilled at the tone of my voice.

I reined in my temper, but not my disapproval. "Don't you ever let me hear you talking about your mother that way," I scolded him.

Nate was wide-eyed. "What way?" he asked. "It's what Paw-Paw said."

I didn't doubt for a minute that was true.

"Your grandfather is who he is," I told Nate. "But you are *my* son and you will show respect to your mother or I'll take this belt off and whip your tail with it."

Nate stared at me in disbelief. I'd never spanked the children. I wasn't opposed to it. Gram had gotten my attention more than once with granddad's old razor strop. And I thought it had probably done some good. But Corrie didn't think corporal punishment was necessary and she always managed, more or less, to make the children behave without it.

I wasn't sure this was the best time to change that system. So I stormed out of the front room before the little guy could make some inappropriate comeback that would force me to follow up my words with action.

I went to the phone to call Corrie's mother. We were drowning and we needed help.

Fortunately for me, it was Doc Maynard who answered the phone. I was able to describe what was going on in our house and he responded like a medical professional.

"She needs to be on some antidepressants," the old man told me. "I'll call Dr. Kotsopoulos tomorrow and get him to see her. Try not to worry, Sam," he told me. "Half the wives in town are on them these days."

By May, when my loan payment came due, it felt like I was living with a Stepford wife. Corrie went about her days, doing what she was supposed to be doing. She cooked now, and cleaned, and the kids were back to having hot meals and help with homework. She puttered about, humming and smiling. But when I tried to talk her about what was going on, she waved my words away.

"Do whatever you think best, Sam," she told me. "I'm sure everything will be fine."

I did not have that confidence.

Since I'd already renegotiated a second mortgage on our house, and we didn't have that much equity in it, anyway, I decided that I was going to have to liquify our remaining assets. I tried to sell the Volvo. I stuck a sign on the windshield and placed an ad in the classifieds. I didn't even get one phone call. So I drove it up to the Volvo dealership in south Tulsa to see what they'd offer me. The manager just shook his head.

"I've got thirty repossessions coming in," he told me. "We're shipping them east for half of what they would have brought on this lot last year. Nobody here is buying, around here everybody is selling."

I drove home, forlorn.

I went to talk with Dad. He was, after all, the crew supervisor, my closest relative and the person I spent the most time with these days.

I drove out to Cherry Dale's double-wide set on the lot next to her parents' bungalow. The place was nicely kept up with attractive faux-wood metal sheeting around the skirt and a decklike front porch with a comfortable cushioned glider surrounded by pots of bright blooming flowers.

Dad had pretty much moved in with Cherry Dale. He still kept some of his stuff at Gram's house, but he'd never really lived there.

"It gives me the creeps," he admitted to me once. "The damn place smells like that old woman. I've smoked a dozen cigars in the living room and left a stringer of fish to rot in the kitchen sink, but I still can't get the stench of her out of the place."

I didn't have a clue as to what he was talking about. But I'd grown up there. It was my childhood home. Of course it would feel differently to me. I knocked on the front door of the mobile home. I didn't see my dad's pickup, but Cherry Dale's blue Firebird was parked under the carport.

I heard movement inside, but there was no immediate answer to my knock. I tried again.

Clearly somebody was home. I thought maybe they'd been in the shower and were getting dressed. I was patient, but eventually knocked on the door a third time, more vigorously.

Reluctantly it opened a few inches. Cherry Dale was on the other side.

"Hi, Sam," she said. "Floyd's not here. He's gone to the beer joint, I think."

She was forcing me to look through the narrow slot of the doorway. Her face was in shadow, but something was wrong.

"You're not at work today?"

"No, I'm not feeling very well," she said. "Didn't think I'd go in today."

I wondered idly who ran the place when she wasn't there. As far as I knew, her fitness center had always been a one-woman show. But she didn't seem particularly eager to talk.

"Well, I'll try to catch Dad downtown," I told her, and turned to walk away. Just as I reached the step, I turned and waved. "Hope you get to feeling better."

The perspective from the step was different, and for one instant I caught a glimpse of her face looking dark and swollen. The sight stopped me in my tracks. Abruptly the door shut and she was gone.

Thoughtful, concerned, I started back across the porch to knock on the door again but thought the better of it. Instead I made my way to the car and drove down to the beer joint. Sure enough, Dad's pickup was parked in front. I angled the Volvo in beside it and went inside.

There was a pretty good crowd in the place. More than I would have expected on a weekday afternoon. I'd sent my crew home because I didn't have anything for them to do. I suppose other employers might have done the same.

Dad was sitting near the doorway on a stool at the bar. His back was to me and there was a bottle of Bud in front of him. He was in the middle of one of his long, drawn-out stories about a lazy drunk and his complaining wife. He dragged through every line with an accentuated accent and deep baritone drawl. Every eye in the room was focused on him. His good looks and perfect smile made him stand out in every crowd, but with that wonderful charm added, he just drew people to him. It was a charisma that I envied. Like the rest of the patrons in the bar, I waited patiently for the punch line. It was as raunchy as expected.

I walked up and slapped him on the back.

"Hey, Dad," I said. "Do you want to buy me a beer?"

He grinned at me. "You're the boss, you should be buying for me."

I shrugged and shook my head before calling out to the bartender to bring me two. I settled down on the stool next to Dad.

"I was just at Cherry Dale's," I told him. "What's wrong with her? She looks awful."

Dad didn't answer immediately, instead he took another swallow of beer.

"Car wreck," he said finally.

"Car wreck?"

"Nothing messes up your face like a car wreck,"

Dad said. "Even a little fender-bender can make you look like hell."

"Yeah, I suppose so," I said. "Wow, that's too bad. She didn't say anything about it. Was anybody else hurt?"

"No, no, she was all alone. I don't think she's told anybody. Probably too embarrassed by her own stupidity. Women drivers," Dad commented, warming up to the subject. "It's downright scary to have 'em on the road. Cherry Dale's just fine. She'll be back out on the highway in a couple of days, as bad at it as ever."

There was some lingering question that niggled at my brain, but I ignored it. I had something important that I had to bring up. I glanced around the room. There was certainly no sense of privacy here. Maybe this wasn't the place to bring it up, but I felt as if I couldn't wait longer.

"Dad, we need to talk," I told him.

"What about?" His question was gruff, defensive.

"About the house," I said.

"What house?"

"Gram's house," I said. "I'm going to borrow some money against it."

He looked at me, strangely guarded.

"Oh, yeah?" he asked evenly.

I nodded. "My business loan is up for renewal," I explained. "We haven't really been making enough money to make the payment. Normally, a guy would just go in at this point and renegotiate. But with the entire industry in such terrible shape, the banks have their backs against the wall. They're going to want some more collateral to sweeten the pot. I've already got a second on my house. Gram's house isn't much, but I think it will keep them from calling the loan."

He took another long draw on his beer, followed by a breathy sigh.

"Not a good idea," he said.

I was a little surprised at his response, but it was not completely unexpected. I'd learned working with him over the last few years that Dad was what they called in the oil fields a *size forty-seven jacket with a size five hat*. Healthy and strong, but not too clear on the complexities of the business.

"Well, in fact, Dad," I told him gently, "it's a very good idea." I took a deep breath, glanced around to make sure nobody was paying any particular attention and then continued. "The downturn in the price of oil is severe. But it's not going to last forever. The businesses that manage to stay in business through this crisis are going to come out of it bigger and stronger and with a larger market share. I want to be one of those businesses."

Part of the time Dad was looking at me. Part of the time he was looking at his beer.

"The bank doesn't really want to bankrupt me," I explained. "They've already got enough foreclosure equipment to make the stuff almost completely worthless. All they need is a tiny excuse to keep me on. Just a small piece of real property to give them cause to renegotiate my loan. If I can get another year, maybe I can pull out of this. I'm just trying to buy a little time."

Dad continued to look at me, saying nothing.

I glanced around nervously again and then lowered my voice. I hated even speaking the next words aloud.

"The alternative is that I go in there with nothing but a drooping balance sheet and a big smile," I said. "That won't get us anything. They'll call in my loan and I won't be able to pay. I'll lose the business, Dad. I'll lose everything. Do you understand what I'm saying?"

He nodded slowly. He set down his beer and lit up a cigarette.

"I get it," he said. "Oh, I get it completely. I'm supposed to lose my house so you won't lose yours. That's it, isn't it?"

"No."

"That's exactly it," he insisted. "I give you my damn house to prop up your fly-by-night business. I get nothing so you can get everything."

I was shocked, even stunned by his words. Six months earlier I had given him the house, just signed it over because he'd asked me for it. He'd never even lived in the place and now he talked like I was trying to cheat him somehow.

"It won't be for nothing," I assured him. "Putting up collateral is like putting money in the company. I'll give you a partnership, like Corrie's brother, Mike. It will be your company as well."

"Big freaking whoop-ee," Dad said facetiously. "Like I want a part of a company that's about to go belly-up?"

"We're not going belly-up."

"You are if I don't hand over my house," he said.

"You don't have to hand anything over," I said. "You'll still have the house. It will just have its address listed on the loan papers."

"And what happens next time you can't make the payment?" he said. "Then they take my house. No way. It's not worth the risk to me."

"Dad, this is your job as well," I said. "If the company goes down, you're out of work."

He snorted. "I never much liked the damn job, anyway."

I couldn't believe what he was saying. I couldn't believe that he wasn't willing to help me. And his crappy comment about the job just went through me like ice. I was suddenly furious.

"I pay you twice what anybody else in this town—what anybody else in this state—would pay you. And if you had been anyone else but my father, I would have fired you for being the lazy, incompetent, son of a bitch that you are."

My anger delighted him. He laughed. "So you can get pissed off, I see," he said. "I was beginning to think that you were completely candy-ass like your mother. At least that's good. I got something out of this thing. I got a smelly old woman's house and a rise out of my son. That's more than I ever hoped to get from that side of the family." He rose to his feet. "You don't have to fire me," he said. "I was getting ready to quit, anyway. That woman of mine makes a pretty nice dollar. I don't need to punch a damn time clock anymore."

He got up and walked out the door.

I followed him and stood on the sidewalk as he got into his pickup and drove away.

I went to my own car, sat down in the driver's seat and grasped the steering wheel with both hands to keep them from trembling. My heart was pounding as if I'd just run a marathon. The stress of the last months swelled up in me and I wanted to just sit there and cry. I wanted to cry like a little boy.

As a little boy, of course, I hadn't cried. The memories suddenly came back to me in a flood that washed all the optimism out of my brain. Dad's smiling face and charming stories were always for somebody else.

When he came home to us, he was mostly mean. He'd get mad about something, nothing, anything, and he'd slap me hard. If I cried, he'd slap me harder.

"Crybaby! Crybaby, just a crybaby like your mama!"

He did the same to her. She tried to please him, but she never could. When he'd hit her and she'd cry, it made him want to hit her harder. It was just the way he was. He was a bully. Exploiting weakness was like a drug to him. The more he did it, the more he wanted it.

In all my worrying, plotting, planning, maneuvering, I had tried to think of every possibility, every situation that could go right, every detail that could go wrong. In all of those, I had taken comfort in my fallback position. Never had it occurred to me that my fallback would be foiled. I had allowed myself to be deluded by Dad. To believe that he was a man like me, rather than the man he was. He had let me down. But it wasn't his fault. He was only what he was, and at least now I was pretty clear on what that meant.

The fault was mine. I was the one who'd given Gram's house away. I had lost my own business. I had no one to blame but myself.

The truth was so painful to me that I could hardly hold it in my mind. My thoughts kept pushing away from it, wanting to focus on anything, anything but the reality of where I'd gone wrong.

It was at that precise moment when I figured out the question that had niggled at my brain earlier. If Cherry Dale had been in a car wreck, how come there wasn't a scratch on that Firebird?

Corrie
1987

$\longrightarrow\!\!\!\longleftarrow$

White noise. That's how I think of my recovery from depression. I had been drowning in blackness. Until I was dragged into the world of white noise.

It was Mike and my dad who got me help. Mom just kept yelling at me. Ordering me to snap out of it. Accusing me of faking it to attract attention. Claiming that my deliberate agenda was meant solely to embarrass her among her friends.

I didn't even have the strength to fight back.

I knew the children were suffering. Nate drew even further away from me. He kept his distance as if I had the plague. Lauren seemed to want to emulate my role. If she was playing, giggling, laughing, I'd see her stop herself, as if she believed that being an ordinary happy child was somehow bad behavior.

I could see this. I could see what I was doing. But I couldn't seem to stop. I couldn't drag myself out of the abyss. I just wanted to sit in the garage in Gram's chair. I just wanted to sit there until I could die. It was too hard to face living anymore.

"You need to be on medication," Mike told me. "You have to see a doctor. This can't go on."

"I can't see a doctor," I told him. "What would Mom say? What would Sam say?"

"Mom knows when to keep her mouth shut," Mike insisted. "And Sam's the one who called us for help."

I told him I would do it. But I made no moves in that direction. Mike took the reins out of my hands. He made the appointment. He told me when I had to be there. Then he showed up to take me.

I was still in my bathrobe.

"I can't go today," I told him. "I don't even feel well enough to dress."

"Then don't," Mike said. "You can go just like that."

"I can't go see some stranger dressed in my bathrobe."

"This doctor is a friend of mine," he told me. "The guy's seen just about everything. I don't think he'll be fainting from shock at the sight of a housewife in a bathrobe."

Just that threat got me to bathe and dress. I looked like hell. All my muscles had turned to fat. The only dress in my closet that fit me was a muumuu that Mom had brought me three years earlier from her Hawaiian vacation. My hair was styleless, dull and overlong. The best I could manage was to run a brush through it and pull it into a ponytail at the nape of my neck. My makeup-free skin was so pale and sallow, I almost looked jaundiced. But when I opened my cosmetics case, with the intention of at least putting on some foundation, the process seemed so difficult that I gave up without even starting.

Mike took me in his car. On the new expressway, the drive into Tulsa was barely twenty minutes. And Mike found his way unerringly.

"You drive in Tulsa as if you live here," I told him.

"I do," he told me. "Lumkee is more a suburb than a small town these days. I come down this way three or four nights a week."

"Are you seeing someone special?" I asked him.

He grinned at me. "You've still got that Mom gene," he said. "No, Edna, no one special."

I smiled. It was the first time in a long time.

The psychiatrist, Dr. Muldrew, put me on an anti-depressant the first day and started me on weekly therapy. Mike had to take me to my first few appointments, where I mostly just sat and cried through my thirty-minute session.

As definitively as turning on a light switch, after thirty days on the medication, I was suddenly out of the darkness and into the white noise. I drove myself then. I chatted through the sessions, baring my deepest darkest secrets. My anger at Mom for not loving me enough. My love/anger conflict about my brother being the favorite. My disappointment in myself for not making anything of my life. My uncertainty as to whether I really loved my husband.

Dr. Muldrew listened, nodded, took notes.

He was an interesting guy. The first openly gay man I had ever met. It made me feel sort of sophisticated, as if I was stepping out of the ordinary, boring world I'd grown up in. I was curious and I asked him about it.

"Is my sexual preference going to be a problem for you?" he asked.

"No, oh no," I assured him. "I just find it interesting. I mean, I've never actually met anyone gay before."

"Really?"

"Really. I mean, I live in Lumkee," I pointed out. "Nobody is gay in Lumkee."

He nodded only slightly and then wrote something in his notes before changing the subject.

For most of the rest of that year, I took my medicine, went to my sessions and lived in the world of white noise.

If I noticed that Sam's world seemed a good deal different, it didn't make much of an impact. He was home every night, working at his desk. I'd walk by and see him poring over papers, checkbooks, contracts. I'd wake in the middle of the night to hear the adding machine going.

He told me that he was worried about the business. It was a bad time for everybody. You could hear that all over town. I knew that Floyd was no longer working for him. That was good news. And I assumed that firing his father was what had led to the distance between the two. Gone were the days when the two spent their every waking moment together.

Of course, Floyd continued to see Nate. I would drive him over there nearly every Saturday morning. Unlike every other child in elementary school, my son preferred Paw-Paw to cartoons.

One day in July, Sam came home in the middle of the afternoon. I was looking through cake recipes, wanting to plan something special for Nate's birthday. He stopped in front of my chair and just stood there until I looked up.

"It's over, Corrie," he said.

My heart flew to my throat. I thought he was divorcing me.

"What's happened?" I asked, suddenly shaken, frightened, regretful.

"The bank's called my loan," he answered. "I can't pay. I've lost the business, and with it, all our assets, our savings, your brother's money, this house. It's all gone. We're broke and I'm unemployed."

Relief flooded through me. Sam wasn't leaving. I was amazed at myself for having jumped to such a conclusion. A very inappropriate little chuckle bubbled through to the surface.

"Oh, is that all," I said.

"Is that all?" Sam repeated loudly. "Good God, Corrie, is that you talking or those happy pills you take? We've lost it all, everything we've worked for, everything we've wanted for our kids. We're destitute. We haven't got a pot to piss in or a window to throw it out. We're going to be out on the street, living under a bridge, trying to raise our children while carting all our worldly goods around in a stolen grocery cart."

He was so scared, so overwhelmed with it, my heart went out to him. Immediately, I rose to my feet, wrapped my arms around him and pulled him tightly against me.

"Shh, it's going to be okay," I told him. "Samuel, listen to me. It's going to be okay. Shh, it's going to be okay."

My comforting seemed to help him. He got a grip on himself and regained his composure, but he continued to hold me. After a long moment he spoke.

"Did you hear what you called me?"

"What?"

"You called me Samuel," he said. "That's what Gram always called me."

I nodded. "Yeah, I guess she did."

"Do you know what it means? The name Samuel?"

"No."

"Gram said it meant 'a man with a special calling,'" he said. "It made me believe that I might do something special. I'm glad she didn't live to see this. She would have been so disappointed."

Sam's eye's welled up with tears; he was gritting his teeth to hold them back.

"That's the stupidest thing you've ever said, Samuel Braydon. And believe me, I've known you long enough to have heard you say plenty of stupid stuff."

I smoothed his forelock away from his face.

"Gram was always proud of you and none of it ever had anything to do with money or business or anything we could own," I reminded him. "She was proud of you because you are an honest, hardworking, honorable man. Nothing about that has changed. Nothing about you has changed. We've got each other. We've got two great kids. We've got our health. This business, this house, all the rest of this, it's just stuff. We'll kick the dust off our sandals and move on."

It was brave talk. I meant it. I meant it that day. And more as the weeks went by.

Newspapers talk about how stock markets *crash*. But they talk about families *sliding* into poverty. Our family's descent into the realms of the unmonied was definitely on the crashing side of *slide*.

The day he told me about the loan we were down to less than one hundred dollars in our checking account. Within a week, a stranger had come in the middle of the night to repossess my minivan. Coming to grips with losing the house was made easier when the gas, electricity and water were shut off. We had a huge yard sale, trying to generate as much cash as we could while making our household goods smaller to cart around.

Fortunately, one of the big advantages of going broke in an economic downturn is that you're not the only one without money. Everybody is in the same boat. The bank foreclosed on our house. But without any conceivable chance to resell it in the near future, they allowed us to stay in it to keep it from sitting empty until it could be liquidated. We were grateful. Without the house, we'd have been forced to move in with Mike or my parents. We didn't want any more upheaval for the children than was necessary. Knowing that their father didn't have a job was undoubtedly scary enough. Now all we had to do was scrape together enough money each month to keep the utilities on.

Sam was doing his best. He was out job hunting every day. There was no work at all in Lumkee, so he drove to Tulsa to fill out applications, sit for interviews or sometimes just stand at the employment office on Archer Street trying to get picked up for day labor. There was not much luck there. Hundreds of guys waited for the half-dozen pickups that came by to pick up two or three guys with strong backs. Local unemployment had gone from the lowest rate in history— 2.9 percent in 1981 to the current high of 9.7 percent. The whole town was like some strange throwback to the depression era.

At least that was my impression on the day of my last visit to Dr. Muldrew. With no company there was, of course, no company health insurance, even if we could have afforded to pay the premiums.

He didn't seem all that surprised. He even suggested that I'd come so far that I really didn't require further therapy, and he put me on a regimen where I slowly decreased the antidepressants until I was off of them completely.

I thanked him and said goodbye.

"I hope that we meet up again sometime under different circumstances," I told him.

He gave me a little hug and smiled. It was a knock-out smile. Dr. Muldrew was one very handsome guy. "I'll tell you the truth, Corrie," he said. "I'm hoping the exact same thing."

We shook hands and I left.

I got into my car and headed home. My mind was on a thousand things. I got turned around and lost. I tried to get my bearings, but it was high noon. North, south, east and west, all looked the same to me. When I came across a street that dead-ended into a tank farm, I knew I was way off the beaten track. I stopped at the QuickTrip on the corner to ask directions. The guy working there was eager to strike up a conversation. He was another out-of-work oilman, lucky to have a job.

He got me headed in the right direction for the expressway. I was several miles out of my way. Finally I could see it up ahead of me a couple of blocks away, when I was stopped at a red light.

The sky was gray and overcast. It wasn't cold, but it looked like it should be. As I sat waiting I watched a group of boisterous children playing on a wood-chip-covered playground behind a wire fence high enough for a prison. The place was called Candy Cane School and the front sign was a converted barber pole. I noticed a woman was taping a piece of paper to it. The light turned green just as I realized what the paper read: Help Wanted.

Horns blared and drivers cursed at me as I swerved across three lanes of traffic and, having missed the entrance ramp, bounced over the curb to pull into the front parking lot.

The woman taping up the flimsy homemade sign looked at me, startled, as I got out of my car.

"What kind of job is it?" I called out to her when I was still a half dozen yards away.

She waited to answer until I got closer.

"We need an assistant teacher for the preschool room," she told me. "We only pay minimum wage and you have to be here at five-thirty in the morning."

"It sounds perfect," I told her, offering my hand. If she'd said they needed a plumber I would have responded in exactly the same way.

"I'm Corrie Braydon."

"Trixie Creekmore," she said. "I'm the manager."

"Are you related to any of the Creekmores in Lumkee?" I asked.

She grinned at me. She had a gold filling in one of her eyeteeth.

"Probably my ex was," she said. "But I sure don't claim none of them folks. I just keep the name for my kid's sake."

I nodded.

"I'm really interested in the job," I told her. "I don't have a degree, but I did do some college."

That was stretching my semester ten years earlier at Oklahoma State. But it didn't seem to bother her.

"We sure don't require college," she said. "Do you have any experience with children?"

"I have two," I told her. "A girl, nine, and a boy, seven and a half."

"Who'll get them ready for school while you're working in the morning?" she asked.

"My husband's out of work."

She nodded.

"Come on inside, we'll talk," she said.

Within forty minutes I had the job. I felt as if I was walking on air.

Sam was surprised.

"Are you sure?" he said, his brow furrowing in concern. "I don't want you to have to work if you don't want to. I'm sure to find something soon."

"Honestly, I'm excited about it," I told him. "It's right near the expressway and we need the money. The whole thing seems ideal."

Of course it wasn't ideal. I was leaving the house at 4:45 a.m. The only other person out was the newspaper delivery boy. The preschool, in a westside working-class neighborhood, was filled to capacity. It was solely staffed by me and the cook for the first hour. During which time almost all of the shift workers and medical personnel dropped their kids off. It was nerve-racking to be so totally responsible for so many. Once my co-workers showed up it was better. By the time everybody had breakfast and the requisite morning crisis was resolved, we divided the children by age groups. The layout of the building was basically open. The different class groups had different sections, with the only differentiation being the color of carpet on the floor. In the center of the building were two enclosed rooms. One was the baby room, with its cribs and rockers. The other room was the preschool classroom. The two walls that were exposed to the day care were floor-to-ceiling glass. Which gave me the feeling of being forever in a fishbowl.

That was where the comparison stopped, however. While the day-care areas were replete with cheery rugs and wall hangings in bright primary colors, the preschool was dull and stark. Fourteen little brown desks sat in neat rows upon a tan carpet surrounded by white walls. I had seen more style and energy at the Department of Motor Vehicles. It perfectly reflected the personality of the head teacher of the class, Clarissa Klempner.

Miss Clarissa was a real teacher. She was a graduate of Northern Oklahoma College in Tonkawa and held a state teaching certificate. But when she'd arrived in the real environment of public elementary education, the seven-year-olds that she was hired to teach were far too frightening for her timid soul. Miss Clarissa walked through the world on a path of endless eggshells.

After her scary experience with second grade, she'd retreated to the relatively insulated surroundings of Candy Cane School. She'd been teaching this class for five years.

And she wasn't terrible. She had empathy, a huge capacity for love and endless patience. The class was extremely well behaved. Perhaps because they somehow realized how upsetting boisterous behavior would be to her.

I liked Clarissa. I liked the class. In fact, I liked almost everything about my job. Getting up in the quiet darkness of my house, waking my husband with a kiss as I left, driving through the frosty mornings into the lights of the city. I loved that. It made me feel a part of things. All over the world people were getting up and going to work. And I was one of them. And I loved bringing home a paycheck.

Sam hadn't even got a nibble on a job. He was going door to door as a fix-it man for the old folks in town. On a good day he might bring home ten dollars. Half the time he was too ashamed to accept the money from the poor old widows he worked for. But I could walk through the door with bags of groceries and change in my pocket. It was a totally victorious feeling.

But naturally, there would have to be a fly in the ointment. That came in the person of Candy Cane's owner, Fern Davis. I met Mrs. Davis after I'd been employed at the school about two weeks.

We were finishing up our classroom day. Miss Clarissa took the class to recess. They would play until the after-school program began when they would join up with the older kids. I was not a part of this. Coming in at 5:30 a.m. meant that I went home at two.

Trixie opened our door and handed a note to Clarissa. She read it and then came over to me.

"Mrs. Davis is here," she said. "She wants to meet you."

"Okay, as soon as I finish with Kaitlyn."

"I'll take care of Kaitlyn," Clarissa said. "Go ahead. Be sure to clock out *before* you go in to talk to her. And watch your back." This last was spoken in a warning whisper.

I shrugged off the advice as just more evidence of Clarissa's chicken heart.

But I did clock out before going into the front office. That was fortunate, because it was the first thing she asked me.

"I hate having my staff sitting around jabbering with me paying for it," Mrs. Davis said.

I could have pointed out that usually when people are off the clock they are allowed to go home, not obliged to sit and talk with the employer, but I thought perhaps our discussion was meant to be only a friendly, after-work chat.

However, it didn't really have that feel. In fact, the tone was more suggestive of a spotlight and rubber hose. She wanted to know, in fine detail, who I was, who I knew and what I thought. After a lifetime of similar interrogations from my mother, I handled myself very well. Maybe too well. When the questions stopped and her subject matter turned to other employees, I relaxed.

She complained bitterly about the woman I was replacing. She had taken a big chance on Misty, given her a wonderful opportunity. She'd thrown it away to follow her out-of-work husband to his new job.

That didn't seem so terrible to me, but I had the good sense not to say so. Instead I tried to change the subject.

"Where did they go?" I asked her.

"Someplace up north," Mrs. Davis said.

"Oh," I said, nodding. "Like New England? Michigan? Minnesota?"

"No, one of those states with North in the name."

"North Dakota?"

"No, not there. North Carolina, that's it."

I thought she was making a joke. I laughed.

"What's funny?"

"You're kidding, right?"

I should have known that a woman like Mrs. Davis probably didn't have that much of a sense of humor.

"Kidding about what?"

"About North Carolina being north."

"It *is* north," she said adamantly. "Otherwise they wouldn't call it North Carolina."

I didn't say anything.

"I'm right," she insisted. "Admit that."

I should have.

"It's certainly north of Florida and Georgia and South Carolina," I told her. "But it's east of here, almost due east. And it's considered a southern state."

My mother had warned me since childhood that being a know-it-all gets you liked by no one.

Mrs. Davis wouldn't give it up. She insisted that we consult a map, and then she couldn't find the state in the area where she thought it should be, up around Ohio and Indiana. When I showed her where it was, it was as if she didn't believe me or the map. She called in Trixie, who reluctantly verified that, indeed, North Carolina was exactly where the map said it was.

I left feeling queasy and nervous, but Trixie reassured me the next day.

"Mrs. Davis hardly ever comes in here," she said. "They live in one of those big old mansions near Swan Lake. Most days the farthest she ventures out is to shop at Miss Jackson's in Utica Square. Just stay out of her way. She may never forgive you or forget it, but she'll not bother to do anything about it."

I hoped Trixie was right, and as the weeks passed I got back into my routine and forgot all about my brush with the owner.

One afternoon, when I was feeling especially creative, I broached the subject of the preschool classroom's boring decor with Clarissa.

"I don't understand why all the group areas in day care are so bright and colorful and we have to work in the big, drab void."

Clarissa glanced up, surprised.

"It's my fault," she said, very quietly, defensively. "The teachers are responsible for the decoration of their area. I just…well, I couldn't decide what to do and I'm not very…well, artistic. So I just never got around to doing anything."

"Would you let me decorate it?" I asked her.

She sighed with relief. "Oh, would you!" she said.

"I've been so afraid that somebody was going to say something. I kept thinking I should do something, because you can see right in here and it looks so...so unfinished. But I thought if I did something, somebody might not like it."

"Don't worry about it anymore," I told her. "I'll come up with something. Something that we'll both like perfectly."

My plans for the room didn't come together that day or even that week. I let my ideas simmer in the back of my mind. I wanted more than just some paint and pictures on the wall. I wanted a theme that would inspire the students, enliven us as teachers and yet fit into the class image that we had already formulated for ourselves.

I was lying in bed with Sam, who was watching Jay Leno, his favorite comedian, guest host for Johnny Carson. I'm not sure if it was something Leno said, or just that all my musing finally came together. But it suddenly hit me.

"Fishbowl!"

"What?" Sam looked at me as if I'd lost my mind.

"That classroom is a fishbowl," I told him. "So that's how I'm going to decorate it."

Having no money proved to be as much a help as a hindrance. I went through leftover paint cans at my house and at my mom's. I even had Clarissa show up with hers. We had about four different kinds of blue. I thought about mixing them and then decided that the best was just to go from light to dark, as if we were in the ocean. The floor was perfect. Its tan carpet was the exact color of sand. I scrounged through Lauren's stuffed animal collection for sea creatures. I looked through books on the oceans and painted the lower walls with undersea flora and fauna. I dabbed our bookshelves with wood putty and painted them as pink as a coral reef. Driving home one afternoon, I'd seen a huge pile of pallets used for hauling cement to well sites left as scrap. I loaded up the trunk and used the lumber to make shell-like fronts for the desks. The students, with the help of Clarissa and I, made fish of every kind and color, which I suspended from the ceiling, at a height unreachable by even a student standing on a desk. I even drew a snorkeler on the top of the water above us, peering down through his swim goggles at us.

The kids loved it. Clarissa loved it. The parents were delighted. The other teachers got excited about their own areas and began brainstorming with me about how they could liven things up. Trixie even showed up one morning with a colorful découpaged sign for the door that read: Preschool Fish Bowl.

Two short weeks after completion, Mrs. Davis showed up. Took one look at my handiwork and fired me on the spot.

"You've vandalized my building," she told me. "It will cost me hundreds of dollars to have that monstrosity cleaned off the walls and the furniture. I'm taking that out of the pay that I owe you."

I begged and pleaded, I cried. Finally she agreed that if I would spend the weekend repainting the walls white at my expense and cart out every piece of fishbowl decoration that we had made, then I could leave with my paycheck intact and two weeks' severance.

I thought of my husband, my children, our checkbook. I didn't have any other choice.

Sam went to paint it on Saturday morning. He told me just to stay home with the kids.

"This is something I can do to help," he told me. "Just stay home, rest up, spend some time with the kids. I'll take care of it."

I thanked him and watched him leave. I was so disheartened. But I tried to be strong. I tried not to think of the kids I'd become attached to and would never see again, or the wonderful classroom that was about to be destroyed.

Sam returned less than two hours later.

He handed me a disposable camera. "I took some photos for you," he said.

"Thanks," I told him. "I didn't expect you so soon. You really got it done quickly."

"I didn't do it," he said.

"What?"

"I didn't do it," he repeated. "I left it exactly like it was."

"But Mrs. Davis—"

"To hell with Mrs. Davis," Sam said. "Corrie, that was the neatest, coolest classroom I've ever seen in my life. Painting over it would have been like…like painting over the Mona Lisa. If Davis wants to paint it over, she can do it. I won't. Besides, it gives the kids a few more days to enjoy it."

"But the money," I said.

Sam waved my concern away. "There're some things a guy just won't do for money," he said. "And destroying something fabulous that his wife created, well, that's one of them."

Sam
1988

In some ways, losing the business was just one tremendous relief. By the sheer force of my own will, I had been trying to keep things together. The stress had been overwhelming. Just the finality of knowing that there wasn't anything else I could do was a kind of reassurance. And I got Corrie back. From the moment I told her that it was all over, she became my partner again. The trouble rejuvenated her in a way that the antidepressants hadn't.

After her time at Candy Cane School, I encouraged her to think about going back to college. At first she acted as if I'd lost my mind. With no money and no jobs, it didn't seem to her like the time to be thinking about making education expenditures.

"Take a couple of classes," I told her. "We can get them paid for with a Pell Grant. All it will really cost us is your time. And it seems to me with both of us out of work, there's a lot of free time available."

So she started driving into the city three days a week to go to Tulsa Junior College. She loved it.

My situation was not as hopeful. With oil companies maintaining a hiring freeze and a hundred men applying for every job that came up, I became less certain about my future. My skills were no longer in demand. And the high school equivalency I got in the army was not considered sufficient education for even the most menial jobs.

"I've got petroleum engineers flipping hamburgers," one fast-food manager told me.

"If you're interested in getting a job," a guy at the employment office told me, "then you should pack your bags and get out of here. All over the rest of the U.S. the economy is booming. People are getting rich. But living here is like being stuck in a Third World country. No matter how hard you work, there just isn't anything to work with."

I thought about leaving. I heard guys on Main Street talking about Atlanta, Seattle. There were jobs in those places. They were screaming for hardworking guys like us.

I even talked to Corrie about it. Her pretty little brow furrowed.

"If that's what you want, Sam," she said. "Then I'm with you. But I think we really need to think about the whole picture. Here we've got a place to live and my family to fall back on, if we need to. Out there...well, we'll just be out there."

I nodded. "Yeah, I guess that's true."

"And think of all the Michigan folks," she said.

The so-called Michigan folks had come to Oklahoma during the 1970s when the automobile industry started closing plants and laying people off. They'd left their families and friends to come for jobs in the oil patch. By and large, they didn't seem to like it much. Michigan folks earned such a reputation for complaining about Oklahoma that among natives a new slang phrase was coined. When something was messed up, screwed up or fouled up, we'd say, "I'll bet this is not how they do it in Michigan."

"What about the Michigan folks?" I asked her.

"They gave up on where they lived and came down here and tried to start over," she said. "Now, after spending a decade trying to settle in here, they're back in their cars headed elsewhere. Is that what we want for ourselves? Is that what we want for our kids? Just new-wave Joads looking for the next crop of grapes?"

It wasn't what I wanted.

But what I wanted wasn't about to come to pass. I wanted to turn the clock back ten years and make things turn out differently. How exactly, I wasn't sure.

For the time being, I could only do what I could do. I got up early every morning. I kept the house, the yard, the car, in tip-top shape. I was more involved in the children's lives than I'd ever thought possible. I assigned their chores, checked their homework, coached their soccer teams. When I got the near-hysterical phone call from Lauren, I scrounged through the secret caverns of unmentionable stuff under the bathroom sink. Carried emergency supplies up to the school, dried her tears and assured her that being the first girl in the fifth grade to get her period didn't make her a freak, it made her a woman.

All this while constantly looking for work, taking every low-paying labor job I could find, and fending off my son's incessant teasing about being Mr. Mom.

Nate was still very much Paw-Paw's boy. My relationship with my father continued to be little more than a nod in passing. He continued to live with Cherry Dale and had been unable to find work. His days were spent touring the local beer joints, and rumors about bruises on Cherry Dale circulated with growing frequency. I tried to convince myself that it was more gossip than fact.

Dad told me he planned to sell Gram's house. Fortunately with the flood of real estate on the market, there weren't any buyers. In my daydreaming moments I fantasized about buying it but, of course, I would never have done that. I had given the house away for nothing. Well, technically, the agreement read *one dollar and other considerations*. But I hardly remembered any discussion with Dad about it, I couldn't even recall my thinking process. But I did sign the papers with no reservations at the time.

"Everything happens for a purpose," Gram had always told me. "Sometimes we don't like what happens and don't understand the purpose, but that don't mean it's not there."

I suppose if there was a purpose in me handing over that house, it must have been to allow me to recognize Floyd Braydon for the man that he was. It seemed like a high price to pay for seeing the light. Or maybe it was seeing past the light, the blinding glare of wanting a dad kept me from seeing the truth about the man who fathered me.

I wanted to protect my son from the same lack of vision. But it was an impossible task. It was hard to figure out where Nate's idolization of his paw-paw had come from. He didn't suffer from the lack of a father figure like I had. His own real, biological dad, me, had been in his life always. Maybe we weren't as close as some father/son teams, but we got along okay. And I had been, and continued to be, a permanent person in his life.

Then there was Corrie's dad. Doc Maynard was, in my estimation, about as perfect a grandpa as a guy could have. He was smart, hardworking, easygoing and had a great sense of humor. He was an upstanding citizen with a prosperous business. He also liked to read and fish and play golf. I admired him tremendously. And he was crazy about Nate. But Nate far preferred braggart, foul-mouthed, ex-convict Paw-Paw. I tried to limit their time together as much as possible.

Which wasn't all that difficult. For all that the city limits of Tulsa were encroaching down Main Street, Lumkee was still a very small town and everybody knew what everybody else was doing.

Except, of course, for my brother-in-law, Mike.

Corrie's brother had invested in my business. The money had been a big boost when it came. It had freed up my own cash so that I could afford to buy a house for my family. I'd just begun to pay him dividends when the oil patch turned sour. Now his investment was down the tubes with mine. It had happened to a lot of folks. And I was sure that Mike had interest in other local companies besides mine. But we were family and that made everything different. In a big corporation, if some anonymous stockholder loses their life savings, you send them a form letter. In a small family business, when your brother-in-law loses so much as a nickel, you owe him an explanation.

Mike had lost more than a nickel.

I wanted to talk to him privately, away from the drugstore. But it was very hard to catch him. I went by his house dozens of times and never found him at home. I eventually realized that he was leaving work, driving straight to Tulsa and not coming back until the next morning.

That was none of my business. Ultimately, I just

called up and tried to make an appointment to meet
with him. He put me off two or three times. When I
persisted, he finally agreed to see me and then canceled at the last minute. The more he avoided me, the
worse I felt and the more insistent I was on seeing him.
He was Corrie's only brother. They were very close. I
couldn't allow anything that I had done, any mistakes
that I had made, to put a damper on that.

Finally we met for dinner one Tuesday evening. He
suggested Gambling Steaks, a place out by the entrance ramp to the expressway. It had been a really
popular place just a couple of years earlier. It was fixed
up to look like a casino with lots of flashing lights and
a salad bar set up on a craps table. It still looked good
and I heard it served great food, but the owner had apparently lost this restaurant wager. There was a foreclosure notice on the front door and a sign on the mar-
quee that read Last Big Week!

Mike ordered a steak. I just asked for coffee. The
waitress gave me an exasperated look, but I didn't
have a spare twenty to put down on a meal. And if I ordered something, Mike would probably try to pick up
the check. With what I owed him already, I couldn't
stomach that.

He was nervous, fidgety.

I assumed that he was as concerned as I was about
the danger of this financial loss causing hard feelings
in the family.

I took a deep breath and calmly began my presenta-
tion of the facts. I tried to put what had happened in
the industry within a historical perspective. I tried to
be very honest about how the business had been set
up, assumptions that I had made and problems that I
had not foreseen. Enough time had passed that I knew

he was aware of how dire the situation had become. I didn't delude myself that the loss was minimal to him. The price of crude had fallen on Wall Street, but ultimately it was Main Street where the crash was felt. If people in Lumkee didn't have jobs, then they didn't pay their bills, they didn't buy their drugs. I wanted Mike to know that I understood that. That I was aware of his own financial balancing act.

I'm not sure when I realized that he didn't seem to be paying much attention. But I suddenly knew that he wasn't. He was sitting there, politely, looking in my direction, but his eyes were completely glazed over as if he were a million miles away.

My initial reaction was to be annoyed. Here I was leveling with him in a totally honest and self-condemning way and he wasn't even listening.

Fortunately, I reminded myself that I was the one in the wrong and I was probably boring him to death with my explanations. I immediately moved to the summation.

"I take full responsibility for this debt, Mike," I told him. "I know that it legally falls into the bankruptcy with everything else. But it is personal to me and I give you my word, I will eventually pay you back, but it may be years, even decades in the future."

I stopped talking and just sat there. He was looking at me closely. I had no idea what was going through his mind, what he thought about my promise. Finally he spoke, and I was more confused than ever.

"I don't care about the money," he said. "Forget about it. It's not important."

"It's important to me," I began.

He waved my words away. "Sam, I need you to do something for me."

"What?"

He hesitated. I thought maybe my response had been wrong.

"I'll do anything you ask, Mike," I assured him.

"I need…"

He hesitated again. He just kept looking at me so intensely.

"I need…" He stopped again, this time he shook his head. He jerked his wallet out of his back pocket and threw a couple of bills on the table. "I need you to eat the steak that I've ordered," he said. "Don't worry about owing me anything. Take care of your wife and kids, that's all the payback I'll ever want."

He got up to leave.

"Where are you going?"

"I can't…I don't feel like eating," he said. "Please, eat the steak."

Stunned, I watched him walk across the room and out the door. I jumped up and hurried after him. I didn't know what was happening, but I couldn't just let him go.

"Mike!" I called out to him as soon as I got outside.

He was almost at his car. He glanced back but kept going. I broke into a run.

"Mike! Wait!"

I was a few feet away when he turned toward me. I came to a halt and waited. He leaned against the car as if he was too tired to stand up.

"Mike, what's going on?"

He raised his chin and looked me in the eye.

"I have AIDS," he said.

I just stood there staring at him. Until that moment, all that I had known about him, I didn't really know.

And suddenly, everything that I'd ever known or wondered or suspected about him made perfect sense.

"I don't know what to do," he said. "I don't know how to tell them. I've been thinking about just killing myself, making it quick and sparing Mom the disappointment. But I want to live. Now, more than I've ever wanted to live in my life. Oh God, Sam, I didn't want to put this on you, but I don't know what to do."

I stood there looking at him and thinking about Corrie. Corrie loved him so much. They shared more than just genetic material. They had shared a life together. They had been kids together in their backyard, running through sprinkler hoses, falling into piles of leaves, making snowmen. He had always been her heroic older brother, friend, counselor, protector. She had been his devoted little sister, always looking up to him, always trying to make him proud. I loved her. And losing him would hurt her so deeply, profoundly. It made my heart ache to think about it. My heart ached for Corrie. It ached for the Maynards. It ached for Mike.

I took the two steps that separated us and I wrapped my arms around my brother-in-law.

"Oh God, Mike, I'm so sorry," I told him. "I'm so damned sorry."

We cried then. We both cried.

Corrie
1989

◄——►

What is so unexpected about life is that we keep learning things about people we thought we knew.

Mike's illness was a terrible shock to the family. Without any doubt it brought out the best and the worst in all of us.

Mom's reaction was to be anxious and frightened. It was what I'd expect from anyone, except somehow it didn't quite ring true with her. It was almost as if she was playing the part of the brave, loving mother of the dying gay man. Which is exactly what she was. I suppose my mom's real dramas seemed feigned because her everyday, artificial dramas were always portrayed so realistically.

On her worst days she was as narcissistic as anyone might have predicted. Her beloved Michael, for whom she had worked and sacrificed all her life, had, she claimed, deliberately gotten himself sick with this terrible homosexual disease in order to embarrass her in front of her friends.

Fortunately, this very Mom-centered view was fleeting and shared only with me, her special confidant of the occasion. In front of the community, she was chin-raised, gloves-off, mother/protector. Anyone who even hinted at intolerance or homophobia would be dealing with her directly. Not a pleasant prospect for the fainthearted. Mom made me go with her to face down the Methodist preacher. She went carrying a threat and a promise. The man didn't have a chance. But he hadn't needed one. Reverend Shue was all compassion and caring. Which saved him the fate of Darlene Gillam, a lifelong friend and a member of Mother's bridge club. She offered sympathy to Mom's face and then behind her back espoused the view that AIDS was a punishment from God for the disgusting sin of homosexuality. Darlene would never be dealt another card. And Mom didn't even want to associate with those who would associate with her.

Even more important than Mom's face to the world, was the face she showed to Mike. Sam and I went together to tell Mom and Dad. I was still so shaken myself, I could hardly speak. When the words came out of Sam's mouth, Mom looked at him for an instant and then slapped his face. But by that time we were all in the car and on the way to Mike's house. She was solidifying her composure. She was still strangely angry at Sam. But to Mike she was concerned, courageous and infinitely loving.

For the first months, it was all learning. We drove into Tulsa to attend AIDS information groups. We read everything we could get our hands on. Our conversation became one big alphabet soup, the problems had names like HPC, PCP, CMV, the treatments were AZT, ZDV, SMX, and the reports we learned about them came from CDC, FDA and NIH.

Mom decided that she would go with Mike to all his doctor visits. And that Sam would drive them. The fact that both Mom and Mike were perfectly capable of

Suburban Renewal 155

driving to Tulsa or that most thirty-five-year-old men didn't need Mama to go with them to the doctor didn't keep Sam from making trip after trip with the two of them in Mom's big Lincoln.

I was mostly out of the loop on all this. I was in Tulsa every day, going to classes and holding down two jobs.

Fern Davis had held my final paycheck and had certainly not been willing to write me a letter of reference. But amazingly both Trixie and Clarissa gave me fabulous recommendations. I applied for, and was hired, to do part-time work in a Head Start program on the north side. It was the same sort of early morning/ teacher assistant job that I'd done at Candy Cane. The supervisor, a huge black woman named Mildred Conner, eyed me critically.

"Now, tell me what exactly you're looking for here and why you're interested in working with black children."

I answered honestly. "I need a job and I want to work with children. I applied here because you have an opening."

Mildred laughed. "Okay, then, we'll give you a try."

The job was fabulous. The teacher I worked with, Emma Stabler, was retired from the school system after twenty-seven years. When it came to kids, she'd seen it all and still wanted to be a part of their lives.

And who could argue with her. The children in our class were adorable. Once we got past the first few days, when I was known and referred to as "that white lady," we all got along great.

It was Emma who urged me to get the second job. When she found out that I was attending classes at TJC she asked me what I was going to do next. The junior college couldn't offer me a bachelor's degree.

"Well, I guess I'd hoped I could finish out at Oklahoma State," I told her. "Of course, I don't know how I'll manage that drive to Stillwater and hold a job, too. It's too bad that none of the state universities have programs in town."

She nodded agreement.

"Have you thought about Tulsa University?" she asked me.

I sighed and shook my head. "I can't pay private-school tuition. Even with grants, I'd never be able to come up with the money."

"You know if you work full-time at TU," she said, "you can go to college there for free."

I hadn't known that. So I checked it out. Sure enough, once you've been on staff for two years, your tuition rate goes down. And after five years, you can attend for free.

It would have been great if I could have worked there doing child care but, of course, there was no such job available. Since I got off work at two-thirty, I was able to take a second-shift custodial job. Not only was I getting a plan together to finish my education, I was bringing home two paychecks, which was really helping our bottom line. The downside was that I was leaving the house at five in the morning and getting home just a little before midnight.

Sam was doing a great job at home, so on the weekends I was able to split my time between my children and Mike.

While I tried to be there for my brother, sometimes it felt as if Lauren needed me more. She was in those terrible 'tween years where every day is a new crisis. As soon as a hint of a breast appeared, she assumed she

was fat and decided she would live on sugar-free bub-
blegum.

Thank God the child didn't have the self-discipline
to be anorexic. I got her hooked up with Cherry Dale.
We couldn't really afford to keep a membership, but
the rest of the town was in the same boat. Cherry Dale
was having trouble just keeping the lights on. So she let
Lauren work out for half price in the hope that she
would bring her girlfriends to join.

Her girlfriends did, of course. They all did what everybody else did. Which was another major issue.
About twice a week there was some blowup, usually
involving screaming conversations, rude phone hang-
ups and lots of tears.

These dramas were my dinner entertainment every
evening when I called her from the break room to see
how the day had gone.

Nate had nothing much to say to me. He was spending less time with Floyd Braydon. That was the good
news. Now, however, his life was taken up with video
games. He was down at the arcade constantly and it
was all he talked about. I heard him explain to Sam in
minute detail the differences in Sega Genesis and Nin-
tendo.

When he showed up one day with his own Game
Boy I was surprised. It was a Saturday morning. Cartoons were still on, *Slimer* was being ignored as Nate
sat in the chair, totally intent on the plastic box in his
hands.

"Is that a Game Boy? Where'd you get it?" I asked
him.

At first he just ignored me and kept on playing.

"Nate! Whose Game Boy is that?" I asked louder,
getting his attention.

He glanced up at me.

"It's mine," he answered simply.

"Where'd you get it?"

He raised his chin to glare at me in challenge. "Paw-Paw gave it to me," he said.

I was surprised at his defensiveness. I didn't like Floyd, but I tried hard not to show it in front of Nate. And I certainly wouldn't have taken away a gift. Especially one like this—one that I knew Nate wanted so badly and was so unlikely to get from us.

I didn't think anything more about it until the next Tuesday when I got a call at work from the school principal.

"I'm sorry to bother you at work, Mrs. Braydon," she said. "Your husband wasn't at home."

"He had to take my brother to the doctor," I said. "Is something wrong? Are Nate and Lauren all right?"

"Yes, your children are fine," she said. "Do you know Stuart Llewellyn?"

"Yes, of course," I answered. Stuart was a little fat kid who had been in Nate's class since kindergarten.

"I have Stuart and his parents here in my office, Mrs. Braydon," the principal continued. "And Stuart is saying that Nate took away his Game Boy last week and refuses to give it back. I've talked to Nate and he insists that the Game Boy that he has is his own. Is that true?"

I wanted to immediately affirm that it was, but something in the memory of the defiant look Nate had given me kept me from defending him. "I don't know," I admitted. "He told me that his grandfather gave it to him."

"Would you mind if I call Doc Maynard and confirm that?" she asked.

"No, not my father," I explained. "Nate said Floyd Braydon gave it to him."

"Oh, well, may I call Mr. Braydon?"

"Better let me do it," I suggested. "I'll call you back."

Nobody answered at Cherry Dale's home phone, so I called Pepxercise.

"Do you know anything about a Game Boy that Floyd gave to Nate last week?" I asked Cherry Dale.

"Last week? Nate didn't see Floyd last week," she said.

"Are you sure of that?"

"I'm sure all right," she said. "The son of a bitch has been up in Tahlequah shacked up with some whore he met in a honky-tonk in Sand Springs."

Her anger and candor were momentarily stunning. I didn't know quite what to say.

"I...oh, Cherry Dale, I'm so sorry," I sputtered out. "I didn't realize the two of you were broken up."

She laughed but there wasn't any humor in it. "I *wish* we were broken up. He'll never let a meal ticket like me go. The only way out I'll have is the same one Sam's mother got."

It was a shocking thing to say. A scary scenario to imagine. But Cherry Dale's problems were not mine. My main concern was for my son. If Nate hadn't gotten the toy from Floyd, then he'd stolen it from Stuart.

I left a message with the receptionist at Mike's appointment and Sam called me back.

"I had no choice but to tell the principal that it might be true," I explained to him.

"It was the right thing to do," he agreed.

"She's suspended Nate for three days," I told him. "She has to release him to a family member, so I asked my father to go pick him up. He says he'll keep Nate with him at the drugstore until you get back to town."

"Okay, Corrie," Sam said. "Don't worry about it. I'll be home in a couple of hours and I'll get things straightened out."

"I should be there, Sam," I admitted guiltily. "I should be at home for my kids."

"Don't get crazy on me," Sam replied. "You're working two jobs and keeping food on the table for them. Your kids are lucky to have you. Just leave this to me."

So I did. I finished my day at Head Start and then called home before I clocked in at the college. Lauren answered but told me she couldn't talk. Sam and Nate were in the office and she was trying to listen through the door.

By the time I walked into the house that night, all was quiet. Sam was sitting up in bed reading, a hobby he'd acquired lately and was frequently engaged in when I got home at night.

"What happened?" I asked immediately.

He set his book aside and rose to his feet to give me a welcome hug.

"Hey, baby," he said. "I'm glad you're home at last." He held me tight for a moment and then kissed me on the top of the head. "Go get your clothes off and take a shower," he said. "There's no news so bad that it can't wait fifteen minutes."

I followed his order. When I returned to the bed, slightly damp and wearing my bathrobe, Sam had a tray with two glasses of wine and some cheese and crackers. Occasionally we'd have wine with a fancy dinner, but never at home.

"What's this about?"

"It's not a celebration, just a snack," he said.

"Tell me what happened, I can't wait any longer."

"Nate stole the Game Boy," Sam said simply.

"Oh, my God," I moaned. I had held out hope that it wouldn't be true. "Why would he do that?" I asked.

"Because he didn't have one."

"What?"

"That was his excuse." Sam raised his hand in the three-fingered Boy Scout's honor.

"Was he sorry?"

"Not much," he said. "Nate told me that Stuart was a 'totally lame dweeb.' That he was lousy at video games. His reaction times are 'pathetic.' And therefore, he doesn't 'deserve' to have the Game Boy."

"What did you say?"

"Oh, just about everything," Sam admitted. "I used the entire stern-father playbook, plus the smarmy scene from every old *Father Knows Best* episode that I could remember. What it all came down to is that he's grounded from TV for a week and from the arcade for a month, and that he has to write a letter of apology to Stuart, which I will be checking over for appropriate sincerity and spelling."

"Wow."

"I wanted to threaten grammar," Sam said, "but my own is so iffy, I didn't want to promise what I couldn't deliver."

"Okay. How did he take it?"

"He was furious," Sam said. "He screamed. He threw things. He said more curse words than I even knew existed when I was his age. And he told me it was my fault, not his."

"Your fault?"

"Yep," Sam nodded. "He said that if I'd get a decent job, I'd be able to pay for things that a kid needs."

"He said that?"

Sam actually laughed. "That's not all," he told me. "He said I was pussy-whipped, a chump and a loser."

"Why would he say something like that? It's so disrespectful. Did you spank him?"

"It crossed my mind," he admitted. "If ever there was a time to get out that razor strop, this was it. But I managed to stay cool, not take it personally."

"Your own son makes a personal attack and you don't take it personally?"

"He's a kid," Sam said. "He was angry and kids say things, especially when they know they're in the wrong and they're cornered."

"I can't believe you're taking this all so well."

He heaved a heavy sigh. "Well, in the grand scheme of things, it didn't seem like such a big deal."

"What do you mean?"

Sam picked up a glass of wine and handed it to me. "Your brother's T-cell count is down to forty," he said softly. "And the banker called. They've decided to auction the house. We have to be out by the end of the month."

He picked up his own glass and raised it to mine in a toast.

"To better days than this one," he said.

Sam
1991

—▶ ◀—

The world was moving, changing, things were happening. The Berlin Wall came down. The Soviet Union was breaking apart. A despot named Saddam Hussein had invaded Kuwait. American soldiers had gone there to fight a war.

The price of oil was finally back on the way up, though domestic production was not really rebounding. Tulsa was going in new directions. The little town of Lumkee was now inseparably linked with the city's path. New industry, a new technological economy had arrived. Most of the men in town had found work or were back in school. A change for Tulsa meant changes for us. In fact, local developers wanted to rename the town. Lumkee sounded so unappealing, they argued. Why would high-tech, upwardly mobile families want to move into a town with such a *yesterday* name? They proposed changing the official name of Lumkee Township to Eagle's Bluff.

"It's aesthetic, it's suburban, it's now," Mayor Dixon explained. "And it's not really a change. It's merely an Americanization of the name we now have."

Lumkee, being the Muscogee language word for *eagle*, had been a community, a tribal town since the removal of the Creek Nation from the Deep South. The name came from the river bluff just north of town, which had once been a prime nesting spot for the birds. Eagles had recently been reintroduced to the habitat and were now a tourist draw for enthusiasts with binoculars.

The mayor, backed by a long line of identically suited real estate hopefuls, supported the amendment to the town charter.

Harjo Peeples, an old, frail leader of the few members of the tribe still left in town, was opposed. Doing away with the Creek place name was, to Harjo, equal to throwing away the town's history. Miss Pruitt at the public library was equally incensed. Slowly all the people began to take sides.

Citizens for a New Century is what the pro-name-change forces called themselves. Let Me Live in Lumkee the signs of the traditionalists proclaimed.

I was sitting on the sidelines, watching.

Not that I wasn't busy.

When we'd been evicted from the house we'd been forced to split the family temporarily. Corrie and Lauren moved in with her parents. That was wonderful for Edna. It was a great diversion for her to be forced to devote more time to the life of a thirteen-year-old who loved shopping and gossip. And it was good for Corrie, too. At least she wasn't still working two jobs. An opening had come up in the university's Early Childhood Education Center, and with the excellent references she had from the north-side Head Start, the human resources department was happy to allow her to transfer. She'd become so accustomed to her rigorous schedule that she'd decided she could study full-time taking night classes. She was now more than halfway to graduation. The luxury of having her mother to come home to at night didn't seem like a bad thing.

Nate moved in with Cherry Dale and Floyd. I was opposed to this. Corrie was opposed to this. I think even Cherry Dale and her kids were opposed to it. But when Nate and his paw-paw decided on something, it was very hard to stand against them. And it made sense in some kind of way. Floyd had gotten a job as the custodian at the high school. Of course, it wasn't really the high school anymore. When the local school district had consolidated with Tulsa Public Schools, the high school where Corrie and I graduated was turned into a middle school, where the kids attended. A new huge high school complex was being constructed outside of town where Lumkee kids would attend along with teenagers from the nearby suburban housing developments.

With Floyd working at Nate's school, it was easy for him to see that Nate was there every day and on time. The fact that Lauren attended the same school and walked to class didn't seem to enter into the equation.

I was living at Mike's house. His health had steadily worsened over the last two and a half years. He was no longer able to care for himself. Since I was the one who didn't have a job, it was reasonable that I was the one who should stay with him.

He still had days when he felt good. Sometimes the doctor would order an IV of what the nurses jokingly called "Immune System in a Bottle." It would perk him up for a few days and he'd want to see friends, drive down Main Street, visit the drugstore.

The last I tried to discourage. Not because his presence cast a pall upon the Maynards' loyal customers, which it did. But because I didn't want him to see how bad business had become.

With big discount stores out near the expressway offering cut-rate prescription service while you shopped for clothes, wastebaskets and power mowers, Maynard Drug, a fixture on Lumkee's Main Street since 1947, was about to go under.

Even sadder than that was the fact that Doc Maynard didn't seem to care. This fine, gentle man who was shouldering most of the financial burden for all of us, had lost heart. He had seen the battle before him and was too war-weary to fight it. I think the only reason he didn't just put a For Sale sign on the front door was that he didn't want Mike to see it. His son's death was inevitable. And I was pretty sure that when the business closed for the funeral, it would never reopen again.

But I could only worry about that on Mike's good days. On his bad days, I only had time and energy to worry about him.

I would help him bathe and dress. He wanted to walk to the living room and eat in the dining room for as long as he could. He knew that his life would most likely end in bed, so he wanted to spend as little time there as possible.

He wasn't crazy about watching TV. But he loved movies, especially obscure art movies. So I would rent videos, dozens at a time, and he would watch them for hours.

Mike had always been an avid reader. But his sight began to fail. We got him new glasses, but the eyestrain problem was caused by his tear ducts malfunctioning—not keeping his eyes wet enough.

So I read to him.

I had, since being unemployed, discovered the thrill of thrillers. I regularly borrowed the latest from the public library.

But what Mike read was different. He was interested in science and history and philosophy. Subjects I knew almost nothing about. But you don't have to understand in order to read. And, amazingly, as you read, eventually you begin to understand.

Sometimes we would even discuss the books. One day while I was reading an essay by Emerson, Mike stopped me in midsentence.

"Do you believe that?" he asked.

I glanced down at the page I was on.

"Compensation?"

Mike nodded. "Yes, do you believe that? That somehow over a lifetime all the good things and bad things that happen equal out."

I looked down at his frail body and pale face, blemished with ugly skin cancers.

"I don't know," I told him honestly.

"I think it does," Mike told me. "Over the whole lifetime, I think it does."

But what if you don't get a whole lifetime? I wanted to ask him. Could there ever be any compensation for that?

I guess it could be said that some of Mike's pain was compensated by the fun he had with his friends. After a lifetime of being a closet homosexual in a small conservative town, Mike had suddenly been "outed," and now his friends from Tulsa showed up in Lumkee to visit. What the town might have thought of that, I don't know. But they were an interesting group. I'd never had any dealings with gay men in my life. And my inclination was just to treat them as if they were straight.

That mostly worked. But some of them were so...
girly...that it just felt more natural to talk to them like
women. So I just went with that.

For the most part, I didn't know what they thought
of me. I assumed I stood out as the straight guy. But apparently not. One evening when the house was literally crowded with people, I was fixing drinks in the
kitchen when Josh, a big, beefy cowboy type asked me
if I was Mike's partner. I think my jaw must have
dropped to the floor, I was too surprised by the question to answer.

"Oh, for heaven's sake, they are not lovers," Daryl, a
close friend of Mike's, told the guy. "He and Mike are
brothers."

I regained my composure enough that I could have
pointed out that Mike was actually my brother-in-law.
But somehow I felt no need to make the correction.

Local people dropped by from time to time as well.
The pastor, some of Mom's friends, occasionally somebody Mike knew from the Chamber of Commerce or
the Optimists Club.

Surprisingly the most faithful visitor was Cherry
Dale. They had been friends for years. She would come
and talk to him. Tell him the stupidest jokes and enter-
tain him with all the gossip from the gym. It was on
one of those days when I heard more things than I expected.

I'd been in and out of the house doing the lawn. I'd
come in the kitchen door and had sat down at the
breakfast nook. I hadn't meant to eavesdrop, it just
happened.

Mike was saying, "So I want you to know that the
money I've loaned you all gets wiped out in the will.

You'll own the gym free and clear and nobody will be able to touch it."

"Mike, I don't know why you've always been so good to me," Cherry Dale answered.

He laughed. "You're the only girl who ever volunteered to cure me."

She laughed. "I'm *so* embarrassed. What an idiot you must have thought I was."

"I didn't think you were an idiot," Mike said. "I thought you were a nice person who was attracted to me and didn't understand why I wasn't attracted back. You know, you're the only person in this town that knew I was gay. I never trusted anyone else."

"I can't believe you trusted me," Cherry Dale said.

"Well, I was right. You never told anyone."

"I told Floyd," she said. "Probably the worst person in town. That's who I told."

"I don't blame you for that," Mike said. "Floyd... well Floyd is like your personal brand of AIDS. He's a painful, sickening source of misery in your life. A plague that you never wanted but can't blame anyone else for."

"And something I'll probably die of," she added.

She said it as a joke. There were always lots of jokes. But there was nothing funny about Mike's battle with AIDS.

He took more medication than we had room for on the kitchen counter. He counted them once.

"One hundred and fourteen per month," Mike told me. "As a pharmacist, I expected to count a building full of pills in a lifetime. I just didn't think I'd be expected to swallow them."

Some days, swallowing was the biggest challenge he could face.

It was easy to tell why the Africans called AIDS Slim Disease. Mike's weight went down to 134 pounds. On his wide-shouldered, six-foot-two frame, he was like a walking skeleton.

I was determined to feed him to try to keep up his strength. He never felt much like eating. Part of that was fatigue, he was just too tired to make the effort. The medicines altered his ability to taste anything. And his mouth was full of thrush, a yeast infection that actually made eating painful.

I had never been all that spectacular in the kitchen. I wasn't even one of those guys who liked to throw steaks on the grill. But when you can see the flesh falling off another person's body, well, you just know that you've to do more than heat up a can of soup and grill a cheese sandwich in the toaster.

I began trying to fix healthy, tasty meals. I talked to Edna and Corrie. I tried to recall some of the special things that Gram had sometimes cooked for me. I borrowed recipe books from the library.

Mike cheered my efforts, though often he didn't eat much of them. I knew I was getting better when everybody seemed to be interested in my leftovers. Even Nate, on his compulsory one-afternoon-a-week visit, spent most of his time raiding the fridge.

On a cold autumn day I stood in the kitchen surrounded by cookbooks, trying to think of something special. It needed to be fairly soft, Mike could hardly chew. Meat loaf? No, that was too bland. It needed to be a little bit spicy, so he could taste it. Spaghetti? Too messy. He'd never be able to feed himself that and it was so demeaning when I fed him. Then, from far in the back of my brain, I remembered a warm spring day, a beautiful wife and a hotel on the move.

Tamales? Tamales.

My mouth watered as I thought of the taste that I remembered.

I went through all the cookbooks looking for a recipe. I couldn't find one. Finally I called Miss Pruitt at the library.

"I'll see what I can find," she told me, and, true to her nature, she called me back in twenty minutes.

There were lots of different recipes. I went by and got copies of them all and sort of scrambled them together in a workable way. Several of the ingredients were not in my cabinets. Masa flour. *Hojas. Anchos.*

I didn't try to fix them that day. But the idea was born. I called around to specialized groceries until I found one that had masa flour and *anchos* and that promised to get me some *hojas.* The next time I took Mike to the doctor we stopped by and got the stuff.

"You're going to have to help me with this," I warned him. "Tamales are not a one-person creation."

He agreed to help. I made up the tamale filling by itself a day early. Then I helped Mike get comfortable in the breakfast nook. I mixed the masa flour and spices with the lard. I used warm beef broth to keep it all from gumming together in a big glob. It had to be cohesive enough to hold together without being so sticky it stayed on our hands.

We'd just started experimenting with the masa paste, smearing it on the corn-shuck hojas. Corrie, Edna and Lauren showed up to help us. We all sat around the table together trying to do it. When all else failed, I read the directions aloud.

"Tear down a wet *hoja* to the width of your hand. Place it in your palm making sure the smooth side is facing up and the tapered end is pointing in the same direction as your fingertip."

Everybody looked down at their hands, trying to get the corn shuck going in the right direction.

The spoonful of masa paste had to cover the hoja completely with no holes, but still be spread thinly enough not to overwhelm the filling.

The giggling and finger-pointing almost got out of hand before it was decided that Edna and Lauren were not up to the challenge and were promoted to being filling fillers.

With more than our share of stupid mistakes, we finally got the tamales rolled up and into the pressure cooker.

"No wonder we buy these in cans," Edna said. "By the time they're cooked it will be nearly midnight."

"Then we'll eat them tomorrow," Mike said.

And we did. For breakfast. He and I couldn't wait and I dished them up in lieu of scrambled eggs or oatmeal.

"Sam, these are great," Mike told me. "I think this is the best thing I've ever eaten in my life."

"Once I week," I vowed. "I don't care how time-consuming and complicated these are. I'm going to make a batch once a week."

I kept my word on that.

Thursday became tamale day. I devoted the entire waking hours of Thursday to the project. Mike began to look forward to it. People dropped in to help out. We made bigger and bigger batches to share.

When Mike's friend Daryl tasted them, he was very complimentary.

"I've got to take some of these back to the city," he told me. "They are simply awesome."

Like the ladies from the San Antonio church, I wrapped them by the dozen in aluminum foil and put them in brown paper bags for delivery. I took them to the pastor, both mine and the Maynards'. I dropped some off at the firehouse and to the ladies at the library. I'd leave several bags at the Maynard home. They not only ate them, but Edna served them at her parties. I even took some by Cherry Dale's place, since I knew how much Nate loved them.

When I stopped by with my ration for the drugstore, Doc thanked me and then motioned me to come to the back.

"I need a favor from you," he said.

Once we got into the harsh light of the back room I could see his expression was very grave.

"What's happened?" I asked him.

"Nothing," he said. "Nothing has happened." He handed me a wide-mouthed, plastic-topped brown medicine bottle. The familiar Maynard Drugstore label was blank except for the name Mike.

"What are these?"

"Pills. Mike asked me for them," Doc said. He hesitated as if reluctant to say anything more.

"The doctor didn't order anything new," I told him, confused.

"They're schedule-two drugs, not one of his prescriptions."

I looked for dosage directions on the label. It was blank.

"Mike asked me for these," Doc repeated. "I've had them here in this bottle for almost a month and haven't been able to give them to him."

"I don't understand."

"He said that he wanted something…" Doc's lower

lip began to tremble. He bit down on it, but that didn't help much. "Mike said that if it got too bad, he wanted something to be able to end it. That if it came to that, he wanted…"

The trembling shuddered into a sob. Doc Maynard suddenly looked a thousand years old. I took the bottle out of his hand and embraced him.

"Don't think about it again," I said. "I'll see that Mike gets these. That will be his choice, one way or another. Just let it go, Doc. We love him and we've done all we can. Now we do what we think is right and not ever look back on it again."

Corrie
1992

><

As Mike lingered painfully on through spring, his condition grew more and more grave. He developed endocarditis and the doctors told us he'd never be able to fight off the infection. Somehow he did. He suffered a bout with pneumocystis pneumonia, they warned us that it was highly unlikely that he would recover, but he did.

All through those first months of the year, we lived in daily expectation of my brother's last breath. We were ready for it. He was ready for it. But his life dragged on and on in obvious suffering.

I was sitting the final exam of Russian History: 1917 to the Present when my pager began to vibrate. I glanced down and saw Mike's home number. Sam knew I was in the middle of a test. He would only call if it was an emergency. I knew my brother was dead. My beloved brother, who had been my closest buddy, my hero. I'd wanted to be with him when he died. I'd wanted to be holding his hand when he stepped into the next world. But, as always, I'd been out doing my own thing, pursuing my own goals, seeking my own life. My brother was dead. I'd missed his last moment and there was nothing I could do about it.

Guilty, grieving, I wanted to just sign the test paper and hand it in. But I got a grip on myself. Nobody would be helped by me wasting time and money failing a class. Mike had been proud of me. He was proud of my determination to take control of my own life, to go after what I wanted. I gathered my composure, took a deep breath and finished the exam.

As soon as I handed it in I hurried to the block of pay phones out in the commons. I was crying now, thinking of Mike, as I dialed his number.

"He's gone," Sam said simply.

"I'll be right there" was my only reply.

The next two days remain a blur in my mind. Friends and family filled Mike's house. There seemed not to be any place to retreat to from the noise and the conversation. Arrangements for the funeral had already been made by Mike himself. He'd picked the order of service, the music, the friends to speak. He told the Reverend Shue that it was one of the few perks of knowing you're going to die young—getting a hip send-off.

I don't know if *hip* would have been the correct word to describe the funeral. It certainly had its hip moments.

The pallbearers were all in tuxes with matching cummerbunds. There was original music, some of it strange, almost free form. A black woman with dreadlocks played a medley of Broadway hits on the xylophone. An old fashioned barbershop quartet sang a very unique rendition of "I'll Be a Sunbeam for Jesus."

For the scripture reading, instead of the comfort of the Psalms or the hopefulness of the New Testament, Mike had chosen a passage from Job.

In lieu of eulogies, there were poetry readings. Most

of the poems were about Mike. Others were about AIDS. Some of the verses were brimming with good humor. Others welling with sadness.

One young man got up to read and his words were so angry and in-your-face I was startled. It was like an indictment of all the friends and family who were not homosexuals. Protectively, I looked over at my parents. My mother was looking straight ahead, her expression was completely blank. She wasn't hearing anything. Dad had his head bent, discreetly crying into his handkerchief.

Of course the service moved on, through more music, more poems, more prayers. Still, it was the poem of the young man that stayed with me.

At the cemetery, I shook hand after hand of people I'd known all my life and people I'd never seen before. They all were touched by Mike's life in some way.

Under the bright green awning I was claustrophobic. As if he sensed what I was feeling, Sam took my hand. I thought of how many times when I was little and afraid that Mike had done the very same thing.

The gravesite was so covered in flowers that if I squinted, I could almost imagine that no casket was even there. But I didn't have the luxury of such a fantasy. Mike was gone. Mom and Dad would be depending upon me.

When the last prayer was spoken and the final admonition to turn to dust was made, we headed for the long black limo. The funeral director drove us back to Mike's house, which was immediately filled with flowers.

The family formed an impromptu reception line as neighbors, visitors and consolers of every sort made a path to the door.

I shook hand after hand, often of people I
didn't know.

"Thank you, so much."

"You are so kind."

"I'm sure Mike would have appreciated you being
here."

My own responses began to sound automatic and in-
sincere even to my own ears.

In a long line of men I'd never met, I looked up and
saw a familiar face. The sight was as welcome as a life
preserver to a drowning victim.

"Dr. Muldrew," I said, surprised.

He ignored my offered hand and wrapped me in a
big, generous hug. "Corrie, I'm so sorry for your loss,"
he said.

"Thank you," I answered. Then at the risk of being
rude to people waiting to talk to me, I asked to speak to
him privately.

We moved away from the front entry, through the
house and out the sliding glass door to the little brick
patio. The day was as gray and overcast as my mood,
but the shoots of green in the lawn and on the trees
weren't quite the dull colorlessness that I felt.

We sat down across from each other at the picnic table.

"When I said I wanted to run into you on another occasion, this wasn't it," I told him.

He nodded and gave me a little smile.

"I've been here several times to see Mike," he told
me. "I've met your husband. He's a nice guy. I like
him."

"Me, too," I said.

"How are you doing?" he asked.

"I don't know," I admitted. "I feel mostly numb. It's

strange how you know this is going to happen, you expect it to happen, you're waiting for it to happen, and when it does, it just feels like a terrible surprise."

"I want to reassure you," he said. "That although I'm sure you'll quite naturally feel tremendous sadness and grief for a while, don't worry that you'll fall back into that dark place you were in before. We're just beginning to understand the physiological components of psychological distress. But statistically, you're not a lot more vulnerable than anyone else."

"Oh," I said, a little bit startled. "I hadn't even thought about the possibility of getting depressed again."

"That's good," he told me. "It's very positive to just keep moving forward. But if you begin to feel like you're relapsing, give me a call. We can get you back into treatment, back on the medication very quickly."

"Okay, sure."

"That wasn't what you wanted to ask me?"

"No, it wasn't," I told him. "I really wanted to find out about the young man who read that poem, the one about our 'straight' jacket."

"Ah," Dr. Muldrew said, nodding. "Cliff." He hesitated as if collecting his thoughts. "Cliff is an angry guy," he said finally. "I'm sorry if what he said hurt you."

"It did hurt," I admitted. "More than that, I really didn't understand it. Everybody who was here, everybody who supported Mike during his illness and showed up at his funeral…we all loved Mike…gay or straight, we all loved him."

Dr. Muldrew agreed. "But sometimes love itself can be a burden. It can hold us back."

I glanced at him skeptically. "I'm not sure I believe that," I told him.

"Did you ever wonder why Mike didn't have a partner?" he asked. "Why he didn't have one permanent man in his life?"

"I guess I never thought about it," I said. "He never mentioned anyone. Whenever I'd asked him about his love life, even before I knew he was gay, he always said that there was nobody special."

"Because there wasn't," Dr. Muldrew said. "Mike could never commit to anyone because he felt as if it was unfair to do so while he was in the closet. He was in the closet because he loved you and your parents. And he thought that admitting that he was gay would be a terrible disappointment to his family. So he *played* it straight even if he wasn't. And he cheated himself out of the kind of intimate relationship that every human being deserves to enjoy."

"So it's our fault, because he loved us?"

"No, ultimately everyone is responsible for his own life," Dr. Muldrew said. "If Mike cheated himself out of a life partner because he was afraid to trust his family with the truth about himself, then that was his mistake and his loss."

"I honestly don't know how we would have felt if he'd have told us he was gay, without telling us that he was dying," I said.

"From what I've seen," Dr. Muldrew said, "all of you, even your mother, would have done just fine."

"Still, Cliff probably does have cause to be mad at us," I said.

"In a way, I guess he does," he said. "Cliff isn't mad at you specifically. He's angry because sometimes it seems that even when our heterosexual families and friends love us, they never seem to make much effort to understand us."

I was beginning to think I didn't understand anyone.

Cherry Dale showed up at the funeral, virtually unrecognizable beneath the bruises. All the rumors that had been whispered around town for years now were suddenly evidenced and it wasn't pretty. Even the Reverend Shue was aghast at the sight of her.

"What happened?" I asked her, though in my heart I already knew the answer.

"Floyd didn't want me to come to Mike's funeral," she told me. "I never go out when I'm beaten up, so he beat me up to keep me from going out."

I felt a rush of anger and hatred for Floyd, but they were almost overshadowed by my guilt about Cherry Dale.

"Mike was a good friend to me," she told me. "Floyd would have had to break my neck to keep me away from here."

The thought of what the woman was going through made me nauseous.

"What can we do to help you, Cherry Dale?" I asked her.

"Don't worry about me," she said. "I know how to handle Floyd. I'll be fine."

She didn't look as if she was going to be fine.

"Nate's not going back to that house," I whispered to Sam as I passed him in the hallway.

He nodded agreement.

"Even seeing it, I can't believe it," he said. "Do you think I should call the sheriff?"

"She says that she can handle it," I told him. "If she won't help herself, can anyone else really help her?"

It was a rhetorical question and Sam didn't try to answer. I knew he felt as badly as I did. We had both been so busy with our lives and distracted with our situation, we'd tried to ignore what was happening. We could no longer do that. If we couldn't help Cherry Dale, at least we could take our son away from there.

At Mike's house friends continued to drop by. Mom was so much at her best, dressed in a suit that Mike had picked out for her years ago, she was the elegant caring hostess. As the afternoon dragged on forever, she was still smiling, but I knew that she was emotionally exhausted. I hope that I never know what it is like to bury my own child. My heart went out to her. I wanted to help.

Lauren and Nate were becoming very bored, so I asked Mom to take them to her house. I whispered in Lauren's ear that it would be a good idea to get her grandma to take a nap. She gave me a wink to signal her willingness to be a co-conspirator. It was amazing how suddenly my little girl who needed all my attention and protection had turned into a strong young woman that I could depend upon.

As the circle of people dwindled, the reminiscences became more bittersweet. Ultimately, it was just me and Sam and Doc remembering Mike and laughing about things that may have happened ten years earlier.

"I always felt bad about losing his money," Sam said.

My dad patted him on the knee. "I'm sure he was much happier to give it to you than to the doctors and hospitals and drug companies."

"Yeah, I guess so."

"We'll have to sell his house to pay off what he owes," my father continued. "We'll be lucky if that gets his estate in the black. He left his half of the drugstore to me. It's not worth much. I don't think we could even find a buyer if we looked for one."

"Probably not," I agreed.

A thoughtful silence settled among the three of us. It was Sam who finally broke it.

"He hung in there a long time," he said. "I never would have believed that he'd hold on as long as he did."

It was true. We'd seen him come back time and time again when the doctors had warned us that he was nearly gone.

My father nodded. "You never gave him the drugs, did you?"

Sam seemed surprised.

"Yes, of course I did," he said.

"When?"

"The day that you gave them to me," Sam told him.

"What did he say?"

"Not much," Sam replied. "I handed the bottle to him and he looked inside and thanked me and said that it was perfect."

"What are you talking about?" I asked them.

My father hesitated for a moment, as if not sure how much to reveal. Then with a sigh he explained it all.

"Mike asked me to give him something to end it," my father said. "He said if it got too bad, he wanted to be in control of how and when to go."

My heart caught in my throat.

"Oh, Daddy, that must have been so terrible for you," I said.

He shrugged. "Mike told me exactly what he wanted. He'd thought it through completely. He even showed up to sign the schedule, so that if an auditor ever questioned the discrepancy, it wouldn't put my license in jeopardy."

"That's Mike," Sam said. "Always looking out for somebody else."

"He never took them," my father said. There was a puzzling question in his tone.

"Maybe he did," Sam said.

"No." Dad was shaking his head. "Digitalis and morphine in those doses—it was enough to kill a healthy man at twice Mike's weight. He would have gone very quickly."

"The last two days," Sam said sadly, "he had so much fluid in his lungs it was as if he were drowning in slow motion."

"He'd planned it all through so thoroughly," my father pointed out. "When someone is that focused... well, I was sure he was going through with it."

"I guess he just decided to tough it out," I said.

Dad didn't seem as convinced as he did worried.

"Do you have any idea what he did with the drugs?" he asked Sam.

"He put them in the drawer of the bedside table. They're probably still there."

Sam got up and went into the bedroom.

The expression on my father's face was pained.

"I don't know how to feel," he said to me. "When Mike asked me for the drugs, I tried to talk him out of it. But he was adamant, certain he didn't even want to discuss it. I'm happy that he didn't take his life. I'm happy that I had no part in causing his death. But I know how determined he was. He was like the Mike we'd always known, seeing something that had to be done and taking charge to do it. In that way, I was kind of proud."

Dad's eyes welled up with tears and I took him in my arms. We had both cried a lot that day. But not like this, not together. Somehow the connection made the hurt more painful and the release more cleansing.

We were still clutching each other for support when Sam came back into the room.

"They're not there," he said. "No pills, no bottle, no nothing."

Sam
1993

—▶ ◀—

After Mike's death my priority became getting a job and providing for my family. That didn't seem like it should be an unreasonable expectation. That's what husbands and fathers did. They worked every day, brought home paychecks, bought houses, saved for a rainy day. I was thirty-five years old. I hadn't held a regular full-time job for five years. My oldest was getting ready to start high school and I didn't have one thin dime saved toward a college education.

The job market was encouraging. Tulsa had really begun to turn the corner on its future, no longer solely dependent upon the oil industry. I was not, however, the ideal candidate for a job in the new economy. I had a high school diploma and a big hole in my résumé. When I'd left the workforce, computers were big machines that office personnel had on their desks. Now even the fast-food restaurants were using them. I had no computer skills. I couldn't even type.

I had more than one human resources receptionist look over the top of her glasses at me like I was an idiot. I got into a night class at the vo-tech center. I never could learn to keyboard worth a damn, but if you could click it with a mouse, then I could run a computer.

Mike's parents sold his house for a good price and managed to cover his debts. I moved into the Maynards' along with the rest of my family. It was a large, three-bedroom home, luxurious by Lumkee standards fifty years earlier. But with all of us crowded into it, it was very close quarters. Since Corrie was already sharing a room with Lauren, I was obliged to share with Nate.

It had been so long since my wife and I had had a room together, I could hardly remember what that was like. As for sex, well I guess when you're in your thirties, sex just ceases to exist.

What seemed to me as the logical thing to do was to move the family into a nice, good-size apartment in Tulsa. We could be near Corrie's work and school and there would be a lot more opportunities for me to find a job.

Of course, what is logical is not always possible. The kids went ballistic at the mention of a new school. Lauren lay on her bed and cried for half a day. Nate cursed and threw things and threatened to run away. Corrie's parents didn't say a word to discourage us, but they looked so old and so fragile. It was hard on them having us underfoot, but it was also a little frightening to be left on their own.

As it happened, we didn't have to move out into our own place just yet. Cy Walker, one of my old clients who'd lost his company, was now a contractor for a major oil subsidiary. He offered me a job.

"I've got a CO_2 push going in West Texas," he told me. "And I'm trying to start up a steam flood out near

Bakersfield, California. I know you can do the work and I could sure use the help."

It was a great opportunity and good money. I couldn't turn it down. Corrie drove me to the airport. She walked with me down to the gate and waited with me for the plane.

"It's kind of crazy," I told her. "We've never really been apart, but lately it seems like we haven't been together."

"What?" she said. Obviously distracted, she hadn't heard what I'd said.

"Hey, I love you, Corrie," I responded.

She smiled. "You're a good man, Sam," she told me. "Be careful out there and don't take chances."

"I won't," I assured her.

"I don't know how Lumkee will get along without tamales once a week," she said.

"I suspect they'll manage."

They called my flight and Corrie jumped to her feet, almost as if she was eager to see me go.

"I'll phone home a lot," I promised. "If anything happens, don't hesitate to call me on the cell. I'll have it with me all the time."

She nodded. "We'll be fine, don't worry about us."

That was, of course, impossible.

I checked in for an extended stay at a reasonably priced chain motel on the interstate. Nothing there but cable TV and a restaurant, but there was enough work to keep me from getting too bored.

The oil field we were working was in the middle of a cotton field. It had a number of low-producing wells. Steam flooding, infusing high-pressure steam into the rock, is a technique used to thin the syrupy molecules of oil that are trapped in rifts and crevices. By changing the viscosity, the oil flows from the fissures into the main reservoirs so that it can be pumped out. I'd never done it in Oklahoma, where the crude is graded as light and sweet. But the oil in Bakersfield was heavier and more susceptible to the steam flood. Injection wells had to be drilled, three times as many as those producing. Fortunately, they could be shallow, just a little over 3,000 feet. Once they were completed and attached to the steam generator, the small bits of trapped oil would coalesce into the larger pools that were retrievable with conventional methods.

It was work that I understood and was good at doing. I didn't mind working for somebody else and I quickly earned the trust and confidence of the crew. But I was not one of the decision-makers. Neither the problems nor the solutions were mine to stew over. Somehow, that took a lot of the satisfaction out of the job.

But I was glad to be working, glad to be providing for my family at last. When Corrie told me that she was thinking about going on to graduate school, it felt great to say, "Yeah, honey, I think you should go. And I think you should go full-time."

"It just gives me so many more options," she explained. "I love teaching, but I think you can burn out too quickly. I want to be able to choose my classroom, not be imprisoned by it."

"You've got to go for it," I agreed. "They're going to keep me really busy out here, at least for the next couple of years. While I've got the chance to make some money, you ought to be going after what you want."

It wasn't hard to convince Corrie to do it, but it was nearly impossible to convince her to do it and not feel guilty about doing it.

But I was happy just to get to talk to her. My life in California was terribly lonely. I was friendly with the other guys in the crew. A number of them, like me, were away from their families. We'd eat dinner together occasionally or drive into town to catch a movie, but once we'd worked all day together, we really weren't all that keen about socializing in the evening.

I read a lot. My year taking care of Mike had broadened my scope of reading interests and, in my off time, I pretty much always kept a book in my hand. That's how I got my nickname. One morning at the restaurant I was enjoying a book with my breakfast when Diedre, one of the waitresses, passed by my table.

"What about you, Mr. Bookworm?" she said. "Do you need some coffee?"

I don't remember what I answered. But none of the guys within earshot could forget what she called me. Within the space of three days, every man and woman on the crew called me Mr. Bookworm. It quickly spread up the corporate chain until even Cy, who'd known me as Sam for twenty years, began calling me that.

"Diedre, you've ruined my life," I told her a few weeks later.

I was just kidding with her, but I guess I shouldn't have been. She was a cute girl, probably in her mid-twenties. She always wore a bright smile and too much makeup.

She leaned her hip against the edge of my table.

"You give me a chance, Mr. Bookworm, and I can make it up to you," she said.

I was momentarily dumbstruck. Everybody back in Lumkee knew that I was very married. It had been so long since a woman had hit on me, I just didn't quite expect it.

"I've got some free time this weekend," she continued. "We can have a few beers together or something."

"I don't think my wife would like that much," I replied.

My answer dimmed her smile. "You've got a wife?" she asked. "You don't wear no wedding ring."

"When we got married, we couldn't afford to buy one," I told her. "We were lucky to get the plain gold band my wife wears."

Diedre didn't give up easily. "How come she's not out here with you?"

"We've got two kids in middle school," I said. "And Corrie's going back to college."

"Corrie? That's your wife's name?"

I nodded.

"How long you been married?"

"Fifteen years."

Diedre's eyes widened. "I didn't think you was that old."

I wiped a hand across my hair. "That Grecian Formula—it's like a miracle."

She laughed then and went on her way.

I sighed a little in relief, but I felt a little sad as well. It would be nice to have a woman to talk to, to laugh with.

I went back to my room and called home. Corrie wasn't there. Lauren said that she'd gone to the library. Nate was out somewhere, as usual. I talked to my daughter for a few minutes. Then I was alone in my room again.

Boredom was to be expected when a guy was far from home. The important thing was not to give in to it and not let it give me permission to do something really stupid.

I became determined to "un-bore" myself. What would I do for fun if I were at home?

"I'd be making tamales," I answered myself aloud.

I got up, put on my jacket on and headed to the grocery store. Fortunately, a lot of Mexicans live in Bakersfield. I found everything I needed. And I bought two six packs of Dos Equis to insure that I was going to have some help.

I invited over all the on-the-loose guys in the crew. I put a basketball game on the TV and talked them into helping me. They turned out great.

"These are real Texas tamales," one of them told me.

"Forget that, Mr. Lone Star State," I answered him. "These are genuine Okie tamales."

We ate the leftovers the next day.

It was early Monday morning and I was just getting ready to walk out the door when the phone rang. It was Corrie.

"What's wrong?" I asked as soon as I heard the tone of her voice.

"Sam," she said calmly, "your father passed away last night."

When Floyd Braydon had walked into my life ten years earlier, he'd turned everything about my world upside down. I'd wanted to believe in him so badly, I had done it in the face of lots of evidence to the contrary. But now that he was gone, I couldn't help but feel sorry. Not sorry that we hadn't been closer. I'd known more about the man than I wanted to know. Not sorry we hadn't had more time together. I was glad I would never have to see him again. But somehow I was sorry that he'd been the man that he'd been.

He was half of me. Half of everything that made me human. And he was half of everything I'd passed on to my children. I was sorry that his half was something about myself that I could never be proud of.

I called my boss, got a week's leave and caught a plane into Tulsa. Corrie met my plane and filled me in on the details as we drove to Lumkee.

"It was a heart attack," she told me. "He'd stayed late at the bar. Cherry Dale made pasta for dinner and had already fed the kids."

Corrie glanced over at me. "Are you sure you want to hear this?"

"Everything you know," I answered.

"Floyd came home drunk and got mad that she'd fixed pasta. He beat her up really bad. He had her down on the floor banging her head against the bottom of the refrigerator when Cherry Dale's kids pulled him off."

Her words actually made me queasy.

"After he got control of himself, he told Cherry Dale to fix him something to eat. She heated up a can a chili. He ate it and lay down on the couch to watch TV. Cherry Dale didn't disturb him until morning. When she realized he was not breathing, she called old Dr. Billups."

"She called Billups?" I was surprised. "Why would Cherry Dale call that old quack instead of the EMS?"

Corrie shrugged. "I guess she thought he was closer, or maybe she just wasn't thinking."

"Dr. Billups said that Floyd just fell asleep and never woke up. He had a heart attack and died right there on the couch."

By the time we got to the double-wide, Cherry Dale was behaving very calmly, but she did look like hell.

One eye was completely swollen shut, her mouth was at a strange angle, and the lower part of her face so black and blue I worried that something might be broken.

"Did you have Dr. Billups look at your jaw?" I asked her.

"Billups? No, I never use him. I went to my usual doctor in Tulsa. He's patched me up several times," she said. "I've got a black veil I can wear to the funeral. Nobody will know."

It was a weird thing for her to say. And, of course, anything that happened in Lumkee everybody already knew.

I didn't remind Cherry Dale of that fact. I just sat there, wishing that I could think of something to say. She had always been so cheerful and funny when she was visiting with Mike. Now she was as ill at ease as I was.

"This kind of thing happens a lot," she said finally.

I was momentarily startled. Of course, I knew that. You couldn't read the paper or watch the TV without being familiar with domestic violence.

"It's mostly middle-aged guys," she said. "But Floyd wasn't much older than that."

"Middle-aged guys?" I repeated, uncertain.

"Yes, they talk about it in the exercise magazines all the time," she said. "Middle-aged guys often overexert themselves, but they don't have the heart attack during the exertion. It's afterward, when they rest."

When I realized how wrong-tracked I was, I had to stifle the impulse to chuckle. My father was dead. His girlfriend was beaten to a pulp. There was nothing about it that was remotely funny. It was a serious moment and I had something very serious that I had to say.

"I'm sorry that my dad beat you like he did," I said. "It was wrong of him to do that. I'm sorry he did it. And I'm sorry I didn't do anything to stop it."

I could see the tension in Cherry Dale's shoulders relax.

"Thank you, Sam," she said. "You couldn't have stopped him."

"I could have got him thrown back into jail," I said.

"Not for long," she answered. "And that wouldn't be a thing that I'd want you to have on your conscience. He was your flesh and blood, no matter what. I don't blame you. Believe me, I don't blame anyone but myself."

We didn't have much of a funeral service. Although I was the official next of kin, Cherry Dale suggested a cremation. It seemed all right to me. It was quick and inexpensive. Floyd never had any interest in churches, so we had a little private memorial for him at Cherry Dale's house. Not many people showed up. There were a half dozen of his buddies from the bar, the assistant principal from the middle school where he worked, Corrie's parents, Corrie and the kids, Cherry Dale and me. Though I was told that his other children, my half sisters, had been informed of his death, neither of them made an appearance. Even Cherry Dale's own kids spent the afternoon elsewhere.

Mr. Howell, the assistant principal, agreed to say a few words. Steering clear of any mention of Floyd's personal life, he made it sound more like an annual employee evaluation than a eulogy.

Every soul in attendance was dry-eyed except Nate.

He cried for his paw-paw as if his little heart was broken.

The ladies auxiliary from Gram's church, where my family still attended on an irregular basis, catered the dinner with a big ham, potatoes, greens, fresh bread and warm berry cobbler. It was a better send-off than the man deserved.

After everyone had gone, Corrie sent Cherry Dale to bed with some pain medication. She was still far from healed. I sent the kids home with Doc and Edna and stayed to help Corrie. I wanted to be near her, to hold her. In some strange way, I needed to be comforted.

Corrie was quiet and distant.

"I'd really rather do this myself," she said.

I was hurt, but I shrugged off her mood as a result of the funeral atmosphere, coupled with Cherry Dale's beaten face.

"I just want to do something to help," I said.

"Why don't you go clean up that mess of garbage by the alley," she said. "Cats or dogs or something got into it and they've spread trash all over the backyard. It needs to be done before tomorrow's pickup. You know they only come once a week these days."

"Sure," I agreed.

If she wanted space, I could give it to her. Even if it meant picking up trash in the alley.

I grabbed a garbage bag from the carport and walked back there. There were old smelly cans, ripped-up cereal boxes, banana peels and bathroom tissues.

Suddenly there was a strange tug on my memory as I picked up, from the tall grass around the edge of the trash can, a wide-mouthed, plastic-topped brown medicine bottle. The familiar Maynard Drugstore label was blank except for the name Mike.

Corrie
1993

◄—►

My graduation should have been a time of celebration. I'd worked so hard and waited so long. It had taken me six years to get a bachelor's degree, but I'd finally done it. It was a tremendous accomplishment. It should have been one of the happiest, proudest moments of my life. What it felt like was just one more event that I was expected to show up at, this one wearing a robe and mortarboard.

Sam had gotten a job. That was great news. I admit, I'd begun to wonder if he liked not working so much that he might just hang around forever. I know it's unfair of me even to say that. He couldn't find a job, and then, thank God, he was unemployed and able to stay with Mike and take care of him. Still, after the first little glow of pride at being sole support of my family, the honor wore thin.

Sam inherited Gram's house after Floyd's death. Or rather he didn't inherit it. We found out that we'd owned it all the time. Although Sam had signed the title transfer papers, Floyd had never gotten around to filing them. We don't know if he was balking at the title transfer fee or if he just didn't want those pesky tax bills coming in his name.

Either way, we were able to take possession of the house and set up a payment schedule to catch up the taxes on the place. It had been so long since we'd had a place of our own that we'd weeded our possessions down to the essentials. Only the children's rooms were significant moving challenges.

Gram's house was small. Since Lauren and Nate both needed their own rooms, I decided that Gram's sewing porch, a little multiwindowed room that had been added to the east side of the house, would serve as our master bedroom. It was small, but with Sam living his life in some distant motel, it was plenty big enough for me.

Lauren was gearing up to start high school in the fall. She was more able to take care of herself and help around the house. She loved being at Gram's place. The neighborhood was in the middle of a revitalization. Lots of the new people, moving into the area for Tulsa's high-tech jobs, liked the big trees, sidewalks and picket fences that evoked memories of small town America. Though it was all just window dressing. The city sprawl now spread far past Lumkee. The new high school had an enrollment close to 1,500, almost three times the size it had been when Sam and I attended.

Lauren was popular and had lots of friends. She also participated in nearly everything, which brought its own share of conflicts. She loved ballet, but worried her horseback riding was making her look too muscular. She had been first-chair flute in the middle school. But if she was in the marching band, she couldn't go out for cheerleader. She was elected president of Salon France, but bemoaned that all the athletes and the really cool kids signed up for Spanish Club.

Nate's problems were different. He had few friends.

He spent most of his time in his room. While I was thrilled that he enjoyed computers and bragged that my "geeky son was destined to be the next Bill Gates," I also worried. Since his paw-paw's death, Nate had become increasingly more isolated. I was aware of several occasions when he'd stayed on the Internet all night. He was also quite capable of cutting classes, or even the entire school day, to sit in front of his screen. I didn't know if he was hacking into the defense department, viewing porno or just chatting with lonely kids like himself. Just not knowing was disturbing enough. And I was not likely to find out.

The anti-woman, especially anti-Mom, seeds that Floyd Braydon had nurtured in my little son had come into full bloom. Nate was way too smart to openly defy me, blatantly disobey me, to talk back to me or to show me disrespect. He knew just where those lines were and he kept to them with great care. But he didn't like me. He didn't want to see me. He didn't want me in his room. And he had nothing whatsoever to say to me.

"I think he should see Dr. Muldrew," I told Sam one evening on the phone.

"What does Nate say about that?" he asked.

"He says he's not interested," I admitted. "But that doesn't mean that we just sit on our hands."

Ultimately we decided that if Nate was unwilling to go, the sessions, which weren't covered by insurance and which we really couldn't afford, wouldn't do him much good.

Sam decided that as soon as school was out, he'd take Nate with him to California. Not yet fourteen, there was no way that he could be out at the job sites. But Sam was going to look into some summer day programs for teens in Bakersfield.

So, on the day of my graduation, I could look at my life and say that it was busy, full, complicated.

It was also messed up. I'd messed it up. I'd fallen for another man.

I never meant for that to happen. Never thought it could happen or would happen. I don't even know how it happened.

I guess it really started even before Sam left for California. That's when I met him. That's when we struck up a friendship.

I was sitting at a table in the library, surrounded by books and papers. I took notes in class on my laptop, but there were always little pieces of paper where I'd jotted down things from books and I liked to enter those into the computer so that I could organize everything together.

I smelled him before I saw him. A faint whiff of woodsy aftershave caught my attention. My fellow students weren't all that keen on shaving. I glanced up and he was looking at me. He was tall and slim, with nice features, reddish-brown hair and wonderful blue eyes.

"Hi," I said immediately. I grew up in Lumkee, where there was no such thing as strangers, just people you hadn't met.

"Hello," he answered. "Are you putting together your final exam?"

The question momentarily puzzled me. "I'm studying," I replied, uncertain. "Oh, you think I'm a professor." I could see immediately that I was right and I laughed. "No, no, I'm old enough, but I'm still a student."

He smiled. It was a wonderful smile. And then he sat down across the table from me.

"Well, aren't we always saying that learning is life-long," he pointed out. "That must mean that I'm a student, too."

"Good save," I told him.

"I do my best." He offered his hand across the top of the table. "Hollace Rivers Harrington, my friends call me Riv, but I always use the whole name when I introduce myself, so people will recognize it when they see it on a book jacket."

"Book jacket? Are you a writer?"

"I'm a novelist," he answered. "An unpublished novelist with a time-consuming and humdrum second job as an English professor."

I laughed. "Time-consuming and humdrum? Hey, mister, I'm studying to be a teacher."

"Oh, I like *being a teacher*," he hastened to clarify. "I'm just not that enamored with actually teaching."

He was fun and flirty and I enjoyed his company. It couldn't be a bad thing to make a new friend. Just because he was a man didn't mean he wasn't friend material. The whole thing was completely acceptable and aboveboard. We both revealed up front that we were married. We each had children. I cannot stress to you enough how totally innocent it all was.

Except maybe it wasn't. I never mentioned Riv to Sam. Occasionally one of us would suggest that we get together as couples some time, but neither of us ever followed up on it. We started meeting for lunch a couple of times a week. Then we were seeing each other every day.

Once we were discussing films and he mentioned one he'd just seen, *The Scent of Green Papaya*. I admitted that I'd never seen a Vietnamese film, in fact I'd never seen any film with subtitles.

Riv invited me to see it with him. I had a great time, watching the movie and talking about it afterward with him. After that Riv and I started going out to the movies together regularly.

Sam was far away in California. I was not. Riv and I never talked about being together as if we were sneaking around. We never discussed what our families might have thought that we were doing. We just met each other at the front of the theater. We each bought our own ticket. It wasn't dating. We were just enjoying a movie together, enjoying time together, enjoying popcorn together.

He was smart, interesting, educated. He'd grown up in Connecticut, a place so far away and exotic to me it might as well have been Djakarta or Khartoum. He'd gone to prestigious schools back East. He'd spent two summers living in Europe. He'd backpacked through Nepal. He'd been on every continent except Antarctica and he'd even seen it from a ship. I was fascinated by his stories, flattered by his attention.

He was so different from Sam, in every way. He'd been places, done things. The most exciting thing my husband had ever done was learn how to cook tamales.

I began thinking about Riv in every spare moment. He was the first thing on my mind when I got up in the morning. He was the last thing on my mind when I went to bed at night.

Lauren would be sharing her latest drama and talking to me, but I was thinking about him.

On the weekends that Sam was home I was annoyed that I was forced to stay in Lumkee and have family time.

I avoided my mom, my friends. I didn't have time for them anymore.

I wanted to be with Riv. And I began to resent everything and everyone that stood in my way.

So when I walked across the stage to get my diploma on that beautiful spring afternoon I was less than happy. My husband was there. My children were there. My parents were there. And they were all cheering and applauding me. All I could do was wonder whether Riv was there. Was he in the audience somewhere watching me? I wanted him to be there.

After commencement, my parents took the whole family out to a lovely dinner at The Fountains. Mom was in her element, sweetly scolding the waiter to get us a better table. Lauren followed her lead with such a pretty and pleasant facade of condescension. Nate was bored and sullen. My dad was quiet, as he was most often was since Mike's death.

Sam stood and offered a toast on my behalf.

"To the smartest woman I've ever known," he said. "Now she has the paper to prove it."

Everybody laughed.

He grew more serious. "I think everyone at this table knows, or should know, that this family wouldn't have survived the last few years without you, Corrie. You have worked, sometimes at two jobs, making sure that our bills were paid. And you've done it generously, selflessly and without a word of complaint." He grinned wryly. "Oh, we had the occasional whine, but no actual complaints." More laughter. "Through all of these terrible times in our family, through all the emotional stress and financial struggle, you never lost sight of your goals. I'm not sure if I can express how proud I am of you. But just let me say that if our children and their children and grandchildren grow to have half the strength and heart of Corrie Braydon, the world will be a better place."

Sam's eyes were filled with tears. I was also swept with emotion. Mine was mostly shame.

The following Tuesday I drove into the city to meet Riv for lunch at the Interurban. He seemed so thrilled to see me. As if we'd been apart for a month instead of three days. The blood was pounding through my own veins.

The place was really too busy and noisy for the discussion that we had to have, but I steeled my determination.

"I don't think we should see each other anymore," I told him as soon as I was seated.

There was a moment of complete silence between us. He was looking at me closely as if trying to decipher my plainspoken words. Finally, weaving his fingers together and resting them on the edge of the table in front of him, he nodded to me thoughtfully.

"You don't need to threaten me, Corrie. I realize that it's time for us to move to the next level," he said. "I've felt it myself. We're more than friends. Relationships are either growing or they're dying. I believe I'm ready to let us grow."

"What do you mean?"

"I'm ready to expand our relationship to include physical intimacy," he said. "And I can't tell you how much it means to me that you've chosen to explore this with a rational and interactive discussion. So many women just want to be caught up in the moment and be swept away by passion. I realize that this alleviates for them any sense of their personal responsibility in their own decision-making. But we are adults here, I think we're capable of being honest with each other."

He paused only to take a studied breath. "I've been wanting to have sex with you," he continued. "I've even been working on the logistics of it. I have a friend in the math department, he keeps a little place off campus for this sort of thing. I'm sure he'll allow us to use it a couple of afternoons a week."

"Riv, I don't think—"

He cut me off with an upraised hand. "Please don't get anxious about any of this," he said. "You're a very attractive woman. I'm certain that we'll be as compatible together in bed as we are in conversation. I mean intercourse is intercourse, that's what I always say."

"Riv, I don't have affairs," I stated bluntly.

He smiled. "Corrie, I think you've got the verb wrong in that statement. You haven't *had* affairs. Okay, that's nice to know. But that's all past tense. Now that you're breaking the constraints of middle-class mores, you'll come to understand that affairs are as much a part of marriage as wedding cake and kids."

I was stunned by his words and shook my head.

"I know you haven't studied much anthropology," he said. "What they've determined is that humans are not naturally monogamous."

"Maybe not when we were nomads on the savannahs," I said. "But we've been that way at least since written language."

He patted my hand. "Yes, well, monogamy was forced upon us earlier than that," he explained. "As soon as we began to walk upright. It was a type of socio-physiological adaptation."

"That certainly sounds like a three-dollar word," I told him. "I'm not sure I understand what you mean."

His tone was patient, almost tutorial. "Because of the change in our pelvic tilt," he said. "Women had to birth their babies at an earlier stage of development. If you look at other mammals, you can see that most newborns can walk within hours."

I nodded. That was true.

"Our offspring require much more care," he said. "They could never survive on their own outside the womb."

"No, of course not," I agreed.

"The human mother is busy with her offspring for years," he said. "While she's doing that, she had less ability to feed and protect herself."

That made sense.

"So the species evolved the necessity for a family unit," Riv said. "With the father a more constant presence. Modern man simply institutionalized that into a vow of fidelity."

"You don't think God or values or morality had anything to do with it?" I asked.

He laughed. "No, of course not," he said. "When that societal modification came about, the human life span was significantly shorter than it is now. I think it's right and reasonable for a couple to commit to an exclusive child-rearing relationship when their children are small. But five to seven years of monogamy is sufficient for that. To expect healthy, intelligent men and women to remain monogamous longer than that, well, that's just silly."

I sat across the table from him for a long moment. He was so good-looking. He was interesting. He was sophisticated. He was like no one I'd ever met in Lumkee. I would never meet anyone like him there. But what seemed *silly* to Riv, seemed to me a very basic question of honesty.

"I see it differently," I told him. "What I see is that if

you're married, then you're married. If you don't want to be married, society says that you don't have to be. One of my in-laws would have said 'either fish or cut bait.' And if this is what you think of the future of our relationship, then it's time for me to cut bait.''

Sam
1993

◄──── ►◄

Having Nate spend the summer with me out in Bakersfield was one of those things that seems like the best idea at the time and turns out to be a near disaster.

I moved from the motel to a small furnished apartment in a nice working-class neighborhood. There was no cable TV and no computer. I thought, for the summer, he should give his mind a rest. I enrolled him in a summer day camp at St. Jude's Church just down the street. The staff seemed like a reasonable bunch, mostly guys, which seemed like the best idea considering Nate's issues with the opposite gender. The program had a curriculum that included swimming, basketball, wood shop and choir.

We went down there and met everybody. It all seemed fine. Nate was easygoing and appeared happy to meet everybody. I gave the director, Mr. Perez, my cell phone number and asked him to call me if there were any problems. He assured me that he would.

I anticipated that everything wouldn't go smoothly. There are always kinks to be worked out of every new operation. But none materialized. Every evening, I would come home from work and Nate would be there, wearing his camp T-shirt. Sometimes the music on the radio would be too loud. Or he would have already eaten everything in the refrigerator. But those were normal expectations for a kid his age.

He looked good. He'd shot up in height over the summer and was nearly as tall as I was. He had a healthy-looking summer tan. He ate heartily and was consistently in a better mood than I'd seen back in Oklahoma.

On Monday mornings I would leave a check for his tuition. On Monday afternoon, there would be a receipt from the church. I even got a mid-summer progress report. Mr. Perez had written that Nate was blending in very well, though he felt that he was below average in both his religious-education level and his music skills.

I was so pleased, and because it was Nate's birthday we went out for pizza to celebrate.

So you can imagine how shocked I was when I returned home one Friday afternoon and he wasn't there. I walked through the apartment then around outside. He wasn't anywhere. I knocked on my neighbor's door. They hadn't seen him. There was an old man always sitting on his porch across the street. He said Nate had left in the morning and he hadn't seen him come back.

I went back to the apartment and called the camp director's number. Of course there was no answer. The program had closed an hour earlier. Surely someone was there. I let it ring until the answering machine picked up. Then I hung up and called again to let it ring some more.

Any parent who's ever been separated from their child knows the sense of panic that I felt. I tried to maintain my cool. There was no need to assume that on his walk home he'd been beaten by muggers and left for dead. I simply needed to retrace his steps.

I walked the seven blocks between the apartment and St. Jude's. I was calm. But I was also aware. I looked in every store window and down every alley.

When I got to the church I went through the gates and into the building. It was empty except for an old woman praying in the front. I walked around outside, through the school-yard area and the back parking lot. I sighed with relief when I spotted a group of kids playing basketball, but Nate wasn't with them.

"I'm looking for my son," I told them. "Nate Braydon. Have you seen him?"

They all shrugged and shook their heads.

"Don't know him" was the general consensus.

"He goes to the summer camp here," I said.

"I go to that," one of the boys said. "But I don't know him. Is he one of the little kids?"

"He's fourteen."

The boy raised his eyebrows. "Then he'd be in my group, but he ain't," the guy said definitively.

"About six foot, brown hair, blue eyes?"

The kid shrugged.

"Mr. Perez is in the gym," one of the other guys said. "Maybe you should ask him."

"I thought it was locked up," I said.

"You can get in this back door."

"Great, thanks."

I hurried over to the entrance they'd indicated and, sure enough, I found Mr. Perez lifting weights.

"Hey, sorry to barge in on your workout," I said. "I'm Sam Braydon, Nate's dad."

He wiped his sweaty palms on a towel and stepped forward to shake my hand.

"Hi, yeah, I remember you, Mr. Braydon. How ya doing?"

"Not as well as I could be. I got home this afternoon and Nate wasn't there," I explained. "Do you have any idea where he might be?"

The guy's brow furrowed. "Me?"

"Yeah."

"I haven't seen him since he left here," Perez said.

"Do you remember what time he left?" I asked. "Or which direction he went? Or if anyone was with him?"

Perez was looking at me very strangely, and when he spoke his words were slow and considered.

"I meant, I haven't seen him since he left the program in June. He transferred over to Peter & Paul about two days after he started here," he said. "They have that marine biology intro study. We lose boys to that program every year."

"What? You're the one that sent me the report," I pointed out. "You said he was fitting in very well. But that he wasn't doing well in music class."

"We don't send home reports," he replied. "It's a summer program. The students aren't working for grades."

"The report was signed by you," I said.

The puzzled look on Perez's face disappeared completely and he was suddenly very professional, very in-charge.

"I think we'd better go up to my office and start making some phone calls."

Over the next hour and a half we didn't find Nate, but the truth about his summer activities slowly came out.

He had brought a letter to school from me, informing the staff at St. Jude's that I had decided to move Nate into the summer program at Peter & Paul. It was a very well-written adult-sounding letter. I'm not sure something I'd actually written would have sounded that good. Perez called the director at Peter & Paul and determined for a certainty that Nate had never attended there.

"The receipts could be just as fake," I said. "But the checks are cashed."

"Have you seen the canceled checks?"

"No, those go to my wife in Oklahoma," I said. "But I know the money was taken out of my account."

"He may have washed the checks," Perez told me.

"Washed them?"

"There's a process where you can get the ink off," he said. "Then you just fill in the payee and the amount and forge the name. I bet if you go to one of the little check-cashing places around your apartment, they'll tell you that Nate's been cashing checks there made out to him."

"Where would he learn to do something like that?"

"Bad companions, I suppose."

"He doesn't have any companions," I said.

Perez nodded. "Does he use the Internet?"

Ultimately, we contacted the police. Officer Reynolds very quickly discovered that Nate did indeed cash checks at the Korean grocery around the corner. And that very morning, he'd cashed one for three hundred dollars.

"Three hundred? I don't know if I even have that much money in my account."

"The woman thought it was a lot," the officer told me. "But he's been cashing checks there for a couple of months and they've all been good."

Officer Reynolds told me that Nate spent most of his

mornings in front of a computer screen at the public library. Several people in the building easily recognized his picture. Beyond that they weren't quite sure what he did with his days. Although he was known to hang out at the mall, flirting with a girl at the pretzel stand named Lisa.

"Lisa thinks he was going up to L.A. today," the policeman told me. "She says he's been talking about it for a while."

"L.A? Why would he go to L.A.?"

The policeman looked grave but answered a very official "I wouldn't want to speculate about that."

I checked Nate's room. He'd taken his backpack and some of his clothes.

"That's a good sign," Officer Reynolds told me. "If he was planning never to come back, he would have taken everything."

The words *never come back* went through me like a cold chill.

"We should be able to locate the ticket agent at the bus station to verify if that's how your son is traveling," he said. "And, of course, we'll notify LAPD to be on the lookout for the boy."

I sat alone, stunned, in my little apartment. I needed to call Corrie. But I had no idea what I was going to tell her. With a terrible sense of dread, I picked up the phone.

"Oh, hi, Daddy," Lauren said. "Listen, can we call you back, I've got somebody on the other line."

"No, honey," I answered. "Tell your friend goodbye and let me speak to your mother."

She hesitated, momentarily surprised by the unusual request.

"Sure, Daddy," she said.

A minute later Corrie was on the phone.

"Sam? What's wrong?"

"Nate's run away."

Corrie flew into L.A. the next day. I didn't even ask her how much the ticket must have cost. I drove down to pick her up at the airport. I had told her not to come. That there was nothing that she could do, but she couldn't stay away.

We talked to the police, visited drop-in shelters for runaways, but mostly we spent the day aimlessly driving up and down the streets.

We arrived back at the apartment in Bakersfield in the wee hours of the morning. We fell into bed, exhausted, but we couldn't sleep. We lay awake wondering aloud where we had gone wrong, how we had failed.

Corrie told me that Nate had slipped away from her years ago. That my father had stolen him from her.

"I'm sorry, Corrie," I told her. "I should never have brought that man into our house."

"He was your father, Sam," she told me. "Of course you wanted to be close to him. Even Gram understood that."

"She did?"

"She told me so."

"Thanks, Corrie," I said.

"Hold me, Sam," she answered.

We made love that night. The sweetest, saddest, bittersweet passion that we'd ever shared. Then, exhausted, we fell asleep.

We awakened a little after dawn, groggy and still tired. I went out to get the paper while Corrie was making coffee. The paper wasn't on the step as it usually was, but I shrugged and went back inside. As soon as I stepped in the door, I saw it on the lamp table. I was puzzled and glanced up at Corrie. She was standing beside a backpack carelessly dropped in the front hall.

Our eyes met for one moment.

I went charging into his room. He was there, a little dirty, a little smelly, but sleeping like an angel.

I immediately started shaking him awake.

Crying with joy and screaming at him with anger at the same time.

"Where have you been?" I demanded. "What have you been doing? Do you know that you scared us half to death?"

He awakened, startled. With no answers to the questions.

"What's Mom doing here?" he finally asked.

"What do you think she's doing here? Her son ran away. He scared his parents to death. 'Cause his parents didn't know that he was lying and stealing and God only knows what else while they were trusting him."

I let go of Nate and he crumpled into a seated position on the bed. I wanted to slap him so hard, I stepped back all the way to the other side of the room. Corrie was in the doorway, pale and scared and joyous and anxious.

"Everything's cool," Nate told us. "Don't get like wigged out over this. I went to see a friend in L.A. I thought if I told you, you might not let me go."

"Why would you do such a thing?"

He gave a little shrug and a smirk. "Because I can," he answered.

Corrie
1994

➤ ◀

I took my first full-time teaching job at Brightwood Elementary in Lumkee. There were better paid, more interesting and innovative positions elsewhere, but I chose my hometown. It wasn't because I was tired of the commute, but that I worried about being away from home.

After the summer shock in California, Nate continued to feel empowered somehow by doing exactly what he wanted whenever he wanted. Especially if it scared us, annoyed us, embarrassed us. I couldn't tell how much of his behavior was normal teenage rebellion, how much of it was following the example of his paw-paw or how much was actually a genetic predisposition to be a slimy, low-life snake.

The last was a postulate that I never uttered aloud. Nate's genes were our genes, and although he looked like a throwback to Floyd Braydon, we had to believe that there was more of us in him than his grandfather.

He still spent way too much time sitting in front of the computer. I talked to one of the Computer Studies grad students, who gave me some pointers on monitoring his Internet usage by using a cookie-trail software that could show me every Web site he visited.

That worked okay for a while, until I began being shocked and horrified. Fortunately I realized that he knew I was trailing him and was probably (I hoped) visiting the bomb-making sites and the violent porno just to get to me.

Although Sam had told him that he would be paying back the money he stole from us by doing chores, he never did anything unless Sam was with him. I wasn't sure if this was a streak of pure laziness on his part or just more of his "because I can" philosophy. Because there was so much tension between the two of us, I was trying to pick my battles. To stand my ground only on those things that I thought were really critical. Taking out the garbage and washing dishes didn't fit into that criteria.

Lauren complained that he wasn't doing his share.

"I don't do bitches' work," he told her.

Lauren slapped him hard enough to make his ears ring.

I wanted to applaud but instead, of course, I was forced to get between them and stop the confrontation. I couldn't allow any physical reprimand with Nate. I felt as if I were handling nitroglycerin. If we weren't careful with Nate, he might blow us all to kingdom come. The same traits that made him look like Floyd and talk like Floyd might make him a woman batterer like Floyd. That was my greatest fear. That my sweet little son would become that evil old man.

It was my worry about nature over nurture that skewed the direction of my graduate study. Instead of following an administrative track, I turned my attention to school counseling. I wanted the psych courses and the socialization theory. I needed help and reassurance that Nate was going to be okay. I was especially interested in nurture over nature. I wanted to create the best kind of environment, one that would enhance the positive in my son's life.

Occasionally I saw Riv on campus. He always smiled and acted like he was glad to see me, but we never ate lunch together, we never sat down for a conversation.

I don't think he really missed it. I saw him a few months after our "breakup" sitting with another woman at *Hamlin & Mimi's.* I hoped that it was his wife, but I had my doubts as I watched them holding hands over their grilled lemon *Tawook.*

I wish I could say that I felt nothing. That I'd completely come to my senses and realized what a better man Sam had turned out to be, and how much better suited I was to him. But I still felt the painful tug and the longing for what might have been.

In the fall, there were some new developments with my son that I thought might be, surprisingly, good. As he entered high school, the solitary, loner guy in front of the computer with no friends or social skills just blossomed. In some way, Nate's experience with taking on the world gave him a weird kind of confidence that the other kids at school found attractive. He would never be in Lauren's little group of the social elite. But he was outspoken and well liked, by the students, if not by the staff.

I was called down to his school by Mrs. Isenhart, Nate's homeroom teacher. She was beside herself. She had administered the trial for the standardized tests that sophomores are required to pass.

I assumed that Nate had failed the test, otherwise I wouldn't have been called in. I was prepared to advocate for my son, point out that it was only the trial, that he would get another chance.

Mrs. Isenhart wasn't disappointed in Nate's performance—she was furious.

"He didn't even try," the woman told me angrily. "I explained to the entire class how important these tests are, not only to them but to the rating of the school system as a whole. He didn't care. He didn't make any effort at all. He just went down the score sheet and made *x*'s. He got every answer wrong."

I eyed her curiously as she pushed the paper in front of me. I glanced down. Sure enough, every answer was wrong. I turned it over. Every answer was wrong on that side, too.

"Nate is always just on the edge of disrespect for me," Mrs. Isenhart said. "But I've tried in every way I know how to be open and helpful to him in class. And this is how he repays me! He doesn't even try!"

The woman was so upset, she wasn't even thinking straight.

"Mrs. Isenhart," I told her, "I don't think we can accuse him of not trying. Just think how hard it is to get every answer wrong. If he'd done what you're saying and just marked *x*'s down the page, statistically he'd get at least get some right. In order to miss every question, he had to know the correct answer, then deliberately mark it wrong."

If we'd ever had questions about Nate's intelligence, we didn't after that.

We tried again to get him into therapy. That was a waste of time and money. We tried four different doctors. If a patient doesn't cooperate there isn't much anyone can do. I talked to Dr. Muldrew about it.

Dr. Muldrew had never treated Nate, he'd become

far too close to the family for that. But he defended the boy.

"Corrie, he's not drinking and he's not on drugs," he said. "These days that's the definition of a good kid."

He spoke too soon.

Halloween night Nate just walked out the front door without a word about where he was going or when he might be back. He returned home in the wee hours of the morning, drunk and stumbling around. I met him at the front door.

"Where have you been?" I asked him, standing my ground.

He laughed. "It's Halloween," he told me. "I've been out chasing down my own ghosts."

"You've been drinking."

He shrugged. "A few beers," he said.

"You're only fifteen years old."

"Paw-Paw told me once that the earlier a guy starts to drink the better he can hold his liquor."

"This bit of wisdom from a man who knew a lot about getting drunk," I said.

Nate's eyes narrowed and he shook his finger at me.

"Don't you say a word against him," he warned me.

"I don't have to," I told him. "You can get poor opinions of that man on any corner in this town."

He shook his head. "That's not true," Nate said. "Everybody liked him. He was *the man*, the life of every party he ever showed up at."

"Oh, yeah, right," I said sarcastically. "And that's why he had twelve people at his funeral and half of those only showed up because they had to."

He drew in a sharp breath and I knew I'd wounded him. I wanted to take the words back. Nate was my baby. I didn't want to hurt him. But I knew I had.

"Paw-Paw loved me," he screamed. "He loved me and you drove him away. You made him unwelcome in our home."

"He made himself unwelcome by his bad behavior," I countered.

"You never liked him, he told me so. You caused trouble between him and Daddy and you tried to keep me from him altogether."

"He was a bad influence," I said. "I was doing the right thing."

"It wasn't fair! It was never fair! He loved me!"

Nate raised his fist. I knew he was going to hit me. I was trembling. Floyd Braydon's anger and abuse came out from behind the mask with the help of alcohol. I was scared, so scared, that in that, too, Nate might be like him. I was not just afraid that he might hurt me, which he could. He was as tall as Sam now and beginning to show some sinew of muscle on his long, lean frame. But the danger of any physical damage paled behind the reality of what would happen emotionally to our relationship if he struck me.

As he swung his fist, I closed my eyes and raised a hand in protection.

A loud bang to my right popped my eyes open.

Nate had put his fist through the Sheetrock of the wall beside me. I just stared at the dent in the wall and my son's still-clenched fist.

"What's going on?"

Lauren had come running into the living room, dressed in flannel pajamas, her hair mussed from sleep.

"Get out of my sight, bitch!" Nate screamed at her.

"You can't talk to me like that, you stupid jerk-off!" she responded.

"Stop it! Both of you!" I said loudly. "We're all going to bed. Right now. Not another word from anyone. We'll talk about all this tomorrow."

I don't know if it was the tone of my voice or if they could sense that I was near hysteria, but after exchanging dirty looks, they each went to their own bedroom.

I stood there, shaking. I made my way over to Gram's old rocker, which was back in its place now by the window, next to the mantel. I couldn't do this by myself. If I was a single mother, then I guess I would have to, but I wasn't single. I was married. I had deliberately chosen to be married.

It was only a little after midnight in California, but I knew that with the hard days that Sam put in, he'd already be asleep. I called him, anyway.

"Hello," he answered groggily on the fourth ring.

"Sam, it's me," I told him. "You've got to come home. You've got to come home for good."

Sam
1994

—▶ ◀—

Corrie needed me. She asked me to come home. After living through all those years of unemployment, I was not particularly keen on giving up a good job that paid well and returning home to Lumkee to explain to people who knew me why I was once again content to allow my wife to support me. But I did.

Cy Walker had been good enough to give me a job when I needed one, and I didn't feel right about walking out on him, leaving him in the lurch. The first phase of the steam-flood pilot was scheduled for completion at the end of '94, so I talked to him, let him know that if a second phase was approved, and it looked like it would be, I would not be available. I fudged a little on my excuse, suggesting that I was trying to line up the financing to start up my company again. I wasn't. I was pretty sure that I couldn't. But it was a good camouflage for the truth. In the oil business, a guy can't just say that he's leaving for personal reasons. Oil companies don't want to know that you have personal reasons. It was never good to even hint at the suggestion that you didn't want to be away from home. Being willing to go to wherever the work happened to be was a part of the industry on just about every level. This year it was Bakersfield, next year Alaska, after that Thailand. If you weren't prepared to do that, then you should be looking for another line of work.

I didn't know any other line of work.

My family was having a crisis. Corrie needed me at home. I was willing to do that, but I wanted to be sure that I didn't burn any bridges behind me. I was hoping that in a few months things would settle down with Nate. If I couldn't get my job back with Cy, he at least would give me a recommendation to work with someone else.

I don't know how I expected to explain why I hadn't started my company back up. The way things turned out, I didn't have to.

The first week of December, Corrie called to tell me that her father was in the hospital. Doc had collapsed in the drugstore. One of his customers had called EMS.

"The doctors say it's a stroke," Corrie told me on the phone. "He's holding his own right now. The way I understand it, every hour that he's still here, his chances of surviving get better."

"Do you want me to fly home?" I asked, though I'd already grabbed my duffel from under the bed and had begun throwing things in it.

"No," Corrie said. "Mom and I are all right, I think."

"It won't be a big deal if I leave a couple of days early," I assured her.

"Well, come as soon as you can, but not any sooner than that."

I called Cy, and he was very understanding. I worked out the rest of my schedule with the guys on the crew. By the next afternoon, I was flying into Tulsa.

Lauren met me at the airport. I was really surprised

to see her. She'd grown into such a pretty girl. She had hair like her grandmother's and the same warm host-ess-with-the-most-est smile. But she was long and lean, like me. She looked more so that afternoon. She was wearing what looked to me like workout sweats. But I was fairly certain that nobody went to the gym with those big, boxy high-heeled shoes.

She'd just gotten her driver's license and this was her very first trip on the expressway into the city. Apparently a trial by fire.

"It was really scary," she admitted to me. "There were these humongous trucks and people zipping past me on both sides at like a million mph. I mean, I am absolutely the worst in-the-traffic person in my driver's ed class. And I wanted to say, no way that I'm driving my first time to Tulsa all alone. But then, I just reminded myself that for Grandpa, having this stroke was having to face new, scary things. And that Grandma, worrying about him, was dealing with some all-new stuff. And then, of course, you and Mom. So if I'm going to be like almost an adult, too, then I'm going to have to face some crap I don't want to. So I said, 'Mom, you stay with Grandma. I'll go get Daddy.' And I said to myself, 'Lauren, get out there. Stay in your own lane and drive.'"

To support this newfound independence, I let her drive back home, though I was white-knuckled most of the way as she crept along through the five o'clock rush hour at a snail's pace, infuriating the honking drivers around us.

We pulled into the driveway. I had more a sense of coming home than I could remember in years. Gram's house was my house, the house my family was growing up in. Somehow that felt so right to me, that I once again refused to get into the mental gymnastics that always accompanied my ownership of the house. Gram had left me the house, but I gave it away. I wouldn't have gotten it back if my father hadn't died. But my father had died. And Mike's suicide bottle was in Cherry Dale's trash.

I pushed all those thoughts away. Someday, when I had time and energy, I'd sort it all out. But today there were things to do, people to take care of, obligations to be met.

I carried my duffel into the house. The first thing I saw was the smashed-in drywall in the living room. I'd heard about it, of course, but it was bigger than I expected. And I didn't really expect it to still be there.

"Where's Nate?" I asked Lauren.

She shrugged. "If he's here, he's probably locked in his room."

She was right. He was lying on the bed, eyes closed, listening with his headphones to his CD player.

"Nate!"

He opened his eyes, sat up, turned down the music and pulled the plugs out of his ears.

"Hi, Dad," he said. "I didn't know you were coming home."

I was surprised that he seemed so uninformed with what was going on in his own house.

"You know your grandfather is in the hospital?" I asked.

"Oh yeah, sure," Nate said with genuine concern. "How's he doing?"

"I don't know, I'm just now going out there."

He nodded.

"What's the deal with the wall in the living room?" I asked.

His eyes widened.

"Didn't Mom tell you?"

"Yeah, she told me you got drunk and knocked a hole in the wall," I replied. "But that doesn't tell me why it's still there."

He just looked up at me, clueless.

"This is *my* house, young man," I told him. "You knock a hole in *my* wall, then you go to the lumber yard, get some gyp board, replace the drywall, tape it, float it and repaint it. That's what men do when they screw up, they go back and they fix it."

His jaw fell open.

I didn't bother to explain any further. I walked out of the room, went back to pick up my duffel which I carried out to the sunporch. It wasn't much of a master bedroom, but it was all we had. I felt like I was covered with some kind of travel sludge and decided I had to shower before I went to the hospital. I put away my clothes as best I could, wrestled some clean jeans out of the little armoire that Corrie was using for a closet and walked back through the house to the bathroom. The door was closed. I knocked.

"Leave me alone!" Lauren responded.

The response was so mean, I assumed it wasn't for me.

"Sugar, I need to take a shower," I said through the door.

"Oh, Daddy," she responded, surprised. "I thought you were Nate. I need fifteen more minutes."

"Fifteen minutes?"

"I'm doing my bikini zone and I just put the hair remover on. I can't move for fifteen minutes."

"I need to get to the hospital," I pointed out.

"Sorry, Dad, but I've done this before," she answered. "It takes the full fifteen minutes."

I just stood there for a long moment staring at the door. Then I shook my head. I walked back into the front of the house, through the living room to the sunporch. I tossed my clean jeans on the bed. Picked up the car keys and headed for the driveway.

It took me twenty minutes to drive to the hospital, another ten to find a parking space, and even longer than that to locate the floor that Doc was on. I almost missed Corrie as I walked past a little alcove with an angle of uncomfortable-looking chairs that resembled box crates with seat cushions. She was all alone.

"Hi!"

Corrie looked relieved to see me and even jumped up and hugged my neck.

"I got here as soon as I could."

She nodded. "You still smell like an airplane," she told me.

"I wanted to shower," I told her. "But there was some kind of bikini emergency and I couldn't get into the bathroom."

She was sympathetic. "It's that time," she said. "Two teenagers in the house is always a challenge. But getting used to one bathroom is an adjustment."

"How's Doc?" I asked her.

She shrugged. "His color is a little better, I think. He's conscious most of the time now. He can't move his leg at all and his arm only slightly. But he tries to talk. The nurses say that's a good sign. Mom's in with him now. The room is so small and there's only one little seat, so we take turns. We don't want to leave him alone. The doctor told us that at this time, his attitude is everything. He has to want to get better. I know that scares Mom. He hasn't really seemed interested in anything since Mike died."

"At least he reopened the drugstore," I told her. "I didn't think he'd even do that."

"He's just letting it drift away," she said. "He's not fighting for customers, he's hardly trying to stay afloat."

"Sometimes you just lose hope," I told her. "It happened to me. When I wasn't working, I had to force myself to get up every day. I just lost my way. It happens."

We sat down and she leaned her head over on my shoulder. I wrapped my arm around her.

"And now I've asked you to do it all over again," she said. "Once again you're hanging around Lumkee looking for a job."

"At least this time it was our choice," I told her. "And there are more jobs to be had now. I'll find something. Maybe something I'll like a whole lot better than being gone all the time."

I pressed a little kiss on the top of her head. She looked up at me and smiled.

"It's good to have you home," she told me. "Did you see Nate at the house?"

"Yeah, I told him to fix the hole in the living room wall."

Corrie glanced at me curiously. "He doesn't know how to do anything like that," she pointed out.

"Then I guess he'll ask for help or read a book or look it up on the Internet," I said. "He's a smart kid. He can figure it out."

"How did you decide to handle it that way?" she asked me.

I shook my head. "I didn't really decide," I admitted.

"I just saw the damage and I thought how displeased Gram would have been if she'd seen it. And then it just sort of followed, how would Gram have handled it, if the culprit had been me. It was almost like she was speaking through me. I wasn't angry and I didn't take any of the weird guilt stuff I feel about Nate in the room with me. It was just Gram and her words and how she would have handled Floyd Braydon's boy."

"And it worked?"

"I think that remains to be seen," I told her. "But at least we're heading in a new direction."

In a few moments Edna came out. I hugged her and she clung to me. "I can't lose him, too," she told me. "What will I have to live for?"

I could have reminded her that she had a daughter who stood by her through everything and two healthy grandchildren, but I was sure she didn't mean it as a real question.

"Hang in there, Edna," I told her instead. "Doc is going to need you. You can't fall apart."

Immediately she raised her chin and straightened her shoulders, as if infused with determination.

"You're right, you are absolutely right," she said. "What good will I be if I turn into a sappy puddle? I despise women who are all heart and no gumption."

In that spirit it was decided that she should go home and rest. I insisted that Corrie go with her.

"Doc and I can handle tonight by ourselves," I assured them.

I introduced myself to the CCU staff and they directed me to one of the narrow, glassed-in rooms that ringed the nurses' station. It was a small space made more so by all the equipment built into the wall above the bed.

Doc looked old and frail as he lay there. He was always so neatly groomed and dressed. Now he was tied into a rumpled hospital gown, his thin hair was mussed, revealing a lot of previously hidden balding, and without his glasses, his face looked sharp and bony.

His eyes were open.

"Hi, Doc, how you doing?" I asked him.

"Sam?"

I could clearly make out that word. And the surprise in his tone.

"I know you didn't think you were going to see me until Christmas," I told him. "But I just finished up and came home early."

He took that statement in, examining it for a long time before responding.

"I'm going to die, then? They sent for you because I'm going to die?"

It took me a minute to understand what he was saying. His words were slow and slightly slurred, but I listened carefully and finally understood him.

"No, no," I assured him. "I came home because the family needed me."

If it had been my mother-in-law lying there, or Corrie, I probably would have left it at that. But my time with Mike had convinced me that men prefer the truth. Once we've got a handle on that, we can deal with whatever it's going to mean.

"The doctors don't know yet if you're going to be all right," I told him. "So far, so good. They say twenty percent don't make it through this part. That means eighty percent do."

He gave me a weird, slightly off-center grin.

"When I talk to them," I said, "I'll tell them to be straight with you."

"Thanks."

He closed his eyes as if the conversation had exhausted him. There was a small metal chair on one side of the bed, near the privacy curtain that could be drawn across the glass. I walked over there and seated myself.

"You tired?" The question came from the bed.

"No, Doc," I answered. "It's been a long day but, amazingly, I'm feeling pretty good. Must be getting my second wind."

He struggled to respond and finally got the words out. "Wish I'd get mine," he said.

I chuckled.

We sat there together in the silence. His eyes were closed.

"You find those pills?" he asked.

I sat up straight in my chair. Even in the middle of the hospital with medications coming and going every minute, I didn't have to ask him what pills he meant. I knew immediately.

"I didn't find the pills," I told him. "But I found out what happened to them."

From beneath the sheet, his good arm came out and his hand beckoned me closer.

"Tell me," he said.

I scooted closer and took his hand in mine.

"Not tonight, Doc," I told him. "When you get stronger, I promise, I'll tell you everything."

His expression was hurt and disappointed.

"Tell me tonight," he said.

I hesitated. The whole thing was speculation. I didn't know anything for sure. Except what seemed to be the obvious conclusion. I had never voiced it aloud. Never let myself put the pieces together. There was too much pain and regret to express.

But Doc was in pain. From the stroke and from the loss of his son. Doc was still grieving. If voicing my suspicions gave him a reason to stay here on earth and find out the truth, then that was reason enough to speak out.

I sat down beside him and shared what I knew and what I suspected.

His eyes widened and he drew a gasp of indrawn breath.

"You think she killed him?" he asked me. "With Mike's help? You think Mike set it up?"

"There's no way to know," I told him. "Unless she tells us, and why would she?"

Doc was smiling. It was a crooked smile, a damaged smile, but he was smiling.

"Isn't that something?" he said. "Poor Cherry Dale. Not a man in this town willing to defend her. And our Mike comes to her rescue from the grave."

Corrie
1995

— ◆ —

The New Year began with things going very well. My father was in physical therapy and recovering slowly. Mom was transporting him to and from the rehab center twice a week. She'd wanted Sam to drive them, just as he had for all of Mike's appointments, but Doc flatly refused.

"If you can't drive me, then I'll get the senior citizens transport," he threatened, knowing Mom would be humiliated to go in the big gold bus with all the "really old people." "Sam's too busy to fool with my troubles. And somebody's got to watch the drugstore."

The drugstore didn't truly require that much watching, but Dad wanted to keep it open. We hired a part-time pharmacist. She came over every afternoon to fill the day's prescriptions. She was a cute young girl in her twenties. She was Korean-American, which I thought really added a nice bit of diversity to Lumkee's old Main Street.

I pushed Lauren to manage the store after school. We needed the help, of course, but more than that. I wanted her to get close to Hye Won. A bright, hardworking woman was just exactly the kind of role model I wanted for my daughter. And if Lauren got interested in pharmacology, that would just be icing on the cake. What she mostly did was visit with her friends at the soda counter and read all the fashion magazines on the sale rack.

A new big home-improvement store opened and Sam was hired. It was a good job with decent pay and stock shares. And, most important, it was ten minutes from the house. He worked the four-to-midnight shift, Friday through Tuesday, which freed him up to spend most of his days working at the drugstore.

It also made him eligible for an employee discount, which we really needed. Since Nate's introduction to drywall repair, he had suddenly become our personal house restorer. Carpentry work was all new to him and he found he had a knack for it. And it kept him close to home. Paint and lumber were not cheap, but Sam gave his son a reasonably free hand in doing what he could to get the house in shape. The work seemed to give him a sense of accomplishment and spur his creativity. He was good at it and, surprisingly, methodical and meticulous. The kid who could never bother to iron a shirt would painstakingly plane a board to a one-thirty-secondth tolerance and sand putty until all imperfection virtually disappeared.

"This is wonderful," I told Sam one night, crowded together in our little narrow bed on the sunporch. "He likes construction and it is obviously an outlet for his artistic side. He could be an architect or a…"

Sam put a finger over my lips.

"Don't even start thinking it," he admonished. "The worst thing that we can do is try to push Nate in *any* direction. He's so determined to be contrary that he'll go against us no matter what it is."

I don't know when or how Sam had become so wise

a parent, but I'd learned to trust him on it. I was the one taking all the psychology courses, but he was the one who always seemed to know just the right thing to say to the children. Even Dr. Muldrew described Sam as *the nurturer.*

Mike's friend, and my former doctor, called me one day to ask how I was doing, how things were going. I told him that we'd never been able to get Nate to talk to a counselor.

"He found something wrong with everybody I suggested," I explained. "He just wouldn't go. He's doing better now. But I still worry about what goes on inside him."

"Well, there's still plenty of time to find out," Dr. Muldrew said. "Why don't you try family therapy."

"Family therapy?"

"The whole family is in the room together," he said. "That way no one feels really singled out. In that kind of environment, Nate might be prompted to share at least some of what is going on inside him."

I talked to Sam. He liked the idea, but he wondered how we would pay for it. With both of us working full-time we were fortunate to have health insurance, but neither his company's plan nor the school system offered any mental-health coverage beyond hospitalization. With our financial situation as precarious as it continued to be, there was no way we could make a long-term therapy commitment.

"Why don't we ask Dr. Muldrew if he could take us for a few sessions," Sam said. "We can see how this family therapy works and maybe he can teach us how to hold them ourselves."

That's exactly what we did. We set three one-hour appointments for family therapy with Dr. Muldrew.

He tried to teach us how to focus on what one another was saying. How to get past any initial feelings of anger that might crop up. And how to negotiate together for a reasonable solution to problems.

We didn't focus on Nate. In fact, in the sessions with Dr. Muldrew, the time was almost completely dominated by conflicts over who should be cleaning the house. I was teaching all day, taking graduate courses and studying in the evening. So I felt that my time was better utilized in things other than vacuuming and scrubbing toilets. Lauren was going to class all day and working in the drugstore afternoons. Sam was working the drugstore all day and his real job all night. Nate was in high school and did work around the house.

"And besides," he admitted, "I don't know anything about housekeeping and don't want to learn."

What Dr. Muldrew had us do was figure out how we could manage it fairly together. We drew up a list of all the tasks and then had everybody pick until they were all taken.

By session three, Dr. Muldrew was just sitting and watching us.

"You have to make a commitment to do this," he told us. "If you don't schedule meetings and have them every week and have everybody in attendance, you'll be back to where you started."

We decided Wednesday night was the best. Everybody agreed they would be there. The first night I arrived late and got quite a surprise. The house smelled of spicy cooked meat. Nate and Lauren were already at the kitchen table, laughing in high spirits.

I walked in and Sam, wearing his cook's apron, walked over to give me a kiss.

"I thought if we had something to do with our hands," he said, "the talk might go easier."

"Plus, everybody in town is hungry for tamales," Lauren said.

I shook my head, but I could hardly fault him.

"I could eat a couple myself," I admitted.

The evening session went great. Lots of worries were vented. Plenty of grievances were aired. And dozens of *hojas* were smeared with masa.

Later, as Sam and I lay in bed together, I told him what a good idea it was.

"Let's do it every time," he said.

I grinned at him, though I knew he couldn't see it in the darkness.

"Are we back to tamale day, Mr. Braydon?"

Indeed we were. Sam no longer delivered. If you wanted tamales, you came down to the drugstore to get them, because we couldn't afford to feed the whole town on Thursday night. Sam began charging two dollars a dozen. Nobody seemed to mind paying. Our life was good.

On a beautiful sunny morning in April, I'd just gotten my class through their morning meeting where we greeted one another and shared the legislatively mandated moment of silence. The children started doing their "jobs," such as getting news, choosing a poem to read, or filling in a crossword puzzle on their table. Just then, Mrs. Wiley, the assistant principal, unexpectedly came to my classroom.

"Could I speak to you for a moment?"

Just from the tone of her voice I knew something terrible was wrong. My heart in my throat, the faces of my family flashed before my eyes.

"What's happened?" I asked immediately as the door closed behind me.

"Somebody has bombed the Federal Building in Oklahoma City," she said. "It's...it's terrible."

Her description had been far from adequate. Our school was locked down for the rest of the day. We tried to shelter the students from what was going on. But we couldn't hide behind our doors forever.

The next few weeks were a complete blur of angry tears, horrifying revelations and grief. The town, the community, the whole state was mobilized to do something to help.

We went to the Red Cross to give blood. Nate lied about being sixteen and he was tall enough that they didn't card him. We cleaned out the pharmacy of extra supplies and donated them.

The Lumkee firefighters were part of the rescue. The local guardsmen were all called up to help. We wanted to help, too. Our budget was too close to the edge to make much of a donation. But at the next family meeting it was unanimous that we tighten our belts to help as much as possible.

The terrible tragedy, so close to home, affected us all. But none more deeply than my Lauren. The images somehow burned into her brain: the senior citizens visiting the social security office, the tellers working at the credit union, the children, the sweet young children, in the day-care center and their mothers and fathers throughout the building. And the injustice of it galled her innocent soul.

I suppose it was the first time that Lauren had come face-to-face with the senseless evil that could be done in the name of honor or patriotism or religion. Like any parent, I had wanted to shelter my children from that.

Now it was on Lauren's radar scope, front and center. My bubbly, outgoing cheerleader was suddenly infused with deeper, more profound needs and the empathy that inspires.

"Mom, I want to start going to Gram's church again," she told me.

For the last several years she and I had been attending Sunday service with my parents at the Methodist Church.

"Okay," I said. "I think that would be okay."

"I want Daddy and Nate to come, too," she insisted.

I shook my head. "I don't know about that, Lauren. Your father doesn't like to go," I told her. "It makes him miss Gram too much. And you know Nate, he'll only do what he wants to do. Nobody can really make him do anything."

She nodded thoughtfully and I thought that ended the discussion, but she brought it up again during our Wednesday tamale session.

"I want our family to go to church together," she announced. "I want us to go together to Gram's church."

Sam glanced up at her, momentarily surprised.

"No way," Nate stated flatly.

Sam shook his head. "Sugar, I haven't darkened the door in years," he said.

"Please, Daddy," she begged him. "Would you do it for me?"

Sam was clearly taken aback by her entreaty. Lauren was our easy child. She never asked for anything and stayed as far away from conflict and trouble as any teenager could.

"Is this really important to you?" he asked her.

She nodded. "I want our family to go together," she

said. "I want our family to be together and sit together. It's very important to me. I want us to be safe, Daddy."

Safe.

Sam looked at her strangely and then glanced over at me. The world had become a very scary place. We couldn't make it less so. But if our daughter thought she could feel safe one morning a week in the Ninety and Nine Baptist church, it didn't seem like that much of a sacrifice.

"Okay, Lauren," he said. "If it will make you feel better, we'll all go."

"Not me," Nate said.

Lauren turned to him. Her tone was not pleading, but matter-of-fact. "I'll do all your house chores from now on if you'll come," she said.

Sam's jaw dropped open and I'm sure I must have looked just as shocked.

"Praise the Lord, my prayers are answered!" Nate shouted blasphemously. "You've got a deal, sis."

So began the family's commitment to the congregation that I will always think of as Gram's church.

We were not the only lost sheep or new lambs who had come into the fold. Attendance was way up there, and at the other religious services in town. The tragedy had made a lot of us look more deeply at our spiritual values.

As time passed, we were less stalwart. Nate found numerous excuses to miss. And Sam and I occasionally groaned in dread as the alarm went off early on Sunday morning, but Lauren never wavered. In fact, quite the opposite. As she began her senior year in high school, her concern about her social clique and own popularity waned as she began to choose youth discipleship meetings over pep rallies. It was unexpected, but we couldn't regard it as negative.

Things began to change at the drugstore, as well. The Thursday tamales became so popular that people were showing up as soon as the doors opened to make sure they got their share. Because they were there, anyway, they bought merchandise and had their prescriptions filled. By the time my father was back to working part-time, the drugstore was beginning to show a profit again.

"So the business is going well," I said to Sam.

He nodded, but was still concerned.

"The pharmacy can only improve so much," he told me. "Most of the big insurers and HMOs have contracts with the big chain drugstores. Only the people who pay out of pocket or are uninsured can afford to patronize us these days."

"Well, that's not fair," I said.

Sam playfully pinched my nose. "Since when did somebody promise you that life was going to be fair?"

I could hardly argue with that.

"Things are going great for us, Corrie," he said. "We're both healthy and working, our kids are doing fine. Your parents are hanging in there. We've got it so good, it would be greedy to even wish for more."

But that didn't stop me from wishing.

Nate decided over the summer that we should enlarge the house. He drew up some rough plans for a new addition with a family room, a third bedroom and a bath. He even added a little deck area and sketched out the location of where he'd eventually like to put a swimming pool.

When he presented his little booklet of efforts Sam

and I were stunned. He'd even costed out the plumbing and electrical work.

"This is so totally cool," Lauren told him, excited. "I can't believe my baby brother actually put this together. Can you really do all this yourself?"

"Well, not everything," Nate admitted modestly. "But I can do most of it myself. If Dad can help me with some of the two-man work, I think I can manage. We really need the room."

Sam looked it all over carefully.

"This is really impressive, Nate," he told him. "It's well thought out. The materials list and the codes included. I don't think we could hire a remodeler who could have presented a clearer, more thorough estimate. I wish we could do it. But, you know we don't have eight thousand dollars."

Nate was immediately on the defensive.

"It would easily cost you thirty if I wasn't doing the work myself," he pointed out.

"I'm not denying that," Sam told him. "It's a good deal and if we could afford it, I'd jump at the chance in a New York minute."

"Can't you get some kind of home improvement loan?" Nate asked.

"Maybe," Sam answered. "We've still got the bankruptcy on our record. I don't know how keen they'd be about it. But even if we could, we can't. I don't think we should go into debt right now. Our first priority has to be you kids. You'll both be heading off to college in the next couple of years. Just paying for that is going to be the biggest financial challenge your mom and I have ever faced."

Nate shrugged away the idea. "Lauren will get some

kind of scholarship," he said. "And me, I'm not going to any college."

His response was so adamant, I was startled.

"Of course you are," I told him, too quickly.

"I'm not," he confirmed flatly. "I'm not wasting four more years. I'm getting a job and getting on with my life."

"Maybe you'll feel differently when the time comes," Sam said, giving me a warning glance. We both knew that if I started insisting on something, Nate would dig his feet in even more deeply. "Or there might be a vocational course you'd want to take. If you're thinking to work in construction, maybe you could get certified in one of the trades."

Nate shrugged. "What will teach me more than any class is actually doing this work on the house myself," he said. "Let's take the money you're willing to waste on me at some state university and put it into something that will actually help me and provide payback for you, too. It will give me something to do this summer." He hesitated a moment. "Otherwise, I'll have to come up with some other plan for my free time."

It was a threat, plain and simple. We'd known Nate long enough to know that rarely was a warning from him solely idle chatter.

Ultimately, Sam came up with a solution. He always does.

Sam
1995

——▶◀——

Nate's idea of expanding the house was terrific. I really wanted to do it. But I'd already learned my lesson about debt. Maybe I was gun-shy, but I didn't want to take a second mortgage on Gram's house. I'd become too attached to the place to be willing to lose it.

At the same time, the house was an investment. Adding on to it would not only make it more livable, it would make it more valuable. And there would never be a better opportunity for getting it done inexpensively than having Nate devote his entire summer to it. Having something purposeful for Nate to do was a big consideration, as well. A kid like Nate with time on his hands and disappointment too—there was no telling what he might come up with as an alternative activity. I just couldn't bring myself to borrow money.

I thought about getting a second job. Of course, it wouldn't be a second job, it would be a third. Although Doc was back to work, I was still putting in a lot of time at the drugstore. There was no way I could work sixteen to eighteen hours a day and still help with the remodel.

I could ask Lauren to get a job. She'd agree if I suggested it. She was a good worker at the drugstore. I'm sure she would have been able to find a full-time summer position that would pay enough to help us out. But I also knew that she'd made other plans for her summer. She was going to work in an educational enrichment program for the children of migrant workers. She was going to travel with the pickers, ostensibly to do day care and summer learning programs. But the organization's main goal was really to help insure that the little ones didn't work in the fields.

Corrie wasn't teaching this summer. She'd signed up for a couple of classes. However, I knew that she'd be willing to work somewhere instead. I didn't want to ask her. She had pulled the full load for our family for so many years, I wanted her to take the time off. I wanted this not to be her problem. I guess I just wanted to figure it out myself.

The truth is, I didn't come up with the solution myself. Cherry Dale actually did. She was in the drugstore, picking up a prescription, looking good and young, as always these days. Things were going well for her. She was opening up a big new gym closer to the city. The new place would have a lap pool, racket ball courts, sauna, whirlpool—the works.

"I guess with you working in the city, we won't see you as much," I said.

"Oh, no," she said. "I'm staying right here in Lumkee. Harlan is managing the new place."

Harlan was Cherry Dale's oldest, now in his early twenties. He was a troubled young man. Both her boys seemed to have their share of problems. I couldn't imagine that she was trusting either of them with her biggest, riskiest venture. But as the father of a troubled kid myself, I admired her courage.

"Do you have any tamales?" she asked me.

I shook my head apologetically. "Sorry, I got rid of the last dozen before ten o'clock," I told her.

She sighed with disappointment. "You do know that you could sell three times as many of these as you do," she said.

"I know, but they require a lot of time and work. Why would we want to do more?"

"Well, a businessperson like me would tell you you should be reimbursed for your time and work," she said. "Raise your prices to compensate yourself with a little profit. That will be just the incentive you need to pump up your production."

I thought about it and realized that she was right.

I called a special family meeting to bring it up for discussion.

"If we raised the price to a profit margin," I explained, "we could use the money we make toward the addition on the house."

Nate's interest was immediately piqued.

"It would involve more planning for you," I told him. "You'd have to do the work as money came in. You'd never have a big chunk of cash to work with. You'll have to divide the whole addition into a connecting series of smaller projects with their total cost requirements. You'll be working on one while we're trying to make enough money to afford the next."

Interrelating projects was a lot more difficult than just meshing them together. That was as tough as any professional building contractor's job. Most of us would have found it intimidating. Nate was young enough and cocky enough to rise to the challenge fearlessly.

"I can do that, Dad," he assured me. "It'll take me

some time, but what else will I have to do while we're raising the money?"

"Finishing your classes would be a good idea," Corrie suggested. "And studying for finals."

Nate rolled his eyes.

"Your mother is right about that," I told him. "You can't just blow off the rest of the semester. It would really put a crimp in the plan if you have to take summer school."

That he at least took seriously.

"I'll talk to Doc," I said. "I think we can sell our food on his premises utilizing his business license, but he'll have to agree to that. And it would be completely reasonable and proper if he asked us to pay a monthly fee or a share of our profit."

"Grandpa won't ask for that," Lauren said, with complete certainty. "It would be like asking Grandma to fork over half of the rent."

The kids laughed aloud at that. I shared a wink with Corrie.

"We're going to have to price our tamales exactly right," I said. "I think we should start at three dollars. That gives us a dollar profit per dozen."

Corrie shook her head. "That's not enough, Sam," she told me. "If we only make a dollar per dozen we'll have to sell nearly 100,000 tamales. Our arms will fall off. I think we should charge five dollars a dozen. That makes a lot more sense."

I shook my head, unsure. "That's more than twice what they cost to make."

"Labor is always the most expensive cost," she said.

"And people think stuff is more valuable when you charge more for it," Lauren added. "I'd bet we'll get more people buying at five dollars a dozen than we ever did at two."

She was right. A week later Lauren and Corrie made a very bright, eye-catching sign that read Okie Tamales $5 Per Dozen. I set it atop the cooler. Within an hour they were all gone.

The next Friday night, when I got home from work, I could smell tamales cooking. Corrie, Lauren and Nate were in the kitchen.

"We decided not to limit ourselves to Thursday for tamales," Corrie told me. "There is an entirely different crowd on Main Street on the weekends. We want them to start buying as well."

The next day the Okie Tamales sign was in the front window. We sold out before noon.

By the time summer was in full swing the tamale business was booming. They were cooking on the stove almost constantly. Also ongoing was the house addition. Nate was up at dawn and worked until bedtime.

He ran into plenty of snags in the process. There had been other add-ons over the years and some had better construction than others. All had to be supported in such a way that they could naturally hang together.

The pier and beam of the original house would not converge easily with the cheaper, easier slab foundation that Nate had hoped to use. The wiring was far too old to be added on to and we had to hire an electrician to do complete rewiring. And the plumbing with its original lead pipes and gravity flow would have been a challenge for an experienced engineer.

Nate, who had never impressed me with having virtues like patience or tenacity, didn't get mad, throw stuff around and curse when things went wrong. Or at least, I never saw him doing any of that. He'd take a break, stand back for a few minutes and try to work it out in his head.

The experience of dividing the addition into financially manageable projects had given him a component vision of the entire remodel. On days when it was raining and he couldn't work outside, he'd pick up the next task that could be worked on indoors. When he ran out of materials or if something didn't show up on time, he easily made use of his time in another way.

The addition wasn't finished by the end of summer. But the new bathroom was usable, if not yet painted and cabineted. And Corrie and I moved into our new bedroom.

The sunporch was a sunporch again, for about a week, before it was turned into the business office for Okie Tamales. Making money meant paying taxes, filing reports, completing forms. We were buying our ingredients in bulk, including importing new easier handling Mexican *enconchada* (conch shaped) corn husks for our hojas. We gave up our three pressure cookers, with every burner on the stove going at once, to embrace a new steam oven that was as big as our old refrigerator. The new commercial refrigerator now sat in Gram's dining room, where we were able to get more space for production.

Cooking in bigger batches added some problems. We began squeezing lime into the masa flour to make it pliable for longer periods. We ground our own meat. We laid out washed cornshucks to dry on every flat space in the house.

I wanted to somehow mechanize the process. I got an old sausage maker at a salvage yard and, using the mechanic's skills I'd learned in oil well service, I refurbished and jury-rigged it to squeeze out the paste, lay a line of tamale filling and cover it over.

That was actually fairly easy. But I had no luck with coming up with a way to automatically wrap the tamale. Cornshucks, being a natural, organic product were all unique. They varied in size, shape and the grooves on them were as distinctive as snowflakes.

I called several commercial tamale producers to ask questions. The response was that to wrap them mechanically, I would have to use paper. We tried that. But cooking in paper just didn't create the flavor we got with the cornshuck wrap. We couldn't compromise taste over ease of production.

We used our revamped sausage maker to produce an endless line of tamales, but every one had to be folded by hand.

Customers started sitting at the drugstore's soda fountain and ordering a drink with their tamales. There was so much "consuming on the premises" as they say in restaurant lingo, that we brought in some more tables to expand the seating. And if people were going to eat in the drugstore they didn't want a brown paper bag with a dozen inside. They wanted a plate with a tamale or two, a choice of salsas and a bag of tortilla chips. This meant new pricing, napkins, dishes and flatware.

We were serving four days a week. And lunch times had become so busy that Hye Won was running back and forth between the pharmacy and helping me wait tables. Finally she started bringing her sixteen-year-old sister to help. With her bright smile, cute figure and waist-length black hair, Jin had half the love-starved guys from Lumkee High crowding one another for seats.

Things were going so well that for Nate's birthday we got him a new, professional-grade table saw. I knew that most boys at his age, including myself, would have much preferred a car, even the worst old junker. Nate was so happy, I was sure I detected moisture gathering in his eyes. He blinked it back, but he was still too choked up to even speak.

That night alone in our bed, Corrie and I talked about it.

"There were times when I thought by sixteen Nate might be dead, on drugs or in prison," I admitted.

Corrie snuggled up close to me. "I've been scared for him since he was five," she said.

"I'm not saying our worries are over," I told her. "There are a lot of stupid mistakes a guy can make between here and the rest of his life. But at least now we know he has a fighting chance."

"I'm so proud of him," she said. "I'm so proud of you."

"Me? What did I do?"

"You understood him and you found a way to help him."

I shrugged off the compliment and she gave me a little kiss.

"Are you tired?"

"Completely exhausted," I answered.

"Me, too," she said. "I guess that means we can't have sex, huh?"

"I'll try if you'll try," I said.

"I'll try, but you've got to try *harder*," she shot back.

We laughed together at her little naughty joke. And then we made love.

In September, Lauren returned home, happy and

tanned. Her Spanish was much improved and her outlook on the world brighter and more filled with hope.

She started her senior year by stepping down as cheerleader. It was the kind of action that shocked the neighborhood as deeply as some terrible scandal. Apparently cheerleaders only gave up their positions when their pom-poms were pried from their cold, dead hands.

Lauren claimed she simply was no longer interested. And she never showed even the slightest indication of missing it. She continued to put in hours after school at the drugstore and tamale duty in the evenings. But other than that, she was totally immersed in her church work, her studies and her plans for the future.

One surprising development that came from Lauren's summer with the Mexican migrant workers helped our business—she brought home a half-dozen new recipes for tamale filling.

"When the moms of my kids heard that I liked to make tamales," she told us, "they all wanted to share their recipes with me."

She had recipes for beef tamales, chicken tamales and brown-bean tamales.

We tried them all and we liked them. We were all getting creative with the cooking and added and improved on what we made.

"If we want new recipes," Corrie said, "I'm sure there are millions on the Internet."

Nate checked it out for us and came back with ideas we'd never expected. Catfish tamales, chiles-and-cheese tamales, shrimp tamales, bacon tamales, spinach tamales, pineapple-corn tamales.

It was almost more than a family, in danger of serious tamale fatigue, could even take in.

We decided that along with our original pork filling, we'd try one new recipe per week for eat-in customers only.

It was a smashing success. The people of Lumkee had an insatiable appetite for tamales. We'd paid for our new rooms on the house. We were banking money in savings for the kids' education. We gave the tired old Volvo to Lauren and bought a brand new car.

In early November the Food Section of the *Tulsa World* wrote one little paragraph about Okie Tamales in Lumkee. After that, I quit my job and purchased the empty five-and-dime building next to the drugstore. Our new sign was created from three-foot-high neon instead of felt pen.

Corrie
1996

――→ ◄――

The phenomenal success of Okie Tamales came as a big surprise to me. I guess it came as a surprise to everyone. One minute we were sitting around our kitchen making tamales for family therapy, and the next our product was being sold in grocery stores all over the state.

Well, maybe it wasn't that fast, but almost.

Sam quit his job and devoted himself full-time to the business. But he couldn't do it all himself.

Although I was proud and pleased, and Sam spoke of our streak of good fortune as a "true family venture" where everybody's efforts had counted, it was Sam who got patted on the back from people around town. It was Sam who was nominated for businessperson of the year by the Chamber of Commerce. It was Sam who was a guest speaker at the Oklahoma Grocers Association.

I found this vague feeling of jealousy haunting me. For so long now I had been the star player in our family. All the years that Sam was out of work, I was the person to keep things going. I was the one who'd pursued my education. I was the one who'd tried to better myself. I was the one who worked to get ahead. After years of sacrifice and struggle, my master's degree was only a thesis away from completion. Yet the added income that it would mean was no longer critical to sending the kids to college. For ten years I had been the one to bring home the biggest paycheck. I liked that. I'd grown so accustomed to it. I was buoyed by it. Sam's sudden, seemingly undeserved, falling-into-a-pot-of-jam success was, for me, somehow deflating.

I found myself denigrating his achievement, minimizing his accomplishment. There was no one better to aid me in this unkind pursuit than my own mother.

"It's not like he's found a cure for cancer," I complained to her. "He's making tamales, for heaven's sake. Any illiterate Mexican grandma across the border can do it."

Mom nodded in complete agreement. "I just hope and pray every day that the children are not lured away from their potential intellectual achievements by the fast, easy money of their father's get-rich-quick scheme."

I nodded in agreement. Although, the terms "fast, easy money" and "get rich quick" didn't quite jive with the reality of my husband tiptoeing around the house in the morning before leaving for work at 5:00 a.m.

"I just hate having the Maynard name associated with such a déclassé enterprise," Mom continued. "It was bad enough when Sam was in the oil business. Oil is necessarily dirty. But food service? And not even a nice restaurant with tablecloths. He actually sells food in brown paper bags."

It was true. Fresh tamales were sold at the door and the only change in the packing was that the bags now had the *Okie Tamales* name and logo. Even the vacuum-sealed packs that went into the grocery stores were designed to look like brown paper.

"And the jabbering that goes on in that factory," Mom continued. "Well, I know that's as much your father's fault as your husband's, but it is just so offputting."

The jabbering that she referred to was Korean.

Though business in the drugstore was doing much better, my dad decided that he was as recovered as he was going to get and that he much preferred semi-retirement to the headaches of owning the store.

He sold Maynard Drug to Hye Won and her older brother, Song, a thoracic surgeon in Tulsa. They turned around and hired Dad to be her part-time, backup pharmacist. It was just a few hours a week and perfect for him.

Hye Won bought a nice big home in Lumkee and moved her parents and her two youngest siblings in with her. Mr. Chai had been a gardener and Mrs. Chai, a housewife. Sam hired them both to work for him in the tamale factory. It was mostly sit-down work and they were right next door to their daughter every day. As the business expanded, the Chais brought along relatives, friends and acquaintances. Sam hired them on as he needed them. Mr. Chai was the natural manager and kept everybody on time and on task. Okie Tamales was the only downtown Lumkee business where Korean was the spoken language.

The Chai teenagers, Jin and Chano, helped after school both at the tamale factory and in the drugstore. Jin was Nate's age, cute, popular and the brightest student in her class. Chano was just starting out in high school. He made good grades, although he was not considered as smart as his sister. But he was athletic, which guaranteed him success at Lumkee High.

I liked the family. At the university, I'd met lots of different people and I thought diversity was good for our community. It was Sam who'd accomplished that. It was just another reason for me to be annoyed at him.

I tried to work through it—to rationalize my way through my irrational envy. I concentrated on my thesis: Designing Classrooms for Optimal Learning. My idea was to assess student-task completion in class-rooms designed to be psychologically positive for specific age behavior and contrast those numbers with classrooms of traditional design that focused on work-place needs of teachers. It was a daunting undertaking, forcing me to create the test environment, formulate the assessments and then do them, both in the new classroom and the traditional one.

For the first time in all my studies, the Internet be-came my prime source for research. The computer had been part of the library for years now. And with a cer-tifiable geek in our midst at home, I was certainly fa-miliar with the World Wide Web. But it was not until this thesis that I learned so much of the latest and best was out there at the touch of my fingertips. I was able to contact teachers with experience in classroom de-sign from all over the country. And by connecting with them, I quickly discovered that my ideas were in the forefront of new thinking on the subject.

I also discovered some software programs online that were used by dot.com home-decoration sites and could be modified for use in classrooms. In fact, I be-came very excited about some of the knowledge base I discovered in home decor and how flawlessly it could be transferred to learning spaces.

I quit competing with Lauren and Nate for computer time and went out and bought myself an updated, high-powered, high-dollar laptop. Doggedly I pursued my own interests and concentrated on my goals. And tried not to compare them to those of Sam or Okie Tamales.

I was rudely jerked out of my personal quest and preoccupation with a bombshell dropped by my daughter.

Lauren, with her perfect features and long, chestnut hair, had grown into a tall, lean beauty, the kind you see staring back at you from all the fashion magazines. She was not the number-one student in her class, but she was easily in the top five. A National Merit Scholar, she made 1420 on her SATs. We were thrilled. Along with her extra-curricular activities, volunteer work and social activism, she was as incredibly impressive on a college entrance application as she was in person.

Sam and I had high expectations. Certainly we expected a scholarship from some good local colleges. We might even get some from distant, more prestigious institutions. And we were both agreed that if she was accepted at some fabulous Ivy League school, we'd see that she got the education she wanted, no matter how we had to pay for it.

With all the paperwork in the mail, we waited to see what would happen, what she would decide and where she would go.

Sam and I were on pins and needles. And when letters came from all over the country from universities wanting her to attend, we were thrilled. All that was left was her decision.

I was torn between wanting her to stay close to home where we could see her often, and wanting for her the adventure of a faraway school where the educational standard was phenomenal and everyone and everything was a brand-new experience.

"I've decided," she said one evening when it was just the three of us at home.

"That's wonderful," I told her. "Your father and I are so excited and anxious to hear."

Truly, we were both on the edge of our seats.

Lauren hesitated, as if she was loathe to share the news with us.

"Mom, Dad," she said, first biting her lip and then taking a deep breath for courage, "I've chosen the Latin American studies program at Living Waters Bible College in Earline, Mississippi," she said.

For a long moment there was a complete stunned silence in our family room.

Sam and I looked at each other.

"Is this a joke?" Sam asked.

"No, Daddy," she said. "There is nothing to joke about."

"Bible college?"

"Earline, Mississippi?"

Our questions bordered on the incredulous.

"They have the most intensive program in the country," she said. "I can get a bachelor of Bible degree in three years. And with my major as Latin American studies, well, the opportunities are tremendous."

"Latin American studies?" I asked. "You're planning to teach?"

"Oh, no," she said, and then corrected herself. "Well, on some level you could say that I am." Lauren took another deep breath and gave us a bright smile. "I've received my call."

I couldn't imagine what she meant.

"This Living Waters Bible College called you?"

"No, no, God has called me," she said. "He's called me to tend his sheep, his poor forgotten sheep in countries like Bolivia, Ecuador and Paraguay. I'm going to be a missionary."

"A missionary?" Sam and I responded in unison.

"I'm taking up my cross and following Christ's admonition to go unto all the world and teach the gospel," she said. "I've been called to take the message of Christ to the people of South America."

"I thought the people of South America were all Catholics," Sam said.

"Catholicism may be the state religion," Lauren corrected him, "but most of the poor people, the native peoples, still worship as they did a thousand years ago."

Sam shrugged. "If it's worked for a thousand years, why mess with it?"

Lauren was in no frame of mind to appreciate humor.

"I knew that you wouldn't be accepting," she said with a sigh. "I've put off telling you for months because I was afraid you'd be like this."

"It's just such a shock," I told her.

"Why is it a shock?" she asked me defensively. "Did you think that I would follow along in this clean comfortable place I've always been sheltered in? That I would never have the courage to look out to a broader world and say, 'Where can I do some good?' Do you just want me to marry some nice fellow from the next suburb over, and drive a couple of overindulged, overprotected children around in a minivan? Is that what you want for me?"

"No, of course not, Lauren," I assured her. "Have

your father and I ever suggested that we didn't want anything but for you to fly as high as you can? We want you to reach your potential. You are a bright young woman. Of course you want to make a difference in the world. But there are a lot of ways to do that. A lot of ways that don't involve Bible college or mud huts in the Andes."

"Think of what a smart mind like yours might be able to come up with in a research lab or behind a telescope," Sam said. "I'm not saying that what you're proposing isn't a good thing, but with all the brains and talent that you have, you could be put to better use in a broader way."

"This is where God wants me," she stated adamantly. "You're my parents, I love you and honor you. But I must go where God leads me. *The harvest is truly heavy, but the laborers are few.*"

There is never any way to have a rational discussion with someone who answers all questions with biblical quotes.

"You may think I'm wasting my life," Lauren said. "But Gram would be proud of me. I know if Gram was here, she'd be proud of me."

"She would," Sam agreed. "She was always proud of you. And we are, too."

That night as Sam and I lay in the bed in our new, spacious master bedroom suite at the back of the house, we tried to shore up our disappointment by being philosophical.

"She's barely eighteen," I pointed out. "If we give her some space, then somehow she will find herself and her own direction."

"Our children are truly amazing," Sam said. "One tries to be so bad, we never know what he might do.

And the other one tries to be so *good*, we never know what she might do."

"I'm afraid for her out in the world," I admitted. "I'm afraid for both of them."

Sam nodded. "Me, too. When they were little I thought that if they could just get big enough then I wouldn't worry. The worries get bigger as fast as the kids."

"I don't think that ever stops," I told him. "I remember having a talk with Gram after Floyd Braydon came to town. She was worried, but she had faith that you'd turn out all right."

"I guess that's something to hold on to," Sam said. "We haven't been perfect parents, but we've tried our best. I suppose we just have to hang in there and hope that it was good enough."

I sighed in agreement.

"I loved what you said about her brains and talent being used in a broader way," I said.

"I believe that," Sam said. "I've never been as smart as you and the kids. I'm not an idiot, I read a lot and I can figure things out. I've got common sense and I'm a hard worker. But I just don't have the same level of intelligence as the rest of you. Making tamales is good, honest work. I like doing it, it keeps me close to home and it pays the bills. But I want more than that for my kids. I'd want more than that for you."

"And I have more than that," I pointed out. "I've wanted to teach. Now I've achieved that. I have my class and my little guys and girls. It's a real dream come true for me."

There was a long moment of silence between us.

"Then why have you seemed so dissatisfied with it lately?" he asked me.

"I'm not!"

"You are," he insisted. "At first I thought that you were angry at me for something. Then I realized I hadn't done anything. You're angry at yourself and I don't know why."

I didn't try to deny it further.

"I don't know what's wrong," I told him. "I guess I'm just plain old jealous. You've become such a grand success and everybody's talking about you. And I'm the little wife, an average, ordinary elementary school teacher. It sounds pretty blah."

Sam laughed at that.

"It may sound that way to you," he said. "But that's not the way it is. I see how the other teachers, especially the younger ones, come to you for advice. Everybody admires the way you think through your classrooms. Your students do better because they love to come to school. This classroom-design thing you do—it's unique and special."

"Oh, you're sweet, Sam," I told him, waving away the compliment.

"I'll never forget that fishbowl you put together in that very first classroom in Candy Cane School. Remember that?"

"How could I forget it?" I answered. "It got me fired."

"But it meant so much to those kids," he said. "I know that they learned more and loved learning more because it was such a cool place to hang out."

"Thanks."

"It's just too bad," Sam went on, "that it's only twenty kids a year that get the benefit of the way that you look at a room. I wish there was a way that you could design every classroom in the country."

That fall we drove Lauren down to Mississippi to start college at LWBC. And I started up my own part-time classroom-design firm, EducationEnvironments.com.

Sam
1997

—▶◀—

Corrie started her dot.com business. That was good news. I started branching out Okie Tamales all over the state. That was good news, too. By the end of our first year of wholesale/retail production we were providing jobs for ten full-time employees and cooking 10,000 dozen per day. I retired my makeshift sausage maker for a shiny, stainless steel $45,000 tamale maker imported from Mexico. For that authentic Okie Tamale flavor, every one was still hand rolled and cooked in cornshuck.

Nate started his last year in high school. He was even more secretive than usual, but we kind of knew he was dating. He started showering before he went out on Saturday nights. And although he was still far from preppie, his oversize jeans and T-shirts were more often clean and fairly new. He never said a word to us. I'm sure he thought it was none of our business. But Lumkee is a very small town and secrets don't stay secrets forever. I thought Nate having a girlfriend was great until Hye Won broke the news to me that it wasn't.

"My parents are very upset," she told me. "They won't approach you directly, because you are their boss. But they are very upset and want you to put a stop to what is going on."

"What's going on?" I asked her, completely clueless. "Everything seems to be running smoothly. Is it the production increases?"

"It's not about work," Hye Won assured me. "My father would speak to you if it were about work. It's about your son, Nate."

"Nate?"

"He and my sister, Jin, have been dating," she said. "They tried to keep it a secret. But Chano knew that he had an obligation to speak to my father about it."

"Nate and Jin are dating?"

I admit I was delighted to hear it. Jin was smart and hardworking, as well as sweet and personable. I would have loved for those qualities to rub off on Nate. At the least, I was delighted that he found those qualities attractive.

"I haven't heard a word about it," I told Hye Won.

I was grinning and realized that she wasn't. I immediately became serious myself.

"Your parents don't like Nate?" I suggested.

"We do not dislike him," she assured me. "My family has no opinion of your family at all."

I doubted very seriously that could be true, but I didn't call her on it.

"But you don't want Nate dating Jin," I said.

Hye Won was very straight-faced, obviously trying to be diplomatic. "My parents are a traditional Korean family," she explained. "They love America and take great pride in their American citizenship and the American citizenship of their children." Here she hesitated. "But among traditional Korean families...we do not date non-Koreans."

"Ah," I said.

"It is not about Nate," she added hurriedly. "We would feel exactly the same about her dating any non-Korean boy."

I nodded, accepting her explanation.

"But you know, Hye Won, there's not a whole lot of Korean boys around here," I pointed out. "If she only dates Koreans, then basically, she doesn't date."

She didn't immediately respond, and with sudden unexpected insight I wanted to slap myself in the head.

"Of course! That's why you don't ever date," I said.

Hye Won shrugged. "I just haven't met the right guy," she said.

"The right Korean guy," I amended.

"Yes," she admitted quietly. "My older brother has a friend who knows someone. They are hoping to arrange an introduction for us very soon."

Her offer of information was defensive. It pricked my own conscience.

"I understand," I said.

"Many Caucasian Americans don't want their young people dating Asians," she pointed out.

"Yes, for some families that's true," I told her. "I'll talk to Nate. I can't promise anything, but I'll do what I can."

"If you order him not to see her, then he won't," Hye Won told me with certainty.

"I'm not sure that'll work," I admitted. "We'd probably have more luck at keeping them apart by trying to fix them up. But I'll talk to Nate. Please tell your father that I'll talk to him."

Before I did, of course, I talked to Corrie.

She was defensive. "So the Chais don't think our Nate is good enough for them!"

"Corrie, you sound like your mother," I told her. "Mr. Chai is trying to do what he can to help his children."

"By not allowing them to date whomever they might fall in love with?"

"We don't know that these two are in love," I said. "All we know is that they're dating."

"Well, kids ought to be able to date anyone they want," she stated firmly.

I grinned at her. "And if Nate comes home with a hopped-up cocaine addict with six tattoos and five illegitimate kids, can I quote you on that?"

She stuck her tongue out at me.

"It's some kind of reverse racism or something," she said.

"I don't think it's racism," I said. "I don't think they hate us or our son. I think all Mr. Chai wants is a happier, easier life for his children than he's had for himself. Dating is ultimately about marrying. And marrying somebody that doesn't share your culture, your religion, your history, even just your background is just plain harder. He doesn't want things to be harder for his kids. As a father, I understand it. But it's like trying to hold back a river flood with a rope and a couple of pieces of plywood. I'm sure he's looking for any help he can get."

"He won't get any help from me," Corrie said. "As a mother, I think my son is good enough for anybody anywhere! And anyone who says otherwise, well, they better not say it to my face."

I laughed. She was a lot like Edna. It was amazing to me—after being married to Corrie for twenty years to see one of the same traits that had so intimidated me in her mother.

Corrie was working a lot these days. She would come home from school, start dinner and get to work answering e-mails and laying out rooms for clients. She tried to grow by word of mouth. She wanted to do such excellent work that it would loudly speak for itself, and that required a lot of commitment from her.

She began to travel more. Attending conferences and trade shows, where she could connect with the market for her services, was essential. The school system was amazingly cooperative, allowing her to take an inordinate amount of unpaid leave to pursue her sideline. I thought they were just being generous until the principal let it slip that their lawyer was investigating whether or not the school system was due a percentage of future profits based on the intellectual-property clause in her teaching contract.

Corrie and I were both stunned, but as there were no profits yet forthcoming, we let it ride.

I cheered her on and urged her to go, but I missed her—both when she was away and when she was home in front of her computer screen.

In May both Nate and Corrie graduated. Nate wore shorts and sneakers under his cap and gown. It was easy to pick him out of the crowd for photographs. He had written in Wite-Out across the top of his mortarboard: *Hell Froze Over!*

"That's our boy!" I told Corrie, rolling my eyes.

"And we are so proud," she countered facetiously.

He had made no moves whatsoever as to his future prior to graduation. He took the SAT only because we insisted. But he'd made it very evident to us that he was not remotely interested in pursuing a college degree.

The summer after graduation, Nate spent lying

around. He went out every night and stayed late, which kept him sleeping most of the day. I didn't know if he was still seeing Jin. I hadn't heard any more from Hye Won, so I figured their romance had cooled. That was okay with me.

But living as a bum in my house, that was not okay. On a hot August evening as he was getting ready to leave the house, I confronted him.

"I'm willing for you to live here as long as you like," I said. "But if you're not going to school, then you have to go to work."

He just looked at me curiously and made no response.

"I'll find a job for you at Okie Tamales if you want one," I continued. "But it will be a real job. And you'll really have to work at it."

"No thanks, Dad," he answered. "I'm leaving day after tomorrow for Maine."

"Maine? You mean like the state of Maine."

"Yeah," he answered. "There's a woodworking school up there, it's one of the best in the country. It's a twelve week course."

"You're taking a woodworking course?"

"Yeah?"

"How much is this going to cost?"

"I've already paid for it."

"Where are you going to stay?"

"Room and board is included."

"How are you going to get there?"

"Airplane," he answered and then added. "Duh, like I'm going to hitchhike fifteen hundred miles. I'm a slacker, but I'm not stupid."

I admit to being completely dumbfounded by this

development. Nate had, if not his future, at least his own plans all worked out.

Just before he left, Lauren came home for a two week visit, before heading back to Bible College. She'd spent the summer building a church/hospital facility in Oaxaca, Mexico.

Once the kids were gone it was just Corrie and I alone. Our first time alone together in twenty years. And it was busy.

Corrie's master's degree was almost anticlimactic. She was becoming so widely known and respected in her field that being a master was a given. At her orals exam she defended her thesis so well that two members of the faculty committee asked if they could recommend her company to their own administrative board. It was shortly after that at a national education technology conference that she was approached by a venture capital firm. They were blown away with what Corrie could do. They wanted to help her do it bigger and sooner.

She called me on my cell. I was delivering a minivan load of tamales to our grocery distributor. Between her excitement and the terrible static on the connection she was literally screaming at me over the phone.

"They want to give me $500,000 in start-up money!" she said.

"What! You're already started up. Why would you need that money?"

"It saves me from having to bootstrap my way up," she said. "They believe in me, they believe in my company. They want to help me make it work."

I know that it felt to Corrie as if she'd won the lottery. Better. This was a lottery awarded not by chance, but because you deserved it. What an endorsement!

But as I wandered around our house and worked at my job, I began to think about it more and more.

By the time Corrie was back in Lumkee, I was certain it was the wrong way to go.

"Look, Corrie, you don't need this money," I told her. "If you were strapped for employees or equipment, okay, but you're not. You're doing all the work yourself and I'm not sure you'd want to take on ten people and teach them what you know."

"But think how much faster we'll grow," she said.

"There is such a thing as growing too fast," I said.

"Changing the landscape of American education can't be done quickly enough," she shot back.

"I'll give you that," I said. "It would be nice if your vision could be implemented overnight. But would it still be your vision? If it's yours, then all the success is yours and all the risks are yours and so all the vision can be yours. If other people are putting in their two cents or their half-million dollars, they are taking most of the risks and seeking most of the success, so they're going to want most of the vision."

Corrie didn't have a response, but she was angry and disappointed, and in her eyes, I was the culprit.

"Look at your own business plan," I said. "The revenue streams are iffy at best. Schools, even expensive private schools, are not big money-making machines. They don't have big discretionary funds for improvements. And they don't have incentives for doing a better job. They won't improve their bottom line by turning out smarter kids."

"I know teachers," she insisted. "They want to do everything they can to help their students succeed."

"Teachers may want to do it," I pointed out. "But teachers aren't the target of your business plan, it's the school administration and their priorities have got to be the bottom line."

"Why are you so negative?" she accused. "Venture capital is what every dot.com out there is shooting for."

"Honey, listen to me," I told her. "We've been in this place before, almost exactly this place. During the oil boom, all the bankers wanted to give us money. It was burning a hole in everybody's pocket and they wanted it out there working for them. I couldn't have made a go of that business without the bank's money, I had no choice but to take it. And it came around to bite us in the butt. I can't help but worry that this may turn out the same way."

"What do you know about it?" she shouted back. "You don't know anything about the new economy or public offerings or stock valuations. Why should I listen to you on any of this?"

"Because I am the one person you can always count on to be on your side in everything you do," I told her.

"Oh, really? Well, it sounds to me like you're just jealous of my success," she said. "Does it hurt your pride to think that somebody wants to give me a boat-load of money for ideas I come up with on my very own? They are my ideas, Sam. Mine. And I don't need to smother them with salsa to get somebody to buy!"

More was said. Much more. It was a terrible fight, complete with long-ago grievances and even unexpected confessions.

She told me that she'd seen another man. She said she hadn't slept with him, but that she'd wanted to. She'd wanted another man because he was her intellectual equal. I thought the top of my head was going to blow off with that one. I was still reeling from that when she got onto my father. I had brought him and his evil into the sanctuary of our home. He'd damaged the psyche of our son and Nate would never recover.

"My father was a bad man, I admit that. I'm sorry I brought him into our home, but that's over. And Nate is going to be fine."

"You should have known what kind of man he was," Corrie yelled. "He murdered your mother."

"It was an accident."

"How many years are you going to say that?" she asked with searing sarcasm. "I don't know what your genealogy is like, Sam Braydon, but in my family we don't *murder* people."

"Oh, yeah? Well, when you get up to heaven, you'd better ask your sainted brother why Cherry Dale had his suicide medicine and how Floyd Braydon really died."

"What are you talking about?"

"You know those suicide pills Doc put together for Mike? I found the empty bottle in Cherry Dale's trash the morning of my dad's funeral. There is no way she could have gotten hold of those pills without Mike handing them to her himself. So your family knows a little bit about murder, too."

Corrie
1997

━━━━◀━━━

That fall alone together turned out to be the longest, most miserable time we had ever spent. Sam and I have never been one of those couples who squabble all the time. Both of us are basically nonconfrontational people, and although I believe my confidence and assertiveness has improved as I've gotten older, I am still never "up for a good fight."

When it came to the venture capital money for EducationEnvironments.com, a good fight is not what we had. It was a down-in-the-mud, no-holds-barred, below-the-belt, emotional slugfest. The kind only married couples can manage, because they know each other's vulnerabilities so well.

I had never intended to tell Sam anything about Riv. I had been mentally unfaithful, but I hadn't been actually so. To my way of thinking, that didn't matter. Confession might be good for the soul, but I wasn't all that sure it was good for the marriage. After observing the world of couples, my impression was that the confessor felt much better after getting the truth off his or her chest. But the person confessed to, the injured party, didn't feel better. He or she felt…well…injured.

I had injured Sam. And he, in turn, lashed out at me

with that ridiculous story about my brother. As if Mike would have had anything to do with Floyd Braydon's death. It was ludicrous. Mike had been in his grave for almost a year when that horrible man died. If it hadn't been from natural causes, and I had no reason to believe it wasn't, then it was Cherry Dale or one of her boys who killed him. Mike had nothing to do with it. Why would he?

As certain as I was of that, I was also bothered by the hint of a memory that I couldn't quite shake. On the morning after our fight, I was standing out on the deck with my coffee. My eyes were drawn to the old washhouse that still stood like some rustic relic in our backyard.

I walked down the brick path to the doorway. It was locked. It was Nate's workshop now. Filled with his saws and clamps and all the accoutrements of a man who worked with his hands. Sam knew where the key was. I was not about to ask him.

Standing on the path, I vividly recalled standing in that same spot hearing Mike and Braydon arguing. The Mike I'd heard that day was not the man I knew as my brother. He'd been cold, powerful, threatening on behalf of those he loved. Could he have engineered Braydon's death? Would he have given those drugs to Cherry Dale for the purpose of getting rid of the man?

Impossible, I firmly decided. Sam might believe that, but I would not. My brother, Mike, was good, all good, up and down, inside out, every way good. Sure he had his problems, his failings. But I was not going to believe this about him—ever.

I spent the rest of the year working on my business, stalling Dan Lyle at the venture capital firm and walking on eggshells with my husband whenever we were in a room together.

I missed the buffer that the children would have provided. We never heard from Nate from the time he left until the time he returned. Lauren e-mailed me regularly to let us know that everything was okay, but in early September I received an unexpected tearful phone call.

"I just can't believe it," Lauren choked out. "I can't believe he would let this happen."

"Who?" I asked anxiously. "Who let what happen?"

"God," she answered. "God let this happen. Both of them dead in one week."

The "both of them" to whom Lauren referred were her beloved fashion plate, Princess Di, and her spiritual beacon, Mother Teresa. Certainly the deaths were a loss. So many people were saddened. To Lauren, however, it provoked a crisis of faith. She left school and came home at the end of the semester.

It was hard for me to really empathize very much with her pain and doubt. People died. People we love. People we don't even know. I couldn't imagine that losing these total strangers from half a world away should mean so much. I had no idea how to snap her out of it.

"It's more than just the terrible loss of these lives," she said. "It's...it's...I don't know what it is, Mom. I just feel so angry. I don't like feeling angry."

I didn't know what to say to her or how to help her.

The answer came from a very unexpected source— Lauren's little brother came through for her.

It was a Sunday morning, Sam and I were up and dressed for church. Lauren just refused to go. We thought the only way she could snap out of her grief was to get reenthused about her life. We were pressing her to make the effort when Nate intervened.

"Leave her alone," he said. "If she doesn't want to go, nobody should make her."

"Just because you've got no faith," I told him, "doesn't mean your sister should abandon hers."

"If God let her down, that's exactly what she should do," Nate said. "I wouldn't want a God who wouldn't follow my directions."

Lauren's head shot up. "Nate, you are such a stupid jerk!" she said. "You shouldn't even try to talk about things you don't understand. God doesn't need to take directions from anybody. I wouldn't want him to take mine. He sees a broader picture, an eternally broad picture. Humans have such a limited vision, we can't even fathom what his purposes might be."

"Hey, don't carp at me," Nate answering. "You're the drama queen who's pissed off at the *Divine*."

"I'm not pissed off!" Lauren insisted. "You don't understand anything."

Lauren got up and headed out to the family room in a huff.

"Can't stand a little sibling conflict?" Nate called out at her. "Can't deal with a little truth from your baby brother?"

"Go to hell!" she shot back. "And that *is* exactly where you are going. I'll pray for you in the service. Right now, I've got to go upstairs and get dressed."

Once she was out of earshot, Nate turned and actually winked at us.

"You guys owe me one," he said.

Nate had returned from Maine invigorated and outgoing. Like his runaway episode in L.A., getting out on his own had made Nate more confident, more ready to pursue his goals. What those goals happened to be wasn't immediately apparent to Sam and myself.

"Son, you can't just live here without a job," his father told him.

Nate just grinned at him. "Why not?"

Sam glanced at me for support. I was pretty sure that nothing that I might say would do anything but confuse the issue.

"Because people work, Nate," he replied. "Everybody is supposed to work. You're a young, healthy guy. And personally, I'm not willing to work my butt off to pay the bills while a young, healthy guy lies around my house and does nothing."

Nate nodded. "That's fair enough," he said. "But, Dad, not everybody can work for somebody else. I'm a lot like Paw-Paw, you know."

"You're not like him at all!" Sam said quickly.

Nate's eyebrows shot up. He looked surprised at his father's words.

"No, really, Dad," he said. "I'm just like Paw-Paw, I really don't work well with other people. I don't think he would have ever been able to hold that supervisor job in the well-service company if you hadn't been the owner. I doubt anyone else would have put up with him."

Sam didn't dispute that.

"Paw-Paw kept the janitor job at the school because everybody there was so busy with their own stuff that they never got in his way."

It was the kind of disparaging observation I might have made myself. But the tone of Nate's phrasing made it seem as if he were speaking of a personality quirk rather than a character failing.

"I'm that same way," Nate continued. "Just like

Paw-Paw, I hate other people telling me what to do, I hate having to go with somebody else's plan."

"Even if that were true," Sam said, "you have to live your life. Everybody has to work."

"Yeah, but I think I'm going to work for myself," he said.

"For yourself?"

Nate nodded. "I made a couple of pieces up in Maine and I sold them, pretty easy."

"You made a piece of furniture that somebody bought?"

"Don't sound so shocked, Dad," Nate told him, laughing. "You're living in a house I built, or mostly built, anyway."

Sam stared at him for a long moment and then he smiled.

"You've done a lot for this house," he said. "You repaired it, modernized it and doubled it in size. But don't forget that my grandfather was the one who built this house. In 1937 he borrowed the plans from Mr. Tatum who had a house on Poplar Street. He put it together with salvaged timbers worked with hand tools. He knew where every nail was, because he'd hammered them all in himself. Maybe you got some of your skill from him."

Nate shrugged, but he did look pleased.

The washhouse/workshop became his place of business. He worked there at his own pace on his own time. No one could fault him for not being productive. He turned out a half dozen pieces that fall. They were beautiful. He was very taken with the mission style, which he constructed out of quarter-sawn oak and darkened by fuming with ammonia. But he also made some handsome pieces in cherry. And some artsy small things in rosewood and ebony. Sam and I were both very impressed with the quality of his work. I honestly wanted to buy them all myself. Sam discouraged me.

Sales of his work had become a very discouraging obstacle. Nate sat his finished pieces out in the yard with price tags on them. Lots of people stopped to look, lots of people admired his work, but nobody would buy.

"The people here in Lumkee just don't want quality furniture," he complained one night at supper. "They treat my stuff like it's some kind of garage sale find and they ought to be able to load it up in their pickup for five bucks!"

"That's because they're not used to buying their new furniture out on somebody's lawn," Sam told him. "You're going to have to get a furniture store to carry your stuff."

Nate shook his head. "I've tried, Dad," he said. "All the dealers contract with big factory suppliers. They don't want to use their floor space for handmade stuff. It's too expensive and the profit margin is too low."

Sam nodded.

"In Maine, we just set the stuff out on the grounds and people came to buy it," Nate said. "I know there are people somewhere who'll want this furniture. I just don't know where to find them and they don't know where to find me."

"What about the Internet?" I asked him.

He looked at me strangely.

Sam's expression I recognized. It was skepticism.

"People might buy a book over the Internet or contract for a service," he said. "But for something like this, something like furniture, people will want to look it over, touch it. I can't imagine that people would buy furniture sight unseen."

"I could upload digital photos," Nate said.

"More than that," I said. "You can have reference letters from your teachers in Maine and the people who've bought your pieces. You can even talk about your philosophy of woodworking, the designs, how they are put together. You can educate your customers, teach them why they should buy your furniture."

Nate was grinning ear to ear. "Rocks!" he said, in a tone that was unmistakably positive.

With Nate's computer savvy and my recent business experience on the Web, we brainstormed some great ideas for Nate's new business, Lumkee Woodcraft Industries.

"It's sounds big and stodgy and respectable," he said.

I agreed.

"If they only knew the truth," he teased, pretending to wax a nonexistent mustache.

The next few days were some of the best I'd spent with Nate since he was a little boy. I let my own work wait, so that we could get his project up and running. Nate's computer skills had helped me learn the Internet. He'd made it possible for me to start up my business. Now I was getting the opportunity to return the favor.

The Web page had to be designed—that was the creative part. Helping him come up with the kind of content he wanted and displaying the photos in a way that was both appealing and informative was a challenge. Especially when we didn't want any long waits for the page to load. We did the whole inventory in thumbnails with clicks to a set of more comprehensive pictures.

The purchasing segment had to be secure and flexible. We signed the company up for online payment systems and I loaned him money to pay for the privilege of accepting credit cards.

We worked together so closely those few weeks that we began to finish each other's sentences. And we laughed. Oh, how we laughed. I couldn't remember a time when my son and I had ever had so much fun together before. I felt so close to him. This was how it was supposed to be. This was what I felt I'd been cheated out of. I was grateful to have that opportunity back.

For his part, Nate was excited, happy and carefree. For once he treated me as if I were just another person, not some resident bad news inflicted upon him. Our relationship was different than it ever had been. But the simple fact that we could manage to have a positive relationship seemed like an incredible breakthrough to me.

And I suppose I treated him differently, too. I was able to quit thinking of him as a younger version of Floyd Braydon and recognize him as the young man that he'd turned out to be.

I also noticed how much he was like Sam. He had that unflagging enthusiasm and commitment, just like his father.

Working with Nate started me thinking more about my husband and the anger and resentment I'd held against him for months now. Sam was just a regular hardworking guy, as transparent as glass. I couldn't believe that I'd accused him of trying to sabotage my business. If he'd wanted me to quit, he'd simply have asked me to. And if he were jealous of my success, he'd confront me to my face, not work against me behind my back.

One afternoon when I left work, instead of hurrying home, I drove by Okie Tamales. The production room was already cleaned and, in the alley, Chano and his father were washing down the inside of the delivery van.

I found Sam where I expected, in his little nook of an office on the second floor.

His surprise when I walked in was evident. "What are you doing here?" he asked me. "What's happened?"

"Everything's fine," I assured him. "I just wanted to talk to you."

"Okay," he said.

He offered me the worn wooden chair with the cracked vinyl upholstery and carefully shut the door. He walked back around the desk and sat in his own chair, the scarred, paper-strewn desk between us.

"I've decided not to take the venture capital money," I began.

He nodded. "Okay," he said.

"I'm not convinced that it would be a mistake, but I trust you, and if it worries you, then it should worry me."

His brow furrowed.

"Corrie, I don't want you to give it up to please me," he said. "You're right, I don't understand anything about this dot.com stuff. I mean, I can see how Nate can make money, he's got a product to sell and he just needs to connect up with customers. But for the rest of it, the information brokering and providing free services, I'm not sure how money is actually going to be made. Advertising for an industry can't carry the whole industry."

"I'm not sure I understand it all, either," I admitted. "But these people with the money must know something that we don't or they wouldn't be investing the kind of dollars that they are."

He nodded. "Corrie, please do whatever you think is best for you to do," he said. "And we'll all just go forward and live with the consequences."

"I am doing what I think is best to do," I told him. "I'm following your advice, because it is your advice. And it's like you said, you are the one person I can trust to always have my best interests at heart."

We looked at each other across the desk. He nodded.

"And this is a part-time business," I continued. "I don't need a half million dollars of seed money to do something part-time."

"We're doing well here," Sam said. "If you need seed money, we can take it out of tamales."

"I wonder what you can grow with tamale seeds?" I asked him, teasing. "Little baby tacos?"

He laughed .

"I also wanted to tell you how sorry I am about... about the man I met at TU."

Sam's expression immediately sobered.

"You said you didn't have an affair with him," he pointed out, looking at me closely as if attempting to discern deceit.

"I didn't," I assured him. "But I spent time with him, I went to the movies with him. I did have a crush on him. I'm sorry. I was never technically unfaithful. But I think that fidelity should be based on more than technicalities. I'm sorry, Sam. I'm sorry that it happened.

I'm sorry that you found out about it. I'm sorry that I used it as a weapon to hurt you."

"I forgive you," he said. "I think we should just move on like it never happened."

I nodded. Then after a moment, I asked a question.

"Is that what we're doing about your father's death?" I asked. "We're just pretending that it never happened?"

Sam thought about that and shrugged.

"I don't know what to do about it," he admitted. "He was my father. And despite everything that I know to be true about him I still…well, I guess I still love him and I'm sorry he's dead. But I can hardly fault Cherry Dale for trying to defend herself. I know that he killed my mother, but I still believe it was an accident. All the same, it was an accident that would never have happened if he hadn't been a brutal, vicious abuser. I'm sure Mike must have felt the same way. Otherwise why would he have given her those drugs?"

"I still don't believe he did that."

"How else would Cherry Dale have had them?"

"I don't know, but I really don't believe that Mike could help murder anybody," I told him. "Even Floyd Braydon."

We agreed to disagree on that subject.

Two days after Christmas that year, the subject came up unexpectedly.

Early on the morning of December 30, we received the call. Cherry Dale's younger son, Rusty, was found dead in Tulsa of a crack overdose.

Sam
1998

◀——▶◀

Rusty's funeral was on New Year's Day. It was a sad and sobering occasion. To lose a twenty year old is always going to be tragic, but somehow being killed by cocaine seemed such a terrible waste of human life.

I had no idea that Rusty used drugs. That fact was frightening to me. I saw the kid on a fairly regular basis. I knew that he had some problems. Both Cherry Dale's boys had their issues and I figured my father had had plenty to do with that. I just never thought things were as bad as they were.

The morning of the funeral I was determined to become more informed. I could hear Nate in his workshop and I went down there. He was making a complicated cherry armoire to be used as an instant office. There was a place for a computer, shelves, files and a pullout desk. The whole thing could be closed up, hiding the entire working space.

"It's my own design," he told me proudly.

"It's neat."

"The first one is for Mom," Nate said. "You know, as like a 'thank you' for helping me get the business part of the Lumkee Woodcraft off the ground."

"That's nice, Nate," I said. "I'm sure your mom will be thrilled."

He smiled and nodded.

"There's something that I need to know," I said.

"What?"

"Do you do drugs?"

"No," he answered. It was a quick response that didn't completely satisfy me.

"I want the truth, Nate," I said. "With what happened to Rusty, I just…I just didn't have a clue. But Rusty's not my son, you are. I need to have a clue with you."

"Rusty's been doping heavily since high school," Nate answered. "He drank too much and did pills on top of snort on top of smoke. I'm sorry the guy's dead. But I'm not surprised."

"What about you?"

"I've smoked some weed, but I had to quit," he said. "You can't do that kind of shit and work with power tools. It's a safety issue, but more than that. You can't compromise your concentration. Musicians and artists, they think they do better after smoking some dope. Sort of takes the edge off and helps them create. In woodworking, if you take the edge off you'll make some really stupid mistake and you'll be lucky just to cut your finger off."

I was tremendously relieved. His words sounded like the truth.

After the funeral, we stopped by Cherry Dale's double-wide. The poor woman was inconsolable. I understood that. I couldn't imagine how I would feel if something happened to Lauren or Nate. No matter how careful you were, no matter how closely you watched, life was full of pain and danger. As a parent all you could do was hope that neither would find your child.

Corrie sat down on the couch next to Cherry Dale. The distraught woman grabbed her hand and did not let it go. The evening wore on. People came, people left. Cherry Dale held on to Corrie and we stayed.

Lauren and Nate finally left without us. Cherry Dale's mother went back to her own house. Even Harlan gave his mom a kiss and told her he'd call her the next day.

We were alone with Cherry Dale.

"I can't forgive myself," she said. "If I had done things differently, if I had made better choices, none of this would have happened."

"You can't blame yourself," Corrie told her. "Rusty was the one who made the bad choices. And he was so young, he really didn't know any better."

"No, it was me," Cherry Dale insisted. "I brought that man into this house. If it hadn't been for that, Rusty would have never been like he was. He blamed himself."

Corrie glanced over at me, puzzled. I shrugged slightly, equally at a loss.

"Rusty blamed himself," Cherry Dale repeated. "He loved that son of a bitch and he blamed himself for what happened."

"What are you talking about?"

"Floyd," Cherry Dale answered. "Rusty was like your Nate. When Floyd treated him special, he felt like he was on top of the world. Rusty would do anything to please that man."

Corrie looked concerned.

"He was a charming man," she admitted.

"That night," Cherry Dale continued. "That last

night when he was beating me...he would have killed me. I think he was going to kill me. If Rusty and Nate hadn't pulled him off me, I'd be dead now."

"Nate?"

Corrie and I spoke the name in unison.

"Nate was here?" Corrie asked.

Cherry Dale nodded. "He was over with Rusty, they were playing some game on the computer. He left after the fight...or in the morning. I'm not sure. I was pretty groggy. I had a concussion."

"Yes, I remember," Corrie said.

"They pulled him off me," Cherry Dale continued. "And Rusty hit Floyd. He hit him really hard. He'd never fought the man, never defended me. But that night he hit him really hard."

"He deserved it," Corrie said.

Cherry Dale nodded. "But Rusty wasn't able to forget that. He thinks that he killed Floyd. He thinks that one blow to the side of that old bastard's head was what killed him. I told him it wasn't. I must have told him a hundred times, but he never believed me. I know what killed Floyd. It wasn't Rusty."

Cherry Dale dissolved into tears and over the top of her head, I caught Corrie's glance.

Later that night as we drove home in the quiet darkness inside the car, Corrie spoke.

"I hope you are wrong about Cherry Dale killing Floyd," she said. "If she did, how will she live knowing her son destroyed his life because of it?"

"I hope I'm wrong, too," I told her. "But that pill bottle. How could it have gotten there if Mike didn't give it to her? Cherry Dale fed him dinner just before he went to sleep on the couch. She must have ground them up into the food. That's how it had to happen."

Beside me, Corrie sighed. It was such a sad sound.

"Did you know that Nate was there that evening?" I asked her.

"No," she told him. "He never said a word about it. I knew that sometimes he was over there when he was supposed to be someplace else, but I didn't know he was there."

"Can you imagine what he felt when he saw his beloved paw-paw beating the crap out of Cherry Dale?" I said.

"It must have been such a wrenching disillusionment," Corrie said. "I suppose it's no wonder that he never spoke about it."

"Poor kids," I whispered. "All of them. Floyd Braydon was just bad. In one way or another, he hurt everyone he touched, including me."

The week after Rusty's death was a busy one for our family. Lauren decided to return to school for the spring semester, but she wanted to transfer to Baylor. She had never mentioned Baylor to us and we had no idea that she was even thinking about attending there. She'd gone through all the motions of getting a permanent job in Tulsa, but college was what we'd always wanted for her. We jumped at the chance. And unlike Living Waters Bible College, we'd actually heard of Baylor.

Most students don't try to do a school transfer in three days. But Lauren hardly blinked an eye at all that was required to get her accepted, enrolled and moved in.

Corrie drove her down to Waco, the car packed to overflowing with her clothes and books and furniture.

I volunteered to go as well, but Corrie urged me to

stay at home. I think she wanted to try to find out what was going on in Lauren's head.

She stayed overnight, getting Lauren settled in, and then called me from the road on her cell phone just a little before noon.

"You'll never guess what prompted Baylor."

From her near giggling tone I assumed it wasn't something scary, like they'd agreed to send her to a leper colony for spring break.

"I can't guess," I admitted. "Just tell me."

"It's a guy."

Lauren, easily being the prettiest girl in her high school, had never shown any interest in the opposite sex. She rarely dated in college and, by her own unwelcome admission, was "saving herself for marriage."

"A guy?"

"Yeah, you know," Corrie teased. "One of those tall, muscular, good-looking humans."

"I hope you don't mean the ones with a penis."

"I think this guy's got one," Corrie said. "But I don't think he's shown it to Lauren yet. He's just cute as a button."

"As a button," I repeated. "Sounds macho to me."

"She apparently met him when she was in Mexico," Corrie said. "He seems very taken with her."

"Is he planning to be a missionary?"

"Oh, this is the best news, the very best news," Corrie said as a buildup.

"What already?"

"He's in premed."

"Okay."

"My son-in-law, the doctor!" Corrie announced. "Our little Lauren could be set up for life."

"Doctors don't make as much as they used to," I told her. "And be careful what you wish for, he might be dreaming of opening a hospital in Botswana."

Corrie laughed. "You're probably right," she agreed. "I'm just happy she's back in school, dating and having a regular twenty-something kind of life again."

"Me, too."

I was still smiling when I got off the phone. When I got back to the line, the workers were just finishing up the last of the tamales and getting them ready for delivery. Mr. Chai had everything under control. I told him I was headed out for lunch.

When I stepped outside the bright sunshine and the unseasonable sixty-degree weather inspired me. I left the van and walked home. It was only a half dozen blocks and it felt good to get out into the world. I was whistling by the time I walked through the front gate and up the steps to the porch. I thought Nate would be in his workshop, but when I heard the sound of somebody in the house and saw his bedroom door was closed, I assumed that he was working on his Web page.

I was headed to the kitchen to fix a sandwich and I thought I'd ask him if he wanted one. I opened the door.

"Nate, do you want—"

A woman screamed.

"Damn!" my son cursed.

Hurriedly I shut the door.

I walked into the kitchen. I just stood there, trying to figure out what to do. Was I supposed to be cool with this? Men are men and boys will be boys. Was I supposed to be enraged? No sex as long as you live under my roof. Or was the good father supposed to react somewhere in the middle? I had no idea. I'd never had a good dad. And as from the first day of my children's lives, I was making it up as I went along.

I opened the refrigerator and began putting together a sandwich.

A few minutes later I heard the front door slam. Nate came into the kitchen shortly afterward.

He stood there. I guess he didn't know how he was supposed to behave, either.

"How long have you been sleeping with Jin?" I asked him.

"Since high school." He hesitated and then added, "She's flying out tomorrow."

Jin had a scholarship for Syracuse.

"Do her parents know you're seeing each other?" I asked.

"Sheesh! No. She promised them she wouldn't go out with me. We keep trying to break up," he said. "Every time she goes back to school we agree to date other people. There are lots of Koreans at Syracuse. She's trying to find somebody else."

"And when she comes home, you two get back together," I said, trying to understand.

Nate shrugged. "We're just good together, Dad. We know it can't really work, but we see each other and…well, we just…you know."

I did know. I'd been nineteen once myself.

Corrie
1998

——→ ←——

EducationEnvironments.com was coming along very well. As the technology got better, I was able to look at more classrooms online and make observations. I began doing a weekly column, for want of a better term, on whatever I happened to be thinking about. What a luxury! To be able to just spout out whatever observations I had on teaching and find an immediate outlet for them. Other teachers were responding with their own take on things, and early that year I began a new feature on the site called The Front of the Class: Teachers Speak Out. Initially, I expected it to be about the classroom-design issues, but it quickly broke out of those parameters into a spectrum of opinion on everything from discipline and school violence to teachers who "don't dress nice."

One thing that began to stand out to me was the growing chasm between classroom teachers and school administration. It was as if there was some great paradigm shift that had occurred in American education. School boards and administrators had begun to see teachers and parents as different constituencies and decided that their best interests lay in siding with parents. Teachers were left hanging. They faced the day in their classrooms knowing that if anything went wrong, *anything,* from Johnny not learning to read to Janey having a potty accident, the teacher was going to be held at fault. And nobody in the principal's office was going to back her up.

"It's hard to concentrate on the correct placement of the science nook," one participant wrote sarcastically, "when I've got to keep my eye on the kid who sharpens his plastic ruler into a stabbing weapon."

"These days the schools are run by education executives in business suits," another complained. "It's been so long since they've been in a classroom, they haven't a clue what goes on there."

"This is a teaching job? I thought my principal hired me as a prison guard!"

The open forum with its venting and controversy brought more and more teachers to the site. Unfortunately, it also brought administrators and school board members and the lawyers and lobbyists representing every side.

My first hint that this was not going to be good for me was when the flood of new clients began to drop off. I wasn't worried. School funding is cyclical and I thought maybe second-semester money was tight. I got my wake-up call when overnight my advertisers dropped me, one even threatening me with a lawsuit if their logo was not taken down from my site immediately.

"Apparently, I've stepped on too many toes," I told Sam and Nate one morning at the breakfast table.

My husband was sympathetic.

"I thought talking things out was supposed to be a good thing," I complained. "This country was built on free speech. Now the educational establishment is virtually endorsing censorship."

"Take 'em to court, Mom," Nate told me. "That's what everybody does when they get their rights trampled."

"I can't do that," I said.

"Why not?"

"Well, because they really haven't stopped me from talking," I explained. "They've just stopped me from making money and talking at the same time."

Nate just looked at me for a minute and then asked, "What do you need money for, Mom? Aren't we still selling tamales?"

"Sure we are," I answered.

"Then you don't need anybody else's cash," he said.

"Well, yes, that's true," I admitted. "But everybody wants to be rewarded for what they do."

"Monetary rewards are not the only rewards," Sam pointed out. "Nate's right. You got into this to help teachers help students. You can still do that."

"Yeah, I guess I could."

"You've got the luxury to do what you want and not *have* to get a paycheck for it," he said.

"But I've always made money," I argued. "And this business should make money. Think of all that venture capital that people have been trying to throw at it."

"I'm always a capitalist," Sam told me as he sliced a banana into his oatmeal. "But sometimes giveaways can be great promotion. Think of all the underfunded school districts that can't even pay for textbooks, let alone any classroom design, no matter how inexpensive you make it."

What he was saying made sense.

"I've been looking at this as a setback and I need to

view it as an opportunity," I said. "I need to retrench, get back to my basics and do what I do best."

Sam and Nate looked at each other. Nate raised a hand and Sam slapped it in a high-five salute.

"What is that about?"

"Oh, you've been whining around here for a week," Sam said. "Nate and I just decided that we would give you a little push to get back to the onward-and-upward trail."

"You're so easy, Mom," Nate told me.

"You guys were manipulating me?"

"We're only pushing you in the direction you want to go," Sam assured me.

I playfully stuck my tongue out at him. But a few weeks later I was called upon to do my own share of urging people I loved in the direction I thought they should go.

I was home on spring break. Following my new mandate, I was voluntarily working up a design for a New Jersey public school. The photos I got of the room looked like the film sets for *Blackboard Jungle*. I took on both the challenge of making the room "learning positive" and doing it with virtually no money.

Lauren was still at Baylor. Most of the colleges had scheduled their break for the following week, so I was trying to get my work done, freeing myself for a full week of laughing, shopping and talking with my daughter.

Nate had started working with some new imported woods and had taken Sam's truck to a lumberyard in Sapulpa. Sam had, in turn, borrowed my car, so I was going to be blissfully alone in a quiet house all morning.

My new armoire/desk that Nate had made for me

was wonderful. I'd located it in the corner of the family room where it could be closed up and out of sight when I wasn't working. And it put me in front of the backyard views from the deck windows when I was.

I was deep into my work when I caught a movement out of the corner of my eye. I looked up to see Jin Chai walking toward Nate's workshop. When she saw the place was locked up she turned and walked to the house. I'd just risen to my feet when she reached the back door.

I expected her to knock and I was ready to walk over, open it and greet her. To my amazement, without even a tap on the glass, she jerked open the French doors. Apparently not seeing me in the family room, she hollered toward the kitchen.

"Damn it, Nate! Are you in there?"

I was momentarily taken aback, but having raised two children, I was not unaccustomed to rowdiness and loud voices.

"He's gone to pick up some lumber," I answered.

Jin's expression was strictly deer-in-the-headlights.

"Mrs. Braydon, I…I didn't know you were here…I thought you'd be at work. I didn't see your car. I thought Nate…I'll come back later."

"No, no, come on in, Jin," I said.

The young woman had always impressed me as being cool as a cucumber and totally in control of every situation she encountered. Today, however, she seemed anxious, jittery. I assumed that she and Nate remained friends, although I could never remember seeing them together in public. I was sure her parents probably still didn't approve. That undoubtedly explained her nervousness at being around me. I wanted her to feel at home. I wished that she and Nate were still dating. I couldn't say that to her face. It would be like saying, "I'm right, your parents are wrong." But I thought by being open, friendly, welcoming, she'd get the message.

"Come in and let me make you some tea," I said. "I've got some new herbal stuff that I got in Tulsa at Wild Oats Community Market. It's fabulous."

Jin looked like she wanted to refuse, but she didn't.

She followed me into the kitchen and made herself at home at our breakfast nook.

"Nate built that," I told her, indicating the wainscoted benching and the half-moon table.

"I know," she answered. Her tone was so sorrowful and sad, I turned to give her another look. Her eyes wouldn't meet mine and I couldn't read the expression on her face. I decided to be upbeat.

"So, how's school?" I asked, falling back on the requisite grown-up-to-student question. "Hye Won tells me that you're majoring in chemistry. Are you going to go into pharmacology, too?"

Jin shrugged. "Maybe drug research," she answered. "I don't want to be tied down to a pharmacy counter all my life."

I nodded. "Drug research is certainly important," I said. "And a growing field."

"Uh-huh."

The conversation was dying. I tried again.

"You're home for spring break already?" I said. "Lauren gets hers next week."

"Me, too," she said. "I came home early."

"Jin, is something wrong?" I didn't really need to ask. I knew there had to be a reason for this bright, sunny young woman to be sad and monosyllabic.

"You can talk to me," I assured her. "Tell me what's wrong?"

She didn't answer immediately, and when she did, she was defensive.

"I need to talk to Nate, that's all."

Her hands were folded in front of her on the table. I don't know what caused me to reach out to her, but I did. She jerked back, but I held her hand gently, but firmly, in my own.

"If you can talk to Nate about it," I said, "you can talk to me. Something is terribly wrong, I can tell. You've got to tell someone. Nate's not here, tell me."

She looked at me then, directly, her eyes locked with my eyes. She was so young and so pretty and so sad.

"Tell me," I urged.

"I'm pregnant," she said.

Strangely, the admission came as a total surprise. I'm sure my expression must have been incredulous. I was sure I hadn't heard her correctly.

"You're pregnant?"

She wasn't looking at me anymore, she was looking down at our hands, still entwined across the table.

"Who's—" I began, but I knew the answer before the question got out of my mouth. "It's Nate's."

She nodded ever so slightly, ever so stalwartly. Her face was a mask of calm, but one tiny tear escaped her eye and trailed down her cheek.

"Everything will be all right," I assured her, rather lamely. I felt as if the roof had fallen in on me. "It will all be fine. This kind of thing happens all the time."

"It doesn't happen to me," she said with a choke, struggling against her emotions before dissolving into tears.

Her breakdown snapped me into action. I was the

adult here. I was the one who had to keep a perspective.

I scooted around the bench seat until I was beside her. I put my arm around her shoulders and allowed her to cry.

"Only stupid girls get pregnant," she snapped angrily. "I'm stupid, stupid, stupid!"

"Shh, honey, that's not true," I whispered.

"I've been on birth control for years," she said. "I've always been careful. Always. But I was away at school and it didn't seem important. I thought I wasn't going to need it. And then when I came home at Christmas we started up again. I started back on the pills right away." She shook her head regretfully. "I guess it wasn't soon enough."

I listened to her tears, her anger, her self-reproach, and I remembered my own. It had been so very long ago. But it felt like only yesterday.

She began to gain control, but she was sniffling. I couldn't get up to get her a tissue. I thought if I let her go, she might run away. I handed her a pile of paper napkins and she blew her nose.

"I don't suppose your parents know," I said.

"No, absolutely not," she said, shaking her head. "They can't ever know. You've got to promise you won't tell them."

"Jin, they'll have to find out eventually," I said. "If you got pregnant at Christmas, you'll be showing in a couple of months."

She turned to glare at me.

"I'm not having a baby!" she said. "I can't have a baby."

Momentarily I was puzzled.

"I came to get Nate to go with me," Jin explained.

"I'm going to go see a doctor, get an appointment for an abortion."

"Oh." I must have pulled away from her. I don't remember doing it, but now my hands were over my mouth.

"I'm sorry, Mrs. Braydon," she said. "I can't have a baby. I have a scholarship. I'm halfway to my degree. I want graduate school and a career. I can't have a baby, not now."

"I see."

"No, you don't," Jin said. "You can't understand what it's like. For my parents, Korean parents, their children's achievement is everything to them. They gave up their home, their friends, their family, their careers, everything that was familiar and that they held dear, to come to America and be laborers. They live their lives here, where they will always be outsiders and always suspect. They did that so that my brothers and sister and I would have a brighter future. If I don't finish school, if I don't do something with my life, it's a slap in the face to them. It's like saying their sacrifice meant nothing to me."

"They will understand," I assured her. "Parents, all parents, they understand. Yes, they'll be disappointed, but when they see this baby, their first grandchild, they'll feel differently."

Jin shook her head. "They'll feel differently, all right," she said, sarcastically. "Their first grandchild and he's only half Korean. That will go over real well."

I shook my head. "It's hard to dislike a baby, any baby. Especially one that's your own flesh and blood."

"They don't like Nate at all," she said. "I think they must hate him. Every time his name even comes up, my father gets angry and my mother has something mean to say about him. They forbade me to date him years ago. I told them I wouldn't. I've just kept lying to them."

"Then it's time to stop," I told her. "It's time to own up to everything and start moving forward from here."

"But I can't have a baby," Jin repeated. "A baby would ruin my life. It would ruin all my plans."

"Yes, it would," I agreed. "But, Jin, honey, you can always come up with new plans. I make up new plans for my life every day. And if there is anything that I can testify to, it's that the things I *haven't* planned have turned out to be best."

"Don't you believe in a woman's right to choose?" she asked me.

"I do," I told her. "I absolutely do. No woman should bear a child because somebody else tells her she has to. Every baby born deserves to be wanted."

She nodded, but there was still question in her eyes.

I continued. "The word *choose* implies there are at least two answers to the question. Or in your case, two different paths in front of you. You're at a crossroads."

I was thinking of my own crossroads and I was hoping, praying that some wisdom I might have gleaned would help.

"You can continue down the path you've been on," I told her. "You can keep lying to your parents about being in love with Nate. Or you can stop loving him, stop seeing him. You can continue your education and go toward all those things that you think that you want. But in order to really choose, you've got to give some thought to that other path, the one that you'll leave behind forever."

She frowned. She looked so young, so scared. I

smoothed a stray hair away from her face and laid my hand against her chin.

"You're afraid of that other path," I said. "You're afraid because you don't know what may be down there and you think it might be bad. Your family may be disappointed in you. Your life may be harder than you hoped. Your dreams may get postponed or even canceled. All those things may happen, but they may not. The truth is, you don't know what's really around the corner of either one of these paths. Do you?"

"No," she admitted.

"You're a scientist, Jin. Scientists don't make decisions based upon what frightens them or what they _think_ they know."

Sam
1998

——▶ ◀——

We knew immediately the day that Jin finally told her parents. I remember that morning perfectly. It was still early on Main Street, no one but the store owners were there. The business district of my childhood had developed into a very slick retro look in keeping with the city's new motto prominently displayed on billboards along the expressway: Lumkee, Oklahoma: Small Town America.

The truth was that Lumkee had long since ceased being "small town America." It was suburbia with a small core of tourist-friendly streets kept like a living museum of the 1950s.

But it was what had kept the downtown from dying completely. There were lots of little communities, once Lumkee's rivals, that were now nearly deserted, their buildings boarded up and their young families moving elsewhere. We were close enough to Tulsa to have been swallowed up by it. Yet, we had enough local people who wanted the old Lumkee to linger that we'd managed to save a few vestiges of the past.

I drove down the alley to my parking place behind the back door. Hye Won came out of her store immediately, as if she'd been watching for me. She approached me carrying some papers. I gave her a big grin, but she wasn't smiling.

"Good morning, Mr. Braydon. I hope that you and your family are well."

Her words and the expression of her greeting were very formal, as if we hadn't been friends and business associates for years.

"We're fine," I told her. "Is everything okay at your house?"

She nodded but didn't elaborate on that.

"My father and mother have asked me to convey their abject apologies," she said. "They will not be at their jobs today, and they have asked me to humbly present these letters of resignation."

I accepted the proffered papers and quickly glanced through them. They were formal and generic, without complaint or explanation.

I glanced up at Hye Won. She gave me a little nod as if our discussion was finished.

"Wait," I insisted. "This is about Jin and Nate, isn't it?"

She didn't say anything and her expression was unreadable.

I took a deep breath, trying to figure out what to say.

"I can only apologize for my son," I finally managed. "I am very sorry if Nate's behavior has…has insulted your family or…dishonored your sister. I…they are grown, adult people. I…"

Hye Won held up her hand and shook her head.

"Please Mr. Braydon," she said. "Do not concern yourself with this. My father does not hold you accountable for any bad behavior. It is not that at all."

"Then what is it?"

"It's hard to explain," she said. "It is very Korean.

The relationship between our families is now forever changed. My father cannot be employed by the family of his daughter's lover. It just cannot be done. It would be a shame and an embarrassment for him. I am sorry."

So that was it. Mr. and Mrs. Chai never set foot in Okie Tamales again. Their son Chano came in that afternoon to retrieve their personal items from their lockers. He requested that their last paychecks be mailed.

The rest of the Korean staff showed up on time, but most immediately gave notice. They didn't want to work for me. They had only stayed because they worked for Mr. Chai. I managed to convince them, with bonuses, to stretch out their termination dates so that I would have time to hire replacement staff.

The last of the Korean employees were gone by the first of June. I was employing anybody that I could. Over the summer, it was mostly high school kids. But the wonderful life I'd been leading, with a dependable, hardworking, trustworthy production line, was a thing of the past.

Not that non-Koreans weren't good workers. Many were. But the commitment to a difficult, monotonous job was hard to maintain. The turnover was constant. I eventually found three middle-aged women who I could count on to stay, and they kept the revolving door of other employees trained. But I was now fulltime production manager as well as working sales, delivery, human resources and payroll. Twelve- to fourteen-hour days now became the norm.

The Chais bought a small building across the street. It had been a dry cleaners when I was a kid. For the last several years it had been a gift shop. They opened a small grocery. The bins of produce were kept out on the sidewalk. That was a good idea since the interior of the place, crowded with merchandise, was hardly big enough for a half dozen customers. It was quite a contrast to the huge supermarkets where we all shopped. I was certain that nobody would come downtown to buy groceries.

And I couldn't understand why the Chais didn't just retire. Their oldest son was married now, well off and appeared quite capable of supporting them. Hye Won had a thriving business as well and looked after her parents in her own home. Chano was graduating high school. Although he wasn't brilliant, like the rest of the kids, he was a good-looking, affable guy. Plenty smart enough for any reasonable purpose. He'd gotten an athletic scholarship to run track at Kansas State.

And there was Jin. Jin was living at our house. She and Nate were still not married. I couldn't begin to know what was going on between those two. But with Lauren off to school and mainly involved in saving the world, Corrie and Jin had somehow become very close.

"We have *mo-jeong*," Corrie explained to me one night as she sat up in bed reading. Her stack of books on Korean history and culture was on the bedside table.

"Moo-junk?" I asked. "Is that like the Korean word for *bullshit?*"

She gave me a look, not appreciating my humor at all.

"*Mo-jeong*," she corrected. "It's a bond of trust between two people. Jin and I recognize that we are inevitably connected by ties of caring, respect and nurturing."

I nodded.

"You're really getting into this Korean stuff, huh?"

"It just helps me understand what's going on so much better," she said. "So much of Korean culture is left unsaid. They all understand what's meant, but those of us from Western culture are just clueless."

I shrugged.

"Weren't you confused about the Chais' attitude to Jin finishing her semester at Syracuse?"

"Yeah," I admitted. "It would have been stupid to drop out in April when she could easily do two more months of school and have that many more credits toward her degree."

"That's what I thought exactly," Corrie said. "As long as she's healthy, she should finish the courses she'd signed up for. The Chais are so keen on education, I thought they should see that. But in Korean culture they believe that the lessons the baby is learning inside the mother's womb are as important as the first ten years of education after birth. They want the mothers-to-be to refrain from stressful endeavors, live in peaceful surroundings, read only good literature, look at beautiful pictures and eat colorful, exquisitely prepared food. Knowing this, of course, they wouldn't want her to return to a dorm room, eating in the cafeteria and knuckling down to the rigors of education."

"The Chais are very smart people," I pointed out. "They wouldn't believe all this stupid stuff like a pregnant woman looking at beautiful pictures and reading good books helps the baby."

"What about that finding on classical music?" she asked me. "Now the pregnant American moms are playing Mozart with the headphones on their belly because they think it makes the child's brain form more intricate neural connections, which will raise the kid's math scores ten years later."

"Okay, maybe there is something to that," I said.

"Besides, it's a difficult and confusing time for Jin's family," Corrie said. "In difficult and confusing times, we all fall back on what we know and what we perceive as familiar."

Around my house, there was very little that I perceived as familiar. Jin had moved into Nate's room, which Corrie had totally redecorated in pale yellow. The curtains and bedding were patterned in Asian-style flowers. Nate had been banished to his workshop, where he'd carved out a corner for his own living quarters. I didn't know if his living separately had to do with them not being married or was more of the Korean birth preparation.

On September 28 at 3:55 in the afternoon, Makayla Moon Braydon was born at Hillcrest Medical Center in Tulsa. She weighed six pounds, five ounces.

Mr. Chai, Jin's brother Song and I spent about three hours hanging around the waiting room together. Mr. Chai was open, friendly, cheerful—just as I remembered him when he used to work for me. Song carried most of the conversation. He had been in this very room only six weeks earlier when his wife gave birth to their firstborn son.

Nate and all the women were all in the labor room with Jin. Corrie had studied for this day as if it were a final exam. She was determined to win over the entire Chai family and heal the breach between Jin and her mother by being rigorously attentive to the *taegyo* and *samchilil.* Whether that actually worked or not, I don't know. But in the three weeks after Makayla came home from the hospital, Mrs. Chai or Hye Won were in my house more than I was.

I had snuck home from work one afternoon, to try to

get caught up on paperwork without being interrupted from the production floor every five minutes. Mrs. Chai had left early and Hye Won wasn't coming over until after the drugstore closed. Corrie was watching over the new mother and baby. She came into the family room where I was sitting at her little home-office desk.

"Jin and the baby are both asleep. I've got to run to the store for more diapers," she told me. "Here's the monitor." She plunked down a piece of blue-and-white plastic that looked like a teddy bear walkie-talkie. "If she calls for anything just tell her I'll be right back. Don't let her get out of bed!"

The not-out-of-bed thing was Korean. She was supposed to recover for three weeks. Corrie had recovered in three days. But she was now completely committed to these ancient rules from the Koryo dynasty.

"Okay," I said. "If she needs something, I'll help her."

It was only a few minutes later when I heard a voice on the monitor.

"Who's there?" Jin asked.

"It's Sam, honey," I answered. "What do you need?"

"Was that Corrie's car I heard leaving?"

"She went to get diapers," I said. "She'll be back in fifteen or twenty minutes."

There was a long pause.

"Do you need something?"

"Sam, I'm going to jump into the shower real quick," she said. "If you hear the baby cry, come up and check on her."

"You're going to take a shower?" Corrie had explained that not only were traditional Korean mothers not supposed to get out of bed, there were no showers or bathing for twenty-one days.

"Are you sure you want to do that?" I asked her.

"I promise not to wash my hair," she said. "But I've just got to shower. When it comes to that, I think there's more Oklahoma in me than Korea."

"I won't tell if you won't tell," I said.

Neither of us did and as far as I know, no one ever suspected, though I'm pretty sure Jin sneaked several more showers before her time was up.

Once her lying-in was completed, Jin and Makayla, or Little Mac as Nate and I called her, became the center of our family life. Corrie had taken the year off from teaching to be at home with the new baby. And I think we both found grandparenting as freeing and energizing as parenting had been confining and exhausting.

Little Mac was the prettiest, sweetest, most intelligent baby I'd seen since our own were tiny. And she was loaded for bear with personality. Charming, funny, gleeful, stubborn, willful and rebellious. Exactly the kind of kid you would expect to get from having Nate and Jin as parents!

Finally, since apparently nobody else would, I broached the subject of marriage.

"So when are you two going to tie the knot?" I asked one snowy cold winter afternoon when everything in town was closed up for bad weather.

Little Mac was sitting in her jiggle seat, a sort of vibrating sling chair, looking around as we all watched her inspecting us.

"That's really none of your business, Dad," Nate said.

His words were not angry or disrespectful, but I was stung by them, anyway. Jin tried to soften the blow.

"There's no hurry," she assured me. "Everything is going so well, why would we want to mess that up?"

"Well," I said, "maybe because it's nice for mommies and daddies to be married to each other. You don't want her having to explain things to her little classmates in kindergarten."

"By the time Little Mac gets to kindergarten," Nate said, "most of the kids in her class won't be from families with two married parents."

He was probably right, but I didn't like it, anyway.

"Nate, I know you've made a life out of never doing anything that we want you to do," I said. "But this is not about getting my goat or acting out against your mother and me. You are somebody's father now. You can't be that and still act as irresponsible as a kid."

Nate glowered at me, preparing for a sharp comeback, when Jin reached a hand over and touched my arm.

"It's not Nate," she said. "He's taking the blame for me. But it's not him. I'm the one who's just not sure."

She looked down at Little Mac and then back at me.

"There is so much that I want for my life," she said. "Things that I can't have here in Lumkee. I'm not ready to give up on that. If I marry Nate, then I'm giving up."

Her defense was admirable. And I knew there was some truth to it. But I looked into Nate's eyes and knew this wasn't the whole truth.

Corrie
1999

I had always thought that I loved teaching more than anything. But I soon found out that I loved being home with Makayla most of all. Jin was a very good mother. She did parenting the way she did everything else, consistently overachieving. Because I didn't have to worry that any of the baby's physical, emotional or spiritual needs were not being met, I could concentrate on just loving the stuffings out of her!

Mrs. Chai, Jin's mother, who now allowed me to call her Cho Kyon, was attached to her, too. But she had her grandson, Michael, Song's little boy, with whom to share her time.

I was very hopeful of having a Korean-American wedding very soon, and I read everything I could on the subject. And I put together a folder of ideas and cultural trivia that might be helpful when the time came.

I was able to utilize some of it, but not exactly as I had hoped. Hye Won had finally been introduced to the right young man and a hasty wedding was in the offing.

David Kim was shorter than Hye Won, not nearly as smart, and as the minister at a small Korean Presbyterian church in Oklahoma City, he had much less earning potential. But I liked him.

Jin didn't feel the same.

"Hye Won is selling out," Jin informed me. "She's afraid that she'll never marry, so she's settling for this major loser. The only reason she'd give this guy the time of day is that he's Korean."

"Did she tell you that?"

"No," she answered. "She says that he's perfect for her. That he's the guy she's been waiting for all her life. But I don't believe her. He's Korean. She's only marrying him because he's Korean."

Jin's certainty about that struck me as a bit of "thou doth protest too much," and I wondered how much Nate's not being Korean actually worked against her willingness to commit to him.

I also worried about Nate's willingness to commit to her. Of course, I had heard Jin tell Sam that she was the one who didn't want to marry. But I saw no evidence that my son was ready to make any vows. In fact, he seemed to be extremely content with his life and eager for things to continue exactly as they were.

He worked in his workshop doing what he liked. His father provided the roof over his head and the food on his table. He was back inside the house again with his beautiful live-in girlfriend who put few demands on his time. And his happy, healthy baby girl could be safely left anytime for free baby-sitting with his mother.

Nate was a very fortunate young man. I was afraid he would never take on the responsibilities of a husband and father. Why should he bother?

In April, Lauren brought home a new boyfriend for the weekend. Actually, she called him her "gentleman friend," I suppose because it was difficult to consider him a boy.

Gilkison Oberfeld was nearing forty, closer in age to Sam and myself than to Lauren. While we were aware of that, it seemed to have escaped our daughter's attention. He was tall and slim. His hair was thinning on top and the sides were showing hints of gray. But he was well dressed in expensive clothes and wore a big diamond ring with a lodge emblem.

She had met Oberfeld at her church in Waco. He was a businessman and investments counselor, successful and conservative. He had opinions on everything and he wasn't hesitant about sharing them.

Lauren cornered me in the kitchen in the first fifteen minutes that he was there.

"Don't mention Bill Clinton, affirmative action or immigration," she warned. "He's a really kind, good, Christian man. But he has some very strongly held beliefs and I wouldn't want him to get off on the wrong foot with my family."

We tiptoed around him as best we could, discussing the weather and how Tulsa compared with Waco, his business and the more favorable tax structures in Texas over Oklahoma. We also covered the stock market and how more money could be made investing in stocks than in small business. I asked him questions about his family.

"My father grew up on a ranch near Schulenburg. They're Germans, but they've been in this country practically since the Alamo was new," he joked to me. "And my mama—" he shook his head incredulously "—my mama's family is what passes for royalty in east Texas."

He seemed to think this was very funny. We all laughed politely.

"Braydon is an English name," he informed us. "As is Maynard, your maiden name, Corrie."

"My family seems to think they are some Scot-Irish mix," I told him. "I don't think Sam knows much about his heritage."

"You really should take an interest," Gilkison suggested. "I know it's not politically correct to talk about bloodlines. But science is learning more and more about genetics. It's proving that who we turn out to be is as dependant upon our heritage as we always thought it was."

Neither Sam nor I made a comment on that.

"This spinach dish is wonderful, Mom," Lauren piped in. "You'll have to give me the recipe."

"Jin made it," I told her.

Lauren glanced down to the end of the table where Jin sat feeding Makayla, who was in her high chair.

"I didn't know you could cook," Lauren said.

"I'm just learning," she responded. "I'll give you the recipe, but my mother says the secret is the freshness of the spinach. So it probably doesn't taste the same if you don't buy your produce from her."

The last little facetious comment was meant as a joke. Everybody laughed but our dinner guest.

"So, Jennifer, where are *you* from?" he asked. "You don't mind me calling you Jennifer, do you? I hate diminutives."

"My name isn't Jennifer," she replied. "It's Jin, J-I-N. And I'm from here. I was born in Tulsa."

He chuckled as if she'd made a joke. "Okay, I'll go with that," he said. "But your heritage is Chinese or Japanese, right?"

"Korean, I'm Korean-American."

"Oh, that's good," he said. "Lots of Koreans are Christians."

"Her sister just married a Presbyterian minister," Lauren piped in.

Gilkison nodded his approval.

Bringing up Hye Won's wedding somehow made Jin respond defensively.

"I'm not really religious," she replied.

"Obviously," he said.

He turned his attention back to his grilled chicken breast and I thought that the direction of the conversation might die a natural death. But it wasn't to be so.

"What do you mean by that?" Nate asked.

Lauren's eyes widened and she turned her gaze to me for help. My mind was a blank. I was helpless to change the subject.

Gilkison shrugged and smiled. "I meant that it's obvious that an unwed mother living with her boyfriend in his parents' house is probably not very concerned with moral behavior or religious values."

"You bastard!" Nate responded.

Sam held up his hand for silence.

"Mr. Oberfeld is a guest in our house," he stated emphatically.

"A guest who certainly needs to make an apology," Gilkison said. "Believe me, I meant no disrespect to your…to Jin. And I am in no position to judge the personal life of anyone else. As I'm sure Lauren has told you, I am divorced."

He paused.

"It was my ex-wife who sought the divorce," he went on to explain. "But I do hold myself very responsible for not being able to keep my marriage together.

We have four wonderful children who now suffer from the stigma of coming from a broken home. It shames me and saddens me. And it's a mistake I will not make twice."

The last comment was made with a quick glance toward Lauren.

She gave him a little smile.

The weekend didn't get a whole lot better. We improvised and made him a guest room out on the sunporch. Nate and Jin made themselves scarce, Jin deciding at the last minute to make an unprecedented overnight visit to her brother's house with Makayla. And Nate just went out to his shop and stayed there.

Sam and I persevered.

It wasn't easy. We found Gilkison narrow and rigid, but he could also be thoughtful and kind. And he was conspicuously crazy about Lauren. So Sam and I tried to put the best face on it and stick to topics and activities that no one could object to.

I spent my time showing him photo albums of my little girl when she had truly been that. He admired her over and over again and she preened under his praise.

Sam got him into a business discussion. It went well as long as the talk was about stock sectors, industry growth and market direction. Things got a little dicey when Gilkison suggested Sam should sell his business.

"It's a waste of time and energy to keep slogging at that, day by day," the man told him. "You've made a profitable company. Sell it to a corporate food-service firm. You'll make more money taking your cash and investing it."

"Okie Tamales isn't an investment. It's my job," Sam said. "What would I do if I sold out?"

"You'd do something else," Gilkison told him. "Get

your cash out while you can. Lauren told me you got burned in the eighties oil bust. Don't hang on to this business until it washes out, too."

"It's a food business," Sam said. "People are always going to want food."

Gilkison shook his head. "That's where you little guys get gummed up. It's not the product anymore. It's not about making tamales or toasters or techno-bits. It's about making money. If you can't see that, then you're destined to be run out, bought out or bankrupt."

Quickly I changed the subject. "So, Lauren," I said, "are you going on another mission trip this summer?" Before she could respond, I drew Gilkison into the conversation by directing a comment his way. "We worry when Lauren's away from home, but we're always fascinated by the stories she brings home. She sent us photos last summer of her eating a guinea pig on a stick."

Lauren smiled uneasily.

Gilkison's tone was adamant. "Lauren won't be going on any more of those trips," he said. "I simply can't permit it. It's not safe or even advisable for a young, single woman to be out in those dangerous, dismal places working with people from primitive cultures. I can't imagine how you've allowed it."

Sam and I shared a quick, meaningful glance.

Neither of us had been supportive of Lauren's evangelical treks. And for some of the same reasons that Gilkison voiced. But hearing it said aloud made it sound more priggish and narrow-minded than we'd considered ourselves to be.

"These are church trips," Sam pointed out. "Doing good work for people less fortunate than us."

"Yes, well, I've never been a big supporter of global missions," Gilkison said. "I'm not opposed to sending Bibles or doing radio broadcasts, but I think we have plenty of needs in our own church without looking outside the community for a way to spend money."

By Sunday afternoon, I was glad to see them drive away in his gleaming white Land Rover that was almost too large to fit in our driveway.

We waved goodbye from the porch. When they were out of sight, we turned to go into the house and Sam slipped his arm around my waist.

"Whatever she wants," he said.

I nodded. "I'm hoping this guy isn't it."

Being home, even helping with Makayla's schedule, gave me lots more time for working on Education-Environments.com. I was still doing mostly gratis work for low-income school districts, so the business wasn't really getting bigger.

Amazingly, my vision and philosophy of the needs of the environments was growing tremendously. I owed this expansion in my thinking to Jin's pregnancy and all the research I'd done of Korean culture. I began to see differing cultures as a variable in the success of design. By using what we know about the classroom populations, I was able to utilize diversity as a positive influence.

On an afternoon in early May I was working on a comprehensive work-flow design for a third-grade classroom in a school district in coastal Georgia that had twenty-two black children and eleven Vietnamese. I was so involved in the details, I wouldn't have noticed the weather if Jin hadn't interrupted me. She came into the family room barefoot. Her shirt was still unbuttoned. She'd been nursing Makayla and now had the baby against her shoulder, trying to coax a burp out of her.

"Have you looked outside?" she said. "It's looking really bad out there."

I stopped to save my work before glancing up. As warm as it had been at noon, a little rain would be welcome on the spring flowers.

Looking out the French doors of the family room the afternoon sky had turned a yellow so dark it was almost green.

"Turn on the TV," I said.

Jin grabbed the remote from the cushions on the couch and punched it on. The Tulsa station was giving out the beep-beep-beep warning and they were showing a brightly colored radar map of the state—it was mostly yellow with large red blotches. The voice-over provided an announcement.

"The National Weather Service has issued a tornado warning. Repeat, this is a tornado *warning* for the counties in northeastern Oklahoma. Tulsa County is included in this warning. A funnel cloud, potential tornado is being tracked on Doppler radar and verified by local law enforcement near Prattville, heading north/northeast at approximately thirty miles per hour. Persons in far north West Tulsa, the northern suburbs and Lumkee should seek shelter immediately. If you must remain in your home, take cover in a cellar or a first-floor interior room away from windows."

Jin and I both jumped to our feet.

"Let's go to the cellar!"

"I don't have my shoes," she said.

The civil-defense siren at the fire station began blaring.

"Oh, my God!"

"Let's go!"

The electricity went out. I jerked open the door and Jin ran out ahead of me. Nate was running toward us from the shop. He met us at the edge of the deck and without a word, in one swoop, he lifted Jin up into his arms.

Gram's old storm cellar was at the edge of the property, next to the alley, only about thirty yards from the back door. That afternoon it seemed like miles. By the time we got there an eerie darkness had settled around us, and the wind was full of trash and papers. It was then we heard it—a roaring, an ominous and distinct roaring.

Nate set Jin on her feet beside the cellar door and tugged at it to get it open. We hurried down the steep narrow stairway into the musty blackness. Makayla was crying. I felt like crying, too. The place was cold and dark and I was scared. When Nate pulled the door shut, it was as if we were in a tomb.

"There's a lantern in here someplace," Nate said, fumbling around among the antique canning jars, odd pieces of metal pipe and God-only-knows-what on the shelving behind him.

"There won't be any kerosene in it," I warned him.

Jin and I sat down on the long, hard bench that ran the length of the wall. When this had been Gram's cellar there was always oil in the lantern, fresh water in the jug and clean quilts on the bench.

Nate managed to find a candle and a match. I watched as he lit it, his hands shaking.

Makayla's crying abruptly stopped as Jin began to nurse her.

The quiet inside the closed space made the roar outside sound more frightening.

The light helped a little, though the flame flickered as if the wind was whipped up inside as well. The door rattled slightly and Nate tied the rope to the back of the door, pulled the length of it across the room and looped it twice around the support pillar before sitting in the chair nearby to hold it taut. The door didn't rattle. But my knees did.

It was over in minutes. The roaring moved on. Beside me I stroked Makayla's head.

Nate undid the rope, climbed the stairs and opened the door. It was as if Jin and I were collectively holding our breath.

"Come on out," Nate said. "It's fine. It missed us. The house is okay. No damage, really."

He took Jin's hand. I followed after them. Everything was standing, although the yard was strewn with lumber and trash and shingles.

"What a mess!" I said. And then I laughed. I was so relieved.

That's when the sirens began.

"Is that the all clear?" Jin asked. Even the tone of her question was skeptical.

Then another siren sounded.

"It's fire trucks," Nate said.

"Or ambulances."

Nate was looking along the horizon.

"Oh, God," he said. "I think it's downtown."

If he said anything else I don't remember. I began to run. I ran up the alley to West Hickory. I turned and continued running to town. My thoughts were muddled, scared. I had to get to Sam. Sam was downtown and I had to get to Sam. I was near the end of West Hickory when I got lost. I don't mean I really got lost. It was as if I suddenly couldn't recognize where I was.

A big tree blocked the street and I had to actually walk on somebody's porch to get around it. I didn't recognize the house. It looked like a dilapidated shack. There were no shacks in this part of Lumkee. I recognized the park only by the cement benches along the street. It seemed to be all broken limbs and downed trees and power lines.

I hastily picked my way around that disaster to find myself on Main Street. Or what had once been Main Street. There were no buildings, there was nothing. Yet there was everything. Mountains of bricks, cars standing on end and huge chunks of things I didn't recognize.

Where was Sam?

I'd lived my whole life in this town. I couldn't tell where my father's drugstore had been. I couldn't tell where my husband's business might be. I couldn't tell where the sides of the street once were.

There was no way to run through the piles of debris. I began climbing over it, crawling through it. I was not alone. There were people everywhere, dirty, frightened-looking people, sifting through the mess, calling out names.

I began calling, too.

"Sam! Sam! Where are you? Damn it, Sam! Where are you?"

"Corrie!"

I heard my name and rose to my feet, looking all around. I saw him standing in a pile of rubble, a hundred yards away in a direction opposite to the one I pursued.

"Corrie! Over here." He waved at me.

I was crying then, crying as I made my way to him as quickly as I could. He was covered with dust and sweat and blood. I wanted to throw myself in his arms. But there wasn't time for that.

"Mr. Chai is in here," he said. "Help us dig him out."

It was then I noticed—Cho Kyon was on her knees, tears streaming down her face as she dug through the bricks of her grocery store.

Sam
1999

It was a wonder that there weren't more people killed.
Seventy-six tornadoes in Oklahoma that Monday.
Forty-three people lost their lives. Two of those in
downtown Lumkee. Harjo Peeples, who had been in-
strumental in keeping the name of our town, was driving home from the post office. His old car was tossed
into the bank like a toy. And Brian Gilbert, the new
pharmacist Hye Won had hired to manage Maynard
Drug had been crushed when the walls of the old
building collapsed upon him.

There were serious injuries as well. Broken arms,
broken legs, electrical burns and internal damage.
Some of it permanent and severe.

Mr. Chai's back was broken. He would never walk
again. Loretta, one of my most dependable employees,
had her left eye put out by flying glass.

And Cherry Dale Pepper, taking a day off work to
celebrate her forty-fifth birthday, was in her double-
wide mobile home when it was picked up from its
foundation and rolled end on end for a city block. She
was alive but in a coma.

There were tragedies in the aftermath as well. One
young teenager was electrocuted by stumbling across a

live wire. A telephone repair worker was hurt when he freed a line from the trees only to have it snap back on him and knock him from his perch on the cherry picker.

Corrie's dad was out cleaning up debris in his yard and suffered another stroke.

The damage estimates were over the moon. And because our disaster looked piddling compared to the cities of Moore and Stroud, we didn't get a lot of attention from the news cameras, FEMA or even our own insurance companies.

The path of destruction started just west of the city park, plowed through the main business district and then into the three blocks of houses on the east side. The experts estimated the funnel was less than a mile in length and had touched the ground less than three minutes. But with so much loss.

Building inspectors condemned the few buildings left standing. The entire downtown commercial district was wiped out.

How we got through those first days, first weeks, first months, remains a blur of work and worry. All of us were up at dawn, working until after dark and falling into bed exhausted.

Jin was helping to take care of her father. Corrie was helping with Doc. Nate and I were simultaneously trying to sort through what was left of our building and keeping the business afloat and our employees working. We'd set up the tamale production in our garage. Of course, I couldn't expect the health inspector to sign off on that for public distribution, so we fed the tamales to ourselves, our families and the volunteers downtown. Financially, I wasn't sure how long we could keep that up. But my staff continued to draw paychecks, so they didn't have to take jobs elsewhere.

The interior of Okie Tamales was a total loss. They found part of our huge steam oven in a cow pasture two miles from town. In many ways, the loss of our financial records was more trouble than the loss of the equipment. All the paper was backed up on computer files, but both were literally "gone with the wind." I didn't know who I owed or who owed me. And I had no idea how I would pay my quarterly taxes. I was too busy to worry much about it. Life had become a day-by-day operation. Which was good for me. Emotionally I was kind of tapped out. The enormity of what had happened affected the way I thought about things. Or it made me think about them for the first time in a long time. I'd lived through uncertainty in my job and uncertainty in my finances. I'd even begun to let go of any sense of control over my children's lives and futures. But still, there are things that you take for granted will always be there. The little downtown where I'd spent all my life was one of those things.

What I found was that the loss of that made me value more those things that truly matter to me. I felt a surge of love for my kids, my home and especially for Corrie.

We were so busy, we hardly saw each other all day. At night we were both so exhausted, I didn't have the energy to spell *sex*, let alone have it. But I could lie in our bed and hold her in my arms.

"I love you, Corrie," I told her, probably more often in those frantic, busy months than I had in all the rest of the years of our marriage.

"Me, too," she responded, and turned her back so that she could spoon up to me in the center of the bed.

It was amazing how just the feel of her body next to

mine could ease all the strain and aches and tension that a long, hard day could make.

As soon as her final exams were over, Lauren returned home. Gilkison came with her. When I saw his Land Rover in the driveway, I groaned aloud.

To my surprise, I found him in the garage helping out with the tamale packing. The man wasn't afraid of work.

The next few days proved that as a certainty. He stayed for a week, and Nate and I put his shoulder to every task that came up. To our complete surprise he never grumbled, complained or shirked. Gilk, as Nate and I began to call him despite his dislike of nicknames, salvaged lumber, hauled out trash by the wheelbarrow load and fed Doc chicken soup at the hospital. Wherever we needed him, he was willing to go.

His relationship with Lauren appeared to be very different from what we'd seen when she'd brought him home to meet us. Then he was the man-in-charge and she was trying every minute to get along and smooth things over. But it was different after the tornado. Lauren was amazingly good at crisis management. She could readily see what needed to be done and come up with a plan for doing it.

We had never seen her like this. I assumed that she'd learned these skills on her mission trips. If we were surprised, poor Gilk was virtually stupefied. But when she said "frog," the guy hopped. We all hopped. What else could we do? She spoke with authority and her directions made sense. She brought more out of people than they knew they had in them.

Cho Kyon was struggling with the enormity of her husband's care and rehab. Hye Won had come from her new home in Midwest City and had been designated to help her. It was Lauren who realized that Hye Won was pregnant, and therefore, her mother wouldn't allow her to help. There were no extra hands, so Lauren had Belinda, one of the young women who worked at the tamale factory, trade places with Cho Kyon for a few hours every day. Belinda had started a nurse's aide course once, but dropped out. She was still interested in the medical field and was able to follow the directions of the home health-care staff and the therapist.

Just the few hours that Cho Kyon got away from her house and sat down to do something else seemed to rejuvenate her. And it rekindled Belinda's interest in the medical field.

It was a simple solution. Lauren came up with it, because she looked at a problem as if a solution already existed; it just needed to be puzzled out.

What Gilk thought of this sudden change in his girlfriend, we didn't know. But Nate summed up the situation clearly.

"He's finding out our Lauren is more than just some Christian arm candy."

I was asked to attend a last-minute citizens' meeting one afternoon. I didn't know where Nate was, so I took Gilk with me. It was held out under the mayor's carport, standing room only. It was a semi-secret gathering. There were so many contractors, developers and urban planners running around town that it was difficult for us to differentiate them from the shysters, swindlers and con men trying to make a buck on our misery. We, the people of Lumkee, needed to figure out what to do next, without their self-serving input or the glare of camera lights.

"What we should do is level the whole area and put it in houses," Tim Reynolds suggested. "We can rebuild a business district closer to the expressway."

"I liked Lumkee just the way it was!" Marvin Kredmur complained. "We should build it back like it was."

"It can't ever be what we remember," Pat Dawson said. "They just don't make buildings that way anymore."

"We should take this opportunity to use our insurance money to build better, more modern, efficient buildings."

"I'm thinking I won't bother to rebuild. The cash is good. I'll make more investing it than putting it back into small-town commercial real estate."

I glanced at Gilkison after that comment. Fortunately for him, I didn't read a hint of agreement in his glance.

In the end we formed committees to work out the details. Everything from zoning specs to contract bidding had to be managed. The decisions would lie with city council, but they couldn't begin to take care of the tremendous overflow of detail being thrown at them. The mayor decided to divide the different aspects of the tasks into committees. Each committee would report to a member of the city council.

"But how will the whole thing be coordinated?" Tim Reynolds complained. "Who'll put it all together?"

"I'm the mayor," he answered. "I make the final decisions."

"That's exactly right, Mr. Mayor," Reverend Shue interrupted. "For that very reason, you won't be able to shepherd the deal along."

"I don't get your meaning," the mayor said.

"As an elected official," Reverend Shue continued, loud enough for everyone to hear, "you will be called upon to make final approval of all the infrastructure spending. You'll be making improvements on the city codes and permits. And it will be you who has to ultimately come up with plans that city council can approve. I'm sure you'll do your duty to the best of your ability. But politics will inevitably rear its ugly head. Any 'no' to your political opponents will be suspect. And any 'yes' to your political friends will be deemed favoritism. The fate of this town can't rest on the outcome of elections. The final decisions will have to be yours, but we don't want politics to taint the process."

Everyone was listening closely.

"In a big city, the mayor would hire this job out," Reverend Shue went on. "We can't really afford to do that. We'll have to take a volunteer."

There was some murmuring among the crowd.

The Reverend continued, ostensibly talking to the mayor, but in fact speaking to everyone. "I think you should pick someone outside of your sphere of influence. Not anyone who works for the city or a company that might be bidding for work. Maybe one of the businessmen directly affected by the disaster. And let him coordinate the committees."

"Do you have anyone in mind for this committee coordinator?" he asked the Reverend.

He shook his head.

The mayor briefly scanned the crowd.

"Anybody got any ideas about who we might get to do this?"

People began talking among themselves.

"You," the mayor called on someone. "You, young man with your hand up, in the back. Do you have something to say?"

"I'd like to suggest you ask my dad, Sam Braydon."

I whipped my head around. I couldn't see Nate, but I could hear him.

"My dad is honest, dependable, he works well with people and he knows how to get a job done. I trust him. Everybody in this town trusts him."

I was stunned by Nate's words. Stunned and embarrassed and proud. I had no idea that he held that opinion of me. It touched me as much as anything he'd ever said to me. I glanced over at Gilk beside me. He looked at me as if he'd never seen me before.

Of course, I wasn't picked for the job. Even in small towns, guys who never went to college and sell tamales for a living aren't singled out to be community leaders. But I was asked if I wanted to be on a committee. I requested Architecture and Design. I thought that would be something where my family might be able to help. Corrie understands everything about design. And *architecture* is a three-dollar word for *building*: Nate knows a lot about building, so I figured he could help me with that.

For the next three months I attended committee meetings in a Sunday school room in the basement of the Methodist church. We decided that we weren't going to allow anyone to not rebuild. We formed a downtown consortium. If you wanted your cash you could only sell your business to us, and we were offering only a minimum fair price. We decided that there would be one design. All the buildings would conform to this design, and we accepted bids for the whole Main Street area.

Like me, everyone there had far too much to do to while away their days in book work. I took stacks of proposals, information on city codes and zoning home with me every night to study. There was so much to be worked out, so many snags to be unsnarled.

One night in the family room with Makayla banging on her musical toy, Jin sleeping in front of the TV and Corrie working at her computer, I was deeply immersed in my work. There was so much that had to be kept together. Every decision had to be documented. I finally got everything together in a big file. Across the top of it I wrote, *City of Lumkee: Suburban Renewal*.

Corrie
2000

━━━▶ ◀━━━

I was sitting in a row of dignitaries behind the podium. In front of me, hundreds of Minnesota educators were seated in stackable hotel chairs. They were wearing their convention buttons, funny hats and award ribbons. They sat waiting, their notebooks open to blank pages, their pens held at the ready, as they listened to the speaker at the microphone.

"Nationally recognized as an education innovator, her learning-friendly classroom designs utilizing age, culture and behavioral norms are nationally recognized for flow, function and the ultimate yardstick, student success. And she has done this as a public service for teachers and schools, public and private, struggling against ever more restrictive budgets. Now she's written a book and developed an interactive software program that shares with users some of what she's learned along the way."

The speaker took a breath and turned slightly to glance in my direction.

"Ladies and gentleman, today's undisputed authority on classroom design for the new millennium, author of *A Place for Learning* and the creator of Education-Environments.com, Ms. Corrie Braydon."

The applause was more welcoming than I expected for an education techie. People knew of my work and admired me for my accomplishments. It was a strange concept, but it felt really good.

During the long months of rebuilding after the tornado, Nate and I had spent our evenings escaping from the workday drudge and anxiety by upgrading the Web site. We managed to get our design software interactive. Teachers could come onto the site, enter in their own specifics and be shown designs that had been developed for classrooms similar to their own. They could then, with the new options available, customize that plan to more closely fit their needs. From the day it went up, it was an immediate success. Teachers took to it with the enthusiasm of middle schoolers to video games.

That was great, except it put a tremendous strain on our server and I was going to have to spend more money to keep the site operating. I thought about going back to Jim, the gentleman who managed the venture capital and who had been previously interested in me. But the dot.com bust was widening. His clients had lost their savings and he was out of business. Alternatively, I approached a publishing company. They were as excited as the teachers. They wanted to produce a CD version of the program on the Web to be included with the book.

I wasn't a rich-and-famous author now—even the top sellers at education presses are only moderately successful commercially. But it had done well enough to make it worthwhile to the publisher, and to provide me with a little development money.

As I stood before those teachers, I knew that I had achieved my goal. At eighteen, I had wanted to do something important. I had wanted to meet important people and make a difference in the world. I had done that now and not in a way that I would ever have imagined.

The new century had brought a number of highlights for the Braydon family, including the reopening of Okie Tamales on the new Main Street Mall.

On Gilkison's advice, Sam had taken on interested investors in the company and revamped the plant, utilizing the latest commercial equipment. It was housed in a more efficient, worker-friendly building and the new setup increased production.

Sam's work on Lumkee's rebuilding project had broadened his ambition as well as his knowledge. Plans were now in the discussion stage for a second production unit to be built near Conway, Arkansas. He hoped that by 2003 Arkie Tamales would be on sale in grocery stores from Fort Smith to the Mississippi River.

My father's rehabilitation was going well. Especially for my mother. Although I had done what I could to help her care for Dad after his stroke, most of his care fell upon her shoulders, more than anyone would have thought she would have been able to bear. Mom was always so self-involved. We all knew that she loved Dad, but as in most of her relationships, she was always more interested in being the love-ee than the lover.

This second stroke had left Dad almost totally helpless for weeks. Even as he improved, it was very slow progress. Because of the ongoing crisis all over town, a few hours a day was all that anyone managed to spare. Jin and her family needed more help than they could give. And poor Harlan Larson, Cherry Dale's son, trying to keep her business going so that he could pay for the care she required, began to count on us as the nearest thing he had to family. Mom was forced to fend for herself, with a very sick man totally dependent upon her. And like the rest of us in that dark, sad period, she rose to the challenge.

I worried that she would ruin her own health, trying to do for him. But the result was quite the opposite. Mom had a purpose. Perhaps more feeling of purpose than she'd experienced since Mike's death. The sagging seventy-something socialite was suddenly energized. Twenty-four-hour nursing care didn't even faze her. And as Dad improved, she began branching out, offering advice and assistance to other caregivers.

I guess this was the first time I realized that Lauren's affinity for social activism might not be some strange aberration in our family, but a strength of character she'd inherited from my mother, who had secretly carried it all her life.

In June, Lauren graduated from Baylor. The whole family went down to Waco, including Dad, who was still unsteady on his feet and using a wheelchair most of the time.

We were so proud of her, and we had a wonderful time wandering the well-manicured campus. The college atmosphere was fun and exciting, but I sensed a wistfulness in Jin. She never said a word, nor did she seem angry or jealous of Lauren. But I would catch her in private moments, her expression sad. And she held Makayla close more often than the little girl liked.

After commencement, Gilkison took us all out to dinner. His two younger children, thirteen-year-old Jared and ten-year-old Regan, were also in the party. They seemed like good kids, polite and quiet, though

Regan did show a little bit of underlying nastiness to Lauren.

Their father's unexpected announcement probably didn't make things better.

"With all the exuberance of this very special day," he said, "I wanted to tell all of you, whom we love so much, that Miss Lauren Braydon, a magna cum laude bachelor of arts graduate, has consented to make me the happiest man in the world. As of last week, we're engaged!"

Lauren was all flushed, I think with both excitement and a smidgeon of embarrassment, as well. Gilkison was obviously so happy, much more so than the people at the table with whom he wanted to share his joy.

Sam and Nate had developed a grudging respect for the man, but it was still grudging. Although she never spoke of it, I was fairly sure that Jin didn't care for the man. I, personally, thought my baby girl could do a lot better. And the two Oberfeld children appeared angry enough about the announcement to spit nails.

But we all wished them well and pretended delight, though I felt a definite pall had settled upon the celebration.

Lauren moved home and we both jumped into the plans for the wedding, which she hoped to have in late fall. Fortunately, she didn't want a grand affair, and Gilkison, after suggesting that the wedding be moved to Tulsa where the churches were larger and the reception venues more lavish, seemed to be willing to allow Lauren the sweet little small-town wedding that she wanted.

The plan was to have the ceremony in "Gram's church"—we'd continued to attend Ninety and Nine Baptist all these years. The sanctuary there would only hold a hundred and fifty, which was a great way to limit the growth of a grandiose occasion.

For the reception we chose the Elk's Lodge, which would easily and safely seat that many and still have separate space for dancing.

Lauren played a little trick on us. She planned a nice menu and went around getting bids from local caterers. She came back with an estimate for dinner, including the champagne toast, at thirty dollars a plate.

Having heard the whines of my friends, I knew this was not out of line. Although, I could tell by Sam's expression that it was more than he'd thought to be spending.

"Do you think we can afford this, Daddy?" Lauren asked him.

"If this is what you want, honey," he told her, "then I think I can swing it."

She hugged him.

"I love you so much," she told him. "And what I'd really like to do is have an old-fashioned reception with just cake and punch, and donate the rest of the money to the International Campaign Against Hunger. That would be a very blessed wedding feast."

So we planned a modest celebration and Sam wrote a big check to her charity.

Not that Lauren's generous nature was universally applauded. My mother was horrified.

"What will people think?" she asked me rhetorically, and then answered her own question. "They'll either believe that Sam's business is on the skids, that you don't care very much about Lauren or that you're just cheap!"

The groom-to-be also had reservations.

"If we're not going to feed people, then the least we

owe them is an explanation," he said. "Otherwise, how will people understand that they're participating in a good deed?"

Lauren laughed at that as if he were making a joke. "Oh, yeah, right," she said facetiously. "We'll get the M.C. to make an announcement. 'Your rubber chicken dinner is being donated to a grateful and deserving nutritionally deprived Third World citizen. He needs the calories and you could stand to lose a few pounds.'"

In the end a small, carefully worded acknowledgment was added to the back of the program.

Lauren chose Gilk's daughters to be her bridesmaids. His son was to be best man. By midsummer the hall was rented, the invitations sent, the decorations selected, the cake ordered and the dress altered. Everything was going great, except Lauren seemed to have lost her luster. She didn't seem happy or excited.

I thought maybe it had something to do with Jin. Jin and the baby didn't spend nearly as much time at home anymore. Her relationship with Nate had always been very private. If they were having trouble or estranged somehow, I couldn't tell. But after Lauren returned from school, Jin spent more and more of her nights and almost all of her days elsewhere. She was helping her parents a lot, assisting with her father's care and working full-time in her sister's business. I was glad to see that the hard feelings between her and her family had lessened considerably since the tragedy of the storm. Her father's disability was permanent. They never reopened the grocery, but I would see him in his wheelchair at the new Kim Pharmacy on the Main Street Mall with little Makayla in his lap, talking to her in Korean. We acknowledged each other politely.

Cho Kyon was more forthcoming. But if she knew what was going on with Jin and Nate, she never said anything.

I finally asked Lauren.

"Have you and Jin had some kind of disagreement?"

"What?" Lauren shook her head with certainty. "We get along fine," she assured me. "All we ever talk about is Makayla. And we're both agreed that she is the sweetest, cutest baby girl on earth!"

Lauren's grin was infectious, like the Lauren I knew so well, but it disappeared too quickly and she was back to this strange gray discontent.

"What's wrong, Lauren?"

"Nothing."

"Are you getting nervous about the wedding?" I asked. "Are you having second thoughts?"

She shook her head, but she didn't smile.

"I'm sure it's the right thing," she said. "I'm convinced that God has chosen me to be a helpmate to Gilkison. That's his plan for my life. It's a very special gift." She sighed heavily. "But sometimes, to make room for something new in your life, God has to cut away something that you've cherished."

"What has God cut away from you?"

"My dreams," she answered. "My ambition."

"Are you saying that Gilk won't let you pursue a career?"

"Oh, a career, probably so," she said. "But marrying him means staying in Waco my whole life. Raising children. Volunteering at church. Doing community work. Those are all good things, worthwhile things. I just had my eyes set on something else."

She looked so sad, it was breaking my heart.

"Lauren, if you don't want to marry this guy, you don't have to. Trust me, God will understand."

She reached over and squeezed my hand. "Thanks, Mom," she said. "I do want to marry him. I know he's stuffy and narrow and sometimes he can be downright arrogant about his opinion even when he's completely wrong. But he's also kind and good and caring. He loves me. And he needs someone to love him. I do."

That should have settled things, but it didn't.

She was still unhappy and I felt powerless to do anything about it.

My perspective, of course, was not everyone's, as I found out one hot, humid afternoon in August. That morning, like the last several, UPS had delivered a couple of boxes of wedding gifts. Somehow Lauren had yet to get around to opening them. By late afternoon, the girls had settled into the new backyard swimming pool. Makayla, in her little water wings, was splashing around happily with the full attention of her mom and Aunt Lauren.

When Makayla began tiring and they got out of the pool, I carried the boxes to the deck.

"Maybe you're not curious about what's in these," I told her, "but I sure am!"

Lauren smiled, but she didn't seem too enthusiastic.

"It's more china," she said. "I can tell now by the size of the boxes." She held up the larger one. "This is a place setting. The long, flat one is probably a platter. I don't even have to open them to know that."

"Do you want me to open them?" I asked.

Lauren shrugged. "Sure, if you want to."

Jin snorted. "That is so *major princess!* You can't even be bothered to open your own gifts. Gotta get Mama to do it."

The comment, complete with a feigned whiney voice, was so snide and so unexpected, Lauren and I both just stared at Jin in shock. Then Lauren inexplicably teared up. She rose to her feet, picking up her gifts.

"You are absolutely right," she said. "I am being ungrateful. These people have been so kind to send gifts, I'm going to take them inside and write the thank-you notes immediately."

Jin and I watched her hurry into the house. I was fairly certain that she was crying.

"Well, shit," Jin said.

"Don't talk that way in front of the baby."

Makayla's ears were all perked up, and you could cut the tension in the air with a knife.

"I'm sorry," Jin said. "I'm sorry about the foul mouth. I'm sorry about hurting Lauren's feelings. I'm sorry. I'm just sorry, sorry, sorry."

"Jin," I said, "you'll have to tell me what's going on. There's no way that I can guess. Is there trouble between you and Nate?"

She shook her head.

"Then what?"

"I don't know," she said, shrugging. "No, I do know. I know exactly. I'm jealous of Lauren."

"Jealous?"

Jin nodded. "Yeah," she said. "Why wouldn't I be? Lauren's got her degree. She's got a man who wants to marry her. She's having a beautiful wedding, moving into a home of her own. She's got everything. Everything that I wanted. And I've got…I've got Makayla."

Impulsively she pulled the child into her arms. The toddler tolerated it for a moment and then wrenched herself away. It was too hot.

"Not that I would trade," she assured me hurriedly. "I love my baby. I love being her mother. But…"

She let the word hang there. There was nothing more to say.

As the wedding drew closer, Lauren's melancholy lingered. Finally one evening, I just picked up the phone.

"Gilk," I told her future husband, "I don't know how you can fix this or what you can do, but you're going to have to try."

"I know she's been kind of blue lately," he admitted. "I just thought it was wedding jitters."

"I talked to her about it," I said. "She's certain about wanting to marry you, but it's as if she's grieving for the life she might have had."

I heard Gilk sigh on the other end of the line. "I'm so much older than her, of course she must feel like she's leaving her youth behind her forever."

"I don't think that's it," I said. "I don't think she's noticed yet that you're closer to her father's age than her own. This is something different. I don't know, Gilk. You're going to have to work something out with her. I'm just not all that keen on seeing my daughter walk down the aisle without a smile on her face."

"I'll be there this weekend," he assured me.

He arrived late on Saturday, just as the whole family was sitting down to dinner. His Land Rover was covered with road film. He wasn't his usual impeccably groomed, completely-in-control self, either. He looked tired, mussed, old.

Lauren greeted him with a kiss.

"I didn't know you were coming up this weekend," she said.

He gave me a quick glance over her head. "I couldn't stay away," he told her. "I have a surprise for you."

Lauren smiled, but her heart wasn't in it.

"I hope you didn't buy me anything else," she said. "You've already bought me too much."

"I had to buy this," he insisted. "What's a wedding without a honeymoon?"

I was afraid Lauren was going to profess not to want one.

"Gilk, come sit and eat," I insisted. "Lauren, everybody, back to the table."

I quickly set another place and we all sat down with Nate and Jin and Makayla.

The dinner conversation was pleasant, casual. Gilk seemed changed from the man we'd first met. He was not so stuffy, not so sure of himself. In fact, he seemed downright uncertain. He glanced over at Lauren repeatedly, gauging her reaction to everything that was said.

When Makayla got bored with her high chair, Gilk volunteered to hold her on his lap.

"You're still eating," he told Jin. "I like kids. Remember, I've got four." He glanced again at Lauren. "But it's been a while and I might need to get back into practice."

Makayla wasn't content just to sit, but managed to climb all over the man like he was a jungle gym. Gilk handled it with a good deal of patience, even when the toddler scooted back the hair that he'd carefully combed over his bald spot.

Nate finally took pity on the guy and retrieved his daughter.

"So, tell us about the honeymoon you've got planned," he said.

I could have cheerfully kicked my son under the table. Unfortunately, it was too late to have made any difference.

"Where are you taking Lauren?" he continued. "Fiji? The Caribbean? I hope it's someplace she can show off the tan she's been working on."

Gilk reached into his shirt pocket and pulled out a long envelope with plane tickets. He handed them to Lauren.

"I don't think this is really a bikini place," he said. "Though I've heard that it's very hot."

Lauren opened the tickets. She sat there reading them, then she looked up confused.

"Where's Lilongwe, Malawi?" she asked him. "Is that some obscure island?"

Gilk shook his head. "It's in Africa," he answered. "Sort of tucked in between Zambia and Mozambique."

"Africa?"

"Lilongwe has the airport. We'll travel from there to Nkhotakota where we're going to spend three weeks. They tell me the sunrise over Lake Malawi is like a view of heaven."

Lauren's expression was incredulous.

"The accommodations won't be four-star," he warned her. "Truth is, they'll be Spartan at best. But we won't be in them much. The work schedule calls for twelve-hour days. We're helping to build an orphanage for refugee children."

She just stared at him for a long moment. Then with a squeal of delight, she threw her arms around his neck.

"I can't believe it," she said. "I prayed for it and prayed for it, but I can't believe it."

Gilk shrugged. "I figured if you were willing to give me a lifetime in Waco, the least I could offer in return is an annual mission trip for the two of us."

Sam
2001

—————▶ ◀—

There was three inches of snow on the ground the morning that Harlan called. Cherry Dale, still comatose since May 1999, had died in her sleep.

She was the tornado's final victim. That was kind of hard to get my mind around. So much had happened. As a country, we'd been in mourning since September 11, and after so many lives lost, one more death should have felt inconsequential. But it didn't.

The world went on. We lived our lives. Things changed every day. The rebuilding of downtown into a walking mall, complete with underground parking, was finished. Most of the businesses, including mine, had reopened into new, updated quarters. We even lured a very fashionable anchor store into our project. The old Lumkee Main Street was now functioning as a typical suburban mall. The only difference from the usual mall stores was that there were the small mom-and-pop businesses that made the community special.

The timing had turned out to be golden. With new technology industries expanding in Tulsa, there was a need for more suburban housing. Growth to the east and south had been ongoing for years. Now suddenly the north suburbs were the place to be. Lumkee was the fastest-growing community in the metro area. And all around us, subdivisions were springing up everywhere, populated by those people who didn't want to drive to south Tulsa to shop. So with a brand-new mall, clean and easily accessible from the expressway, store traffic was up over a hundred percent from before the storm.

But, of course, the Lumkee we grew up with, the Lumkee we remembered, was gone. And now, Cherry Dale with it.

Doc called me as soon as he heard.

"I want to do a viewing at the funeral home," he told me. "Edna won't take me. She says I've got no business there, but I feel up to it. Will you take me, Sam? I want to go."

Of course I couldn't turn the old man down. He probably *didn't* have any business there. It was a bitter cold day and the roads were icy. Doc was old and not very strong anymore. He should stay home by the fire. Viewing was ostensibly for family and close friends. We were really neither. But unlike Edna, I recognized the tie the Doc had. Cherry Dale and Mike had killed Floyd Braydon. Just knowing that fact had kept him alive now for years.

For me, it was still a mixed and muddled mess of feelings. Mike was my friend, but Floyd was my father. I felt sorry for Cherry Dale. I don't condone murder, but my dad did kill my mother. I'd forgiven him for that. Could I forgive Cherry Dale and Mike? I wasn't sure if I truly could. It wasn't the kind of moral dilemma that Gram or Sunday school had prepared me for. I just did what I did best. I kept putting one foot in front of the other, moving forward. And tried to take comfort in the old hymn we used to sing, "We'll understand it better by and by."

I sat down for breakfast with Nate, these days known as My Son, the Loner.

Nate worked in his shop, sold his furniture and slept in his room. He never went anywhere, he never saw his friends, he never even talked on the phone.

Jin and Makayla had moved into Tulsa with Jin's brother. Nate hadn't said a word before, during or after the move. It was as if he had no comment on the lives of his baby or the mother of his child.

Corrie and I kept up with her, of course. We missed her around the house. We'd become so used to the noise of a little one underfoot, the place seemed too quiet and empty without Makayla.

Jin was moving on. She was back in school at Oklahoma State's new Tulsa branch campus. It was a comedown from Syracuse, I suppose, but she could leave Makayla with her sister-in-law while she pursued her education. We were happy for her, but sad for Nate. If there had been some big breakup between the two, we never heard any evidence of it. She'd packed up, said goodbye and left. Nate went to his shop as if nothing had happened. Only those of us who loved him could see how much light and joy had walked out with her.

"I'm going to take Doc to see Cherry Dale at the funeral home this morning," I told him.

Nate glanced up, surprised.

"He wants to see her?"

I nodded. "Yeah, they have…I don't know…she was close to Mike. I think for Doc, that means a lot."

That seemed reasonable to Nate.

"I'll go with you," he said.

"What?"

"I'll go with you," Nate repeated. "I was thinking to go up there myself. I can just go with you and Grandpa."

I was surprised, but was glad for any indication that he was interested in something outside his workshop.

We picked up Doc a little after one. Edna scolded him and us all the way to the car. We were all so used to her, we didn't pay any attention.

Mullen Funeral Home was in a grand old brick home across the street from the city park. It had suffered some damage in the twister, but was now restored to a former glory that it hadn't shown prior to the storm.

With Nate on one side and me on the other, we helped Doc negotiate the half-dozen steps up to the front porch. His left leg still didn't work quite right, but he was getting around very well. And when he was determined to do something, there was really no stopping him.

The funeral director, Delbert Mullen, met us at the door. He shook hands with all of us, but with Doc first. At least among morticians, age still commanded respect. Cherry Dale, he informed us, was laid out in the blue parlor.

The little room had lots of windows. But without the sunshine, the place was chilly. There was very little furniture. A table with flowers and a visitor's book were next to the door. A long upholstered bench sat in front of the windows. Along the length of the room, raised on a platform to eye level, was the open casket.

Quietly, as if we thought we might wake her, we walked over and looked inside.

Cherry Dale was hardly recognizable as the woman

that I remembered. She seemed tiny and shrunken in the huge mahogany box.

"Poor girl," Doc said. "I remember when she used to stop by the drugstore with a nickel to buy a candy bar."

"She looks really old," Nate said. "How old was she?"

"A few years older than me," I answered.

"She was forty-seven," Doc piped in. "The same age as Mike."

I saw a tear slip down Doc's cheek. I knew that it was as much for his dead son as for the woman in the casket.

"It's terrible that someone should lie waiting to die so long," Doc said.

I agreed.

Doc grabbed Nate's hand and squeezed it. "I don't want to die like that," he told him. "If I'm just a vegetable, you put me out of my misery. Do you understand me, Nate?"

"Yes, Grandpa," he replied.

"I can't ask Sam," he said. "He'd do it for me, but I already owe him too much. Can you do it, Nate?"

"I can do it, Grandpa," he said with certainty.

"It's hard to understand why somebody should have to live in a coma for so very long," I said.

Doc nodded. "I guess she had to do it for Harlan," he said. "Her lying there, needing care—it's been the making of that boy."

That was true. In his own way, Cherry Dale's older son had been as troubled as the younger one. Drinking too much, unable to settle down, he'd been jumping from one job to another, one relationship to another, since he got out of high school. Even with Cherry Dale handing him the Tulsa branch of Pepxercise, he'd hardly been able to make a go of it. He'd still been playing around, more interested in partying than making a profit.

Her coma, and the care it required, forced Harlan to really knuckle down. Responsibility can sometimes break a strong man down. Sometimes it can drag a weak man to his feet. That's what happened with Harlan. He'd finally shown himself to have the same kind of work ethic and financial savvy as his mother. The business was expanding again. Harlan had wed one of his employees and Cherry Dale's first grandchild was due to arrive in the spring.

Cherry Dale hadn't lived to see it, but somehow I was sure she knew.

We were getting ready to leave when Delbert came in and Doc began asking questions about setting up a burial plan. The two went off to Mullen's office and Nate and I were left with the chilly room and the casket. We took seats on either end of the upholstered bench.

Quite naturally, we talked about Cherry Dale, her boys and memories that we shared. At first we stuck just to the happy ones. But eventually, the less pleasant came to mind as well.

"She had a really hard life," Nate said.

"Yeah, I guess she did."

"I don't think she ever got over Rusty's death," he said.

"No, of course she didn't," I agreed. "She blamed herself."

He furrowed his brow, puzzled.

"Why would she blame herself?"

I sorted my thoughts in my head and chose my

words carefully. This was Nate. Paw-Paw's Nate. I didn't want him dealing with anything more than he must.

"Rusty thought that he'd killed Floyd," I said. "When you boys pulled him off Cherry Dale. He thought that the punch he threw was what killed him."

Nate shook his head, disbelieving. "Well, that's crazy," he said. "Rusty couldn't have decked a marshmallow."

"Yeah, well, Cherry Dale tried to tell Rusty, but he wouldn't believe her."

"He should have asked me," Nate said. "I knew what really happened."

My insides tightened in anxiety.

"Heart attack, just like the doctor said."

He shook his head. "Dr. Billups is a quack," he said. "It was pills. That's what really happened."

"How could you know that?" I asked him. "You weren't even there. You got up and went home."

"I saw the pill bottle," he said. "The bottle with Uncle Mike's suicide pills. It had fallen on the floor and rolled under the couch."

"How did you know about Uncle Mike's pills?"

"He told me," Nate answered. "I asked Uncle Mike once how he could stand the pain. He told me about the pills. He said that as long as he knew that they were there, that he was in control, then he could bear anything."

"And you recognized the bottle when you saw it in Cherry Dale's house?"

He was quiet for a minute and then answered. "I took the bottle to Cherry Dale's house," he said. "I had been carrying them around in my backpack for months."

"What?"

"The day Uncle Mike died," Nate said. "I stole the pills and put them in my backpack. I carried them around with me."

"Why?"

He hesitated. "I was planning to kill myself," he said.

I'm sure I gasped. I felt like a vein in my forehead might pop.

"It's okay," Nate reassured me. "That was a long time ago. I'm not into that anymore."

"You wanted to kill yourself? Why?"

"Because I couldn't stand who I was," he said. "Because I hated myself. I hated everybody else. I just felt bad, worthless."

"That doesn't make any sense," I said.

"It did to me," he answered. "Every day I realized more and more what kind of person I was. And I didn't like myself. I still don't like myself. I don't like myself at all."

"What kind of person did you think you were?"

"I'm like Paw-Paw," he answered. "That's who I've always been like. Everybody says so. 'Nate is just like Floyd. He looks like Floyd, he talks like Floyd. He acts like Floyd.' That was all well and good until I realized that Floyd was a vicious, brutal son of a bitch."

I nodded thoughtfully.

"I figured that out all by myself," he told me. "That year I spent so much more time with him and watched how he was. He was mean, Dad. He was mean all the time. And when he was drinking, he was evil."

"I know," I told him. "I figured it out by myself, too. But you never let on how you felt. You always defended him."

"Because we were the same," Nate said. "When anyone made a comment about Paw-Paw, it was like they were saying it about me."

"That's not true."

He shrugged. "Probably not, but that's what it felt like," he said. "I knew that Mom hated him. I thought she must hate me, too."

I put my arm around my son. "Nate, your mother loves you."

He nodded. "I know that now. But then, I just knew that I was like him," he said. "I didn't want to be like that, so I decided I would kill myself. So I took Mike's pills. But it wasn't that easy. At first I wanted to wait until Mom got over Uncle Mike's death. I thought it was too unfair for me to die right after him. And then I wanted to wait until school was out. And then I wanted to wait until summer was over. I just kept putting it off and putting it off."

He glanced toward the casket and ran a hand through his hair.

"The night I saw him beat up Cherry Dale, I wasn't waiting anymore," he said. "Once everybody was asleep I got up and got the pills out of my backpack. I went into the kitchen to get some water. I guess that woke him up. He was more or less sober by then. The fight, the food, a little rest, he was not his crazy self, just his regular one. He asked me what I was going to do. And I told him. I told him what a terrible man he was. That the things he did were evil, truly evil, and that I didn't want to be that way. I hated being like him. And that I was going to kill myself rather than grow up to be that kind of man."

"What did he say?"

"He said I was making the same mistake that he'd

made," Nate answered. "He said I was killing the wrong person."

"The wrong person?"

Nate nodded. "He said that he'd done the same thing. That he'd hated himself. That he'd hated himself so bad that he'd killed your mother when he should have killed himself. He said it wasn't an accident. He said he'd done it cold-blooded. He'd killed her because she'd had enough. She was going to take you and go home. He knew she was right to go. He knew he was bad. He hated himself. So he killed her."

My jaw trembled and my blood was pounding through my veins so loudly I could barely hear.

"He killed her," I said aloud.

It felt good just to say it, to know it finally, once and for all.

"He killed the wrong person," Nate said. "He told me not to do the same thing. He told me to leave the pills and go home. That's what I did."

I looked at him then as the truth of what happened became suddenly clear.

"He took the pills himself," I said. "It was suicide."

Nate nodded.

"I found the pill bottle the next day. I threw it in the trash before anybody else could see it and suspect."

I sat there beside my son, trying to take it all in.

"I thought Cherry Dale had killed him," I said.

"Cherry Dale? No way," Nate said. "Cherry Dale was too good a person. A good person would never have killed him. A good person wouldn't have even let him take his own life."

"Wait a minute," I said. "You're not blaming yourself for that?"

Nate shrugged and shook his head, indecisive.

"I don't feel guilty anymore about him doing it," Nate said. "I guess I've gotten past that. He was an adult. I was a kid. I never made him do anything in his life. I'm just saying that I let it happen. I should never have stolen the pills. I sure shouldn't have told him how ashamed and angry it made me because of who he was. It made me ashamed of who I was. Ashamed of who I am."

"Ashamed? Nate, you should be proud of who you are," I told him.

"Dad, I'm just like him," he said. "I look like him, I talk like him, I act like him."

"You mean you're like a heavy drinker?" I asked.

"No, you know I don't really drink."

"So you're a braggart, a loudmouth?"

"No, I'm not really like that."

"Are you incompetent with tools? Lazy on the job?"

"I'm good at what I do and I like doing it."

"Do you beat the woman you love?"

"No, of course not."

"Do you lie and cheat and take advantage at every opportunity?"

"Well no, you know I don't."

"Are you in this world for yourself and to hell with anybody that gets in your way?"

"No."

"Then you're not like him," I said. "You're like me. You're just like me."

I pulled him into a big hug. Dads don't get to hug their sons enough and that's what I wanted to do, just hold him safe in my arms.

"You're like me, Nate," I told him. "You're like me. I don't know if my father had crappy genes or if he was abused as a kid. He never said, I just don't know. I guess I won't know. But he didn't raise me. Gram raised me. She raised me to be a decent, upright kind of guy and that's the kind of guy I've tried to be. Nate, I raised you to be that kind of guy, too."

Corrie
2002

Coming into the kitchen that morning, I felt antsy, disturbed, restless. It was a morning that demanded something. Change was in the air.

The house, Gram's house, our house was quiet these days, empty. Nate had moved his business to a warehouse in north Tulsa. And he'd moved himself to an apartment closer to Jin and Makayla. They were not back together, but a happy, active three-year-old could easily consume all the love, energy and patience of two parents.

Jin had switched her major to computer engineering and finished her degree with honors. Her graduation, unfortunately, coincided with the bubble burst of the technology industry. She had managed to keep her job with WorldCom, one of the big new tech employers in Tulsa, but it was an uncertain time.

Lauren and Gilk were expecting their first child. They were both excited and happy. I was, too, but I felt a bit disconnected from the process. When Jin was pregnant with Makayla, I'd been right there for everything. Now, with my own daughter, I only got weekend visits every few weeks and reports on the phone.

My business was both a smashing success and a colossal failure. My ideas, my philosophy, my designs, even my name was known throughout the education community. I was frequently asked to give presentations and speeches—I was nationally lauded as an innovator. But I barely brought in enough income to cover my expenses.

Not that there wasn't money to be made. A number of commercial concerns had cheerfully ripped off things available for free on my Web site, repackaged them, revved up some expensive marketing and sold them at a nice profit.

This was annoying, and I tried to get my ego past it. What I'd wanted was to make a difference. That had happened. That I didn't get credit, or get rich on the deal, well, that would have just been gravy, anyway.

But thank God for tamales! If it had not been for Sam's business, I would never have been able to pursue my dreams.

He'd almost sold out the last year. Investors, looking for a safe place to stash their money, had offered Sam two million dollars to buy the business outright. We'd both gotten eyes as big as saucers. Considering the debt that we owed for expansion, the rising costs of operation and the slim, but steady, profit he was pulling in, it was a very generous offer.

I was already planning European vacations, an updated wardrobe and a flashy new car when Sam told me he was turning it down.

"What would I do?" he asked me. "This is what I know. This is what I like. This pays me to get up every morning and go to work."

"Lots of men would give a lot to retire in their midforties and live off their investments," I pointed out.

He shook his head. "I've been out of work. I sat out

years without a job to go to. I don't see that as a reward."

As a compromise, he took on a partner, someone to help manage the day-to-day operations. Celia Garner was the daughter of one of our former employees. Loretta had been partially blinded by flying glass during the tornado. Though she had worked on and off since then, she'd never regained her vision and had taken disability retirement. Her youngest daughter, Celia, had just earned her degree in hotel and restaurant management. I was pretty sure that she was taking this opportunity with *Okie Tamales* to get some experience and save up some capital to start something of her own. But that was not a bad thing, and it did give Sam time to take a few trips and learn to play golf. And to pass off, to someone younger, those long hours required by a small business.

It was a good life. It hadn't always been easy. Sometimes it was still a struggle, but it was good.

As I poured my coffee in the kitchen that had once been Gram's, I thought about our past. And I wondered about the future.

Sam was sitting on the deck by the pool, reading the paper. He was a handsome guy, maybe more now than when he was young. Back then all the guys looked good. Not all of them had held up as well. I guess that was where that Braydon blood came in. They were attractive people, Floyd, Sam, Nate.

A trim, good-looking guy in his midforties with a decent amount of money and a likable disposition. I figured that in the dating market, some shrewd thirty-something divorcée would snap him up in twenty minutes and thank her lucky stars for the rest of her life. He'd provide for her, dote on her, do for her. He'd be a great stepfather for her troubled kids from the bad first marriage. He'd show up for their soccer games and make sure there was plenty of money for them to go to college. He'd do it without ever expecting even an acknowledgment of his effort.

Sam was a good deal any way you sliced it. I was not unaware of that fact. It just didn't figure into my thinking that morning.

I carried my coffee out to the deck. He leaned over to give me a good-morning kiss and handed me the Lifestyle section of the newspaper. I sat down in the chair across from his.

"Do you know what today is?" I asked him.

He got that deer-in-the-headlights look and quickly checked the date on his watch. He looked up at me, clearly puzzled.

"Well, it's not our anniversary or anyone's birthday," he said.

I knew there wasn't any way that he would guess.

"It was twenty-five years ago today that I came home from college and told you that I was pregnant."

"Aah," he said, drawing the sound out and nodding.

"What do you think about us renewing our wedding vows?" I asked him.

His brow furrowed. "You want to renew our wedding vows?" he asked.

"Yes."

"Like one of those anniversary things? With wedding clothes and a cake and all that?"

"I don't care about the clothes or the cake," I told him. "I'd just like us to repledge our vows."

"You want me to *plight my troth* again?" he asked with a chuckle.

"People don't say that these days," I said. "We'd make up our own vows, say it the way that has meaning for us."

Sam's body language was all squirmy and uncomfortable. "Why would we want to do that?" he asked.

"To make it clear that we're together because we want to be," I answered.

He shrugged off the suggestion. "I'm here. I'm married to you," he told me. "*Because I want to be* goes without saying."

I raised my chin, determined to be demanding. This was important.

"The way I see it," I said. "We either renew our vows and start this marriage all over again or we just call it quits and get a divorce."

From the stunned look on his face, I was sure my statement was unexpected.

"I didn't realize that you were unhappy," he said very carefully.

"I'm not unhappy," I told him. "How could I be? I have a great career, two healthy, well-adjusted kids and a wonderful home. I'm emotionally stable and financially secure. Any woman who has all that can't possibly get away with saying she's unhappy."

"Usually when the *D* word is mentioned, it's because something is terribly wrong," he said. "If you're not unhappy then why has it dropped in today?"

It wasn't that easy to explain. I took a sip of coffee and then looked thoughtfully into the eyes of the man who had been my partner for more than half of my life.

"Things are different now, Sam," I said. "With Lauren married and starting a family, and Nate as settled as he probably will ever be, it's as if we've suddenly got our lives back as our own."

"We've worked hard, we've done our job as parents and, knock on wood, they've both turned out okay," he said. "We have every reason to be proud of that. And I'd say we've earned some life on our own."

"I agree, I totally agree," I told him. "But it's like a door is opening to a whole new life. That old life, those young kids with young kids, they've grown up now. They've gone after what they wanted. Sometimes they succeeded, sometimes they failed. But that's yesterday. Today it's you and me and a whole new future out there."

"That's a good thing," Sam pointed out.

"I'm not disputing that," I said. "But a marriage can't live on memories alone. It's like the tornado going through downtown. Things change. They will never be tomorrow what they were yesterday."

"Of course not," he agreed. "I hope you're not thinking that we're stuck in some kind of rut, because we're not. Both of us are different now than we were when we married."

"My point exactly," I said. "We are different. The things we want are different and the world that we live in is different. My question is, do we want to spend the next phase of our different life together, or on our own?"

"Corrie, I can't even imagine my not being with you," Sam said.

"Well, try," I told him. "Try to imagine that you just met me today, now, this morning," I asked him. "Would you choose to be married to me?"

"Of course," he answered too quickly.

"No, think about it," I insisted. "If we were total strangers, just starting out on our own in our midforties, would you want to date me, sleep with me, spend the rest of your life with me?"

"How can I know?" he answered. "If I hadn't married you, I don't know what kind of guy I'd be. And I don't know what kind of woman you'd be if you'd spent the last twenty-five years somewhere else."

"Okay, that's a fair enough answer," I admitted. "But I have to let you know, I'm not sure that I'm willing to spend the next twenty-five years with you if our only reason for being together is that we always have been."

His brow furrowed with genuine concern.

"Was my pregnancy the only reason that you married me? Can you even remember how you used to feel about me?"

Sam sat there for a long moment just looking at me. For both of us, it was as if our whole lives together were flashing before our eyes. An assault of memories, sweet and sad, special and ordinary. Twenty-five years of being man and wife.

"This is amazing," he said finally, his expression incredulous.

"What?"

"It's amazing that after all this time, being together year after year after year, we still don't know each other any better than this," he said.

"Oh?"

He leaned forward and took my hand in his own. With his finger he traced the little gold band on my left hand. Then he looked up into my eyes.

"Corrie, being pregnant was your reason for marrying me," he said. "It was never my reason for marrying you."

"It was."

"It was not," he insisted. "I married you because I was given a chance to. It was clear to me, even young and crazy and shortsighted as I was back then, that if my life, with all its tragic baggage and uncertain potential, was linked with yours, then nothing we'd face could ever defeat us."

The openness and honesty of his statement nearly took my breath away. "I knew then, like I know now, that you're out of my league," he continued. "You could have had any guy—smart guys, rich guys, important guys. I'm not oblivious to the treasure that you are, Corrie. The day you told me you were going to have my baby, I didn't feel scared or trapped or any of those emotions guys are supposed to feel. I was elated! I thought you'd come to tell me that you'd fallen for somebody else. That's what I expected. That you would dump me for somebody who was smart and well-off and who could offer you a better future. All I ever had to offer was myself and my love."

He held out his strong, work-worn, empty hands before him. "That's still, pretty much, all I have. You, Corrie Braydon, are all the woman I've ever wanted, everything that I ever hoped and prayed for. That pesky little sperm that caused all the trouble in your life was the best friend that I ever had. He gave me the last two and a half decades with you. But I guess you're right. Even a life sentence doesn't usually run over twenty-five years."

Sam stopped and took a deep breath, as if mustering his courage.

"I remember talking with Mike once about Emerson's idea of 'compensation.' How over a lifetime the good things and bad things somehow even out. I know that marrying me meant giving up a lot of good things that you wanted in your life. And that through our years together a lot of bad things have happened to us. I also know that I love you, Corrie Braydon. If you leave, I will still love you. If you stay married to me, then you're right, it needs to be your own free choice."

I sat there, across the table from him, his eyes gazing into mine. What was any lifetime together based on? Passion? Habit? Friendship? Convenience? It was all those things. And it was more. It was a sharing that says, today I'll carry you and tomorrow you'll carry me. It was a hand to hold in grief and arms to embrace in trouble. It was a partner who believed in you when you didn't believe in yourself. A person who could watch you change and be willing to change themselves. Someone you could trust to always have your best interest at heart.

Marrying Sam had taken my life in a different direction than I had planned for, different than I'd hoped for. But what my life had been; the family I had, the success I'd achieved, that would have been impossible without him. I had no plans for the rest of my life. No goals, no aspirations to be fulfilled. I needed to think that through, figure out where I wanted to head next, what I wanted to accomplish. There was a good chance I might live another forty years. I wanted the second half of my time on earth to be as full and exciting and meaningful as the first.

And whatever I chose to do, I knew that it would be better, sweeter, more worthwhile with this man at my side.

"I love you, too, Sam," I told him, and then added the question that needed to be asked. "Will you marry me?"

Nate
2002

➤━━━◆━━━◄

My parents are like the most sappy married couple on planet Earth. They call each other "honey" and "sweetheart" and they still sleep in the same bed after twenty-five years. It's unbelievable! Practically all of my friends' parents divorced years ago. And the ones who are still married, well, it's like inertia or something. But not Sam and Corrie. They are the love bunnies of Lumkee.

So I wasn't really surprised when they called and said that they were going to renew their vows. It was just the kind of deal I would have expected from those two. I marked that Saturday on my calendar, made sure the trousers to my suit weren't crumpled up on the floor of my closet and that I had a clean shirt.

I picked up Jin and Makayla and we drove up there for the event. Her invitation was separate from mine, of course. And there was some discussion of her driving to Lumkee on her own. But eventually she decided that we could go together. If anyone mistakenly assumed that we were a family, she would set them straight.

Setting things straight was Jin's mission in life. Her family, my family, they all made assumptions. Jin didn't want anyone boxing her into anything, especially if it concerned me or Makayla.

But being boxed in was becoming more of a problem for her. She'd just closed on her little suburban house with the thirty-year mortgage and the nice backyard. The ink was barely dry when she was laid off at WorldCom. Of course, she'd get another job. But it probably wouldn't be overnight. I could help her but Jin didn't like much help. The money she accepted from me we called "child support." We had no legal arrangement. I'd just put what money I could spare in an envelope and I'd leave it on her kitchen table. She let me do that, but nothing more. Fortunately, with the growth of my Internet business and my reputation locally, I had orders lined up and waiting lists for pieces months long. So I was able to fork over some cash. But Jin was very proud, very self-reliant. Taking money from an ex-boyfriend was not on her list of things that an independent woman would do.

But, she did let me pick her up that day. And she looked beautiful. She was wearing a shiny, sort of silky, straight dress. It was very simple and conservative, but she still managed to look hot in it.

Maybe I was just horny. Jin didn't sleep with me anymore. She said that since our relationship was going nowhere, it was cruel to give Makayla mixed messages.

Walking behind Jin, the message I was getting, watching those shapely legs in those high-heeled sandals, definitely mixed it up for me. I just wanted her to wrap those legs around my waist.

Instead, she told me to take Makayla's hand.

The church was unexpectedly crowded. They didn't send out invitations, but word got around. Practically everybody in town showed up. The other businesspeople from Main Street, the folks from the church, Mom's teacher friends, all crowded into that little Baptist Church.

I stopped beside my grandparents, already seated in a pew. I knew they'd want to give Little Mac a big smooch.

"How you doing, Doc?" I asked the old man.

He shrugged. "I have good days and bad."

"What about this one?"

He reached a shaky, gnarled hand to Jin. "Any time I see you two kids together is a good day," he answered with a wink.

I glanced back quickly to see if Jin was pissed off. She was smiling at Doc and seemed as glad to see him as he was to see her.

"Hey, who's this hot chick you're with?" I asked as my grandmother rose to her feet to hug me.

"Hot chick? Nate, really," she scolded me, but I knew that any compliments were welcome with Grandma.

"Looks like a great day for a wedding," I told her.

She huffed in disapproval and shook her head. "It's foolishness that borders upon the bizarre," she answered. "To think I'd have to sit through the consecration of this union *twice* in one lifetime."

I couldn't help but chuckle at that.

"Grandma, we all know you're crazy about Dad," I told her.

With raised eyebrows and a sigh, she shrugged. "Well, he's turned out better than he would have without her," Grandma admitted. "And you children were certainly worth the sacrifice."

An instant later her face was suddenly wreathed in smiles.

"Well hello there, little Miss Makayla! Don't you look pretty today."

She was conversing in her singsong granny voice for a couple of moments before turning her attention back to me, smiles disappearing.

"I always think 'only children' miss out on so much."

I ignored the jibe and steered Jin and Little Mac away before any more missiles could be launched.

Jin's parents were up near the front. Her father's wheelchair was in the aisle and her mom sat in the pew beside him with Hye Won and David. Dave had started a new church for the Korean congregation in and around Lumkee. They'd moved back in with the Chais and were able to help on a round the clock basis.

As soon as we walked up, there was a burst of excited Korean chatter as Jin's mother eagerly reached for Makayla.

I bowed deferentially to Mr. Chai.

"*An-nyŏng-ha-sim-ni-kka*? I said, greeting him respectfully with the polite question, "Are you at peace?"

"*Ne, an-nyŏng-ha-se-yo*," he responded positively with only the barest hint of a nod to his head.

From the corner of my eye I spotted Cho Kyon gazing with approval. It was important to them that I was trying to learn Korean. I would never be the guy that they wanted their daughter to marry. But I figured it was maybe not so different from how Grandma felt about Dad. It was hard to look at healthy, happy, giggly Little Mac and be sorry that Jin and I had ever gotten together.

Gilk came walking up the aisle with my sister, Lauren, on his arm. She was looking really pregnant.

"You look wonderful!" Jin told her, gushing.

I agreed, but after listening to Lauren complain about how big the baby was getting, I said, "Yeah, and who knew you could carry them on your butt like that."

Jin jabbed me in the ribs for the insult. But Lauren laughed. She knows me. If I'd been too kind, she would have worried.

We all sat on the front rows. Makayla sat between me and Lauren. She'd been going through this kind of demanding stage where she just refused to do anything her mother even suggests. You have to pick your battles with kids. You can't make them do much, so laying down the law has got to be for the really important stuff.

She was still kind of pudgy, with little round cheeks and the sweetest little voice, which in an instant could turn into a loud, intolerable shriek. She didn't do that much anymore. Being almost four, it was now possible to reasonably discuss things with her without her doing a brat-fit on the floor.

I suppose she was a little spoiled. Everybody made such a big deal over her. As more little cousins were born to Song and Hye Won, and to Lauren, it was sure to get easier.

I said as much to my sister.

"Do what you can," I suggested.

Lauren gave me a raised eyebrow and shot back, "Just don't get her a little brother. That could ruin a girl's life."

I made a face at my sister. Makayla saw it and giggled.

The music began. Mom and Dad walked down the aisle together. They were both smiling, happy, looking more at each other than at the crowd that had come to celebrate with them.

It was as if they had their own private joke going all the time. It had always been that way. I could remember wondering about that, marveling about it. *What can he see in her?* I'd thought. But I guess I'd learned a few things since then. A woman doesn't have to be perfect for a man to love her. And I guess vice versa is just as true, as well.

The preacher gave a little sermonette about the sacredness of marriage and how such a bond can never truly be broken. I don't know about that, but I was pretty impressed with the vows my parents made. They wrote them up themselves, so Mom's sounded the best.

Mom said, "Sam Braydon, I promise to love you, cherish you and choose you for my husband every day of my life for the rest of our lives."

Dad's cut right to the heart of it.

"Corrie Braydon, I promise to be with you, provide for you and care for you always. No matter what happens next week or next year or forever."

It was pretty cool, really, the way they talked to each other, so up-front, no holding back. I wondered how rare that was. I wondered if it was possible for just anyone.

I glanced over at Jin and caught her surreptitiously wiping a tear from her eye. Jin does not cry. Nothing gets to Jin. Jin is in control of the universe. The only time I'd ever even seen a chink in her armor was when we had the tornado. Anything that would threaten the baby could get to her. But nothing else. She was emotionproof. Or was she?

I don't know what made me do it. But at that moment, without really even thinking about it, I picked up her hand and I brought it to my lips.

She turned to stare at me as if I'd lost my mind. But beneath her surprise I saw something, something deeper, something that maybe we could work with.

I'm a lot like my dad. Marriage really worked for him. For the first time in my life, I thought it might work for me.